THE
JOHNNY MAXWELL
TRILOGY

Also by Terry Pratchett

THE CARPET PEOPLE

THE DARK SIDE OF THE SUN

STRATA

TRUCKERS

DIGGERS

WINGS

THE UNADULTERATED CAT (with Gray Joliffe)

GOOD OMENS (with Neal Gaiman)

The Discworld® Series:

THE COLOR OF MAGIC

THE LIGHT FANTASTIC

EQUAL RITES

MORT

SOURCERY

WYRD SISTERS

PYRAMIDS

GUARDS! GUARDS!

ERIC (with Josh Kirby)

MOVING PICTURES

REAPER MAN

WITCHES ABROAD

SMALL GODS

LORDS AND LADIES

MEN AT ARMS

SOUL MUSIC

INTERESTING TIMES

MASKERADE

FEET OF CLAY

HOGFATHER

JINGO

THE JOHNNY MAXWELL TRILOGY

Only You Can Save Mankind
Johnny and the Dead
Johnny and the Bomb

TERRY PRATCHETT

SFBC SCIENCE FICTION

This is a work of fiction. All the characters and events portrayed in these novels are either fictitious or are used fictitiously.

Printing History:

Doubleday (UK) Hardcover 1992
Corgi (UK) paperback 1993

Printing History:

Doubleday (UK) Hardcover 1993
Corgi (UK) paperback 1994

Printing History:

Doubleday (UK) Hardcover 1996
Corgi (UK) paperback 1997

Published by arrangement with the author's agent:
Ralph M. Vincinanza Ltd.
111 Eighth Avenue, Suite 1501
New York, NY 10011

Visit our website at *http://www.sfbc.com*

ISBN: 1-56865-620-3

PRINTED IN THE UNITED STATES OF AMERICA.

CONTENTS

ONLY YOU CAN SAVE MANKIND

Yet another one
for Rhianna

The Mighty ScreeWee™ Empire™ is poised to attack Earth!

Our battleships have been destroyed in a sneak raid!

Nothing can stand between Earth and the terrible vengeance of the ScreeWee™!

But there is one starship left . . . and out of the mists of time comes one warrior, one fighter who is the last Hope of Civilization!

YOU!

YOU are the Savior of Civilization. You are all that stands between your world and Certain Oblivion. You are the Last Hope.

Only You Can Save Mankind!™

Action-Packed with New Features! Just like the Real Thing! Full-Color Sound and Slam-Vector™ Graphics!

Suitable for IBM PC, Atari, Amiga, Pineapple, Amstrad, Nintendo. Actual game shots taken from a version you haven't bought.

Copyright 1992 Gobi Software, 17834 W., Agharta Drive, Shambala, Tibet. All Rights Reserved. All company names and product names are registered trademarks or trademarks of their respective companies.

The names ScreeWee, Empire and Mankind are trademarks of Gobi Software 1992.

1

The Hero With A Thousand Extra Lives

Johnny bit his lip, and concentrated.

Right. Come in quick, let a missile target itself—*beep beep beep beebeebeebeeb*—on the first fighter, fire the missile—*thwump*—empty the guns at the fighter—*fplat fplat fplat fplat*—hit fighter No. 2 and take out its shields with the laser—*bwizzle*—while the missile—*pwwosh*—takes out fighter No. 1, dive, switch guns, rake fighter No. 3 as it turns *fplat fplat fplat*—pick up fighter No. 2 in the sights again up the upcurve, let go a missile—*thwump*—and rake it with—

Fwit fwit fwit.

Fighter No. 4! It always came in last, but if you went after it first the others would have time to turn and you'd end up in the sights of three of them.

He'd died six times already. And it was only five o'clock.

His hands flew over the keyboard. Stars roared past as he accelerated out of the mêlée. It'd leave him short of fuel, but by the time they caught up the shields would be back and he'd be ready, and two of them would already have taken damage, and . . . here they come . . . missiles away, wow, lucky hit on the first one, die die die!, red fireball—*swsssh*—take shield loss while concentrating fire on the next one—*swsssh*—and now the last one was running, but he could outrun it, hit the accelerator—ggrrRRRSSHHH—and just keep it in his sights while he poured shot after shot into—*swssh*.

Ah!

The huge bulk of their capital ship was in the corner of the screen. Level 10, here we come . . . careful, careful . . . there were no more ships now, so all he had to do was keep out of its range and then sweep in and *We wish to talk*.

Johnny blinked at the message on the screen.

We wish to talk.

The ship roared by—*eeeyooowwwnn*. He reached out for the throttle key and slowed himself down, and then turned and got the big red shape in his sights again.

We wish to talk.

His finger hovered on the Fire button. Then, without really looking, he moved it over to the keyboard and pressed Pause.

Then he read the manual.

Only You Can Save Mankind, it said on the cover. "Full Sound and Graphics. The Ultimate Game."

A ScreeWee heavy cruiser, it said on page 17, could be taken out with seventy-six laser shots. Once you'd cleared the fighter escort and found a handy spot where the ScreeWee's guns couldn't get you, it was just a matter of time.

We wish to talk.

Even with the Pause on, the message still flashed on the screen.

There was nothing in the manual about messages. Johnny riffled through the pages. It must be one of the New Features the game was Packed With.

He put down the book, put his hands on the keys and cautiously tapped out: Die, alein scum/

No! We do not wish to die! We wish to talk!

It wasn't supposed to be like this, was it?

Wobbler Johnson, who'd given him the disc and photocopied the manual on his dad's copier, had said that once you'd completed level 10 you got given an extra 10,000 points and the Scroll of Valour and moved on to the Arcturus Sector, where there were different ships and more of them.

Johnny *wanted* the Scroll of Valour.

Johnny fired the laser one more time. *Swsssh*. He didn't really know why. It was just because you had the joystick and there was the Fire button and that was what it was *for*.

After all, there wasn't a Don't Fire button.

We Surrender! PLEASE!

He reached over and, very carefully, pressed the Save Game button. The computer whirred and clicked, and then was silent.

He didn't play again the whole evening. He did his homework.

It was Geography. You had to colour in Great Britain and put a dot on the map of the world where you thought it was.

The ScreeWee captain thumped her desk with one of her forelegs.

"*What?*"

The First Officer swallowed, and tried to keep her tail held at a respectful angle.

"He just vanished again, ma'am," she said.

"But did he accept?"

"No, ma'am."

The Captain drummed the fingers of three hands on the table. She looked slightly like a newt but mainly like an alligator.

"But we didn't fire on him!"

"No, ma'am."

"And you sent my message?"

"Yes, ma'am."

"And every time we've killed him, he comes back . . ."

He caught up with Wobbler in Break.

Wobbler was the kind of boy who's always picked last when you had to pick teams, although that was all right at the moment as the PE teacher didn't believe in teams because they encouraged competition.

He wobbled. It was glandular, he said. He wobbled especially when he ran. Bits of Wobbler headed in various directions; it was only on *average* that he was running in any particular direction.

But he was good at games. They just weren't the ones that people thought you ought to be good at. If ever there was an Inter-Schools First-One-To-Break-The-Unbreakable-Copy-Protection-on-*Galactic-Thrusters*, Wobbler wouldn't just be in the team, he'd be *picking* the team.

"Yo, Wobbler," said Johnny.

"It's not cool to say Yo any more," said Wobbler.

"Is it rad to say cool?" said Johnny.

"Cool's always cool. And no-one says rad any more, either."

Wobbler looked around conspiratorially and then fished a package from his bag.

"*This* is cool. Have a go at this."

"What is it?" said Johnny.

"I cracked *Fighter Star TeraBomber*," said Wobbler. "Only don't tell anyone, right? Just type FSB. It's not much good, really. The space bar drops the bombs, and . . . well . . . just press the keys, you'll see what they do . . ."

"Listen . . . you know *Only You Can Save Mankind*?"

"Still playing that, are you?"

"You didn't, you know, *do* anything to it, did you? Um? Before you gave me a copy?"

"No. It wasn't even protected. Didn't have to do anything except copy the manual. Why?"

"You did play it, didn't you?"

"A bit." Wobbler only played games once. Wobbler could watch a game for a couple of minutes, and then pick up the joystick and get top score. And then never play it again.

"Nothing . . . funny . . . happened?"

"Like what?" said Wobbler.

"Like . . ." Johnny hesitated. He could tell Wobbler, and then Wobbler would laugh, or not believe him, or say it was just some bug or something, some kind of trick. Or a virus. Wobbler had discs full of computer viruses. He didn't do anything with them. He just collected them, like stamps or something.

He could tell Wobbler, and then somehow it wouldn't be real.

"Oh, you know . . . funny."

"Like what?"

"Weird. Um. Lifelike, I suppose."

"It's *sposed* to be. Just like the real thing, it says. I hope you've read the manual properly. My dad spent a whole coffee break copying that."

Johnny gave a sickly grin.

"Yes. Right. Better read it, then. Thanks for *Star Fighter Pilot*—"

"*TeraBomber*. My dad brought me back *Alabama Smith and the*

Jewels of Fate from the States. You can have a copy if you give me the disc back."

"Right," said Johnny.

"It's OK."

"Right," said Johnny.

He never had the heart to tell Wobbler that he didn't play half the games Wobbler passed on. You couldn't. Not if you wanted time to sleep and eat meals. But that was all right because Wobbler never asked. As far as Wobbler was concerned, computer games weren't there for playing. They were for breaking into, rewriting so that you got extra lives or whatever, and then copying and giving away to everyone.

Basically, there were two sides to the world. There was the entire computer games software industry engaged in a tremendous effort to stamp out piracy, and there was Wobbler. Currently, Wobbler was in front.

"Did you do my History?" said Wobbler.

"Here," said Johnny. " 'What it was like to be a peasant during the English Civil War.' Three pages."

"Thanks," said Wobbler. "That was quick."

"Oh, in Geog last term we had to do one about What it's like being a peasant in Bolivia. I just got rid of the llamas and put in stuff about kings having their heads chopped off. You have to bung in that kind of stuff, and then you just have to keep complaining about the weather and the crops and you can't go wrong, in peasant essays."

Johnny lay on his bed reading *Only You Can Save Mankind*.

He could just about remember the days when you could still get games where the instructions consisted of something that said, "Press < for left and > for right and Fire for fire."

But now you had to read a whole little book which was all about the game. It was really the manual, but they called it "The Novel."

Partly it was an anti-Wobbler thing. Someone in America or somewhere thought it was dead clever to make the game ask you little questions, like "What's the first word on line 23 on page 19 of the manual?" and then reset the machine if you didn't answer them right, so they'd obviously never heard of Wobbler's dad's office's photocopier.

So there was this book. The ScreeWee had turned up out of nowhere and bombed some planets with humans on them. Nearly all the starships had been blown up. So there was only this one left, the experimental one. It was all that stood against the ScreeWee hordes. And only *you* . . . that is to say John Maxwell, aged twelve, in between the time you get home from school and get something to eat and do your homework . . . can save mankind.

Nowhere did it say what you were supposed to do if the ScreeWee hordes didn't want to fight.

He switched on the computer, and pressed the Load Game key.

There was the ship again, right in the middle of his sights.

He picked up the joystick thoughtfully.

There was an immediate message on the screen. Well, not exactly a message. More a picture. Half a dozen little egg-shaped blobs, with tails. They didn't move.

What kind of message is that? he thought.

Perhaps there was a special message he ought to send. "Die, Creep" didn't seem to fit properly at the moment.

He typed: Whats hpaening?

Immediately a reply appeared on the screen, in yellow letters.

We surrender. Do not shoot. See, we show you pictures of our children.

He typed: Is this a trick WObbler?

It took a little while before the reply came.

Am not trick wobbler. We give in. No more war.

Johnny thought for a while, and then typed: Youre not supoosed to give ni.

Want to go home.

Johnny typed: It says in the book you blue up a lot of planets.

Lies!

Johnny stared at the screen. What he wanted to type was: No, I mean, this cant happen, youre Aliens, you cant not want to be shot at, no other game aliens have ever stopped aliening across the screen, they never said We DonT Want to Go.

And then he thought: they never had the chance. *They* couldn't.

But games are a lot better now.

They never made things like the old MegaZoids seem *real*, with stories about them and Full-Colour Graphics.

This is probably that Virtual Reality they're always talking about on the television.

He typed: It is only a game, after all.

What is a game?

He typed: Who ARE you?

The screen flickered. Something a bit like a newt but more like an alligator looked back at him.

I am the Captain, said the yellow letters. *Do not shoot*!

Johnny typed: I shoot at you and you shoto at me. That is the game.

But we die.

Johnny typed: Sometimes I die. I die a lot.

But YOU live again.

Johnny stared at the words for a moment. Then he typed: Dont you?

No. How could this be? When we die, we die. For ever.

Johnny typed desperately: No, thats not right because, in the first mission, theres three ships you have to blow up before the first planet. I@ve played it lots of times and there@s always three ships there—

Different ships.

Johnny thought for a while and then typed: What happens if I switch of tthe machine?

We do not understand the question.

This is daft, thought Johnny. It's just a very unusual game. It's a special mission or something.

He typed: Why should I trust you?

LOOK BEHIND YOU.

Johnny sat bolt upright in his chair. Then he let himself swivel around, very cautiously.

Of course, there was no-one there. Why should there be anyone there? It was a *game*.

The newt face had disappeared from the screen, leaving the familiar picture of the inside of the starfighter. And there was the radar screen—

—covered in yellow dots.

Yellow for the enemy.

Johnny picked up the joystick and turned the starfighter around. The entire ScreeWee fleet was there. Ship after ship was hanging in space behind him. Little fighters, big cruisers, massive battleships.

If they all had him in their sights, and if they fired . . .

He didn't want to die.

Hang on, hang on. You don't die. You just play the game again.

This was *nuts*. It was time to stop it.

He typed: All right what happens now?

We want to go home.

He typed: All right no problem.

You give us safe conduct.

He typed: OK yes.

The screen went blank.

And that was it? No music? No "Congratulations, You've Got the Highest Score"?

Just the little prompt, flashing on and off.

What did safe conduct mean, anyway?

2

Operate Controls To Play Game

You never said to your parents, "Hey, I really need a computer because that way I can play *Megasteroids*."

No, you said, "I really need a computer because of school."

It's *educational*.

Anyway, there had to be a good side to the Trying Times everyone was going through in this house. If you hung around in your room and generally kept your head down, stuff like computers sort of happened. It made everyone feel better.

And it *was* quite useful for school sometimes. Johnny had written "What it felt like to be different sorts of peasants" on it, and printed them out on the printer, although he had to rewrite them in his handwriting because although the school taught Keyboard Skills and New Technology you got into trouble if you used keyboard skills and new technology actually to do anything.

Funnily enough, it wasn't much good for maths. He'd always had trouble with algebra, because they wouldn't let you get away with "What it feels like to be x^2." But he had an arrangement with Bigmac about that, because Bigmac got the same feeling when he looked at an essay project as Johnny did when he was faced with a quadratic equation. Anyway, it didn't matter that much. If you kept your head down, they were generally so grateful that you were not, e.g., causing policemen to come to the school, or actually nailing a teacher to anything, that you got left alone.

But mainly the computer was good for games. If you turned the volume control up, you didn't have to hear the shouting.

The ScreeWee mother ship was in uproar. There was still a haze of smoke in the air from the last bombardment, and indistinct figures pattered back and forth, trying to fix things up well enough to survive the journey.

The Captain sat back in her chair on the huge, shadowy bridge. She was yellow under the eyes, a sure sign of lack of sleep. So much to be done . . . half the fighters were damaged, and the main ships were in none too good condition, and there was hardly any room and certainly no food for all the survivors they were taking on board.

She looked up. There was the Gunnery Officer.

"This is not a wise move," he said.

"It is the only one I have," said the Captain wearily.

"No! We must fight on!"

"And then we die," said the Captain. "We fight, and then we die. That's how it goes."

"Then we die gloriously!"

"There's an important word in that sentence," said the Captain. "And it's not the word 'gloriously'."

The Gunnery Officer went light green with rage.

"He's attacked hundreds of our ships!"

"And then he stopped."

"None of the others have," said the Gunnery Officer. "They're *humans*! You can't trust a *human*. They shoot *everything*."

The Captain rested her snout on one hand.

"He doesn't," she said. "He listened. He talked. None of the others did. He may be the One."

The Gunnery Officer placed his upper two front hands on the desk and glared at her.

"Well," he said, "*I've* talked to the other officers. I don't believe in legends. When the full enormity of what you have done is understood, you will be relieved of your command!"

She turned tired eyes towards him.

"Good," she said. "But right now, I *am* Captain. I am *responsible*.

Do you understand? Have you got the faintest idea of what that *means?* Now . . . *go!*"

He didn't like it, but he couldn't disobey. I can have him shot, she thought. It'd be a good idea. Bound to save trouble later on. It'll be No. 235 on the list of Things to Do . . .

She turned back to continue staring at the stars outside, on the huge screen that filled one wall.

The enemy ship still hung there.

What kind of person is it? she thought. Despicable though they are, there's so few of them. But they keep coming back! What's their secret?

But you can be sure of one thing. They surely only send their bravest and their best.

The advantage of the Trying Times was that helping yourself from the fridge was OK. There didn't seem to be any proper mealtimes any more in any case. Or any real cooking.

Johnny made himself spaghetti and baked beans. There was no sound from the living-room, although the TV was on.

Then he watched a bit of television in his room. He'd been given the old one when they got the new one. It wasn't very big and you had to get up and walk over to it every time you wanted to change channels or the volume or whatever, but these were Trying Times.

There was a film on the News showing some missiles streaking over some city. It was quite good.

Then he went to bed.

He was not entirely surprised to wake up at the controls of a starfighter.

It had been like that with *Captain Zoom.* You couldn't get it out of your head. After an evening's concentrated playing you were climbing ladders and dodging laser-zap bolts all night.

It was a pretty good dream, even so. He could *feel* the seat under him. And the cabin smelled of hot oil and overheated plastic and unwashed people.

It *looked* pretty much like the one he saw on the screen every evening, except that there was a thin film of grease and dirt over everything. But there was the radar screen, and the weapons console, and the joystick . . .

Hey, *much* better than the computer! The cabin was full of noises—the click and whirr of fans, the hum and buzz of instruments.

And better graphics. You get much better graphics in your dreams.

The ScreeWee fleet hung in the ai—hung in space in front of him.

Wow!

Although dreams ought to be a bit more exciting. You got chased in dreams. Things *happened* to you. Sitting in the cockpit of a starfighter bristling with weapons was fun, but things ought to *happen* . . .

He wondered if he should launch a missile or something . . . No, hang on, they'd surrendered. And there was that thing about safe conduct.

His hands wandered over the switches in front of him. They were a bit different from the computer keyboard, but *this* one—

"Are you receiving me?"

The face of the Captain appeared on the communications screen.

"Yes?" said Johnny.

"We are ready."

"Ready?" said Johnny. "What for?"

"Lead the way," said the Captain. The voice came out of a grille beside the screen. It must be being translated by something, Johnny thought. I shouldn't think giant newts speak English.

"Where to?" he said. "Where are we going?"

"Earth."

"Earth? Hang on! That's where *I* live! People can get into serious trouble showing huge alien fleets where they live!"

The grille hummed and buzzed for a while. Then the Captain said: *"Apology. That is a direct translation. We call the planet that is our home, 'Earth.' When I speak in ScreeWee, your computer finds the word in your language that means the same thing. The actual word in ScreeWee sounds like . . ."* There was a noise like someone taking their foot out of a wet cowpat. *"I will show our home to you."*

A red circle suddenly developed on the navigation screen.

Johnny knew about that. You just moved a green circle over it, the computer went *binkabinkabinka*, and you'd set your course.

They've shown me where they live.

The thought sunk in.

They trust me.

As he moved his fighter forwards, the entire alien fleet pulled in behind him. They eclipsed the stars.

The cabin hummed and buzzed quietly to itself.

Well, at least it didn't look too hard . . .

A green dot appeared ahead of him.

He watched it get bigger, and recognized the shape of a starfighter, just like his.

But it was a little hard to make it out.

This was because it was half-hidden by laser bolts.

It was firing at him as it came.

And it was travelling so fast it was very nearly catching up with its own fire.

Johnny jerked the joystick and his ship rolled out of the way as the . . . the *enemy* starfighter roared past and barrelled on towards the ScreeWee ships.

The whole sky full of ScreeWee ships.

Which had surrendered to *him*.

But people out there were still playing the game.

"No! Listen to me! They're not fighting any more!"

The starfighter turned in a wide curve and headed directly for the command ship. Johnny saw it launch a missile. Someone sitting at a keyboard somewhere had launched a missile.

"*Listen!* You've got to *stop*!"

It's not listening to me, he thought. You don't listen to the enemy. The enemy's there to be shot at. That's why it's the enemy. That's what the enemy's *for*.

He swung around to follow the starship, which had slowed down. It was pouring shot after shot into the command ship . . .

. . . which wasn't firing back.

Johnny stared in horror.

The ship rocked under the hail of fire. The Gunnery Officer crawled across the shaking floor and pulled himself up beside the Captain's chair.

"Fool! Fool! I told you this would happen! I demand that we return fire!"

The Captain was watching the Chosen One's ship. It hadn't moved.

"No," she said. "We have to give him a chance. We must not fire on human ships."

"A *chance*? How much of a chance do *we* have? I shall give the order to—"

The Captain moved very fast. When her hand stopped she was holding a gun very close to the Gunnery Officer's head. It was really only a ceremonial weapon; normally ScreeWee fought only with their claws. But its shape said very clearly that things came out of the hole in the front end with the very definite purpose of travelling fast through the air and then killing people.

"No," she said.

The Gunnery Officer's face went blue, a sure sign of terror. But he had enough courage left to say: "You would not *dare* fire!"

It's a game, thought Johnny. There's not a *real* person in that ship. It's someone playing a game. It's *all* a game. It's just things happening on a screen somewhere.

No.

I mean, *yes.*

But . . .

. . . at the same time . . .

. . . it's all happening *here* . . .

His own ship leapt forward.

It was easy. It was so easy. Just line up circles on the screen, *binkabinkabinka*, and then press the Fire button until every weapon on the ship was empty. He'd done it many times before.

The invader hadn't even seen him. It launched some missiles—and then blew up in an impressive display of graphics.

That's all it is, Johnny told himself. Just things on a screen. It's not real. There's no arms and feet spinning away through the wreckage. It's all a game.

The missiles arrived . . .

The whole cockpit went blinding white.

He was aware, just for a moment, of cold space around him, with things in it . . .

A bookcase. A chair. A bed.

He was sitting in front of the computer. The screen was blank. He was holding the joystick so hard that he had to concentrate to let go of it.

The clock by his bed said 6:3≡, because it was broken. But it meant he'd have to get up in another hour or so.

He sat with his quilt around him watching the television until the alarm went off.

There were some more pictures of missiles and bullets streaking over a city. They looked pretty much the same as the ones he'd seen last night, but were probably back by popular demand.

He felt sick.

Yo-less could help, Johnny decided.

He normally hung out with Wobbler and Bigmac on the bit of wall behind the school library. They weren't exactly a gang. If you take a big bag of crisps and shake them up, all the little bits end up in one corner.

Yo-less was called Yo-less because he never said "Yo." He'd given up objecting to the name by now. At least it was better than Nearly Crucial, which was the last nickname, and MC Spanner, which was the one before that. Johnny was the official nickname generator.

Yo-less said he'd never said "crucial," either. He pointed out that Johnny was white and never said, "YerWhat? YerWhat? YerWhat?" or "Ars-nal! Ars-nal!" and anyway, you shouldn't make jokes about racial stereotyping.

Johnny didn't go into too much detail. He just talked about the dream, and not about the messages on the screen. Yo-less listened carefully. Yo-less listened to everything carefully. It worried teachers, the way he listened carefully to everything they said. They always suspected he was trying to catch them out.

He said, "What you've got here is a projection of a psychological conflict. That's all. Want a cheese ring?"

"What's that?"

"It's just crunchy cheesy-flavoured—"

"I mean the other thing you said."

Yo-less passed the packet on to Bigmac.

"Well . . . your mum and dad are splitting up, right? Well-known fact."

"Could be. It's a bit of a trying time," said Johnny.

"O-*kay*. And there's nothing you can do about it."

"Shouldn't think so," said Johnny.

"And this definitely affects you," said Yo-less.

"I suppose so," said Johnny cautiously. "I know I have to do a lot of my own cooking."

"Right. So you project your . . . um . . . suppressed emotions on to a computer game. Happens all the time," said Yo-less, whose mother was a nurse, and who wanted to be a doctor if he grew up. "You can't solve the *real* problems, so you turn them into problems you *can* solve. Like . . . if this was thirty years ago, you'd probably dream about fighting dragons or something. It's a projected fantasy."

"Saving hundreds of intelligent newts doesn't sound very easy to solve," said Johnny.

"Dunno," said Bigmac, happily. "Ratatatat-blam! No more problem." Bigmac wore large boots and camouflage trousers all the time. You could spot him a mile off by his camouflage trousers.

"The thing is," said Yo-less, "it's not real. Real's real. But stuff on a screen isn't."

"I've cracked *Stellar Smashers*," said Wobbler. "You can have that if you want. Everyone says it's a lot better."

"No-oo," said Johnny, "I think I'll stick with this one for a while. See if I can get to level twenty-one."

"If you get to level twenty-one and blow up the whole fleet you get a special number on the screen, and if you write off to Gobi Software you get a five pound token," said Wobbler. "It was in *Computer Weekly*."

Johnny thought about the Captain.

"A whole five pounds?" he said. "Gosh."

It was Games in the afternoon. Bigmac was the only one who played. He'd never been keen until they'd introduced hockey. You got a club to hit people, he said.

Yo-less didn't do sport because of intellectual incompatibility. Wobbler didn't do sport because the sports master had asked him not to. Johnny didn't do sport because he had a permanent note, and no-one cared much anyway, so he went home early and spent the afternoon reading the manual.

He didn't touch the computer before tea.

There was an extended News, which meant that *Cobbers* was postponed. There were the same pictures of missiles streaking across a city that he'd seen the night before, except that now there were more journalists in sand-coloured shirts with lots of pockets talking excitedly about them.

He heard his mother downstairs complain about *Cobbers*, and by the sound of the raised voices that started Trying Times again.

There was some History homework about Christopher Columbus. He looked him up in the encyclopedia and copied out four hundred words, which usually worked. He drew a picture of Columbus as well, and coloured it in.

After a while he realized that he was putting off switching the computer on. It came to something, he thought, when you did school work rather than play games . . .

It wouldn't hurt to at least have a game of *Pac-Man* or something. Trouble was, the ghosts would probably stay in the middle of the screen and refuse to come out and be eaten. He didn't think he could cope with that. He'd got enough to worry about as it was.

On top of it all, his father came upstairs to be fatherly. This happened about once a fortnight. There didn't seem to be any way of stopping it. You had to put up with twenty minutes of being asked about how you were getting on at school, and had you *really* thought about what you wanted to be when you grew up.

The thing to do was not encourage things, but as politely as possible.

His father sat on the edge of the bed and looked around the room as though he'd never seen it before.

After the normal questions about teachers Johnny hadn't had since the first year, his father stared at nothing much for a while and then said, "Things have been a bit tricky lately. I expect you've noticed."

"No."

"It's been a bit tricky at work. Not a good time to start a new business."

"Yes."

"Everything all right?"

"Yes."

"Nothing you want to talk about?"

"No. I don't think so."

His father looked around the room again. Then he said, "Remember last year, when we all went down to Falmouth for the week?"

"Yes."

"You enjoyed that, didn't you?"

He'd got sunburnt and twisted his ankle on some rocks and he had to get up at 8.30 *every morning*, even though it was supposed to be a holiday. And the only TV in the hotel was in front of some old woman who never let go of the remote-control.

"Yes."

"We ought to go again."

His father was staring at him.

"Yes," said Johnny. "That would be nice."

"How're you getting on with *Space Invaders?*"

"Sorry?"

"*Space Invaders*. On the computer."

Johnny turned to look at the blank screen.

"What're Space Invaders?" he said.

"Isn't that what they're called any more? Space Invaders? You used to get them in pubs and things, oh, before you were born. Rows of spiky triangular green aliens with six legs kept on coming down the screen and we had to shoot them."

Johnny gave this some thought. "What happened when you'd shot them all, then?"

"Oh, you got some more." His father stood up. "I expect it's all more complicated now, though."

"Yes."

"Done your homework, have you?"

"Yes."

"What was it?"

"History. Had to write about Christopher Columbus."

"Hmm? You could put in that he didn't set out to discover America. He was really looking for Asia and found America by accident."

"Yes. It says that in the encyclopedia."

"Glad to see you're using it."

"Yes. It's very interesting."

"Good. Right. Right, then. Well, I'm going to have another look at those accounts . . ."

"Right."

"If there's anything you want to talk about, you know . . ."

"All right."

Johnny waited until he heard the living-room door shut again. He wondered if he ought to have asked where the instruction manual for the dishwasher was.

He switched on the computer.

After a while, the screen for *Only You Can Save Mankind* came on. He watched the introductory bit moodily, and then picked up the joystick.

There weren't any aliens.

For a little while he thought he'd done something wrong. He started the game again.

There were still no aliens. All there was, was the blackness of space, sprinkled with a few twinkling stars.

He flew around until he was out of fuel.

No ScreeWee, no dots on the radar screen. No game.

They'd gone.

3

Cereal Killers

There was more news these days than normal. Half the time the TV was showing pictures of tanks and maps of deserts with green and red arrows all over them, while in the corner of the screen would be a photo of a journalist with a phone to his ear, talking in a crackly voice.

It crackled in the background while Johnny phoned up Wobbler.

"Yes?"

"Can I speak to Wob . . . to Stephen, please?"

Mutter, clonk, bump, scuffle.

"Yes?"

"It's me, Wobbler."

"Yes?"

"Have you had a look at *Only You Can Save Mankind* lately?"

"No. Hey, listen, I've found a way to—"

"Could you have a go with it right now, please?"

Pause.

"You all right?"

"What?"

"You sound a bit weird."

"Look, go and have a go with the game, will you?"

It was an hour before Wobbler phoned back. Johnny waited on the stairs.

"Can I speak—"

"It's me."

"There's no aliens, right?"

"Yes!"

"Probably something built into the game. You can do that, you know. A kind of time bomb thing. Maybe it's programmed to make all the aliens vanish on a certain date."

"What for?"

"Make things more interesting, I expect. Probably Gobi Software will be putting adverts in the computer papers about it. You all right? Your voice sounds a bit squeaky."

"No problem."

"You coming down to the mall tomorrow?"

"Yeah."

"See you, then. Chow."

Johnny stared at the dead phone. Of course, there *were* things like that on computers. There'd been something in the papers about it. A Friday the 13th virus, or something. Something in the program kept an eye on the date, and when it was Friday the 13th it was supposed to do something nasty to computers all over the country.

There had been stories about Evil Computer Hackers Menacing Society, and Wobbler had come to school in home-made dark glasses for a week.

Johnny went back and watched the screen for a while. Stars occasionally went past.

Wobbler had written an actual computer game like this once. It was called *Journey to Alpha Centauri*. It was a screen with some dots on it. Because, he said, it happened in *real time*, which no-one had ever heard of until computers. He'd seen on TV that it took three thousand years to get to Alpha Centauri. He had written it so that if anyone kept their computer on for three thousand years, they'd be rewarded by a little dot appearing in the middle of the screen, and then a message saying, "Welcome to Alpha Centauri. Now go home."

Johnny watched the screen for a bit longer. Once or twice he nudged the joystick, to go on a different course. It didn't make much difference. Space looked the same from every direction.

"Hello? Anybody there?" he whispered.

He watched some television before he went to bed. There were some more missiles, and someone going on about some other missiles which were supposed to knock down the first type of missile.

* * *

The fleet travelled in the shape of a giant cone, hundreds of miles long. The Captain looked back at it. There were scores of mother ships, hundreds of fighters. More and more kept joining them as news of the surrender spread.

The Chosen One's ship flew a little way ahead of the fleet. It wasn't answering messages.

But no-one was shooting at them. There hadn't been a human ship visible for hours. Perhaps, the Captain thought, it's really working. We're leaving them behind . . .

Johnny woke up in the game.

It was hard to sleep in the starship. The seat started out as the most comfortable thing in the whole world, but it was amazing how uncomfortable it became after a few hours. And the lavatory was a complicated arrangement of tubes and trapdoors and it wasn't, he was beginning to notice, entirely smellproof.

That's what the computer games couldn't give you: the *smell* of space. It had its own kind of smell, like a machine's armpit. You didn't get dirty, because there was no dirt, but there was a sort of grimy cleanliness about everything.

The radar went *ping*.

After a while, he could see a dot ahead of him. It wasn't moving much, and it certainly wasn't firing.

He left the fleet and went to investigate.

It was a huge ship. Or, at least, it had been once. Quite a lot of it had been melted off.

It drifted along, absolutely dead, tumbling very gently. It was green, and vaguely triangular, except for six legs, or possibly arms. Three of them were broken stubs. It looked like a cross between a spider and an octopus, designed by a computer and made out of hundreds of cubes, bolted together.

As the giant hulk turned he could see huge gashes in it, with melted edges. There was a suggestion of floors inside.

He switched on the radio.

"Captain?"

"*Yes?*"

"Can you see this thing here? What is it?"

"*We find them sometimes. We think they belonged to an ancient race, now extinct. We don't know what they called themselves, or where they came from. The ships are very crude."*

The dead ship turned slowly. There was another long burn down the other side.

"I think they were called Space Invaders," said Johnny.

"The human name for them?"

"Yes."

"I thought so."

Johnny was glad he couldn't see the Captain's face.

He thought: No-one knows where they came from, or even what they called themselves. And now no-one ever will.

The radar went *ping* again.

There was a human ship heading towards the fleet, at high speed.

This time, he didn't hesitate.

The point was, the ScreeWee weren't very *good* at fighting. After the first few games it was quite easy to beat them. They couldn't seem to get the hang of it. They didn't know how to be sneaky, or when to dodge.

It was the same with all of them, come to think of it. Johnny had played lots of games with words like "Space" and "Battle" and "Cosmic" in the titles, and all the aliens were the sort you could beat after a few weeks' playing.

This player didn't stand a chance against a real human.

You got six missiles. Johnny had two streaking away before the enemy was much larger than a dot. Then he just kept his finger on the Fire button until there was nothing left to fire.

A spreading cloud of wreckage, and that was it.

It wasn't as if anyone would die, after all. Whoever had been in there would just have to start the game again.

It *felt* real, but that was just the dream . . .

Dreams always felt real.

He turned his attention to the thing by the control chair. It had a nozzle which filled a paper cup with something like thin vegetable soup, and a slot which pushed out very large plastic bags containing very small things like sandwiches. The bags had to be big to get all the list of additives on. They contained absolutely everything necessary to keep a star warrior healthy. Not happy, but healthy . . .

He'd taken one mouthful when something slammed into the ship. A red glare filled the cabin; alarms started to blare.

He looked up in time to see a ship curving away for another run.

He hadn't even glanced at the radar.

He'd been eating his *tea*!

He spun the ship. The multi-vitamin sandwich flew around into the wiring somewhere.

It was coming back to get him. He prodded furiously at the control panel.

Hang on . . .

What was the worst that could happen to him?

He could wake up in bed.

He took his time. He dodged. He weaved. Another missile hit the ship. As the attacker roared past, Johnny fired, with everything.

Another cloud of wreckage.

No problem.

But it must have fired a missile just before he got it. There was another red flash. The lights went out. The ship jumped. His head bounced off the seatback and banged on to the control panel.

He opened his eyes.

Right. And you wake up back in your bedroom.

A light winked at him.

There was something beeping.

Bound to be the alarm clock. That's how dreams end . . .

He lifted his head. The flashing light was oblong. He tried to focus. There were shapes there.

But they weren't saying 6:3≡.

They were spelling out "AIR LEAK," and behind the insistent beeping was a terrible hissing sound.

No, no, he thought. This doesn't happen.

He pushed himself up. There were lots of red lights. He pressed some buttons hurriedly, but this had no effect at all except to make some more lights go red.

He didn't know much about the controls of a starship, other than fast, slow, left, right and fire, but there were whole rows of flashing alarms which suggested that a lot of things he didn't know about were going wrong. He stared at some red letters which said "SECONDARY PUMPS FAILURE." He didn't know what the secondary pumps were, either, but he wished, he really wished, they hadn't failed.

His head ached. He reached up, and there was real blood on his hand. And he knew that he was going to die. Really die.

No, he thought. Please! I'm John Maxwell. Please! I'm twelve. I'm not dying in a spaceshi—

The beeping got louder.

He looked at the sign again.

It was flashing 6:3≡.

About time, he thought, as he passed out . . .

And woke up.

He was at the computer again. It wasn't switched on, and he was freezing cold.

He had a headache, but a tentative feel said there was no blood. It was *just* a headache.

He stared into the dark black screen, and wondered what it felt like to be a ScreeWee.

It felt like that, except that you didn't wake up. It was always AIR LEAK, or *Alert*Alert*Alert* beeping on and off, and then perhaps the freezing cold of space, and then nothing.

He had breakfast.

You got a free alien in every pack of sugar-glazed Snappiflakes. It was a new thing. Or an old thing, being tried again.

The one that ended up in his bowl was orange and had three eyes and four arms. And it was holding a ray gun in each hand.

His father hadn't got up. His mother was watching the little television in the kitchen, where a very large man disguised as an entire desert was pointing to a lot of red and blue arrows on a map.

He went down to Neil Armstrong Mall.

He took the plastic alien with him. That'd be the way to invade a planet. One alien in every box! Wait until they were in every cupboard in the country, send out the signal and *bazaam*!

Cereal killers!

Maybe on some other planet somewhere you got a free human in every packet of ammonia-coated Snappi-crystals. Hey, *zorks*! Collect the Whole Set! And there'd be all these little plastic people. Holding guns, of course. You just had to walk down the street to see that, of course, everyone had a gun.

He looked out of the bus window.

That was it, really. No-one would bother to put plastic aliens inside the plastic cereal if they were just, you know, doing everyday things.

Holding the Cosmiczippo Ray™ hedge clippers! Getting on the Megadeath™ bus! Hanging out at the Star Thruster Mall!

The trouble with all the aliens he'd seen was that they either wanted to eat you or play music at you until you became better people. You never got the sort that just wanted to do something ordinary like borrow the lawn mower.

Wobbler and Yo-less and Bigmac were trying to hang out by the ornamental fountain, but really they were just hanging around. Yo-less was wearing the same grey trousers he wore to school. You couldn't hang out in grey trousers. And Wobbler still wore his sunglasses, except they weren't real sunglasses because he had to wear ordinary glasses *anyway*; they were those clip-on sunglasses for tourists. Also, they weren't the same size as the glasses underneath, and had rubbed red marks on his nose. And he wore an anorak. Wobbler was probably the only person in the universe who still wore an anorak. And Bigmac, in addition to his camouflage trousers and "Terminator" T-shirt with "Blackbury Skins" on the back in biro, had got hold of a belt made entirely of cartridge cases. He looked stupid.

"Yo, duds," said Johnny.

"We've been here ages," said Yo-less.

"I went one stop past on the bus and had to walk back," said Johnny. "Thinking about other things. What's happening?"

"Do you mean what's happening, or sort of hey, my man, what's *happening*?" said Wobbler.

"What's happening?" said Johnny.

"I want to go into J&J Software," said Wobbler. "They might have got *Cosmic Coffee Mats* in. It got a review in *Bazzammm!* and they said it's got an unbreakable copy protection."

"Did they say it was any good?" said Bigmac.

"Who cares?"

"You'll get caught one day," said Yo-less.

"Then you get given a job in Silicon Valley, designing antipiracy software," said Wobbler. Behind his two thicknesses of glasses, his eyes lit up. Wobbler thought that California was where good people went when they died.

"No, you don't. You just get in trouble and you get sued," said Yo-less. "And the police take all your computers away. There was something in the paper."

They wandered aimlessly towards the computer shop.

"I saw this film once, right, where there were these computer games and if you were really good the aliens came and got you and you had to fly a spaceship and fight a whole bad alien fleet," said Bigmac.

"Did you beat it? I mean, in the film, the alien fleet got beaten?"

Bigmac gave Johnny an odd look.

"Of *course*. Sure. There wouldn't be any point otherwise, would there."

"Only you can save mankind," said Johnny.

"What?"

"It's the game," said Wobbler.

"But it *always* says something like that on the boxes you get games in," said Johnny. Except if you get them from Wobbler, he added to himself, when you just get a disc.

"Well. Yeah. Something like that. Why not?"

"I mean they never say, 'Only You are going to be put inside a Billion Pounds Worth of Machine with more Switches than you've Ever Seen and be Blown to Bits by a Thousand Skilled Enemy Pilots because You Don't Really Know how to Fly It.' "

They wandered past Mr. Zippy's Ice Cream Extravaganza.

"Can't see that catching on," said Wobbler. "Can't see them ever selling a game called *Get Shot to Pieces*."

"You still having trouble at home?" said Yo-less.

"It's all gone quiet," said Johnny.

"That can be worse than shouting."

"Yes."

"It's not that bad when your mum and dad split up," said Wobbler, "although you get to see more museums than is good for you."

"Still found no aliens?" said Yo-less.

"Um. Not in the game."

"Still dreaming about them?" said Wobbler.

"Sort of."

Someone handing out leaflets about Big Savings on Double Glazing gave one, in desperation, to Yo-less. He took it gravely, thanked them, folded it in two and put it in his pocket. Yo-less always filed this sort of thing. You never knew when it might come in handy, he said. One day he might want to doubleglaze his surgery, and he'd be in a good position to compare offers.

"Anyone see the war on the box last night?" said Bigmac. "Way to go, eh?"

"Way to go where?" said Yo-less.

"We're really kicking some butt!"

"Some but what?" said Wobbler.

"We'll give them the 'Mother-in-law of All Battles,' eh?" said Bigmac, still trying to stir some patriotism.

"Nah. It's not like real fighting," said Wobbler. "It's just TV fighting."

"Wish I was in the army," said Bigmac, wistfully. "Blam!" He shot the double-glazing lady, who didn't notice. Bigmac had a habit of firing imaginary guns. Other people played air guitar, he shot air rifles.

"Couple more years," he said. "That's all."

"You ought to write to Stormin' Norman," said Wobbler. "Ask him to keep the war going until you get there."

"He's done pretty well for someone called Norman," said Yo-less. "I mean . . . Norman? Not very mackko, is it? It's like Bruce, or Rodney."

"He had to be Norman," said Wobbler, "otherwise he couldn't be Stormin'. You couldn't have Stormin' Bruce. Come on."

J&J Software was always packed on a Saturday morning. There were always a couple of computers running games, and always a cluster of people gathered round them. No-one knew who J&J were, since the shop was run by Mr. Patel, who had eyes like a hawk. He always watched Wobbler very carefully, on the fairly accurate basis that Wobbler distributed more games than he did and didn't even charge anyone for them.

The four of them split up. Bigmac wasn't much interested in games, and Yo-less went down to look at the videos. Wobbler had found someone who knew even more complicated stuff about computers than he did himself.

Johnny mooched along the racks of games.

I wonder if the ScreeWee do this, he thought. Or people on Jupiter or somewhere. Go down to a shop and buy "Shoot the Human" games. And have films where there's a human running around the place terrorizing a spaceship—

He became aware of a raised voice at the counter.

You didn't often get girls in J&J Software. Once, quite a long time ago, during a bit of time she'd set aside for parenting, Johnny's mother had tried playing a game. It had been quite a simple one—you had to shoot asteroids and flying saucers and things. It had been embarrassing. It had been amazing that the flying saucers had even bothered to shoot back. More likely they should have parked and all the aliens could have looked out of the windows and made rude noises. Women didn't have a clue.

A girl was complaining to Mr. Patel about a game she'd bought. Everyone knew you couldn't do that, even if you'd opened the box and it was full of nothing but mouse droppings. Mr. Patel took the view that once the transparent wrapper had come off, even the Pope wouldn't be allowed to return a game, not even if he got God to come in as well. This was because he'd met people like Wobbler before.

The boys watched in fascinated horror.

She kept tapping the offending box with a finger.

"*And* who wants to see nothing but stars?" she said. "I've seen stars before, *actually*. It says on the box that you fight dozens of different kinds of alien ships. There isn't even *one*."

Mr. Patel muttered something. Johnny wasn't close enough to hear. But the girl's voice had a kind of penetrating quality, like a corkscrew. When she spoke in italics, you could *hear* them.

"Oh, no. You can't say that. Because how can I tell if it works without *trying* it? That comes under the Sale of Goods Act (1983)."

The awed watchers were astonished to see a slightly hunted look in Mr. Patel's eyes. Up until now he'd never met anyone who could pronounce brackets.

He muttered something else.

"Copy it? Why should I copy it? I've *bought* it. It says on the box you meet fascinating alien races. Well, all I got was one ship and some stupid message on the screen and then it ran away. I don't call that fascinating alien races."

Message . . .

Ran away . . .

Johnny sidled closer.

Mr. Patel muttered something else, and then turned to one of the shelves. The shop watched in amazement. There was a *new* game in his hand. He was actually going to make an exchange. This was like Genghis Khan deciding not to attack a city but stay at home and watch the football instead.

Then he held up his hand, nodded at the girl, and stalked over to one of the shop's own computers, the ones with so many fingermarks on the keys that you couldn't read them any more.

Everyone watched in silence as he loaded up the copy of the game that the girl had brought back. The music came on. The title scrolled up the screen, like the one in Star Wars. It was the usual stuff: "The mighty ScreeWee fleet have attacked the Federation," whatever that was, "and only *you* . . ."

And then there was space. It was computer space—a sort of black, with the occasional star rolling past.

"There ought to be six ships on the first mission," said someone behind Johnny.

Mr. Patel scowled at him. He pressed a key cautiously.

"You've just fired a torpedo at nothing, Mr. Patel," said Wobbler.

Finally Mr. Patel gave up. He waved his hands in the air.

"How d'you find the things to shoot?" he said.

"They find you," said someone. "You should be dead by now."

"See?" said the girl. "You get nothing but space. I left it on for hours, and there was just space."

"Maybe you're not persevering. You kids don't know the meaning of the word persevere," said Mr. Patel.

Wobbler looked over the shopkeeper's head to Johnny and raised his eyebrows.

"It's like persistently trying," said Johnny helpfully.

"Oh. Right. Well, I persistently tried the other night and *I* didn't find any, either."

Mr. Patel carefully unwrapped the new copy of the game. The shop watched as he slotted the disc into the computer.

"Then let us see what the game looks like before Mr. Wobbler plays his little tricks," he said.

There was the title screen. There was the story, such as it was. And the instructions.

And space.

"Soon we shall see," said Mr. Patel.

And then more space.

"This one was only delivered yesterday."

Lots more space. That was the thing about space.

Mr. Patel picked up the box and looked at it carefully, But they'd all seen him take off the polythene.

They've gone, thought Johnny.

Even on the new games.

They've all gone.

People were laughing. But Wobbler and Yo-less were staring at him.

4

"No-one Really Dies"

"I reckon," said Bigmac, "I *reckon* . . ."

"Yes?" said Yo-less.

"I reckon . . . Ronald McDonald is like Jesus Christ."

Bigmac did that kind of thing. Sometimes he came out with the kind of big, slow statement that suggested some sort of deep thinking had been going on for some time. It was like mountains. Johnny knew they were made by continents banging together, but no-one ever saw it happening.

"Yes?" said Yo-less, in a kind voice. "And why do you think this?"

"Well, look at all the advertising," said Bigmac, waving a fry in the general direction of the rest of the burger bar. "There's this happy land you go to where there's lakes of banana milkshake and—and trees covered in fries. And . . . and then there's the Hamburglar. He's the Devil."

"Mr. Zippy's advertised by a giant talking ice cream," said Wobbler.

"I don't like that," said Yo-less. "I wouldn't trust an ice cream that's trying to get you to eat ice creams."

Occasionally they talked like this for hours, when there was something they didn't want to talk about. But now they seemed to have run out of things to say.

They all looked silently at Johnny, who'd hardly touched his burger.

"Look, I don't *know* what's happening," he said.

"Gobi Software're going to be really pissed off when they find out what you've done," said Wobbler, grinning.

"I didn't do anything!" said Johnny. "It's not my fault!"

"Could be a virus," said Yo-less.

"Nah," said Wobbler. "I've got loads of viruses. They just muck up the computer. They don't muck up your head."

"They could do," said Yo-less. "With flashing lights and stuff. Kind of like hypnosis."

"You said before I was making it all up! *You* said I was projecting fantasies!"

"That was before old Patel went through half a dozen boxes. I'm glad I saw that. You know she actually got another copy *and* her money back, *actually*?"

Johnny smiled uncomfortably.

Wobbler drummed his fingers on the table, or partly on the table and partly in a pool of barbecue sauce.

"No, I still reckon it's just something Gobi Software did to all the games. Cor, I like the virus idea, though," he said. "Humans catching viruses off of computers? Nice one."

"It's not like that," said Johnny.

"They used to do this thing with films where they'd put in just one frame of something, like an ice cream or something, and it'd enter people's brains without them knowing it and they'd all want ice cream," said Yo-less. "Subliminal advertising, it was called. That'd be quite easy to do on a computer."

Johnny thought about the Captain showing him pictures of her children. That didn't sound like hypnosis. He didn't know what it *did* sound like, but it didn't sound like hypnosis.

"Perhaps they're real aliens and they're in control of your computer," said Yo-less.

"OOOO—eee—OOO," said Bigmac, waving his hands in the air and speaking in a hollow voice. "Johnny Maxwell did not know it, but he had just strayed into . . . the Toilet Zone . . . deedledeedle, deedledeedle, deedledeedle . . ."

"After all, you're supposed to be leading them to Earth," Yo-less went on.

"But that's just their own name for their own world," said Johnny.

"You've only got their word for it. And they're newts, too. You could be bringing them *here*."

They all looked up, in case they could see through the ceiling, T&F Insurance Services and the roof to a huge alien fleet in the sky above.

"You're just getting carried away," said Wobbler. "You can't invade a planet with a lot of aliens out of a computer game. They live on a screen. They're not *real*."

"What're you going to do about it, anyway?" said Yo-less.

"Just keep doing it, I suppose," said Johnny. "Who was that girl in Patel's?"

"Don't know," said Wobbler. "Saw her in there once before playing *Cosmic Trek*. Girls aren't much good at computer games because they haven't got such a good grasp of spatial . . . something or other like we have," he went on airily. "You know. They can't think in three dimensions, or something. They haven't got the instincts for it."

"The Captain's a female," said Johnny.

"It's probably different for giant alligators," said Wobbler.

Bigmac sucked a sachet of tomato ketchup.

"Do you think IT might still be going when I'm old enough to join the army?" he said, thoughtfully.

"No," said Yo-less. "Stormin' Bruce'll get it all sorted out. He'll kick some butt."

They chorused "Some but what?" like tired monks.

They went to the cinema in the afternoon. *Alabama Smith and the Emperor's Crown* was showing on Screen S. Wobbler said it was racist, but Yo-less said he quite enjoyed it. They discussed whether it could still be racist if Yo-less enjoyed it. Johnny bought popcorn all round. That was another thing about Trying Times—pocket money was erratic, but you tended to get more of it.

He had spaghetti hoops when he got home, and watched TV for a while. The pyramid-shaped man disguised as a desert seemed to be on a lot now. He told jokes sometimes. The journalists laughed a bit. Johnny quite liked Stormin' Norman. He looked the sort of man who could talk to the Captain.

Then there was a programme about saving whales. They thought it was a good idea.

Then you could win lots of money if you could put up with the game show's host and not, for example, choke him with a cuddly toy and run away.

There was the News. The walking desert again, and pictures of bombs being dropped down enemy chimneys with pin-point precision. And Sport.

And then . . .

All right. Let's see.

He switched on.

Yes. Space. And more space.

No ScreeWee anywhere.

Hang on, he thought. They're all in the big fleet, aren't they. Following me. They followed me out of—out of—out of *game* space. You must be able to get there from here, if you keep going long enough. In the right direction, too.

Which way did I go?

Can I catch myself up?

Can anyone *else* catch me up?

He watched the screen for a while. It was even more boring than the quiz show.

Sooner or later he'd have to go to sleep. He'd thought hard about this, while Alabama Smith was being chased by bad guys through a native market-place . . .

. . . Johnny had a theory about these market-places. Every spy film and every adventure had a chase through the native market-place, with lots of humorous rickshaws crashing into stalls and tables being knocked over and chickens squawking, and the theory was: it was the same market-place every time. It always *looked* the same. There was probably a stallholder somewhere who was getting very fed up with it . . .

Anyway . . .

He'd take his camera.

He went to bed early with the camera strap wound around his wrist. Cameras didn't dream.

The ship smelled *human*.

There were no alarms, no hissing noises.

I'm back, thought Johnny.

And there was the ScreeWee fleet, spread out across the sky behind him.

And the camera, with its strap wrapped around his arm. He untangled it quickly and took a photo of the fleet. It whirred out of the machine after a few seconds. He held it under his armpit for a moment, and it gradually faded up. Yep. The fleet. If he could get it back, he'd have proof . . .

There was a red light flashing beside the screen on the console. Someone wanted to talk to him. He flicked the switch.

"*We saw your ship explode*," came the voice of the Captain. The screen crackled for a moment, and then showed her face. It looked concerned. *"And then it . . . returned again. You are alive?"*

"Yes," said Johnny, and then added, "I think so."

"Excuse me. I must ask. What happens to you?"

"What?"

"When you . . . go."

Johnny thought: What do I tell her? I stay awake in school. I stay in my room a lot. I hang out with Wobbler and the others. We hang around in the mall, or in the park, or in one another's houses, although not my house at the moment because of Trying Times, and say things like "I'm totally splanked" even though we're not sure what they mean. Sometimes we go to the cinema. We live in Blackbury, most excellent city of cool.

I must have the most boring life in the entire universe. I expect there's blobs living under rocks on Neptune that have a more interesting life than me . . .

"It'd be too hard to explain," he said. "I—"

There was a *ping* from the radar.

"I have to go," he said, feeling a bit relieved. Facing someone else in mortal combat was better than trying to tell a giant newt about Trying Times.

There was a ship coming in fast. It didn't seem to notice him. Its screen must be full of ScreeWee ships.

It was in the middle of his targeting grid. Around him, the starship hummed. He could feel the power under his thumb. Press the button and a million volts or amps or something of white-hot laser power would crackle out and—

His thumb trembled.

It didn't seem to want to move.

But no-one dies! he told himself. There's just someone somewhere sitting in their room in front of a computer! That's what it looks like to them! It's all just something on a screen! No-one really dies!

I can fire right into his retro-tubes with pin-point precision!

No-one really dies!

The ship roared past him and onwards, towards the fleet.

On the radar screen he saw two white dots, which meant that it had fired a couple of missiles. They streaked towards one of the smaller ScreeWee ships, with the attacker close behind them, firing as he went.

The ScreeWee burst into flame. Johnny knew you shouldn't be able to hear sound in space, but he did hear it—a long, low rumble, washing across the stars.

The human ship turned in a long curve and came back for another run.

The Captain's face appeared on the screen.

"*We have surrendered! This must not be allowed!*"

"I'm sorry, I—"

"You must stop this now!"

Johnny let his own ship accelerate while he tried to adjust the microphone.

"Game player! Game player! Stop now! Stop now or—"

Or what, he thought—or I'll shout "stop" again?

He raised his thumb over the Fire button, took aim at the intruder—

"Please! I mean it!"

It was plunging on towards another ship, taking no notice of him.

"All right, then—"

Blinding blue light flashed across his vision. He shut his eyes and still the light was there, purple in the darkness. When he opened them again the ship ahead of him was just an expanding cloud of glittering dust.

He turned in his seat. The Captain's ship was right behind him. He could see its guns glowing.

They never did this in the game. They had much more firepower than you, but they used it stupidly. It had to be like that. You could only win against hundreds of alien ships if they had the same grasp of gunnery techniques as the common cucumber.

This time, every gun had fired at exactly the same time.

The Captain's face appeared on the screen.

"I am sorry."

"What? What happened?"

"It will not happen again, I promise you."

"What *happened*?"

There was silence. The Captain appeared to be looking at something beyond the camera range.

"There was an unauthorized firing," she said. *"Those responsible will be dealt with."*

"I was going after that ship," said Johnny, uncertainly.

"Yes. It is to be hoped that another time you can do so before one of my ships is destroyed."

"I'm sorry. I—I didn't want to fire. It's not easy, shooting another ship."

"How strange that a human should say that. Clearly the Space Invaders shot themselves?"

"What do you mean?"

"Were they doing you any harm?"

"Look, you've got the wrong idea," said Johnny. "We're not really like that!"

"Excuse me. Things appear differently from where I sit."

It would have been better if she had shouted, but she didn't. Johnny could have dealt with it if she had been angry. Instead, she just sounded tired and sad. It was the same tone of voice in which she'd spoken about the Space Invaders wreckage.

But he found he was quite angry too.

She couldn't be talking about him.

He picked spiders out of the bath, even if they'd got soapy and didn't have much of a chance. Yet she'd looked at him as if he was Ghengiz the Hun or someone . . . after blowing a ship into *bits*.

"I didn't ask for this, you know! I was just playing a game! I've got problems of my own! I ought to be getting a good night's sleep! That's very important at my age! Why me?"

"Why not?"

"Well, I don't see why I should have to be told how nasty we are! You shoot at us as well!"

"Self-defence."

"No! Often you shoot first!"

"With humans, we have often found it essential to get our self-defence in as soon as possible."

"Well, I don't like it! Find someone else!"

He switched off the screen and turned his ship away from the fleet. He half expected the Captain to send some fighters after him, but she did not. She didn't do anything.

Soon the fleet was merely a large collection of yellow dots on the radar screen.

Hah! Well!

They could find their own way home. It wasn't as if they needed him any more. The game was ruined. Who was going to spend hours looking at stars? They'd have to manage without him.

Serve them right. He was doing things for them, and they were only newts.

Occasionally a star went past. You didn't get stars going past in real space. But they had to put them in computer games so that people didn't think they'd got something like Wobbler's *Journey to Alpha Centauri*.

Interesting point. Where was *he* going?

The radar screen went *bing*.

There were ships heading towards him. The dots were green. That meant "friendly." But the missiles streaking ahead of them didn't look friendly at all.

Hang on, hang on—what colour was he on their radar?

That was important. Friendly ships were green and enemy ships were yellow. He was a starship. A *human* starship.

But on the other hand, he'd been on the same side as the ScreeWee, so he might show up—

He grabbed the microphone and got as far as "Um, I—" before the rest of the sentence was spread out, very thin, very small, against the stars.

He woke up.

It was 6:3≡.

His throat felt cold.

He wondered why people made such a fuss about dreams. Dream Boat. Dream River. Dream A Little Dream. But when you got right down to it dreams were often horrible, and they felt *real*. Dreams always started out well and then they went wrong, no matter what you did. You couldn't trust dreams.

And he'd left the alarm set, even though this was Sunday and there was nothing to do on a Sunday. No-one else would be up for hours.

It'd be a couple of hours even before Bigmac's brother delivered the paper, or at least delivered the wrong paper. And he was all stiff from sitting at the computer, which wasn't switched on.

Maybe tonight he'd put some stuff on the floor to wake him up.

He went back to bed, and switched the blanket on.

He stared at the ceiling for a while. There was still a model Space Shuttle up there. But one of the two bits of cotton had come away from the drawing pin, so it hung down in a permanent nosedive.

There was something in the bed. He fumbled under the covers and pulled out his camera.

Which meant . . .

Some more fumbling found a rectangle of shiny paper.

He looked at it.

Well, yes. Huh. What'd he expect?

He got up again and turned the computer on, then lay in bed so that he could watch the screen. Still more fake stars drifted past.

Maybe other people were doing this, too. All over the country. All over the world, maybe. Maybe not every computer showed the same piece of game space, so that some people were closer to the fleet than others. Or maybe some people were just persistent, like Wobbler, and wouldn't be beaten.

You saw people like that in J&J Software, sometimes. They'd have a go at whatever new game old Patel had put on the machine, get blown to bits or eaten or whatever, which was what happened to you on your first time, and then you couldn't get rid of them with a crowbar. You learned a bit more, and then you died. That's how games worked. People got worked *up*. They had to beat some game, in the same way that Wobbler would spend weeks trying to beat a program. Some people took it personally when they were blown to bits.

So the ships he'd seen, then, were the ones who wouldn't give up.

But the Captain hadn't been at all grateful to him! It wasn't fair, making him feel like some kind of monster. As if he'd like shooting anyone in cold blood! They'd just totally destroyed another ship. OK, it was attacking them after they had surrendered, but after all it was a only a game . . .

Except, of course, it wasn't a game to the ScreeWee.

And they'd surrendered.

That didn't make them his responsibility, did it? Not the whole time? It had been OK for a little while, but he was getting tired of it.

He padded downstairs in the darkened house and pulled the encyclopedia off its shelf under the video. It had been bought last year from a man at the door, who'd persuaded Johnny's father that it was a good encyclopedia because it had a lot of colour pictures in it. It did have a lot of colour pictures in it. You could grow up knowing what everything looked like, if you didn't mind not knowing much about what it was.

After ten minutes with the index he got as far as prisoners of war, and eventually to the Geneva Convention. It wasn't something you could illustrate with big coloured pictures so there wasn't much about it, but what there was he read with interest.

It was amazing.

He'd always thought that prisoners were, well, prisoners—you hadn't actually killed them, so they ought to think themselves lucky. But it turned out that you had to give them the same food as your own soldiers, and look after them and generally keep them safe. Even if they'd just bombed a whole city you had to help them out of their crashed plane, give them medicine, and treat them properly.

Johnny stared at the page. It was weird. The people who'd written the encyclopedia—it said inside the cover that they were the Universal Wonder Knowledge Data Printing Inc, of Power Cable, Nebraska—had shoved in all these pictures of parrots and stuff because they were the Natural Wonders of the World, when what was really strange was that human beings had come up with an idea like this. It was like finding a tiny bit of the Middle Ages in the middle of all the missiles and things.

Johnny knew about the Middle Ages because of doing his essay on "What it felt like to be a peasant in the Middle Ages." When a knight fell off his horse in battle the other side weren't allowed to open him up with a can opener and torture him, but had to look after him and send him back home after a while, although they were allowed to charge for the service.

On the whole, the ScreeWee were letting him off lightly. According to the Geneva Convention, he ought to be feeding all of them as well.

He put the book back and turned the television on.

That was odd. Someone was complaining that the enemy were putting prisoners of war in buildings that might be bombed, so that they could be bombed by their own side. That was a barbaric thing, said the man. Everyone else in the studio agreed.

So did Johnny, in a way. But he wondered how he would explain something like this to the Captain. Everything made sense a bit at a time. It was just when you tried to think of it all at once that it came out wrong.

There was too much war on television now. He felt it was time to start showing something else.

He went out into the kitchen and made himself some toast, and then tried to scrape the burnt bits off quietly so as not to wake people up. He took the toast and the encyclopedia upstairs and got back into bed.

To pass the time he read some more about Switzerland, which was where Geneva was. Every man in the country had to do army training and keep a gun at home, it said. But Switzerland never fought anyone. Perhaps that made sense somewhere. And what the country used to be known for was designing intricate and ingenious mechanical masterpieces that made a little wooden bird come out and go cuckoo.

After a while he dozed off, and didn't dream at all.

On the screen the fake stars drifted by. After an hour or so a yellow dot appeared in the very centre. After another hour it grew slightly bigger, enough to be seen as a cluster of smaller yellow dots.

Then Johnny's mother, who had come to see where he was, tucked him up and switched it off.

5

If Not You, Who Else?

There was a constant smell of smoke and burnt plastic in the ship now, the Captain noticed. The air conditioners couldn't get rid of it any more. Some of the smoke and burned plastic *was* the air conditioners.

She could feel the eyes of her officers on her. She didn't know how many of them she could count on. She got the feeling that she wasn't very popular.

She looked up into the eyes of the Gunnery Officer.

"You disobeyed my orders," she repeated.

The Gunnery Officer looked around the control-room with an air of injured innocence.

"But we were being *attacked*," he said. "They fired the first shots."

"I said that we would not fire," said the Captain, trying to ignore the background murmur of agreement. "I gave my word to the Chosen One. He was about to fire."

"But he did not," said the Gunnery Officer. "He merely watched."

"He was about to fire."

"*About* is too late. The tanker *Kreewhea* is destroyed. Along with half our campaign provisions, I should add . . . *Captain*," said the Gunnery Officer.

"Nevertheless, an order was directly disobeyed."

"I cannot believe this! Why can't we *fight*!"

The Captain pointed out of the window. The fleet was passing several more ships of the ancient Space Invader race.

"They fought," she said. "Endlessly. And look at them now. And they were only the first. Remember what happened to the Vortiroids? And the Meggazzoids? And the Glaxoticon? Do you want to be like them?"

"Hah. They were primitive. Very low resolution."

"But there were many of them. And they still died."

"If we are going to die, I for one would rather die fighting," said the Gunnery Officer. This time the murmur was a lot louder.

"You would still be dead," said the Captain.

She thought: There'll be a mutiny if I shoot him or imprison him. I can't fine him because none of us have been paid. I can't confine him to his quarters because . . . she hated to think this . . . we might need him, at the end.

"You are severely reprimanded," she said.

The Gunnery Officer smirked.

"It will go on your record," the Captain added.

"Since we will not escape alive—" the Gunnery Officer began.

"That is my responsibility," said the Captain. "You are dismissed."

The Gunnery Officer glared at her.

"When we get home—"

"Oh?" said the Captain. "Now you think we *will* get home?"

By early evening Johnny's temperature was a hundred and two, and he was suffering from what his mother called Sunday night flu. He was lying in the lovely warm glow that comes from knowing that, whatever happens, there'll be no school tomorrow.

The backs of his eyeballs felt itchy. The insides of his elbows felt hot.

It was what came of spending all his time in front of a computer, he'd been told, instead of in the healthy fresh air. He couldn't quite see this, even in his itchy-eyeball state. Surely the fresh air would have been worse? But in his experience being ill always came of whatever you'd been doing. Parents would probably manage to say it came of taking vitamins and wrapping up nice and warm. He'd probably get an appointment down at the health centre next Friday, since they always liked you to be good and ill by the time you came, so that the doctors could be sure of what you'd got.

He could hear the TV downstairs. He spent twenty minutes wondering whether to get out of bed to switch on his old one, but when he moved there were purple blurs in front of his eyes and a *goioioing* hum in his ears.

He must have managed it, though, because next time he looked it was on, and the colours were much better than usual. There were the newscasters—the black one and the one who looked like his glasses fitted under his skin instead of over the top—and there was the studio, just like normal.

Except that it had the words "ScreeWee War" in the corner, where there were usually words like "Budget Shock" or "Euro Summit." He couldn't hear what people were saying, but the screen switched to a map of space. It was black. That was the point of space. It was just infinity, huge and black with one dot in it that was everything else.

There was one stubby red arrow in the middle of the blackness. Several dozen blue ones were heading towards it from the edge of the map. In one corner of the map was a photo of a man talking into a phone.

Hang on, thought Johnny. I'm almost certain there wasn't a BBC reporter with the ScreeWees. They'd have said. Probably there isn't even a CNN one.

He still wasn't getting any sound, but he didn't really need any. It was obvious that humans were closing in on the fleet.

The scene changed. Now it showed a tent somewhere, and there was the huge man, standing in front of another copy of the map.

This time the sound came up. He was saying: ". . . that Johnny? He's no fighter. He's no politician. He goes home when the going gets tough. He runs out on his obligations. But apart from that, hey, he's a real nice kid . . ."

"That's not true!" Johnny shouted.

"It isn't?" said a voice behind him.

He didn't look around immediately. By the sound of it, the voice had come from his chair. And that was much more impossible than the ScreeWee being on television. No-one could sit in that chair. It was full of old T-shirts and books and supper plates and junk. There was a deep sock layer and possibly the Lost Strawberry Yoghurt. No-one could sit down there without special equipment.

The Captain was, though. She seemed quite at home.

He'd only ever seen her face on the screen. Now he could see that she was about two metres long, but quite thin—more like a fat snake with legs than an alligator or a newt. She had two thick, heavy pairs about half-way down, and two pairs of thinner ones at the top, on a set of very complicated shoulders. Most of her was covered in a brown overall; the bits that stuck out—her head, all eight hands or feet, and most of her tail—were a yellow-bronze, and covered in very small scales.

"If you parked out in the road Mrs. Cannock opposite will be really mad," Johnny heard himself say. "She goes on about my dad leaving his car parked out in the road and it's not even a thousand metres long. So this is a hallucination, isn't it?"

"Of course it is," said the Captain. "I'm not sure that real space and game space are connected, except in your head."

"I saw this film once where spaceships could go anywhere in the universe through wormholes in space," said Johnny. "That means I've got a wormhole in my *head*?"

The Captain shrugged, which was a very interesting sight in a being with four arms.

"Watch this," she said. "This is very impressive. I expect this will be shown a lot."

She pointed at the screen.

It showed stars, and a dot in the distance. It got bigger very quickly.

"I think I know that," said Johnny. "It's one of your ships. The sort you get on level seven, isn't it?"

"The type, I think, will not matter for long," said the Captain quietly.

The ship was heading away from the camera. Its rocket exhausts got larger and larger. The camera seemed to be mounted on a . . .

"Missile?" said Johnny weakly.

The screen went blank.

Johnny thought of the dead Space Invader armada, turning over and over in the frosty emptiness between the game stars.

"I don't want to know about it," said Johnny. "I don't want you to tell me how many ScreeWee there were on board. I don't want you to tell me what happ—"

"No," said the Captain, "I expect you don't."

"It's not my fault! I can't help what people are like!"

"Of course not."

The Captain had a nasty way of talking in a reasonable voice.

"We are under attack," she said. "Humans are attacking us. Even though we have surrendered."

"Yes, but you only surrendered to me," said Johnny. "I'm just *me*. It's not like surrendering to a government or something. I'm not important."

"On the contrary," said the ScreeWee, "you're the saviour of civilization. You're all that stands between your world and certain oblivion. You are the last hope."

"But that's not . . . real. That's just what it says at the start of the game!"

"And you did not believe it?"

"Look, it always says something like that!"

"Only you can save mankind?" said the Captain.

"Yes, but it's not really true!"

"If not you, then who else?"

"Look," said Johnny, "I *have* saved mankind. In the game, anyway. There aren't any ScreeWee attacking any more. People have to play it for hours to find any."

The Captain smiled. The shrug had been impressive. But the Captain's mouth was half a metre long.

"You humans are strange," she said. "You are warlike. But you make rules! *Rules* of war!"

"Um. I think we don't always obey all those rules," said Johnny.

Another four-armed shrug.

"Does that matter? Even to have made such rules . . . You think all of life is a game."

The Captain pulled a small piece of silvery paper out of a pocket of her overall.

"Your attackers have left us too short of food. So, *by your rules*," she said, "I must ask for the following: fifteen tonnes of pressed wheat extractions treated with sucrose; ten thousand litres of cold bovine lactation; twenty-five tonnes of the baked wheat extraction containing grilled bovine flesh and trace ingredients, along with chopped and fried tubers and fried and corn-extract-coated rings of vegetables of the allium family; one tonne of crushed mustard seeds mixed with water and permitted additives; three tonnes of exploded corn kernels coated with lactic derivation; ten thousand litres of coloured water containing sucrose and trace elements; fifteen tonnes of prepared and fermented wheat extract in vegetable juice; one thousand tonnes of soured lactic acid flavoured with fruit extract. Daily. Thank you."

"What?"

"The food of your fighting men," explained the Captain.

"Doesn't sound like food."

"You are right," said the Captain. "It is disgustingly lacking in fresh vegetables and dangerously high in carbohydrates and saturated fats. However, it appears that this is what you eat."

"Me? I don't even know what that stuff *is*! What are pressed wheat extractions treated with sucrose?"

"It said 'Snappiflakes' on the packet," said the Captain.

"Soured lactic acid?"

"You had a banana yoghurt."

Johnny's lips moved as he tried to work this out.

"The grilled bovine flesh and all that stuff?"

"A hamburger and fries with fried onion rings."

Johnny tried to sit up.

"Are you saying that I've got to go down to the shops and get takeaway Jumboburgers for an entire alien spacefleet?"

"Not exactly."

"I should think not—"

"My Chief Engineer wants a Bucket of Chicken Lumps."

"What do ScreeWee usually eat?"

"Normally we eat a kind of waterweed. It contains a perfect balance of vitamins, minerals and trace elements to ensure a healthy growth of scale and crest."

"Then why—"

"But, as you would put it, it tastes like poo."

"Oh."

The Captain stood up. It was a beautiful movement. The ScreeWee body had no *angles* in it, apart from the elbows and knees; she seemed to be able to bend wherever she wanted.

"And now I must return," she said. "I hope your attack of minor germs will shortly be over. I could only wish that my attack of human beings was as easily cured."

"Why aren't you fighting back?" said Johnny. "I know you can."

"No. You are wrong. We have surrendered."

"Yes, but—"

"We will not fire on human ships. Sooner or later, it has to stop. We will run instead. Someone gave us safe conduct."

The worst bit was that she didn't raise her voice, or accuse him of anything. She just made statements. Big, horrible statements.

"All right," said Johnny, in a dull voice, "but I know it's not real. I've got the flu. You get mild hallucinations when you get the flu. Everyone knows that. I remember I was ill once and all the floppy bunnies on the wallpaper started dancing about. This is like that. You can't really know about this stuff. You're just in my head."

"What difference does that make?" said the Captain. She stepped out through the wall, and then poked her head back into the room.

"Remember," she said, "only you can save mankind."

"And I said I already—"

"ScreeWee is only the human name for us," said the Captain. "Have you ever wondered what the ScreeWee word for ScreeWee is?"

He must have slept, but he didn't dream. He woke up in the middle of the afternoon.

A huge ball of incandescent nuclear fire, heated to millions of degrees, was shining brightly in the sky.

The house was empty. His mother had left him a breakfast tray, which was to say that she'd put together a new Snappiflakes packet, a spoon, a bowl and a note saying "Milk in Fridge." She'd also put her office phone number on the bottom of the note. He knew what it was anyway, but sometimes she used the phone number like other people would use an Elastoplast.

He opened the packet and fished around inside. The alien was in a hygienic little paper bag. It was yellow, and in fact did look a bit like the Captain, if you almost shut your eyes.

He wandered aimlessly through the rooms. There was never anything any good on television in the middle of the day. It was all women talking to one another on sofas. He sneaked a look out into the road, just in case there *were* half-mile-long rocket-exhaust burns. And then he went back upstairs and sat and stared at the silent computer.

OK.

So . . . you switch on. And there's the game. Somehow it felt *worse* thinking about playing it by just sitting in front of it now.

On the other hand, it *was* daytime, so most people would be at school or at least keeping a low profile somewhere. Johnny wasn't quite certain about game time and real time, but maybe the attacks stopped when people had to go to school? But no, there were probably people playing it in America or Australia or somewhere.

Besides, when you died in your sleep you woke up, so what happens now if you die while you're awake?

But the ScreeWee were getting slaughtered out there. Or *in* there. Or in *here*.

The Captain was *stupid* not to fire back.

His hand switched on the computer without his mind really being aware of it.

The game logo appeared. The music started up. The same old message scrolled up the screen. He knew it by heart. Savior of Civilization. Certain Oblivion.

Only You Can Save Mankind.

If Not You, Who Else?

He blinked. The message had scrolled off the top of the screen. He couldn't have imagined that extra last line . . . could he?

And then the same old stars.

He didn't touch the keyboard or the joystick. He wasn't certain what direction he should be going in. On the whole, straight on seemed best. For hours.

He glanced at the clock. It was just gone four o'clock. People would be home from school now. They'd be watching *Cobbers* and *She'll Be Apples* and *Moonee Ponds*. Bigmac would be watching with his mouth open at his brother's. Wobbler would be watching while trying to rob some other poor computer games writer of his just rewards. Yo-less probably wouldn't be paying much attention, exactly; it'd just be on while he did his homework. Yo-less always did his homework when he got home from school and didn't pay attention to anything else until it had been finished to his satisfaction. But everyone watched *Cobbers*.

Except Johnny, today.

He felt vaguely proud of that. The television was off. He had other things to do.

Somewhere in the last ten minutes he'd made a decision. He wasn't sure exactly what it was, but he'd made it. So he had to see it through. Whatever it was.

He went to the bathroom and had a go with the thermometer. It was an electronic one that his mother had bought from a catalogue, and it also told the time. *Everything* in the catalogue had a digital clock built in. Even the golf umbrella that doubled as a Handy Picnic Table. Even the thing for getting fluff out of socks.

"Away with Not Being Able to Know What the Time is All the Time Blues," said Johnny vaguely, and stuck the thermometer in his mouth for the required twenty seconds.

His temperature was 16:04°.

No wonder he felt cold.

He went back to bed with the thermometer still in his mouth and looked at the screen again.

Still just stars.

The rest of them would probably be down at the mall now, unless Yo-less was trying for an A+ with his homework. Hanging out. Waiting for another day to end.

He squinted at the thermometer. It read 16:07°.

Still nothing but stars on the screen . . .

6

Chicken Lumps In Space

He woke up. The familiar smell of the starship tickled his nose. He cast his eyes over the control panel. He was getting a bit more familiar with it now.

Right. So he was back in real life again. When he got back to . . . when he got back to . . . He'd have to have a word with the medics about this odd recurring dream that he was a boy in—

No! he thought. I'm me! Not a pilot in a computer game! If I start thinking like that then I'll *really* die! Got to take charge!

Then he noticed the other ships on the screen. He was still a long way from the fleet, of course. But there were three other ships spread out neatly behind him, in convoy. They were bigger and fatter than his and, insofar as it was possible to do this in space, they seemed to wallow rather than fly.

He hit the Communications button. A plump face appeared on the screen.

"Wobbler?"

"Johnny?"

"What are *you* doing in my head?"

The on-screen Wobbler looked around.

"Well, according to this little panel riveted on the control thingy,

I'm flying a Class Three Light Tanker. Wow! Is it normally like this inside your head?"

"I'm not sure," said Johnny. By the main communication screen was another switch saying "Conference Facility." He had a feeling he knew what it did.

Sure enough, when he pressed it Wobbler's face drifted to the top left-hand corner of the screen. Yo-less's face appeared in the opposite corner, with Johnny's own head above it. The other corner stayed blank.

Johnny tapped a button.

"Bigmac?" he said. "Yo-less?"

Bigmac's face appeared in the blank. He appeared to be wiping his mouth.

"Checking the cargo?" said Johnny sarcastically.

"It's full of hamburgers!" said Bigmac, in a voice like a good monk who's just arrived in heaven and found that all the sins of the flesh are allowed. "Boxes and boxes of hamburgers! I mean *millions*! With fries. And one Bucket of Chicken Lumps, it says here."

"It says on this clipboard," said Yo-less, "that I'm flying a lot of Prepared Corn and Wheat Products. Shall I go and see what they are?"

"OK," said Johnny. "Then that means you're driving the milk tanker, Wobbler."

"Oh, yes. That's right. Bigmac gets burgers, Wobbler gets boring *milk*," moaned Wobbler.

Yo-less's face reappeared.

"Back there it's breakfast cereals, mainly," he said. "In Giant-Jumbo-Mega-Civilization-Sized boxes."

"Then Bigmac'd better bring his ship between you and Wobbler," said Johnny briskly. "We can't risk a collision."

"Snap, crackle, *fababababBOOM*!" said Bigmac.

"Will we remember this when we wake up?" said Wobbler.

"How can we?" said Yo-less. "*We're* not dreaming."

"OK. OK. Um. So will we remember this when *he* wakes up?"

"I don't think so. I think we're only here as projections from his own subconscious mind," said Yo-less. "He's just dreaming us."

"You mean we're not *real*?" said Bigmac.

"I'm not sure if *I'm* real," said Johnny.

"It *feels* real," said Wobbler. "Smells real, too."

"Tastes real," said Bigmac.

"Looks real," said Yo-less. "But he's only imagining we're here. It's not really us. Just the us that's inside his head."

Don't ask me, thought Johnny. You were always best at this stuff.

"And I've just worked out, right," said Yo-less, "that if we send in the boxtops from every single packet back there we can get six thousand sets of saucepans, OK? And twenty thousand books of football stickers and fifty-seven thousand chances to win a Stylish Five-Door Ford Sierra."

The four ships lumbered on towards the distant fleet. Johnny's starship could easily outdistance the tankers, so he flew in wide circles around them, watching the radar screen.

There was an occasional zip and sizzle from Wobbler's tanker. He was trying to take its computer apart, just in case there were any design innovations Johnny might remember when he woke up.

Ships appeared on the screen. There was the big dot of the fleet and, around the edges of the screen, the green dots of the game players.

A thought occurred to him.

"Yo-less?"

"Yeah?"

"Have those things got any guns on?"

"Er . . . what do they look like?"

"There's probably a red button on the joystick."

"Not got one on mine."

"What about you, Wobbler? Bigmac?"

"Nope."

"Which one's the joystick?" said Bigmac.

"It's the thing you're steering with."

"Yeah, wipe the mustard off and have a look," said Yo-less.

"Nothing on it," said Bigmac.

Unarmed, thought Johnny. And slow. One hit with a missile and Wobbler is sitting inside the biggest cheese in the universe. What happens to people in my dream?

"Why does it always go *wrong*?

"I'll just go on ahead," he said, and pressed the Fast button.

There were three players attacking the ScreeWee fleet. It soon became two; Johnny had one in his sights all the way in, curving away through the smoke-ring of the explosion and heading for the next attacker so fast that he was only just behind his own missile.

It was going after the Captain's ship, and the player wasn't paying attention to his radar. Another explosion, already behind Johnny as he looked for the third player.

Johnny realized he wasn't thinking about it. His eyes and hands were doing all the work. He was just watching from inside.

The third player had spotted the tankers. It saw him, turned and actually managed to get some shots away.

Oh, no. Johnny's mind whirred like a machine, judging speed and distance . . .

He felt the ship buck under him, but he held it steady until the crosshairs merged.

Then he pressed his thumb down until a beeping sound told him he hadn't got anything more to fire.

After a while the red mist cleared. He found thoughts slinking back into his mind again. They moved slowly, uncertain of where they were, like people drifting back into a bombed city, picking through rubble, trying to find the old familiar shapes.

There was a metallic taste in his mouth. His elbow ached—he must have banged it on something during the turn.

He thought: No wonder we make rules. The Captain thinks it's strange, but we don't. We know what we'd be like if we didn't have rules.

A light flashed by the communication screen. Someone wanted to talk to him. He flicked a switch.

The face of the Captain appeared.

"Ah, Johnny. What an efficient technique."

"Yes. But I had to—"

"Of course. And I see you have brought some friends."

"You said you needed food."

"Even more so now. That last attack was severe."

"Aren't you firing at all?"

"No. *We have surrendered, I remind you. Besides, we must not stop. Some of us at least will reach the Border."*

"Border?" said Johnny. "I thought you were going to a planet."

"We must cross the Border first. Beyond the Border, we are safe. Even you cannot follow us. If we fight, all of us die. If we run, some of us live."

"I don't think humans can think like that," said Johnny. He glanced out of the cockpit. The tankers were getting nearer.

"You are mammals. Fast. Hot-blooded. We are amphibians. Cold-blooded. Slow. Logical. Some of us will get across. We breed fast. To us, it makes sense. To me, it makes sense."

The Captain's image moved to a corner of the screen. Wobbler, Bigmac and Yo-less appeared in the other three quarters.

"That was brilliant shooting," said Bigmac. "When I'm in the army—"

"There's a frog on my screen," said Wobbler.

"It's . . . *she's* the Captain," said Johnny.

"A woman in charge?" said Yo-less.

"No wonder the aliens always lose," said Wobbler. "You should see the side of my mum's car."

"Um. She can hear you, I think. Don't use sexist language," said Johnny.

The Captain smiled.

"I invite your comrades to unload their welcome cargoes," she said.

They found out how to do it, eventually. The whole of the middle of the tankers came away as one unit. Small ScreeWee ships, not much more than a seat and a pilot's bubble and a motor, nudged them into the holds of the biggest ships. Without them, the tankers were just a cockpit and engine and a big empty network of girders.

Johnny watched the tank from Yo-less's ship drift gently through the hatch of the Captain's ship.

"Er . . . if when you, you know . . . you're pouring them out of the packet," he said, "and you sort of find something plastic falls into your bowl . . . well, it's just a joke. It's not on purpose."

"Thank you."

"If you save all the box tops you could probably win a Ford Sierra," said Yo-less. There was a slight tremble in his voice as he tried to sound like someone who talked to aliens every day. "You could get your photo in *Competitor's Journal,*" he added.

"That would be very useful. Some of the corridors in this ship are very long."

"Don't be daft," said Bigmac. "He'd—she'd never get the spares."

"Really? In that case we shall have to go for the six thousand sets of saucepans," said the Captain.

"How do we get back?" said Wobbler.

"How did you get here?"

Wobbler frowned.

"How *did* we get here?" he said. "One minute I was . . . was . . . and then here I was. Here we were."

"Come to that, where did all the milk and burgers come from?" said Bigmac.

"It's all right," said Yo-less. "I *told* you. We're not really here anyway. We're just anxiety projections. I read about it in a book."

"That's a relief, then," said Wobbler. "That's worth knowing when you're a billion miles out in space. Anyway . . . so how do we get back?"

"I don't know," said Johnny. "I generally do it by dying."

"Is there some other way?" said Yo-less, after a long, thoughtful pause.

"I don't think there is for me. This is game space. You have to die to get out," said Johnny. "I think *you* can probably just fly back. I'm not definitely sure any harm can come to *you*. You're not playing . . . in your heads, I mean."

"Well—" Wobbler began.

"But I should go soon, if I was you," said Johnny. "Before some more players arrive."

"We'd stay and help," said Wobbler, "but there's no guns on these things, you see."

He sounded worried.

"Yeah. Silly of me not to have dreamed of any," said Johnny, kindly.

"Yo-less might be right and we're just stuff in your head," said Wobbler. "But even people in dreams don't want to die, I expect."

"Right."

"You going to be in school tomorrow?"

"Might be."

"Right. Well, then . . . chow."

"See you."

"You hang in there, right, Johnny?" said Yo-less anxiously.

"I'll try to."

"Yeah, give them aliens hell, my man!" said Bigmac, as the tankers turned.

Johnny could hear them still talking as the three ships accelerated away.

"That was a foe-par, Bigmac. Johnny's on the aliens' side!"

"What? You mean they're on our side?"

"No, they're on their side. And so is he."

"Whose side are we on, then?"

"We're on his side."

"Oh. Right. Er. Yo-less?"

"What?"

"So who's on *our* side?"

"Eh? He is, I suppose."

"So is there *anyone* on the other side?"

The ships became dots on the radar, and then vanished off the edge of the screen.

Where to, Johnny had no idea.

I may have wished them here, or dreamed them, or something. But I mustn't do it again. Maybe they're not really here, but I don't want to see my friends die. I don't want to see *anybody* die.

At least *I'm* on my side.

He scanned the sky. After a while the Captain said: *"You are not leaving?"*

"Not yet."

"Until you die, you mean."

Johnny shrugged.

"It's the only way out," he said. "Fight until you die. That's how all games go. You just hope you can get a bit further each time."

There were still no more attackers on the screen. The fleet looked as if it wasn't moving, but it had built up quite a speed. Every second was taking it further from game space. Every second meant that fewer and fewer players would have the patience or determination to go on looking for it.

He helped himself to some of the horrible nourishing soup from its spigot.

"Johnny?"

"Yes?"

"I believe I upset you some time ago by suggesting that humans are bloodthirsty and dangerous"

"Well. Yes. A bit."

"In that case . . . I would like to say . . . I am grateful."

"I don't understand."

"That you are on our side."

"Yes, but *I'm* not bloodthirsty."

"Then I think perhaps a little while ago someone else must have been flying your ship?"

"No. It's hard to explain it to you," said Johnny. First of all, he'd have to be able to explain it to himself.

"Shall I embark upon a less troubling topic of conversation?"

"You don't have to," said Johnny. "I mean, you're in charge. You must have things to do."

"Oh, spaceships fly themselves," said the Captain. *"They keep going until they hit things. There is little to do. Tend the wounded and so on. I seldom have a chance to talk to humans. So . . . What is sexist?"*

"What?"

"It was a word you used."

"Oh, *that*. It just means you should treat people as people and, you know . . . not just assume girls can't do stuff. We got a talk about it at school. There's lots of stuff most girls can't do, but you've got to pretend they can, so that more of them will. That's all of it, really."

"Presumably there's, uh, stuff boys can't do?"

"Oh, *yeah*. But that's just girls' stuff," said Johnny. "Anyway, some girls go and become engineers and things, so they can do proper stuff if they want."

"Transcend the limitations of their sex. Outdo the other sex, even. Yes. It is much the same with us. Some individuals show an awe-inspiring desire to succeed, to make a career in a field not traditionally considered to be appropriate to their gender."

"You, you mean," said Johnny.

"I was referring to the Gunnery Officer."

"But he's a man—I mean, a male."

"Yes. Traditionally, ScreeWee warriors are female. They are more inclined to fight. Our ancestors used to have to fight to protect their breeding pond. The males do not do battle. But in his case—"

A speck appeared on the radar.

Johnny put down his cup and watched it carefully.

Normally, players headed straight for the fleet. This one didn't. It hovered right on the edge of the screen and stayed there, keeping pace with the ScreeWee ships.

After a while, another dot appeared from the same direction, and kept on coming.

This one at least looked like just another player.

There was a nasty equation at the back of Johnny's mind. It concerned missiles. There were the six missiles per level in *Only You Can Save Mankind*. Once you'd fired them, that was it. So the longer he stayed alive, the less he had to fight with. But all the attacking players would have six missiles each. *He'd* only got four now. When they were gone, it'd just be guns. One missile in the right place would blow him up. Losing was kind of built-in, in the circumstances.

The attacker came on. But Johnny kept finding his gaze creeping to the dot at the edge of the screen. Somehow it had a watchful look, like a shark trailing a leaky airbed.

He switched on the communicator.

"Attacking ship! Attacking ship! Stop now!"

They can't speak, Johnny thought. They're only a player, they're not *in* the game. They can't speak and they can't listen.

He found he'd automatically targeted a missile on the approaching dot. But that couldn't be the only way. Sooner or later you had to talk, even if it was only because you'd run out of things to throw.

The attacker fired a missile. It streaked past Johnny and away, heading on into empty space.

Not real, Johnny thought. You have to think they're not real. Otherwise you can't do it.

"Attacking ship! This is your last chance! Look, I *mean* it!"

He pressed the button. The ship juddered slightly as a missile took off. The attacker was moving fast. So was the missile. They met and became an expanding red cloud. It drifted around Johnny's ship like a smoke ring.

Someone, somewhere, was blinking at their screen and probably swearing. He hoped.

The dot was still on the edge of the screen. It was irritating him, like an itch in a place he couldn't scratch. Because that wasn't how you were supposed to play. You spotted some aliens and you shot at them. That was what the game was supposed to be *about*.

Lurking in the distance and just watching made him uneasy. It looked like the kind of thing people would do if they were . . . well . . .

. . . taking it seriously.

The Captain sat in front of her desk, watching the big screen. She was chewing. Anything was better than waterweed, even—she looked at the packet—even Sugar-Frosted Corn Crackles in cold bovine lactation. Sweet and crunchy, but with odd hard bits in . . .

She inserted a claw into her mouth and poked around among her teeth until she found the offending object.

She pulled it out and looked at it.

It was green, and had four arms. Most of them were holding some sort of weapon.

She wondered again what these things were. The Chief Medical Officer had suggested that they were, in fact, some sort of vermin which invaded food sources. There was a theory among the crew that they were things to do with religion. Offerings to food gods, perhaps?

She put it carefully on one side of her desk. In the right light, she thought, it looked a bit like the Gunnery Officer.

Then she opened the little cage beside the bowl and let her birds out.

There had been things very like alligators among the ScreeWee's distant ancestors, and some habits had been handed down. The Captain opened her mouth fully, which made her lower and upper jaws move apart in a way that would make a human's eyes water.

The birds hopped in, and began to clean her teeth. One of them found a small piece of plastic ray-gun.

The watching ship was moving, still keeping at a great distance, travelling around the fleet in a wide circle. It had watched one more attacker come in; Johnny had got rid of this one with a missile and some shots, although a flashing red light on the panel was suggesting that something, somewhere, wasn't working any more. Probably those secondary pumps again.

He found he was turning the ship all the time to keep the distant dot in front of him.

"Johnny?"

It was the Captain.

"*Yes*? Are you watching it?"

"Yes. It is moving between us and the Border. It is in our direct line of flight now."

"You can't sort of steer around it?"

"There are more than three hundred ships in the fleet. That may be difficult."

"It seems to be waiting for something. I'll . . . I'll risk going to have a look."

He let his ship overtake the fleet and run ahead of it, towards the distant dot.

It made no attempt to get out of his way.

It was a starship just like his own. In fact, in a way . . . it *was* his starship. After all, there was only one starship in the entire game, the one You flew to Save Mankind. Everyone was flying the same one . . . in a way.

It hung against the stars, as lifeless as a Space Invader. Johnny moved a bit closer, until he could see the cockpit and even the shape of a head inside. It had a helmet on. Everyone did—it was on the cover of the box. You wore a helmet in a starship. He didn't know why. Maybe the designers thought you were likely to fall off when you went round corners.

He tried the communicator again.

"Hello? Can you hear me?"

There was nothing but the background hiss of the universe.

"I'm pretty sure you can. I've got a feeling about it."

The tiny blob of the helmet turned towards him. You could no more see through the smoked glass of the helmet than you could through a pair of sunglasses from the outside, but he knew he was being stared at.

"What are you waiting for?" said Johnny. "Look, I know you can hear me, I don't want to have to—"

The other ship roared into life. It accelerated towards the oncoming fleet on two lances of blue light.

Johnny swore under his breath and kicked his own engines into life. There was no hope of overtaking the attacker. It had a head start, and a starfighter's top speed was a starfighter's top speed.

It was just out of gun range. He raced along behind it.

Ahead, he could see some of the big capital ships of the fleet manoeuvring clumsily out of the way. They spread out slowly, trying to avoid colliding with one another. Seen from the front, it was like watching the petals of a flower opening.

The attacker roared for the middle of the fleet. Then it rolled gently and fired six missiles, one after another. A moment later, two of the small ScreeWee fighters exploded and one of the larger ships spun around as it was hit.

The attacker was already heading for another fighter. Johnny had to admit it—it was beautiful flying. He'd never realized before how badly most players flew. They flew like people who lived on the ground—from right to left and up and down, woodenly. Like someone moving something on a screen, in fact.

But the attacker rolled and twisted like a swallow in flight. And every turn brought another ScreeWee ship under its guns. Even if they had been firing back, it wouldn't have been hit, except by accident. It *pirouetted*.

The Captain's face appeared on the screen.

"You must stop this!"

"I'm trying! I'm trying! Don't you think I'm trying!"

The attacker turned. Johnny hadn't thought it was possible for a starship to skid, but this one did. It paused just for a moment as its jets slowed it down, and then accelerated back the way it had come.

Right down his sights.

"Look, *stop*!" he shouted. He had a missile ready. Why even bother to shout? Players *couldn't* hear, they only saw the game on the screen—

"Who are you?"

It was a very clear voice, and very human. The Captain sounded as though she'd learned the language out of a book, but this voice was one that someone had really used since they were about one year old.

"You *can* hear me!"

"Get out of the way, *stupid*!"

The two pilots stared at one another across a distance that was getting smaller very, very fast.

I've heard that before, Johnny thought. That voice. You can hear all the punctuation . . .

They didn't crash—exactly. There was a grinding noise as each starship scraped the length of the other, ripping off fins, ripping open tanks, and then spun drunkenly away.

The control panel in front of Johnny became a mass of red lights. There were cracks racing across the cockpit.

"Idiot!" screamed the radio.

"It's all right," said Johnny urgently. "You just wake up—"

His ship exploded.

7

The Dark Tower

It was 16:34° by the thermometer. Time was different in game space.

No matter how often you died, you never got used to it. It wasn't as if you got better with pract—

She'd heard him. Inside the game.

He sat up.

The ScreeWee were inside the game because it was their world. Wobbler and the rest hadn't really been in it; he was pretty sure he'd just dreamed them in because he needed someone to pilot the food tankers.

But he'd heard her in Patel's. That ringing, sharp voice, which made it very clear that its owner thought everyone in the whole world was dim-witted and had to be talked to like a baby or a foreigner.

On the screen, empty space rolled onwards.

He had to find her. Apart from anything else, no-one who flew like that should be allowed anywhere near the ScreeWee.

Wobbler'd probably know who she was.

He found the room moving around him when he stood up. He probably really was ill, he thought. Well, not surprising. What with Trying Times and stupid school and parents trying to be friends and now having to save an entire alien race instead of getting proper sleep, it wasn't surprising.

He made it to the hall and took the phone off its base and brought it back upstairs. He'd just extended the aerial when it rang.

"Um, hello—Blackbury-two-three-nine-nine-eight-zero-who's-that-speaking-please?"

"Is that you? This is me."

"Oh. Hello, Wobbler."

"You ill or something?"

"Flu. Look, Wobbler—"

"You seen the papers today?"

"No. Mum and Dad take them to work with them. Wobbler—"

"Thing in the papers about Gobi Software. Hang on . . . says, 'NO ENCOUNTERS OF THE TWENTY-FIRST KIND.' That's the headline."

Johnny hesitated.

"What does it say?" he said, very cautiously.

"What does 'inundated' mean?"

" 'S'like 'overwhelmed,' " said Johnny.

"Says that Gobi Software and computer games shops have been . . . inundated with complaints about *Only You Can Save Mankind*. Because they made that offer of five pounds if you shoot all the aliens, and it says people aren't finding any aliens. And Gobi Software are in trouble because of the Trades Descriptions Act. And they keep on using the word *hacker*," said Wobbler, in the sneering tones of one who knows what a hacker really is and knows that most journalists *don't*. "And there's a quote from Al Rampa, president of Gobi. He says they're recalling all the games, and if you send back the original discs they'll send you a token for their new game, *Dodge City 1888*. That got four stars in *FAAzzzzAAAP!*."

Recalling the games . . .

"Yes, but you haven't got the original discs," said Johnny. "You hardly ever have any original discs."

"No, but I know the guy whose brother bought it," said Wobbler happily. "So it was just a problem with the game, right? You weren't mental after all."

"I never said I was mental," said Johnny.

"No, but . . . well, you know," said Wobbler. He sounded embarrassed.

"Wobbler?"

"Yes?"

"You know that girl who was in Patel's?"

"Oh, her. What about her?"

"D'you know who she is?"

"She's someone's sister, I think."

"Whose?"

"Goes to some kind of special school for the terminally clever. She's called Kylie or Krystal or one of those made-up names. What do you want to know for?"

"Oh, nothing. Just because she complained about the game in Patel's, I suppose. Whose sister is she?"

"Some guy called . . . oh . . . Plonker. Yeah. Friend of Bigmac's. You sure you're all right?"

"Yes. Fine. Cheers."

"Cheers. You going to be in tomorrow?"

" 'Spect so."

"Cheers."

"Cheers."

Bigmac wasn't on the phone. Where Bigmac lived, people hardly even got letters. Even muggers were frightened to go there. People talked about the Joshua N'Clement block in the same way that they probably once talked about the Black Hole of Calcutta or the Spanish Inquisition's reception area.

The tower loomed all alone, black against the sky, like someone's last tooth.

There wasn't much else around the place. There *was* a row of boarded up shops, but you could see where the fire had been. And there was a pub made out of neon lights and red brick; it was called The Jolly Farmer.

The tower had won an award in 1965, just before bits had started falling off. It was always windy. Even on the calmest day, gales whistled icily through the concrete corridors. The place was some kind of wind reservation. If the Joshua N'Clement block had existed a few thousand years ago, people would have come from all over the country to sacrifice to the wind god.

Johnny's father called it Rottweiler Heights. Johnny could hear them barking as he walked up the stairs (the lifts had stopped working in 1966). Everyone in the tower seemed afraid, and mostly they seemed afraid of one another.

Bigmac lived on the fourteenth floor, with his brother and his brother's girlfriend and a pit bull terrier called Clint. Bigmac's brother was reliably believed to be in the job of moving video recorders around in an informal way.

Johnny knocked cautiously, hoping to be loud enough to be heard by the people but quiet enough to be missed by Clint. No such luck. A wall of sound erupted from behind the door.

After a while there was the clink of a chain and the door opened a few centimetres. A suspicious eye appeared at about the height an eye should be, while a metre below there was a certain amount of confused activity as Clint tried to get both eyes and his teeth into the same narrow crack.

"Yeah?"

"Is Bigmac in?"

"Dunno."

Johnny knew about this. There were only four rooms in the flat. Bigmac's family was huge and lived all over the town, and practically no member of it knew where any other member was until they were quite sure who was asking.

"It's me, Johnny Maxwell. At school."

Clint was trying to push a fifteen-centimetre-wide head through a five-centimetre-wide hole.

"Oh, yeah." Johnny felt that he was being carefully surveyed. "He's down the pub. Yeah."

"Oh, right," said Johnny in what he hoped was a normal voice. "I mean, yeah."

Bigmac was thirteen. But the landlord of The Jolly Farmer was reputed to serve anyone who didn't actually turn up on a tricycle.

His way home led back past the pub anyway. He agonized a bit about going in. It was all right for Bigmac. Bigmac had been born looking seventeen. But Bigmac turned out to be outside anyway, leaning against the bonnet of a car. He had a couple of friends with him. They watched Johnny intently as he approached, and the one who had been nonchalantly fiddling with the car's door handle stood up and glared.

Johnny tried to swagger a bit.

"Yeah, Johnny," said Bigmac, in a vague kind of way.

He's different here, Johnny thought. Older and harder.

The other youths relaxed a little. Bigmac knew Johnny. That made him acceptable, for now.

"Don't often see you up here," said Bigmac. "You drinking now or what?"

Johnny got the feeling that asking for a Coke would definitely be bad for his street cred. He decided to ignore the question.

"I'm looking for Plonker," he said. "Wobbler said you know him?"

"What d'you want him for?" said Bigmac.

On the wall in school, or down at the mall, Bigmac wouldn't have even asked. But there were different rules here. Like, in school Bigmac tried to hide how good he was at numbers, and up here he had to hide his ability to hold a normal conversation.

Johnny saw a way through.

"Actually I'm looking for his sister," he said.

One of Bigmac's friends sniggered.

Bigmac took Johnny's arm and led him a little way off.

"What'd you come up here for?" he said. "You could've asked me tomorrow."

"It's . . . important."

"Bigmac! You coming or what?"

Bigmac glanced over his shoulder.

"Can't," he said. "Got to sort out something else."

One of the kids said something to the other one, and they both laughed. Then they got into the car. After a little while it started up, bumped up on to the pavement and off again, and then accelerated into the night. They heard the tyres screech as it turned the corner on the wrong side of the road.

Bigmac relaxed. Suddenly he was a lot less tough, and a bit shorter, and more like the amiable not-quite-thicko Johnny had always known.

"Didn't you want to go with them?" said Johnny.

"You're a right nerd, aren't you," said Bigmac, in a friendly enough voice.

"Wobbler says you have to say dweeb now, not nerd," said Johnny.

"I usually say dickhead. Come on, let's go," said Bigmac. " 'Cos there'll probably be some unhappy people around here pretty soon. "S'their own fault for leaving a car here."

"What?"

"Dweeb. You don't know nothing about real life, you."

"It's just games," said Johnny, half to himself. "All different sorts. Bigmac?"

Somewhere away in the distance a car horn wailed, and was suddenly cut off. Bigmac stopped walking. The breeze blew his T-shirt against him, so that "Terminator" was superimposed on a chest that looked like a toast rack.

"What?" he said.

"Look, have you ever wondered what's real and what isn't?"

"Bloody stupid thing to wonder," said Bigmac.

"Why?"

"*Real's* real. Everything else isn't."

"What about . . . well, dreams?"

"Nah. They're not real."

"They've got to be *something*. Otherwise you couldn't have them, right?" said Johnny desperately.

"Yeah, but that's not the same as *really* real."

"Are people on television real?"

" 'Course!"

"Why're we treating them as a game, then?"

"You mean . . . on the News—"

"Yes!"

"That's different. You can't have people going around doing what they like."

"But *we*—"

"Anyway, space games aren't real," said Bigmac. He kept looking down the dark street.

Johnny relaxed a little.

"Are you real?"

"Dunno. Feel real. It's all crap anyway."

"What is?"

"Everything. So who cares? Come on, I'm going back home."

They strolled past what had been, in 1965, an environmental green space and was now a square of dog-poisoned earth where the shopping trolleys went to die.

"Plonker's a bit of a maniac," said Bigmac. "Bit of a wild man. Bit of a loony. Lives in a big posh house, though."

"Where?"

"Oh, in Tyne Avenue or Crescent or somewhere," said Bigmac.

A blue light lit his face for a moment as a police car flashed past the end of the road, its siren dee-dahing into the distance.

Bigmac froze.

"What's his real name?" said Johnny.

"Eh? Yeah. Garry, I think."

Bigmac was staring at the end of the road. The blue light was still visible. It had stopped about half a mile away; they could see it reflected off an advertising hoarding.

"Just Garry?" said Johnny.

Bigmac's face was wet in the light of the street lamps. Johnny realized that he was sweating.

"Might be Dunn," said Bigmac. He shifted uneasily from one foot to the other.

Another siren echoed around the night. An ambulance went past on the main road, ghostly under its flashing light.

"Look, Bigmac—"

"Bugger off!"

Bigmac turned and ran, his Doc Marten's crashing on the pavement. Johnny watched him go. He thought of all the things he should have said. He wasn't stupid. Everyone knew what happened to cars around the dark tower. What could he say now?

And his body thought: You don't say anything. You *do* something. It started running all by itself after his friend, taking his brain with it.

Despite a bedroom full of weight-training equipment that would have been of considerable interest if the police had ever bothered much about a recent theft down at the Sports Centre, Bigmac wasn't in much of a condition. He had been *born* out of condition. Johnny caught him up on the bend.

"I told you . . . to . . . buggeroff! Nothing . . . todo . . . withyou!" said Bigmac, as they headed towards the distant lights.

"They crashed it, didn't they."

"Nozzer's a good driver!"

"Yeah? Good at going fast?"

There was a crowd standing around at the traffic lights further down the road. As they ran, another ambulance overtook them and rocked to a halt. The crowd parted. Johnny caught a glimpse of—well, not a car, but maybe what a car would look like after trying to be in the same place as a liquid-cement truck. He knew it was a cement truck, because one had climbed up the pavement and lay on its side. Its load was fast becoming the biggest brick in the world.

In the distance there was the scream of a fire engine, getting nearer.

He grabbed Bigmac's arm, pulling him around.

"I don't think you want to go any closer," he said.

Bigmac shook himself free, just as the police managed to lever the crumpled door open.

Bigmac stared.

Then he turned, tottered over to a low garden wall by the roadside, and was sick.

When Johnny reached him his whole body was shaking, with cold and terror.

"Bugger you, I could have been in that, you—"

Bigmac was sick again, all down the front of Arnold Schwarzenegger. Johnny took his coat off and put it over the other boy's shivering shoulders.

"—they kept goin' on at me, I told them, I said—"

"Yeah. Yeah, that's right," said Johnny, looking around. "Look, you just sit here . . . there's a phone—You just sit there, all right? You just—"

"Don't go away!"

"What? Oh. Yes. Right. Come on then—"

Click!

"Hello, this—"

"Yo-less? It's Johnny."

"Yes?"

"Your mum in the hospital tonight?"

"No, she's on days this week. Why?"

"Can you get her to bring her car down to Witheridge Road?"

"What's up? You sound as if you've been—"

"Look, shut up! Get her to do it, right? Please! It's Bigmac!"

"What's up with him?"

"Yo-less! This is *important*! This is *really important*!"

"You know how she goes on when I—"

"Yo-less!"

"Oh, all right. Hey, is that a siren?"

"We're in a phone box. You'd better get her to bring a blanket or something. And hurry up, it's dead smelly in here."

"That was a siren, wasn't it?"

"Yes."

He put the phone down.

Bigmac wasn't being sick any more. He hadn't got anything to be sick with. He was just leaning against the door, shaking.

"She'll be along right away," said Johnny, as cheerfully as he could manage. "She's a ward sister. She knows all about this stuff."

Outside, one of the ambulances drove away. Firemen were all over the wreck. Some of them were getting equipment off the engine.

Bigmac stared at the scene.

"They're probably fine," lied Johnny. "It's amazing how people can—"

"Johnny?"

"What?"

"No-one's fine who looked like that," said Bigmac, in a flat voice. "There was blood all over."

"Well—"

"My brother'll kill me when he finds out. He said if I have the cops round again he'll throw me out of the window. He'll kill me if he finds out."

"He won't, then. You didn't do anything. We were just hanging out and you felt ill. That's all."

"He'll kill me!"

"What for? No-one knows anything except me, and I don't know *anything*. I promise."

It was gone eight when Johnny got home. He left his coat in the shed until he could sneak it in and sponge it off, and said he'd been round at Yo-less's, which was true, and was a pretty good way of avoiding questions, because his parents approved of Yo-less on racial grounds. To object to him being round at Yo-less's would be like objecting to Yo-less. Yo-less was dead handy.

Anyway, it wasn't as if anyone had cooked any dinner. Mrs. Yo-less had made him a hot chocolate when he was there, but he hadn't accepted a meal, because that suggested you didn't have them all that often at home and you didn't do that. She'd put Bigmac to bed. Bigmac with his skinhead haircut.

He microwaved himself something called a Pour-On Genuine Creole Lasagne, which said it served four portions. It did if you were dwarfs.

The phone went as he was carrying it upstairs. It was Wobbler.

"Yo-less just rang me."

"Right."

"Why didn't you get them to put Bigmac in an ambulance?"

"Who with?"

There was a moment of silence from Wobbler as he worked this out. Then he said, "Yuk."

"Right."

"Anyway, people'd ask questions. Bigmac's been in enough trouble as it is, what with his brother and one thing and another."

"Right."

"Wow!"

"Got to go now, Wobbler. Got to eat my dinner before it congeals."

He put the phone down on the tray, and looked at it. There was something else he was going to do. What was it? Something, anyway.

The lasagne looked real. It looked as though someone had already eaten it once.

The Captain looked up.

Most of her officers were standing in front of her. Except for the Gunnery Officer, who was looking smug, they all wore rather embarrassed expressions.

"Yes?" said the Captain.

To her surprise, it wasn't the Gunnery Officer who spoke. It was the Navigation Officer, a small and inoffensive ScreeWee who suffered for prematurely shedding scales.

"Um," she said.

"Yes?" said the Captain again.

"Um. We—that is, all of us—" said the Navigation Officer, looking as if she wished she was somewhere else, "—we feel that, uh, the present course is, uh, an unwise one. With respect," she added.

"In what way?" said the Captain. She could see the Gunnery Officer grinning behind the little ScreeWee. No-one could grin like a ScreeWee—their mouths were built for it.

"We, uh—that is, all of us—we are still being attacked. And that last attack was a terrible one."

"The Chosen One stopped it, at the cost of his own life," said the Captain.

"Um. He will return," said the Navigation Officer. "Um. Twenty of our people will not."

The Captain wasn't really looking at her. She was staring at the Gunnery Officer, whose grin was now wide enough to hold a set of billiard balls and probably the cue too.

He's been talking to them, she told herself. Everyone's on edge, no-one can think straight, and he's talking to them. I should have had him shot. They wouldn't have liked it, but I could probably have shouted them down.

"So what is it you are suggesting?" she said.

"Um. We—that is, all of us," said the little ScreeWee, with an imploring glance at the Gunnery Officer, "we feel we should turn and—"

"Fight?" said the Captain. "Make a last stand?"

"Um. Yes. That's right."

"And that's the feeling of all of you?"

The officers nodded, one after another.

"Um. Sorry, ma'am," said the Navigation Officer.

"The others stood and fought," said the Captain. "The . . . Space Invaders. And the others. We've all seen the wrecks. All they knew was how to attack. They stood and fought, and fought and died."

"We are dying too, um," said the Navigation Officer.

"I know. I am sorry," said the Captain. "But many are living. And every minute takes us further from danger. We are so near the Border! If we stop . . . you know what will happen. Game space will move. The Border will retreat. The humans will find us. And then they will—"

"Die," said the Gunnery Officer. "And we shall win. Those others were stupid. We are not. We can win. We shall give the humans the mother of all battles."

"Ah, yes," said the Captain. "Mother and grandmother of battles. Battles that breed more battles."

"And this is your leader speaking," sneered the Gunnery Officer. "The leader of the fleet. It is pathetic. Cowardly."

"When we are home—" the Captain began.

"Home? This is our home! We have no other! All this talk of the Border, and a planet of our own . . . Have any of us seen it? No! It's a legend. Wishful thinking. A dream. We lie to ourselves. We make up stories. The Chosen One. The Hero with a Thousand Extra Lives! It's all dreams! We live and breed and die on our ships. That is our destiny. There is no choice!"

8

Peace Talks, Peace Shouts

Johnny awoke in the starship.

Normally he was some way from the fleet, but this time it was around him. There were ScreeWee ships on every side.

They were flying the wrong way.

Immediately, a face appeared on the screen. Except for a few differences on the crest, and a slight orange tint to the scales, it might have been the Captain.

"Calling the human ship."

"Who are you?"

"I am the new Captain. These are my instructions—"

"What happened to the old Captain?"

"She is under arrest. These are my instructions—"

"Arrest? What for? What did she do?"

"She did nothing. Listen to me. You have sixty seconds to get beyond range of our guns. For honour. After that, you will be fired upon with extreme force."

"Hang on—"

"The count has started."

"But—"

"End of communication. Die, human."

The screen went blank.

Johnny stared at it.

It hadn't been a friendly face. The voice had sounded as though it had learned Human out of a book, just like the real Captain. But in this case it had been a nasty book. It also sounded as though it belonged to someone who would count to sixty like this: "One, two, three, four, five, seven, eighteen, thirty-five, forty-nine, fifty-eight, fifty-nine, sixty—firing, ready or not—"

His ship jerked forward, ramming him back in his seat. That was one good thing about game space—you could do the kind of turns and manouevres that, in real space, would leave the human body looking like thin pink lino across the cabin wall . . .

The fleet slid past, dwindling to a collection of dots behind him. A couple of laser beams crackled past, but some way away; it looked as though they were trying to frighten him off rather than kill him.

The ScreeWee had turned around. They were heading back deeper into game space. Why? They'd show up on people's screens soon! There were always some players who'd go looking. Any day now some kid'd switch on his machine and there'd be wall-to-wall ScreeWee, heading straight for him. They weren't safe even now. Yes—there were always some people who'd go looking . . .

And there was a green dot ahead of him. He recognized the way it moved, like a dog creeping around the edge of a sheep field.

He headed towards it.

Now he could remember. You thought better in game space, too. It was as if he was more *him* in game space. Krystal or Kylie or one of those made-up names, Wobbler had said. And Bigmac said the other name was Dunn . . .

He twirled the knob of the communicator panel.

"Krystal?" he tried. "Kylie? Kathryn? Whatever?"

There was just the hiss of the stars, and then: "It's Kirsty, *actually*."

"Don't fire!" said Johnny, quickly.

"Who *are* you?"

"Don't fire, first. Promise? I hate dying. It makes it hard to think."

The other ship had stopped being a dot now. If she was going to fire, he was as good as dead—if dead was good.

"All right," she said, slowly. "No firing. Peace talk. Now tell me who you are."

"I'm a player, like you," said Johnny.

"No you're not. None of the other players talk to me. Anyway, you're on *their* side. I've been watching you."

"Not . . . exactly on *their* side," said Johnny.

"Well, you're not on *my* side," said Kirsty. "No-one is."

"Did they try to surrender to you too? I heard you say in Patel's shop that they'd sent you a message."

There was another silence filled with the whispers of the universe, and then a cautious voice: "You're not the fat one who looks as though he could do with a bra, are you?"

"No. Listen—" Johnny tapped his controls hurriedly.

"The black one who looks like an accountant?"

"No. *Look*—"

"Oh, no . . . not the *skinny* one with the big boots and the pointy head . . . ?"

"No, I'm the one who kind of hangs around and no-one notices much," said Johnny desperately.

"Who? I didn't see anyone."

"Right! *That was me!*"

"They surrendered to *you*?"

"Yes!" Number three missile went ping as it locked on to her ship. Now for number four—

"But you're a nerd!"

Ping!

"I think it's dweeb now. Anyway, I'm more than a dweeb."

Ping!

"Why?"

"I'm a dweeb with five missiles targeted on you."

"You said you weren't going to fire!"

"I haven't yet."

"You said this was a peace talk!"

"*You* did. Anyway, it is. It's just that I'm . . . kind of shouting."

If he concentrated, he thought he could hear music in the background when she spoke.

"You've *really* got missiles targeted on me?"

"Yes."

"I'm amazed you thought of it."

"So am I. Look, I don't want to shoot *anyone*. But I need help. The fleet's turned round. They fired at me!"

"That's their *job*, dweeb. They fire at us, we fire at them. Why did they stop? It's no fun if they don't fire back."

"They surrendered."

"They can't surrender. It's a game."

"Well, they did. Sometimes you change the game. I don't know, Kirsty!"

"Listen, I hate that name!"

"I've got to call you something," said Johnny. "What do you call yourself?"

"If you tell anyone else I'll kill you—"

"I thought you were planning to do that anyway."

"I don't mean just kill you, I mean *really* kill you."

"All right. What's your game name?"

"Sigourney—*you're laughing!*"

"I'm not! I'm not! It was a sneeze! Honest! No, it's a . . . good name. Very . . . appropriate . . ."

"It's just dreaming, anyway. I'm dreaming this. You're dreaming this."

"So what? Doesn't make things unimportant."

There was some more silence with the scratchy suggestion of music in the background, and then: "Ah-*ha!* While we've been talking, Mr. Clever, *I've* targeted missiles on *you!*"

Johnny shrugged, even though there was no way she could see that.

"Doesn't matter. I thought you would, anyway. So we kill each other. Then we'll have to go through all this again. It's stupid. Don't you want to find out what happens next?"

More scratchy music.

"I can hear scratchy music," said Johnny.

"It's my Walkman."

"Clever. I wish I'd thought of that. I tried dreaming my camera, but the pictures weren't any good. What're you listening to?"

"C Inlay 4 Details—'Please Keep This Copy For Your Records.' "

There was another scratchy pause.

Then, as if she'd been thinking deeply, she said: "Look, we can't be in the same dream. That can't happen."

"We could find out. Where'd you live?"

This time the pause went on for a long time. The ScreeWee fleet appeared on the radar.

"We'd better move," said Johnny. "They've started firing. Something's happened to the Captain. She's the one that wanted peace in the first place. Look, I know you live in Tyne Avenue or Crescent or somewhere—"

"How come we live so close?"

"Dunno. Bad luck, I suppose. Look, they're going to be in range soon—"

"*No* problem. Then we shoot them."

"We'll be killed. Anyway—"

"So what? Dying's easy."

"I know. It's living that's the problem," said Johnny, meaning it. "You don't sound like someone who takes the easy way."

C Inlay 4 Details played on in the distance.

"So what do you have in mind?"

Johnny hesitated. He hadn't thought that far. The new Captain didn't seem to want to talk.

"Dunno. I just don't want any ScreeWee to get killed."

"Why not?"

Because when they die, they die for real.

"I just don't, OK?"

Several fighters had left the fleet and were heading purposefully towards them.

"I'm going to try and talk one more time," he decided. "Someone must be listening."

"Nerdy idea."

"I'm not much good at the other kind."

Johnny turned his ship and hit the Go-faster button. A few shots whiffled harmlessly past him and did a lot of damage to empty space.

And then he was heading at maximum speed towards the fleet.

Music came over the intercom.

"Idiot! Dodge and dive! No wonder you get shot a lot!"

He wiggled the joystick. Something clipped one of the starship's wings and exploded behind him.

"*And* you've got the fighters after you! Huh! You can't even save yourself!"

Johnny didn't take his eyes off the fleet, which was bouncing around the sky as he flung his ship about in an effort to avoid being shot at.

"You might try to be some help!" he shouted.

There was a boom behind him.

"I am."

"You're shooting them?"

"You're very hard to please, *actually*."

The Captain tried the door of her cabin again. It was still locked. And there was almost certainly a guard in the corridor outside. ScreeWee tended to obey orders, even if they didn't like them. The Gunnery Officer was very unusual.

That, she thought bitterly, is what comes of promoting a male. They're unreliable thinkers.

She looked around the cabin. She didn't want to be in it. She wanted to be outside it. But she was in it. She needed a new idea.

Humans seemed much better at ideas. They always seemed to be on the verge of being totally insane, but it seemed to work for them. The inside of their heads would be an interesting place to visit, but she wouldn't want to live there.

How do you think like a human? Go into madness first, probably, and then out the other side . . .

Listen! *Listen!* If you keep going this way, you'll all be killed! You're going back into game space! People like me will find you! You'll all be killed! That's how it goes!"

And then he died.

It was 6.3≡. He was lying on his bed with his clothes on, but he still felt cold.

Bits and pieces of his . . . his previous life trickled through his mind.

Sigourney!

Well, Yo-less would say that explained anything. And now it looked as if he'd be spending every night watching the ScreeWee get killed.

It was bad enough fighting off people in ones and twos. But they were just the ones who were weird or lonely or bored enough to go looking. Wobbler said thousands of copies of the game had been sold. Even if most people took them back to the shops, there'd always be someone playing. Once the ScreeWee turned up again, the news would get around . . .

And then, one day, long after no-one played the game any more, there'd be these broken ships, turning over and over in the blank-screen darkness of game space.

And he couldn't stop it. Kir—Sigourney was right. That's what they were *there* for.

It was Tuesday, too. It was Maths for most of the morning. And then English. He'd better write a poem at lunchtime. You could generally get away with a poem.

He got his jacket out of the shed and sponged it off as best he could, and then propped it up by the heater. Then he investigated the fridge.

His father had been doing the shopping again. You could always tell. There were generally expensive things in jars, and odd foreign vegetables. This time there was Yoghurt Vindaloo and more celery. No-one in the house liked celery much. It always ended up going brown. And his father never bought bread and potatoes. He seemed to think that stuff like that just *grew* in kitchens, like mushrooms (although he always bought mushrooms, if they were the special expensive dried kind that looked like bits of mouldy bark and were picked by wizened old Frenchmen).

There was a carton of milk which thumped when he shook it.

Johnny found a cup in the ghastly cavern of the dishwasher and rinsed it under the tap. At least there wasn't much that could go wrong with black coffee.

He quite enjoyed the time by himself in the mornings. The day was too early to have started going really wrong.

The war was still on television. It was getting on his nerves. It was worrying him. You'd really think everyone would have had enough by now.

Bigmac was in school. He'd stayed the night at Yo-less's. Mrs. Yo-less had washed out his clothes, even the T-shirt with "Blackbury Skins" on the back. It was a lot cleaner than it had ever been.

He could feel Wobbler and Yo-less looking at him with interest. So were one or two other people.

Later on, when they were in the middle of the rush which meant that every pupil in the school had to walk all the way across the campus to be somewhere else, Yo-less said: "Bigmac said you pulled him out of the wreck. Did you?"

"What? He wasn't even—" Johnny paused.

It was amazing. He'd never thought so fast before. He thought of Bigmac's room, with its Weapons of the World posters and plastic model guns and weight-training stuff he couldn't lift. Bigmac had been thrown out of the school role-playing games club for getting too excited. Bigmac, who spent all his time trying hard to be a big thicko; Bigmac, who could work out maths problems just by looking at them. Bigmac, who played the game of being . . . well, big tough Bigmac.

Johnny looked around. Bigmac was watching him. It was amazing, given that Bigmac's ancestors were a sort of monkey, how much his expression looked like the one he'd first seen on the face of the Captain, whose ancestors were a kind of alligator. It said: Help me.

"Can't really remember," he said.

"Only my mum rang the hospital and they said there were only two boys and they were—"

"It was dark," said Johnny.

"Yes, but if you'd *really*—"

"It's just best if everyone shuts up about it, all right?" said Johnny, nodding meaningfully at Bigmac.

"She said you did everything right, anyway," said Yo-less. "And she said you aren't being properly looked after."

"Yo-*less*."

"She said you ought to come round our house to eat sometimes—"

"Thanks," said Johnny. "I'm a bit busy these days—"

"Doing what?" said Yo-less.

Johnny fumbled in his pocket.

"What does this look like to you?" he said.

Yo-less took it gravely.

"It's a photograph," he said. "Just looks like a TV screen with dots on."

"Yes," sighed Johnny. "It does, doesn't it."

He took it back and shoved it deep into his pocket.

"Yo-less?"

"What?"

"If someone was . . . you know . . . going a bit weird in the head—"

"Mental, he means," said Wobbler, behind him.

"Just a bit *over-strained*," said Johnny. "I mean . . . would they know? Themselves?"

"Well, everyone thinks they're a bit mad," said Yo-less. "It's part of being normal."

"Oh, I don't think I'm mad," said Johnny.

"You don't?"

"Well—"

"Ah-*aha!*" said Wobbler.

"I mean—the whole world seems kind of weird right now. You watch the telly, don't you? How can you be the good guys if you're dropping clever bombs right down people's chimneys? And blowing people up just because they're being bossed around by a loony?"

"Shouldn't let 'emselves be bossed around, then," said Bigmac. Johnny looked at him. Bigmac deflated a bit. "It's their own fault. They don't *have* to. That's what my brother says, anyway," he mumbled.

"Is it?" said Johnny.

Bigmac shrugged.

"Oh, well, *yes*," said Wobbler. "How? It's hard enough to get rid of prime ministers and at least they don't have people taken out and shot. Not any more, anyway."

"My brother's *stupid*," said Bigmac, so quietly under his breath that Johnny wondered if anyone else even heard it.

"There was a man on the box saying that the bomb-aimers were so good because they all grew up playing computer games," said Wobbler.

"See?" said Johnny. "That's what I mean. Games look real. Real things look like games. And . . . and . . . it all kind of runs together in my head."

"Ah," said Yo-less, knowingly. "That's not mental. That's shamanism. I read a book about it."

"What's shamanism?"

"Shamans used to be these kind of people who lived partly in a dream world and partly in the real world," said Wobbler. "Like medicine men and druids and guys like that. They used to be very important. They used to guide people."

"Guide?" said Johnny. "Where to?"

"Not sure. Anyway, my mother says they were creations of Satan."

"Yes, but your mother says that about practically everything," said Wobbler.

"This is true," said Yo-less gravely. "It's her hobby."

"She said role-playing games were creations of Satan," said Wobbler.

"True."

"Dead clever of him," said Wobbler. "I mean, sitting down there in Hell, working out all the combat tables and everything. I bet he used to really *swear* every time the dice caught fire . . ."

Shamanism, thought Johnny. Yes. I could be a shaman. A guide. That's better than being mental, at any rate.

It was Maths *again*. As far as Johnny was concerned, the future would be a better place if it didn't contain $3y + x^2$. He had problems enough without people giving him pages of them.

He was trying to put off the idea of ringing someone up.

And then there was Social Education. Normally you could ignore Social Education, which tended to be about anything anyone had on their minds at the time or, failing that, Aids. Really the day ended with Maths. SE was just there to keep you off the streets for another three-quarters of an hour.

He *could* try ringing up. You just needed the phone book and a bit of thought . . .

Johnny stared at the ceiling. The teacher was going on about the war. That was all there was to talk about these days. He listened with half an ear. No-one liked the bombing. One of the girls was nearly in tears about it . . .

Supposing *she* was really there? Or supposing *she* said she'd never heard of him?

Bigmac was arguing. That was unusual.

And then someone said, "Do you think it's easy? Do you think the pilots *really* just sit there like . . . like a game? Do you think they laugh? Really laugh? Not just laugh because they're still alive, but laugh because it's . . . it's fun? When they're being shot at for a living, every day? When any minute they might get blown up too? Do you think they don't wonder what it's all about? Do you think they *like* it? But we always turn it into something that's not exactly real. We turn it into games and it's not games. We really have to find out what's *real*!"

They were all looking at him.

"Anyway, that's what I think," said Johnny.

9

On Earth, No-one Can Hear You Say "Um"

Click!

"Yes?"

"Um."

"Hello?"

"Um. Is Sig—is Kirsty there?"

"Who's that?"

"I'm a friend. Um. I don't think she knows my name."

"You're a friend and she doesn't know your name?"

"Please!"

"Oh, hang on."

Johnny stared at his bedroom wall. Eventually a suspicious voice said, "Yes? Who's that?"

"You're Sigourney. You like C Inlay 4 Details. You fly really well. You—"

"You're *him*!"

Johnny breathed a sigh of relief. Real!

Going through the phone book had been harder than flying the starship. Nearly harder than dying.

"I wasn't sure you really existed," he said.

"I wasn't sure *you* existed," she said.

"I've got to talk to you. I mean face to face."

"How do I know you're not some sort of maniac?"

"Do I *sound* like some sort of maniac?"

"Yes!"

"All right, but apart from that?"

There was silence for a moment. Then she said, reluctantly: "All right. You can come round here."

"What? To your house?"

"It's safer than in public, idiot."

Not for me, Johnny thought.

"OK," he said.

"I mean, you might be one of those funny people."

"What, clowns?"

And then she said, very cautiously: "It's really you?"

"*Really* I'm not sure about. But me, yes."

"You got blown up."

"Yes, I know. I was there, remember."

"I don't die often in the game. It took me ages even to find the aliens."

Huh, thought Johnny.

"It doesn't get any better with practice," he said, darkly.

Tyne Crescent turned out to be a pretty straight road with trees in it, and the houses were big and had double garages and a timber effect on them to fool people into believing that Henry VIII had built them.

Kirsty's mother opened the door for him. She was grinning like the Captain, although the Captain had the excuse that she was related to crocodiles. Johnny felt he had the wrong clothes on, or the wrong face.

He was shown into a large room. It was mainly white. Expensive bookshelves lined one wall. Most of the floor was bare pine, but varnished and polished to show that they could have afforded carpets if they'd wanted them. There was a harp standing by a chair in one corner, and music scattered around it on the floor.

Johnny picked up a sheet. It was headed "Royal College, Grade V."

"Well?"

She was standing behind him. The sheet slipped out of his fingers.

"And don't say 'um,' " she said, sitting down. "You say 'um' a lot. Aren't you ever sure about things?"

"U—No. Hello?"

"Sit down. My mother's making us some tea. And then staying out of the way. You'll probably notice that. You can actually *hear* her staying out of the way. She thinks I ought to have more friends."

She had red hair, and the skinny look that went with it. It was as if someone had grabbed the frizzy ponytail on the back of her head and pulled it tightly.

"The game," said Johnny vaguely.

"Yes? What?"

"I'm really glad you're in it too. Yo-less said it was all in my head because of Trying Times. He said it was just me projecting my problems."

"*I* haven't got any problems," snapped Kirsty. "I get on extremely well with people, *actually*. There's probably some simple psychic reason that you're too stupid to work out."

"You sounded more concerned on the phone," said Johnny.

"But now I've had time to think about it. Anyway, what's it to me what happens to some dots in a machine?"

"Didn't you see the Space Invaders?" said Johnny.

"Yes, but they *were* stupid. That's what happens. Charles Darwin knew about that. I am a winning kind of person. And what I want to know is, what were you doing in *my* dream?"

"I'm not sure it's a dream," said Johnny. "I'm not sure *what* it is. Not exactly a dream and not exactly real. Something in between. I don't know. Maybe something happens in your head. Maybe you're in there because—because, well, I don't know why, but there's got to be a reason," he ended lamely.

"Why're *you* there, then?"

"I want to save the ScreeWee."

"Why?"

"Because . . . I've got a responsibility. But the Captain's been . . . I don't know, locked up or something. There's been some kind of mutiny. It's the Gunnery Officer. He's behind it. But if I—if we could get her out, she could probably turn the fleet around again. I thought you might be able to think of some way of getting her out," Johnny finished lamely. "We haven't got a lot of game time."

"She?" said Kirsty.

"She started all this. She relied on me," said Johnny.

"You said 'she,' " said Kirsty.

Johnny stood up.

"I thought you might be able to help," he said wearily, "but who cares what happens to some dots that aren't even real. So I'll just—"

"You keep saying 'she,' " said Kirsty. "You mean the Captain's a woman?"

"A female," said Johnny. "Yes."

"But you called the Gunnery Officer a 'he,' " said Kirsty.

"That's right."

Kirsty stood up.

"That's typical. That's absolutely typical of modern society. He probably resents a wo—a female being better than him. I get that *all the time*."

"Um," said Johnny. He hadn't meant to say "um." He meant to say: "Actually, all the ScreeWee *except* the Gunnery Officer are females." But another part of his brain had thought faster and shut down his mouth before he could say it, diverting the words into oblivion and shoving good old "um" in their place.

"There was an article in a magazine," said Kirsty. "This whole bunch of directors of a company ganged up on this woman and sacked her just because she'd become the boss. It was just like me and the Chess Club."

It probably wouldn't be a good idea to tell her. There was a glint in her eye. No, it probably wouldn't be a good idea to be honest. Truthfulness would have to do instead. After all, he hadn't actually *lied*.

"It's a matter of principle," said Kirsty. "You should have said so right at the start." She stood up. "Come on."

"Where are we going?" said Johnny.

"To my room," said Kirsty. "Don't worry. My parents are very liberal."

There were film posters all over the walls, and where there weren't film posters there were shelves with silver cups on. There was a framed certificate for the Regional Winner of the Small-Bore Rifle Confederation's National Championships, and another one for chess. And another one for athletics. There were a lot of medals, mostly gold, and one or two silver. Kirsty won things.

If there was a medal for a tidy bedroom, she would have won that too. You could see the floor all the way to the walls.

She had an electrical pencil sharpener.

And a computer. The screen was showing the familiar message: NEW GAME (Y/N)?

"Do you know I have an IQ of one hundred and sixty-five?" she said, sitting down in front of the screen.

"Is that good?"

"Yes! And I only started playing this *wretched* game because my brother bought it and said I wouldn't be any good at it. These things are *moronic*."

There was a notebook by the keyboard.

"Each level," explained Kirsty. "I made notes about how the ships flew. And kept score, of course."

"You were taking it seriously," said Johnny. "Very seriously."

"Of *course* I take it seriously. It's a *game*. You've got to *win* them, otherwise what's the point? Now . . . can we get on to the ScreeWee flagship?"

"Um—"

"Think!"

"Can we get into a ScreeWee battleship?"

Kirsty almost growled. "I asked *you*. Sit down and *think*!"

Johnny sat down.

"I don't think we can," he said. "I'm always in a starship. I think things have to look like they do on the screen."

"Hmm. Makes some sort of sense, I suppose." Kirsty stuck a pencil in the sharpener, which whirred for a while. "And we don't know what it looks like inside."

Johnny stared at the wall. Among the items pinned over the bed was a card for winning the Under-7 Long Jump. She wins everything, he thought. Wow. She actually assumes she's going to win. Someone who always thinks they're going to win . . .

He stared up at the movie posters. There was one he'd seen many times before. The famous one. The slavering alien monster. You'd think she'd have something like a C Inlay 4 Details photo over her bed but no, there was this thing . . .

"Don't tell me," he said, "you want to get inside the ship and run along the corridors shooting ScreeWee? You do, don't you?"

"Tactically—" she began.

"You can't. The Captain wouldn't want that. Not killing ScreeWee."

Kirsty waved her hands in the air irritably.

"That's *stupid*," she said. "How do you expect to win without killing the enemy?"

"I'm supposed to save them. Anyway, they're not exactly the enemy. I can't go around killing them."

Kirsty looked thoughtful.

"Do you know," she said, "there was an African tribe once whose nearest word for 'enemy' was 'a friend we haven't met yet'?"

Johnny smiled. "Right," he said. "That's how—"

"But they were all killed and eaten in eighteen hundred and two," said Kirsty. "Except for those who were sold as slaves. The last one died in Mississippi in eighteen sixty-four, and he was *very upset*."

"You just made that up," said Johnny.

"No. I won a prize for History."

"I expect you did," said Johnny. "But I'm not killing anyone."

"Then you *can't* win."

"I don't want to win. I just don't want them to lose."

"You really *are* a dweeb, aren't you? How can anyone go through life expecting to lose all the time?"

"Well, I've got to, haven't I? The world is full of people like you, for a start."

Johnny realized he was getting angry again. He didn't often get angry. He just got quiet, or miserable. Anger was unusual. But when it came, it overflowed.

"They tried to talk to you, and you didn't even listen! You were the only other one that got that involved! You were so mad to win you slipped into game space! And you'd have been so much better at saving them than me! And you didn't even listen! But I listened and I've spent a week trying to Save Mankind in my sleep! It's always people like me that have to do stuff like that! It's always the people who aren't clever and who don't win things that have to get killed all the time! And you just hung around and watched! It's just like on the television! The winners have fun! Winner types never lose, they just come second! It's all the other people who lose! And now you're only thinking of helping the Captain because you think she's like you! Well, I don't bloody well care any more, Miss Clever! I've done my best! And I'm going to go on doing it! And they'll all come back into game space and it'll be just like the Space Invaders all over again! And I'll be there every night!"

Her mouth was open.

There was a knock on the door and almost immediately, mothers being what they are, Kirsty's mother pushed it open. She brought in a wide grin and a tray.

"I'm sure you'd both like some tea," she said. "And—"

"*Yes*, mother," said Kirsty, and rolled her eyes.

"—there's some macaroons. Have you found out your friend's name now?"

"John Maxwell," said Johnny.

"And what do your friends call you?" said Kirsty's mother sweetly.

"Sometimes they call me Rubber," said Johnny.

"Do they? Whatever for?"

"*Mother*, we were *talking*," said Kirsty.

"*Cobbers* is on in a minute," said Kirsty's mother. "I, er, shall watch it on the set in the kitchen, shall I?"

"Goodbye," said Kirsty, meaningfully.

"Um, yes," said her mother, and went out.

"She dithers a lot," said Kirsty. "Fancy getting married when you're twenty! A complete lack of ambition."

She stared at Johnny for a while. He was keeping quiet. He'd been amazed to hear his own thoughts.

Kirsty coughed. She looked a little uncertain, for the first time since Johnny had met her.

"Well," she said. "Uh. OK. And . . . we won't be able to fight all the players when they get back to game space."

"No. There's not enough missiles."

"Could we dream a few more?"

"No. I thought of that. You get the ship you play with. I mean, we *know* it's only got six missiles. I've tried dreaming more and it doesn't work."

"Hmm. Interesting problem. *Sorry*," she added quickly, when she saw his expression.

Johnny stared at the movie posters. Sigourney! Games everywhere. Bigmac was a tough guy in his head, and *this* one kept sharp pencils and had to win everything and in her head shot aliens. Everyone had these pictures of themselves in their head, except him . . .

He blinked.

And now his head ached. There was a buzzing in his ears.

Kirsty's face drifted towards him.

"Are you all right?"

The headache was really bad now.

"You're ill. And you look all thin. When did you last eat?"

"I dunno. Had something last night, I think."

"Last night? What about breakfast and lunch?"

"Oh, well . . . you know . . . I kept thinking about . . ."

"You'd better drink that tea and eat that macaroon. Phew. When did you last have a bath?"

"It's kind of . . ."

"Good grief—"

"Listen! Listen!" It was important to tell her. He didn't feel well at all.

"Yes?"

"We dream our way in," he said.

"What are you talking about? You're swaying!"

"We go on to their ship!"

"But we agreed we don't know what it looks like inside!"

"OK! Good! So we decide what it *does* look like inside, right?"

She tapped her pad irritably.

"So what does it look like?"

"I don't know! The inside of a spaceship! Corridors and cabins and stuff like that. Nuts and bolts and panels and sliding doors. Scotsmen saying the engines canna tak' it anymoore. Bright blue lights!"

"Hmm. That's what you think is inside spaceships, is it?"

Kirsty glared at him. She generally glared. It was her normal expression.

"When we go to sleep . . . I mean, when I go to sleep . . . I'll try and wake up inside the ship," he said.

"How?"

"I don't know! By concentrating, I suppose."

She leaned forward. For the first time since he'd met her, she looked concerned.

"You don't look capable of thinking straight," she said.

"I'll be all right."

Johnny stood up.

10

In Space, No-one Is Listening *Anyway*

And woke up.

He was lying down on something hard. There was some sort of mesh just in front of his eyes. He stared at it for a while.

There was also a faint vibration in the floor, and a distant background rumbling.

He was obviously back in game space, but he certainly wasn't in a starship . . .

The mesh moved.

The Captain's face appeared over the edge of the mesh, upside down.

"Johnny?"

"Where am I?"

"You appear to be under my bed."

He rolled sideways.

"I'm on your ship?"

"Oh, yes."

"Right! Hah! I knew I could do it . . ."

He stood up, and looked around the cabin. It wasn't very interesting. Apart from the bed, which was under something that looked like a sun-ray lamp, there was only a desk and something that was probably a chair if you had four back legs and a thick tail.

On the desk were half a dozen plastic aliens. There was also a cage with a couple of long-beaked birds in it. They sat side by side on their perch and watched Johnny with almost intelligent eyes.

Right. Sigourney was right. He *did* think better in game space. All the decisions seemed so much clearer.

OK. So he was on board. He'd rather hoped to be *outside* the cabin the Captain was locked in, but this was a start.

He stared at the wall. There was a grille.

"What's that?" he said, pointing.

"It is where the air comes in."

Johnny pulled at the grille. There was no very obvious way of removing it. If it *could* be removed, the hole behind it was easily big enough for the Captain. Air ducts. Well, what did he expect?

"We've got to get this off," he said. "Before something dreadful happens."

"We are imprisoned," said the Captain. "What more can happen that is dreadful?"

"Have you ever heard the name . . . Sigourney?" said Johnny cautiously.

"No. But it sounds a lovely name," said the Captain. "Who is this Sigourney?"

"Well, if she can dream her way here as well, then there's going to be *trouble*. You should see the pictures she's got on her walls."

"What of?"

"Um. Aliens," said Johnny.

"She takes a very close interest in alien races?" said the Captain happily.

"Um. Yes." The mere thought of her arrival made him pull urgently at the grille. "Um. There's something on the inside . . . and I can't quite get my hand through . . ."

The Captain watched him with interest.

"Something like wingnuts," grunted Johnny.

"This is very instructive," said the Captain, peering over his shoulder.

"I can't get a grip!"

"You wish to turn them?"

"Yes!"

The Captain waddled over to the table and opened the bird cage. Both of the birds hopped out on to her hand. The Captain said a few words in ScreeWee; the birds fluttered past Johnny's head, squeezed through the mesh, and disappeared. After a second or two he heard the squeak-squeak of nuts being undone.

"What were they?" he said.

"Chee," said the Captain. "Mouth birds. You understand?" She opened her mouth, revealing several rows of yellow teeth. "For hygiene?"

"Living toothbrushes?"

"We have always had them. They are . . . traditional. Very intelligent. Bred for it, you know. Clever things. They understand several words of ScreeWee."

The squeaking went on. There was a clonk, and a nut rolled through the mesh.

The panel fell into the room.

Johnny looked at the hole.

"O-*kay*," he said uncertainly. "You don't know where it goes, do you?"

"No. There are ventilation shafts all over the ship. Will you lead the way?"

"Um—"

"I would be happy for you to lead the way," said the Captain.

Johnny stood on the bed and crawled into the hole. It went a little way and then opened on to a bigger shaft.

"All over the ship?" he said.

"Yes."

Johnny paused for a moment. He'd never liked narrow dark spaces.

"Oh. Right," he said.

Kirsty's mother put down the phone.

"There's no-one answering," she said.

"I think he said his father works late and his mother sometimes works in the evening," said Kirsty. "Anyway, the doctor said he's basically all right, didn't she? He's just run down, she said. What was the stuff she gave him?"

"She said it'd make him sleep. He's not getting enough sleep. Twelve-year-old boys need a lot of sleep."

"I know this one does," said Kirsty.

"And *you* said he's not eating properly. Where did you meet him, anyway?"

"Um," Kirsty began, and then smiled to herself. "Out and about."

Kirsty's mother looked worried.

"Are you sure he's all there?"

"He's all there," said Kirsty, climbing the stairs. "I'm not sure that he's all *here*, but he's certainly all there."

She opened the door of the spare room and looked in. Johnny was fast asleep in a pair of her brother's pyjamas. He looked very young. It's amazing how young twelve is, when you're thirteen.

Then she went to her own bedroom, got ready for bed, and slid between the sheets.

It was pretty early. It had been a busy evening.

He was a loser. You could tell. He *dressed* like a loser. A ditherer. Someone who said "um" a lot, and went through life trying not to be noticed.

She'd never done that. She'd always gone through life as if there was a big red arrow above the planet, indicating precisely where she was.

On the other hand, he *tried* so hard . . .

She'd bet he'd cried when ET died.

She pushed herself up on one elbow and stared at the movie posters.

Trying wasn't the point.

You had to win. What good was anything if you didn't win?

"Stuck? You're an *alien*," said Johnny. "Aliens don't get stuck in air ducts. It's practically a well-known fact."

He backed into a side tunnel, and turned around.

"I am sorry. It occurs to me that possibly I am the wrong type of alien," said the Captain. "I can go backwards, but I am forwardly disadvantaged."

"OK. Back up to that second junction we passed," said Johnny. "We're lost, anyway."

"No," said the Captain, "I know where we are. It says here this is junction ⊨ ⊋ ϴ."

"Do you know where that is?"

"No."

"I saw a film where there was an alien crawling around inside a spaceship's air ducts and it could come out wherever it liked," said Johnny reproachfully.

"Doubtless it had a map," said the Captain.

Johnny crawled around a corner and found . . .

. . . another grille.

There didn't seem to be any activity on the other side of it. He unscrewed the nuts and let it fall on to the floor.

There was a corridor. He dropped into it, then turned and helped the Captain through. ScreeWee might have descended from crocodiles, but crocodiles preferred sandbanks. They weren't very good at crawling through narrow spaces.

Her skin felt cold and dry, like silk.

There were no other ScreeWee around.

"They're probably at battle stations," said Johnny.

"We're *always* at battle stations," said the Captain bitterly, brushing dust off her scales. "This is corridor ≮. Now we must get to the bridge, yes?"

"Won't they just lock you up again?" said Johnny.

"I think not. Disobedience to properly constituted authority does not come easily to us. The Gunnery Officer is very . . . persuasive. But once they see that I am free again, they will give in. At least," the Captain added, "most of them will. The Gunnery Officer may prove difficult. He dreams of grandeur."

She waddled a little way along the bare corridor, keeping close to the wall. Johnny trailed behind her.

"Dreams are always tricky," he said.

"Yes."

"But they'll wake up when the players start shooting again, won't they? They'll soon see what he is leading them into?"

"We have a proverb," said the Captain. "*SkeejeeshejweeJEEyee*. It means . . ." she thought for a moment, "when you are riding a *jee*, a six-legged domesticated beast of burden capable of simple instruction but also traditionally foul-tempered, it is easier to stay on rather than dismount; equally, better to trust yourself to a *jee* than risk attack from the sure-footed *JEEyee*, which will easily outrun a ScreeWee on foot. Of course, it is a little snappier in our language."

They'd reached a corner. The Captain peered around it, and then jerked her head back.

"There is a guard outside the door of my cabin," she said. "She is armed."

"Can you talk to her?"

"She is under orders. I fear that I will only be allowed to say

'Aaargh!'," said the Captain. "But feel free to make the attempt. I have no other options."

Oh, well—you only die a few hundred times, thought Johnny. He stepped out into the corridor.

The guard turned to look at him, and half raised a melted-looking thing that nevertheless very clearly said "gun." But she looked at him in puzzlement.

She's never seen a human before! he thought.

He spread his arms wide in what he hoped was an innocent-looking way, and smiled.

Which just goes to show that you shouldn't take things for granted because, as the Captain told him later, when a ScreeWee is about to fight she does two things. She spreads her front pairs of arms wide (to grip and throttle) and exposes her teeth (ready to bite).

The guard raised the gun.

Then there was a thunderous knocking on the other side of the cabin door.

The guard made a simple mistake. She *should* have ignored the knocking, loud and desperate though it was, and concentrated on Johnny. But she tried to keep the gun pointing in his general direction while she pressed a panel by the door. After all, it was only the Captain in there, wasn't it? And the Captain was still the Captain, even if she was locked up. She could keep an eye on both of them . . .

The door opened a little way. A foot came out, swinging upwards, and caught the guard under the snout. There was a click as all its teeth met. Its eyes crossed.

Someone shouted: "Haiii!"

The guard swayed backwards. Kirsty came through the door airborne and started hacking at the guard's arms with her hands. It dropped the gun. She picked it up in one movement. The guard opened its mouth to bite, spread its arms to grip and throttle, and then went cross-eyed because the gun barrel was suddenly thrust between its teeth.

"Don't . . . swallow . . ." said Kirsty, very deliberately.

There was a sudden, very heavy silence. The guard stayed very still.

"This is a friend of mine," said Johnny.

"Oh, yes," said the Captain. "Sigourney. One of your warriors. Is she a friend of mine?"

"At the moment," said Sigourney, without moving her head. She had tied one of the strips of webbing from the Captain's bed around her forehead. She was breathing heavily. There was a wild glint in her eye. Johnny suddenly felt very sorry for the guard.

"You know, I'm *glad* she's a friend of mine," said the Captain.

"Ee ee ogg ee?" said the guard. Its arms were trembling. The ScreeWee didn't sweat, but this one would probably have liked to.

"We'd better tie her up and put her in the cabin," said Johnny.

"Ees!" said the guard.

"I could just fire," said Sigourney wistfully.

"No!" said Johnny and the Captain together.

"Eep!" said the guard.

"Oh, all right." Sigourney relaxed. The guard sagged.

"Sorry to be late," said Sigourney. "Had a bit of trouble getting to sleep."

The Captain said something to the guard in ScreeWee. It nodded in a strangely human way and trooped obediently into the cabin, where it squatted down just as obediently and let them tie its hands and feet with more bits of bed.

"You've got a black belt in karate too, I expect," said Johnny.

"Only purple," she said. "But I haven't been doing it long," she added quickly. "Huh! Is that the only kind of knot you can tie?"

"I went to karate once, with Bigmac," said Johnny, trying to ignore that.

"What happened?"

"I got my foot caught in my trousers."

"And *you* are the Chosen One? Huh! They could have chosen *me*."

"They tried. But *I* was the one who listened," said Johnny quietly.

Sigourney picked up the gun and cradled it in her arms.

"Well, I'm here now," she said, "And ready to kick some butt."

"Some but what?" said Johnny wearily. He really hated the phrase. It was a game saying. It tried to fool you into believing that real bullets weren't going to go through real people.

Sigourney sniffed.

"Nerd."

They went back into the corridor.

"By the way," said Johnny, "what happened to me?"

"You just collapsed. Right there on the floor. We've got a doctor living next door. Mum went and got her. Unusually bright of her, really. She said you were just tired out and looked as though you hadn't been eating properly."

"This is true," said the Captain. "Did I not say? Too much sugar and carbohydrate, not enough fresh vitamins. You should get out more."

"Yeah, right," said Johnny.

There was something different about the corridor. Before, it had been grey metal, only interesting if you really liked looking at nuts and bolts. But now it was darker, with more curves; the walls glistened, and dripped menace. Dripped something, anyway.

The Captain looked different, too. She hadn't changed, exactly—it was just that her teeth and claws were somehow more obvious. A few minutes ago, she had been an intelligent person who just happened to be an eight-legged crocodile; now she was an eight-legged crocodile who just happened to be intelligent.

Game space was changing now two people were sharing one dream.

"Hold on, there's—" he began.

"Don't let's hang around," said Sigourney.

"But you're—" Johnny began.

Dreaming it wrong, he finished to himself.

This really *is* nuts, he told himself as he trailed after them. At home Kirsty went around being Miss Brains. In here it was all: Make my shorts! Eat my day!

The Captain waddled at high speed along the corridors. Now steam was dribbling from somewhere, making the floor misty and wet.

There wasn't that much in the ScreeWee ships. Perhaps they ought to have sat down and worked out the inside of one in a bit more detail before they'd dreamed, he thought. They could have added more cabins and big screens and interesting things like that; as it was, all there seemed to be were these snaking corridors that were unpleasantly like caves.

Bigger caves, though. They'd got wider. Mysterious passages led off in various directions.

Sigourney crept along with her back against the wall, spinning around rapidly every time they passed another passage. She stiffened.

"There's another one coming!" she hissed. "It's pushing something! Get back!"

She elbowed them into the wall. Johnny could hear the scrape-scrape of claws on the floor, and something rattling.

"When it gets closer I'll get it. I'll leap out—"

Johnny poked his head around the corner.

"Kirsty?"

She took no notice.

"Sigourney?" he tried.

"Yes?"

"I know you're going to leap out," said Johnny, "but don't pull the trigger, right?"

"It's an *alien*!"

"So it's an alien. You don't have to shoot them all."

The rattling got closer. There was also a faint squeaking.

Sigourney gripped the gun excitedly, and leapt out.

"OK, *you*—oh . . . um . . ."

It was a very small ScreeWee. Most of its scales were grey. Its crest was nearly worn away. Its tail just dragged behind it. When it opened its mouth, there were three teeth left and they were huddling together at the back.

It blinked owlishly at them over the top of the trolley it had been pushing. Apart from anything else, Kirsty had been aiming the gun well above its head.

There was one of those awkward pauses.

"Around this time," said the Captain behind them, "the crew on the bridge have a snack brought to them."

Johnny leaned forward, nodded at the little old alien, and lifted the lid of the tray that was on the trolley. There were a few bowls of something green and bubbling. He gently lowered the lid again.

"I think you were going to shoot the tea lady," he said.

"How was I to know?" Kirsty demanded. "It could have been anything! This is an alien spaceship! You're not supposed to get *tea ladies*!"

The Captain said something in ScreeWee to the old alien, who shuffled around slowly and went off back down the corridor. One wheel of the trolley kept squeaking.

Kirsty was furious.

"This isn't going right!" she hissed.

"Come on," said Johnny. "Let's go to the bridge and get it over with."

"I didn't *know* it was a tea lady! That's *your* dreaming!"

"Yes, all right."

"She had no right to be there!"

"I suppose even aliens get a bit thirsty in the afternoons."

"That's not what I meant! They're supposed to be *alien*! That means slavering and claws! It doesn't mean sending out for . . . for a coffee and a jam doughnut!"

"Things are just like they are," said Johnny, shrugging.

She turned on him.

"Why do you just *accept* everything? Why don't you ever try to *change* things?"

"They're generally bad enough already," he said.

She leapt ahead and peered around the next corner.

"Guards!" she said. "And these have got *guns*!"

Johnny looked around the corner. There were two ScreeWee standing in front of a round door. They were, indeed, armed.

"Satisfied?" she snapped. "No hint of Danish pastries anywhere? Right? Now can I actually shoot something?"

"No! I keep telling you! You have to give them a chance to surrender."

"You always make it difficult!"

She raised the gun and stepped out.

So did the Captain. *She* hissed a word in ScreeWee. The guards looked from her to Kirsty, who was squinting along her gun barrel. One of them hissed something.

"She says the Gunnery Officer has instructed them to shoot anyone who approaches the door," said the Captain.

"I'll fire if they move," said Kirsty. "I mean it!"

The Captain spoke in ScreeWee again. The guards stared at Johnny. They lowered their guns.

Suspicion rose inside him.

"What did you just tell them?" he said.

"I just told them who you were," said the Captain.

"You said I was the Chosen One?"

One of the guards was trying to kneel. That looked very strange in a creature with four legs.

Kirsty rolled her eyes.

"It's better than being shot at," said the Captain. "I've been shot at a lot. I know what I am talking about."

"Tell her to get up," said Johnny. "What do we do now? Who's on the bridge?"

"Most of the officers," said the Captain. "The guard says there have been—arguments. Gunfire."

"That's more like it!" said Kirsty.

They looked at the door.

"OK," said Johnny. "Let's go . . ."

The Captain motioned one of the guards aside and touched a plate by the door.

11

Humans!

Johnny saw it all in one long, long second.

Firstly, the bridge was *big*. It seemed to be the size of a football pitch. And at one end there was a screen, which looked almost as big. He felt like an ant standing in front of a TV set.

The screen was covered with green dots.

Players. Heading for the fleet.

There were hundreds of them.

Right in front of the screen was a horseshoe-shaped bank of controls, with a dozen seats ranged in front of it.

It's here, he thought. When I was sitting in my room playing, they were in here in this great shadowy room, steering their ship, firing back . . .

Only one seat was occupied now. Its occupant was already standing up, half turning, reaching for something . . .

"Go ahead," said Kirsty. "Make my stardate."

The Gunnery Officer froze, glaring at them.

"Too late," he said. "You're too late!" He waved a claw towards the screen. "I've taken us back to where we belong. There is no time to turn us round again. You *must* fight now."

He focused on Johnny. "What's *that*?" he said.

"The Chosen One," said the Captain, starting to walk forward. The others followed her.

"But we *must* fight," said the Gunnery Officer. "For honour. The honour of the ScreeWee! That's what we are *for*!"

Johnny's foot touched something. He looked down. Now that his eyes had become accustomed to the gloom, he could see that he'd almost tripped over a ScreeWee. It was dead. Nothing with a hole like that in it could have been alive.

Kirsty was looking down, too. Johnny could see other shapes on the floor in the shadows.

"He's been killing Sc—people," he whispered.

Shoot them in space, shoot them on a screen, and there was just an explosion and five points on the score total. When they'd been shot from a few metres away, then there was simply a reminder that someone who had been alive was now, very definitely, not alive any more. And would never be again.

He looked up at the Gunnery Officer. ScreeWee were cold-blooded and a long way from being human, but this one had a look about it—about *him* that suggested a mind running off into madness.

There was a silvery sheen on his scales. Johnny found himself wondering if the ScreeWee changed colour, like chameleons. The Captain had always looked more golden when she was acting normally, and became almost yellow when she was worried . . .

She was the colour of lemons now.

She hissed something. The guards looked at her in surprise, but turned and filed obediently out of the bridge. Then she turned to the Gunnery Officer.

"You killed all of them?" she said, softly.

"They tried to stop me! It is a matter of honour!"

"Yes, yes. I can see that," said the Captain, in a level voice. She was shifting position slightly now, moving away from the humans.

"A ScreeWee dies fighting or not at all!" shouted the Gunnery Officer.

The Captain's scales had faded to the colour of old paper.

"Yes, I understand, I understand," she said. "And the humans understand too, *don't you*."

The Gunnery Officer turned his head. The Captain spread her arms, opened her mouth and leapt. The male must have sensed her; he turned, claws whirring through the air.

Johnny reached out and caught Kirsty's gun as she raised it.

"No! You might hit her!"

"Why'd she do that? I could easily have shot him! So could the guards! Why just jump at him like that?"

The fighters were a whirling ball of claws and tails.

"It's personal. I think she hates him too much," he said. "But look at the screen!"

There were more green dots. Red figures that might have meant something to a ScreeWee were scrolling up on one side too fast for a human to read.

He looked down at the controls.

"They're getting closer! We've got to do something."

Kirsty stared at the controls too. The seats were made to fit a ScreeWee. So were the controls themselves.

"Well, do *you* know what ⊙ ∇ ∺ ∓ ≧ means?" she said. "Fast? Slow? Fire? The cigarette lighter?"

The fighters had broken apart and were circling each other, hissing. The green and red light from the screen threw unpleasant shadows.

Neither ScreeWee was paying the humans the least attention. They couldn't afford to. ScreeWee walked like ducks and looked like a cartoon of a crocodile, but they fought like cats—it was mainly watching and snarling with short, terrible blurs of attack and defence.

A light started to flash on the panel and an alarm rang. It rang in ScreeWee, but it was still pretty urgent even in Human.

The Captain spun around. The Gunnery Officer jumped backwards, hit the ground running, and sped towards the door. He was through it in a blur.

"He can't go anywhere," said the Captain, staggering across to the controls. "I . . . can deal with him later . . ."

"You've got some nasty scratches," said Kirsty. ScreeWee blood was blue. "I know some first aid . . ."

"A lot, I expect," said Johnny.

"But not for ScreeWee, I imagine," said the Captain. Her chest was heaving. One of her legs seemed to be at the wrong angle. Blue patches covered her tail.

"You could have just shot him," said Kirsty. "It was stupid to fight like that."

"Honour!" snarled the Captain. She tripped a switch with a claw and hissed some instructions in ScreeWee. "But he was right. Sadly, I know this now. There is no changing ScreeWee nature. Our destiny is to fight and die. I have been foolish to think otherwise."

She blinked.

"Take off your shirt," Kirsty demanded.

"What?" said Johnny.

"Your shirt! Your shirt! Look at her! She's losing blood! She needs bandaging!"

Johnny obeyed, reluctantly.

"You've got a vest on underneath? Only grandads wear a vest. Yuk. Don't you ever wash your clothes?"

He did, sometimes. And occasionally his mother had a burst of being a mother and everything in the house got washed. But usually he used the wash-basket laundry, which consisted of going through the basket until he found something that didn't seem all that bad.

"But she said you wouldn't know anything about ScreeWee medicine," he said.

"So what? Even if it's blue, blood's still blood. You should try to keep it inside."

Kirsty helped the Captain to a chair. The alien was swaying a bit, and her scales had gone white, speckled with blue.

"Is there anything I can do?" said Johnny.

Kirsty glanced at him. "I don't know," she said. "Is there *anything* you can do?"

She turned back to the Captain.

We'll all die, Johnny thought. They're all out there waiting. And here's me at the controls of the main alien ship. We can't turn round now. And I can't even read what it says on the controls!

I've done it all wrong. It was all simple, and now it's all complicated.

You think about doing things in dreams, but we're always wrong about dreams. When people talk about dreams they mean *day*dreams. *That's* where you're Superman or whatever. That's where you win everything. In dreams everything is weird. I'm in a dream now. Or something like a dream. And when I wake up, all the ScreeWee will be back in game space and they'll be shot at again, just like the Space Invaders.

Hang on . . .

Hang on . . .

He stared at the meaningless controls again.

On one of them the symbols ≙ ʘ ♃ ≎ ¬ rearranged themselves to form "Main Engines."

This is *my* world, too. It's in my head.

He looked up at the big screen.

All of them. They're all there, waiting. In bedrooms and lounges around the world. In between watching *Cobbers* and doing their homework.

All waiting with their finger on the Fire button, and each one thinking that they're the only one . . .

All there, in front of *me* . . .

"I wasn't expecting to do this," said Kirsty, behind him. "I wasn't expecting to be bandaging aliens. Put a claw on this knot, will you? What's your pulse level?"

"I don't think we have them," said the Captain.

The ship *thumped*.

The distant background rumble of the engines was suddenly a roar.

The seats had bits sticking up where humans didn't expect bits to stick up. Johnny was sitting cross-legged on one, both hands on the controls, face multi-coloured in the light of the screen.

Kirsty tapped him on the shoulder. "What *are* you doing?"

"Flying," said Johnny, without turning his head.

"He said it's too late to turn round."

"I'm not turning round."

"You don't know how to fly one of these!"

"I'm not flying one of these. I'm flying the whole fleet."

"You can't understand the controls!"

Green and red light made patterns on his face as he turned to her.

"You know, everyone tells me things. All the time," he said. "Well, I'm not listening now. I can read the controls. Why not? They're in my head. Now sit down. I shall need you to do some things. And stop talking to me as if I'm stupid."

She sat down, almost hypnotized by his tone of voice.

"But *how*—"

"There's a control that lets this ship steer all the others as well. It's used on long voyages." He moved a lever. "And I'm flying them as fast as I can. I don't think they can go any faster. All the dials have gone into the ⑊ ℏ ⊗—that's ScreeWee for red."

"But you're heading straight for the players!"

"I've got to. There isn't time to turn round . . ."

Wobbler had a pin-up over his bed. It was a close-up photograph of the Intel 80586–75 microprocessor, taken through a microscope; it looked like a street map of a very complicated modern city. His grandfather complained that it was unhealthy and why didn't he have a double page spread from *Giggles and Garters* instead, but Wobbler had a vision: one day, if he could master GCSE maths and reliably pick up a soldering iron by the end that wasn't hot, he was going to be a Big Man in computers. A Number One programmer, with his hair in a ponytail at the back like they all wore. Never mind about Yo-less saying it was all run by men in suits these days. One day, the world would hear from Wobbler Johnson—probably via a phone-line it didn't know was connected to its computer.

In the meantime, he was staring at columns of numbers in an effort to make a completely illegal copy of *Mr. Bunky Goes Boing*. It had been given four stars and declared "megabad!!!," which was what *Splaaaaatttt!* magazine still thought meant pretty good if you were under sixteen.

He blinked at the screen, and smeared the grease on his glasses a bit more evenly.

And that was enough for tonight.

He sat back, and his eye caught sight of *Only You Can Save Mankind*, under a pile of other discs.

Poor old Rubber. Of course, you called people mental all the time, but there *was* something weird about him. His body walked around down on Earth but his brain was probably somewhere you couldn't find with an atlas.

Wobbler shoved the disc in the drive. Odd about the game, though. There was probably a logical reason for it. That's what computers were, logical. Start believing anything else and you were in trouble.

The title came up, and then the bit that Gobi Software had pinched from *Star Wars*, and then—

His jaw dropped.

Ships. Hundreds of them. Getting bigger and bigger. Yellow ships, filling the screen, so that it was just black and yellow and just yellow and then blinding white—

Wobbler ducked.

And then a black screen.

Almost black, anyway.

For a moment the words hung there—

Hi, Wobler—

—and then vanished.

More alarms were clanging and whooping.

Kirsty peered out from between her fingers.

"I don't think we hit anyone," said Johnny, tapping on the keys.

"You flew straight through them!"

"That's right!"

"OK, but they'll still come after us."

"So *now* we turn round. It'll take a little while. How's the Captain?"

A clawed hand gripped the back of his chair, and her snout rested on his shoulder.

"This is very bad," said the Captain. "Our engines are not designed to run at this sort of speed for any length of time. They could break down at any moment."

"It's a calculated risk," said Johnny.

"Really? How precisely did you calculate it?" said the ScreeWee.

"Well . . . not exactly *calculate* . . . I just thought it was worth a try," said Johnny.

"You're turning back towards the players!"

"And we're still accelerating," said Johnny.

"What were you typing just then?" said Kirsty.

"Oh, nothing," said Johnny, grinning. "Just thought I saw someone I recognized. You know, as we flashed past."

"Why are you looking so happy?" she demanded. "We're in terrible trouble."

"Dunno. Because it's *my* trouble, I suppose. Captain, why have all those lights over there come on?"

"They're the ships of the fleet," said the Captain. "The commanders want to know what's happening."

"Tell them to hold on to something," said Johnny. "And tell them—tell them they're going home."

They both looked at him.

"Oh, yes, *very* impressive," said Kirsty. "*Very* dramatic. All very—"

"Shut up."

"What?"

"Shut up," said Johnny again, his eyes not leaving the screen.

"No-one tells me to shut up!"

"I'm telling you now. Just because you've got a mind like a, a *hammer* doesn't mean you have to treat everyone else like a nail. Now—here they come again . . ."

Wobbler took the disc out of the drive and looked at it. Then he felt around the back of his computer in case there were any extra wires.

That Johnny . . . he was the quiet type. He always said that all he knew about computers was how to switch them on, but *everyone* knew about computers. He'd probably messed around with the game and given it back. Pretty good. Wobbler wondered how he'd done it.

He put the disc back in and started the game again.

"Only You Can Save Mankind" . . . yeah, yeah.

Then the inside of the starship. Missiles, guns, score total, yeah, yeah . . .

And stars ahead. The sparkly ones you got in the game. He'd done much better ones for *Voyage to Alpha Centauri*.

No ships to be seen.

He picked up the joystick and moved it, watching the stars spin as the ship turned . . .

There was a ship right behind him. Very much behind him. Dozens of ships, again. *Hundreds* of ships. All getting bigger. Much bigger. Very quickly.

Very, very quickly.

Again.

When he got up off the floor and put the leg back on the chair, the screen was all black again, except for the little flashing cursor.

Wobbler stared at it.

Logic, he said. Not believing in logical reasons was almost as bad as dropping hot solder on to a nylon sock. There had to be a logical explanation.

One day, he'd think of one.

"They're following us! They're following us!"

Little coils of smoke were coming up from the controls. There were all sorts of vibrations in the floor.

"I'm pretty sure we can outrun them," said Johnny.

"How sure?" said Kirsty.

"Pretty sure."

Kirsty turned to the Captain.

"Have we got any rear guns?"

The Captain nodded.

"They can be fired from here," she said. "But we should not do that. We have surrendered, remember?"

"*I* haven't," said Kirsty. "Which one fires the guns?"

"The stick with the button on the top."

"This? It's just like a games joystick," she said.

"Of *course* it is," said Johnny. "This is in our *heads*, remember. It has to be things we *know*."

The screen showed the view behind the fleet. There were green ships bunched up behind them.

"They're coming right down our tailpipe," said Kirsty. "This is going to be really easy."

"Yes, it is—isn't it," said Johnny.

There was a dull edge to his voice. She hesitated.

"What do you mean?" she said.

"Just dots in the middle of a circle," said Johnny. "It's easy. Bang. Here comes the high score. Bang. Go ahead."

"But it's game space! It's a *game*. Why are you acting like that? It's just something on a screen."

"Fine. Just like the Real Thing. Press the button, then."

She gripped the stick. Then she paused again.

"Why do you have to spoil everything?"

"Me?" said Johnny vaguely. "Look, if you're not going to fire, switch the screen back to what's ahead of us, will you? This dial here says we're moving at ⊨ ⊖ per φ ⋝, and that's ⊀ times faster than it says we ought to be going."

"Well?"

"Well, I just think it'd be nice not to run into an asteroid or something. Of course, if you want us to end up five miles across and one centimetre thick, keep looking back."

"Oh, all *right*!"

She took her finger off the screen switch.

And then she gasped.

They stared at the expanse of space ahead of them, and what was in the middle of it.

"What," said Kirsty, after a long pause, "is *that*?"

Johnny laughed.

He tried to stop himself, because the ship was groaning and creaking like a tortured thing, but he couldn't. Tears ran down his cheeks. He thumped his hand helplessly on the control panel, accidentally switching a few lights on and off.

"It's the Border," said the Captain.

"Yes," said Johnny. "Of course it is."

"But it's—" Kirsty began.

"Yes," said Johnny. "The Border, see? Beyond it they're safe. Of course. *No-one* crosses the Border. Humans can't do it!"

"It can't be natural."

"Who knows? This is game space, after all. It's probably natural here. I mean, we've all seen it before."

"But it is still a very long way off," said the Captain. "I fear that—"

There was a dull explosion somewhere behind them.

"Missiles!" said Kirsty. "You should have let me—"

"No, listen," said Johnny. *"Listen."*

"What to? I can't hear anything."

"That's because something's making a lot of silence," said Johnny. "The engines have stopped."

"The engines have probably melted," said the Captain.

"We've still got . . . what is it . . . momentum or inertia or one of those things," said Johnny. "We'll keep going until we hit something."

"Or something hits us," said Kirsty.

She looked at the Border again.

"How big is that thing?" she said.

"It must be huge," said Johnny.

"But there's stars beyond it."

"Not our stars. I told you, that's one place humans can't go . . ."

They looked at one another.

"What happens, then," Kirsty began, like someone exploring a particularly nasty hole in a tooth, "if we're on a ship that tries to go past the Border?"

They both turned to the Captain, who shrugged.

"Don't ask me," she said. "It's never happened. It is impossible."

Now all three of them turned to look at the Border again.

"Is it just me?" said Kirsty, "or is it just a little bit bigger?"

There was some silence.

"Still," said Johnny, "what's the worst that can happen to us?"

Then he wished he hadn't said that. He remembered thinking he'd hear the alarm clock waking him up, that very first time, and then he recalled the shock of realizing that he wasn't being allowed to wake up at all.

"You know, I don't want to find out," he added.

"Without engines, we cannot turn the ship around," said the Captain. "I am sorry. You were too keen to save us."

"It *is* getting bigger," said Kirsty. "You can tell, if you watch the stars behind it."

"I am sorry," said the Captain again.

"At least the ScreeWee should make it," said Johnny.

"I am sorry."

Kirsty stood up. "Well, *I'm* not," she said. "Come on!"

She picked up the gun and strode away into the shadows. Johnny ran after her.

"Where do you think you're going?"

"To the escape capsule," she said.

"What escape capsule?"

"Indeed," said the Captain, scuttling after them, "I ask that too. There is no such thing."

"There can be if we want there to be," said Kirsty, opening the door. "You said the game is made up of things we know? Well, I *know* it'll be right down under the ship."

"But—"

"It's my dream as well as yours, right? Believe me. There'll be an escape capsule." Her eyes had that gleam again. She hefted the gun. "I *know* it," she said. "I've been there."

He remembered her room. He could picture her sitting there, with a dozen sharp pencils and no friends, getting top marks in her History homework, while in her head she was chasing aliens.

"I cannot understand," said the Captain.

The corridor outside was full of steam. The ship might cross the Border, but it was going to have to have a lot of repairs before it ever came back.

"Um," said Johnny. "It's a bit like the models in the cereal packets. It's . . . kind of a human idea."

The ScreeWee hesitated in the doorway. Then she turned to look at the screen.

"We are getting closer," she said. "If you think there is something there, then you must go now."

"Come *on*!" said Kirsty.

"Uh—" Johnny began.

"Thank you," said the Captain, gravely.

"I haven't really done much," said Johnny.

"Who knows? You never thought of yourself. You tried to work things out. You made choices. And I chose well."

"And now we must go!" said Kirsty.

"Perhaps we shall meet again. Afterwards. If all goes well," said the Captain. She took one of Johnny's hands in two of her own.

"Goodbye," she said.

Kirsty caught Johnny's shoulder and dragged him away.

"Nice to have met you," she said to the alien. "Sort of—interesting. Come on, you."

Some of the lights had gone out. The corridors were full of steam and vague shapes. Kirsty ran on ahead, darting from shadow to shadow.

"We'll have to go down," she said over her shoulder. "It'll be there. Don't worry!"

"You're really into this, aren't you," said Johnny.

"Here's a ramp. Come on. We can't have much time."

There was another passage below that, and another ramp, curling away down through the steam.

They came out in a room bigger than the bridge. There was a very large double door at one end, and banks of equipment around the walls. And, in the middle, standing on three landing legs, was a small ship. It had a stubby, heavy look.

"There! See? What did I tell you?" said Kirsty triumphantly.

Johnny walked over to the nearest equipment panel and touched it. It was sticky. He looked at his fingertips.

"It hasn't been here long," he said. "The paint's not dry."

A screen in the middle of the panel lit up, showing the Captain's face.

"How interesting," she said. "I look down at my controls and discover a new one. You have found your escape capsule?"

"It looks like it," said Johnny.

"We have ten minutes until we reach the Border," said the Captain. "You should have plenty of time."

There was a whirring noise behind Johnny. The escape capsule's ramp was coming down.

"I found a switch on the landing leg," said Kirsty.

He joined her. The ramp was a silvery grey-colour. It gleamed in the misty blue light that streamed down from inside the capsule.

"Can you guess what I'm thinking?" said Kirsty.

"You're thinking: We haven't seen the Gunnery Officer lately," said Johnny. "You're thinking: He'll be in there somewhere, hiding. Because this part is *your* dream, and that's how your dream works."

"Only I'll be ready for him," said Sigourney. "Come on."

She sidled up the ramp, turning constantly in a series of small excited hops to keep the gun pointed at any teeth that might suddenly appear.

There were two seats in the capsule, in front of a very small control panel. There was a big window. There were a couple of small cupboards. And there wasn't much of anything else.

Kirsty pointed to a cupboard and made a gesture to Johnny to open it. She raised her gun.

He opened the door and stood back quickly.

Kirsty seriously menaced a stack of tins.

She caught Johnny's expression.

"Well, he *could* have been in there," she said.

"Oh, yes. Sure. Admittedly he'd have to stop to cut his arms and legs off and then curl up really small, but he could have been in there."

"Hah! Smart comment!"

"Why not try looking under the seat cushions? It's amazing what goes down behind them."

Kirsty tried to prod behind the control panel without Johnny noticing. He noticed.

"Maybe aliens don't watch the same kind of films we watch?" he said.

"All right, all right, no need to go on about it," she snarled. She looked at the controls, and pressed a switch. The hatch swung up. The Captain's face appeared on a small screen in the middle of the panel.

"Eight minutes to the Border," she said.

"Right," said Kirsty. She shoved a hand down behind her seat cushion, and then looked at Johnny's grin.

"You see aliens everywhere, don't you," he said.

"What's that supposed to mean?"

"Nothing. Nothing. Just a thought."

She glowered at him.

There were seat belts. They put them on. Kirsty started to drum her fingers on the panel. She seemed to be looking for something.

"How do we open the doors?" said Johnny.

"All right, all right—it's got to be here somewhere."

She pressed a button. Behind them, the ramp rose up and hissed into place.

Johnny looked around. There really *was* nowhere for anyone to hide. They were aboard the escape craft. They were safe.

He didn't *feel* safe. He grabbed Kirsty's arm.

"Wait a minute," he said urgently. "I think something's wro—"

The screen flickered into life.

There was a ScreeWee there.

It was the Gunnery Officer.

"Run and hide, human scum," he said.

They could see the screen behind him; he was on the bridge.

"You? Where is the Captain?" said Johnny.

"She will be dealt with. While you run away."

"No!"

Kirsty nudged him.

"Look, the ScreeWee are *safe*," she said. "The Border is only a few minutes away. We've done it all! You can't chase around after her now! She'll have to take her chances! That's what she'd say if you asked her!"

"But I can't ask her, can I?"

He reached over and pushed a switch. There was a whirring behind them as the ramp slid down.

"I'm going back up there," he said.

"He'll be waiting for you!"

"Fine." He picked up the alien gun. "Which bit's the trigger?"

She rolled her eyes. "This is stupid!"

"Scared, are you?" said Johnny. His face was pale.

"Me?" She shrugged and snatched the gun. "I'll take this," she said. "I'm used to guns. You'll only make a mess of it."

12

Just Like The Real Thing

They ran down the ramp and back to the corridor.

"Got a watch on?" said Johnny.

"Yes. We've got more than six minutes."

"I should have *known*!" said Johnny, as they ran. "*No-one* gets that long to escape! James Bond never turns up with enough time to have a cup of coffee and clean his shoes before he disarms the time bomb! We're playing games again!"

"Calm down!"

"If we find a cat I'm going to kick it!"

The corridors were darker. Water dripped from the ceiling. There was still some steam, hissing out of broken pipes.

They reached a junction.

"Which way?"

Kirsty pointed.

"That way."

"Are you sure?"

"Of course."

They disappeared into the gloom.

About thirty seconds later they reappeared, running.

"Oh, yes, *of course*."

"Well, they all look the same, *actually*. It must be this way!"

This one *did* lead to the wide corridor with the door to the bridge at the far end.

It was open. They could see the blue and white flickering of the big screen.

Kirsty changed her grip on the gun.

"O-*kay*," she said. "No messing about this time, right? No talking?"

"All right."

"Let's go."

"How?"

"You walk in there. When he leaps out at you, I'll get him."

"Oh? I'm bait, am I?"

Kirsty glanced at her wrist.

"You've got four and half minutes to think of something better," she said. "Oh, sorry. Four minutes and twenty-five seconds. Hang on, that's twenty seconds now . . ."

"I just hope you're good!"

Kirsty patted the gun. "Regional Champion, remember? Trust me."

Johnny walked towards the open doorway. He tried to swivel his eyes both ways as he reached it.

"Four minutes and fifteen seconds," said her voice, far, far behind him.

He halted on the threshold.

"How come you weren't National Champion?" he said.

"I had food poisoning on the day, *actually*."

"Oh. Right."

He stepped through.

Multi-toothed death failed to happen to come. He risked a better look to either side and then, swallowing, upwards as well.

"Nothing here," he said.

"OK. I'm right behind you."

On the screen the Border was already much bigger. We're travelling very fast, he thought, and it's still more than four minutes away, and already it's filling the sky. *Huge* isn't the word for it.

"I can see all round the room," he said. "No-one's here."

"There was a control panel, wasn't there?" said Kirsty. "Hang on . . . I'm in the doorway now. Yes. It's got to be behind the controls. Go ahead. I'm ready if it leaps out."

I'm not, he thought. He sidled across the floor until he could just see behind the bank of instruments.

"There's noth . . . hold it."

"What?"

"I think it's the Captain."

"Is it alive?"

"She. She's a she. You know she's a she. I can't tell. She's just . . . lying there. I'll have a look."

"What good would that do?"

"I'm going to have a look, all right?"

"Careful, then. Stay where I can keep an eye on you."

He moved forward, searching the shadows around the edge of the huge room.

It was the Captain, and she was alive. At least, bits of what was probably her chest were going up and down. He knelt beside her.

"Captain?" he whispered.

She opened one eye.

"Chosen One?"

"What happened?"

"He was . . . waiting. While I . . . talked to you . . . he crept in . . . hit me . . ."

"Where'd he go then?"

"You . . . *must* . . . go. Not much time . . . left. The fleet . . . is . . ."

"You're hurt. I'll get Ki—Sigourney over here . . ."

Her claw gripped his arm.

"Listen to me! He's going . . . to blow up the . . . ship! The fuel . . . the power plant . . . he's . . ."

Johnny stood up.

"Is she all right?" Kirsty called out.

"I don't know!"

She was standing in the doorway, outlined against the light.

There was a shadow behind her. As Johnny watched, it spread its arms.

It was bigger than a ScreeWee should be, now. It wasn't a funny alligator—there was still a suggestion of alligator there, but now there was insect, too, and other things . . . things that had never existed outside of dreams . . .

Johnny shouted: "He's behind you!" Then he lowered his head and ran.

Kirsty turned.

You can't *trust* dreams. If you live inside them, they'll turn on you, carry you along . . .

He saw Kirsty turn and look up, and up, at the Gunnery Officer.

The ScreeWee opened his mouth. There were more teeth than he'd had before; rows and rows of them, and every one glistening and sharp.

Her dream, Johnny thought. No wonder she always fights.

"Shoot it! Shoot it!"

She was just staring. She didn't seem to want to move.

"You've got the *gun*!" he screamed.

She was like a statue.

"*Shoot* it!"

". . . oh . . ."

Kirsty shook her head vaguely and then, as if she'd suddenly clicked awake, raised the gun.

"OK," she said. "Now—"

The ScreeWee ignored her. He jerked his head up and focused on Johnny. He hardly had eyes, now. The alien seemed to be looking at Johnny with its teeth.

"Ah. The Chosen One," it said. It slapped Kirsty out of the way. She couldn't even have seen its arm move. One moment she was aiming, and the next she was lifted into the air and dropping in a heap a few metres away.

The gun clattered on to the floor and slid towards Johnny.

"Chosen One!" hissed the ScreeWee. "Foolish! We are what we are! You disgrace your race and mine! For you, and her . . . for you, there's no going back . . ."

Kirsty was trying to get to her feet, her face contorted with anger.

Johnny reached down and picked up the gun.

The ScreeWee waved two arms in a sudden movement. Johnny flinched.

He heard, from a long way away, Kirsty call out: "Quick! Throw it to me! To *me*!"

The alien smiled.

Johnny backed away a little. The alien was concentrating entirely on him.

"To *me*, you idiot!" shouted Kirsty.

"You?" said the alien to Johnny. "Shoot me? You can't. Such

weakness. Like your Captain. A disgrace to the ScreeWee. Always weak. And that is why you want peace. The strong never want peace."

Johnny raised the gun.

The alien moved forward, slowly. His teeth seemed to fill the world. His arms seemed longer, his claws sharper.

"You cannot," it said. "I've watched you. At least the other humans could fight! We could die honourably! But *you* . . . you *talk* and *talk* . . . you'd do anything rather than *fight*. You'd do anything but face the truth. *You* save mankind? Hah!"

Johnny stepped back again, and felt the edge of the control desk behind him. There was no more retreating.

"Will you surrender?" he said.

"Never!"

Johnny saw a movement out of the corner of his eye. Kirsty was going to try to leap on the thing. But the alien wasn't like the guards, now. She wouldn't stand a—

He fired.

There was a small, sharp explosion.

The ScreeWee looked down in shock at the sudden blue stain spreading across his overall, and then back up to Johnny almost in bewilderment.

"You *shot* me . . . in cold blood . . ."

"No. My blood's never cold."

The alien toppled forward. And now he was smaller again, more like a ScreeWee.

"And I had to," said Johnny.

"You shot him," said the voice behind him. He looked round. The Captain had pulled herself to her feet.

"Yes."

"You had to. But I didn't think you could . . ."

Johnny looked down at the gun. His knuckles were white. With some difficulty, he managed to persuade his fingers to let go.

"I didn't think I could, either."

He walked over to Kirsty, who was staring at the thing on the floor.

"Wow," she said, but quietly.

"Yes," he said.

"You—"

"Yes, I shot him. I shot him. I wish I didn't have to, but I had to.

He was alive and now he isn't." There were more alarms sounding now, and red lights flashing on the control panel. On the screen, the Border completely filled the sky. "Can we go? How much longer have we got left?"

She looked hazily at her watch.

"A minute and a half."

He was amazed. He felt he was sitting inside his own head, watching himself. There wasn't any panic. The one who was watching didn't know what to do, but the one outside seemed to know everything. It was . . . like a dream.

"Can you run?" She nodded. "Really *fast*? What am I saying? You've probably won medals. Come on."

He pulled her after him, out of the bridge and along the dark corridors. Kirsty was hardly concentrating any more; the walls glistened less. There were even nuts and bolts again.

They reached the capsule. Johnny ran from leg to leg until he found the button that let down the ramp. It seemed to take ages to come down.

"How long?"

"We've got fifty seconds . . ."

Up the ramp, into the seats.

There weren't many controls. Johnny peered at them.

"What are you doing?" said Kirsty.

"Like you said before. Looking for one marked 'Doors Open.' "

The screen flickered into life.

"Johnny? The doors open from up here," said the Captain.

Johnny glanced up at Kirsty.

"We didn't know that," he said.

"Is the ramp back up?"

"Yes."

"Doors opening."

There was a *clonk* ahead of them, and a hiss as the air in the hall escaped through the widening crack. The twinkling, unreal stars of game space beckoned them.

Johnny's hand hovered over the biggest red button on the panel.

"Johnny?"

"Yes, Captain."

"Thank you. You did not have to help us."

"If not me, then who else?"

"Hah. Yes. And now . . . goodbye. We will not . . . meet again."

"Goodbye."

Johnny looked at Kirsty.

"How long?"

"Ten seconds!"

"Let's go."

He hit the button.

There was a *boom* behind them. The walls flashed past. And suddenly they were surrounded by sky.

Johnny leaned back against the seat. His mind was blank, empty, except for something which kept on replaying itself like a piece of film.

Over and over again, his memory fired the gun. Over and over again, the alien collapsed. Action replay. Pinpoint precision. Just like the Real Thing.

Kirsty nudged him.

"Can we steer it?"

"Hmm? What?" He looked vaguely at the controls. "Well, there's this joystick . . ."

"Turn us round, then. I want to watch them go through."

"Yes. Me too."

The capsule turned gently in the deep void of game space, right up against the Border.

The ScreeWee fleet hurtled past. As each ship reached the Border it flickered and faded.

"Do you think they've got a planet to go to, really?"

"I think they think so."

"Do you think they'll ever be back?"

"Not now."

"Um . . . look . . . when I looked up and I saw that *thing* . . . I mean, it was so *real*. And I thought, but it's alive, it's living, how can I—"

"Yes," said Johnny.

"And then it was dead and . . . and I didn't feel like cheering . . ."

"Yes."

"When it's real, it's not easy. Because people die and it's really over."

"Yes. I know. Over and over. D'you know what?"

"What?"

"My friend Yo-less thinks dreams like this are a way of dealing with real life."

"Yes?"

"I think it's the other way round."

"Yo-less is the black one?"

"Yes. We call him Yo-less because he's not cool."

"Anti-cool's quite cool too."

"Is it? I didn't know that. Is it still cool to say 'well wicked'?"

"*Johnny!* It was *never* cool to say 'well wicked.' "

"How about 'vode'?"

"Vode's cool."

"I just made it up."

The capsule drifted onwards.

"No reason why it can't be cool, though."

"Right."

Game stars glittered.

"Johnny?"

"Yes?"

"How come you get on with people so well? How come people always talk to you?"

"Dunno. Because I listen, I suppose. And it helps to be stupid."

"Johnny?"

"Still here."

"What did you mean . . . you know, back there? When you said I see aliens everywhere?"

"Um. Can't remember."

"You must have meant *something*."

"I'm not even sure there *are* aliens. Only different kinds of us. But I know what the important thing is. The important thing is to be exactly sure about what you're doing. The important thing is to remember it's not a game. None of it. Even the games."

The ship became a dot against the night.

"What do we do to get home? I've always had to die to get out."

"You can get out if you win."

"There's a green button here."

"Worth a try, yes?"

"Right."

* * *

Light was streaming into the room when Johnny woke up. He lay in someone else's bed and looked around through half-closed eyes.

It was like all spare rooms everywhere. There was the lamp that was a bit old-fashioned and didn't fit in anywhere else. There was the bookcase with the books that no-one read much. There was a lack of *small* things, apart from an ashtray on the bedside table.

There was a clock, but at some time in the past the mains had gone off for a while and although people must have sorted out every other clock in the house, they'd forgotten about this one, so it just sat and flashed 7:41 continuously, day and night. But an absence of sound from below suggested that it was still early in the morning.

He snuggled down, treasuring this time stolen between dreaming and waking.

So . . . what next? He'd have to talk to Kirsty, who dreamed of being Sigourney and forgot that she was trying to be someone who was *acting*. And he had a suspicion that he'd see his parents before long. He was probably going to be talked at a lot, but at least that'd make a change.

These were still Trying Times. There was still school. Nothing actually was better, probably. No-one was doing anything with a magic wand.

But the fleet had got away. Compared to that, everything else was . . . well, not easy. But less like a wall and more like steps.

You might never win, but at least you could try. If not you, who else?

He turned over and went back to sleep.

The Border hung in the sky.

Huge white letters, thousands of miles high.

They spelled:

GAME
OVER

And the fleet roared past. Tankers, battleships, fighters . . . they soared and rolled, their shadows streaking across the letters as ship after ship escaped, for ever.

JOHNNY AND THE DEAD

Author's Note

I've bent history a little bit. There really were such things as Pals' Battalions, just as described here, and they really were a horribly innocent device for wiping out a whole generation of young men from one particular area with one cannon shell. But the practice died out by the summer of 1916, when the first Battle of the Somme took place. Nineteen thousand British soldiers died on the first day of the battle.

"Thomas Atkins" really *was* the name used on documents in the British Army in the way that people would now use "A. N. Other," and "Tommy Atkins" did become a nickname for the British soldier.

There were certainly a number of real Tommy Atkinses in the war. This book is dedicated to them—wherever they are.

1

Johnny never knew for certain why he started seeing the dead.

The Alderman said it was probably because he was too lazy not to.

Most people's minds don't let them see things that might upset them, he said. The Alderman said he should know if anyone did, because he'd spent his whole life (1822–1906) not seeing things.

Wobbler Johnson, who was technically Johnny's best friend, said it was because he was mental.

But Yo-less, who read medical books, said it was probably because he couldn't focus his mind like normal people. Normal people just ignored almost everything that was going on around them, so that they could concentrate on important things like, well, getting up, going to the lavatory and getting on with their lives. Whereas Johnny just opened his eyes in the morning and the whole universe hit him in the face.

Wobbler said this sounded like "mental" to him.

Whatever it was called, what it *meant* was this. Johnny saw things other people didn't.

Like the dead people hanging around in the cemetery.

The Alderman—at least, the *old* Alderman—was a bit snobby about most of the rest of the dead, even about Mr. Vicenti, who had a huge black marble grave with angels and a photograph of Mr. Vicenti (1897–1958) looking not at all dead behind a little window. The Alderman said Mr. Vicenti had been a Capo de Monte in the Mafia. Mr. Vicenti told Johnny that, on the contrary, he had spent his entire life being a wholesale novelty salesman, amateur escapologist and children's entertainer, which in a number of important respects was as exactly like not being in the Mafia as it was possible to get.

But all this was later. After he'd got to know the dead a lot better. After the raising of the ghost of the Ford Capri.

Johnny really discovered the cemetery after he'd started living at Grandad's. This was Phase Three of Trying Times, after the shouting, which had been bad, and the Being Sensible About Things (which had been worse; people are better at shouting). Now his dad was getting a new job somewhere on the other side of the country. There was a vague feeling that it might all work out, now that people had stopped trying to be sensible. On the whole, he tried not to think about it.

He'd started using the path along the canal instead of going home on the bus, and found that if you climbed over the place where the wall had fallen down, and then went around behind the crematorium, you could cut off half the journey.

The graves went right up to the canal's edge.

It was one of those old cemeteries you got owls and foxes in and sometimes, in the Sunday papers, people going on about Our Victorian Heritage, although they didn't go on about this one because it was the wrong kind of heritage, being too far from London.

Wobbler said it was spooky and sometimes went home the long way, but Johnny was disappointed that it wasn't spookier. Once you sort of put out of your mind what it *was*—once you forgot about all the skeletons underground, grinning away in the dark—it was quite friendly. Birds sang. All the traffic sounded a long way off. It was peaceful.

He'd had to check a few things, though. Some of the older graves had big stone boxes on top, and in the wilder parts these had cracked and even fallen open. He'd had a look inside, just in case.

It had been sort of disappointing to find nothing there.

And then there were the mausoleums. These were much bigger and had doors in, like little houses. They looked a bit like allotment sheds with extra angels. The angels were generally more lifelike than you'd expect, especially one near the entrance who looked as though he'd just remembered that he should have gone to the toilet before he left heaven.

The two boys walked through the cemetery now, kicking up the drifts of fallen leaves.

"It's Halloween next week," said Wobbler. "I'm having a disco.

You have to come as something horrible. Don't bother to find a disguise."

"Thanks," said Johnny.

"You notice how there's a lot more Halloween stuff in the shops these days?" said Wobbler.

"It's because of Bonfire Night," said Johnny. "Too many people were blowing themselves up with fireworks, so they invented Halloween, where you just wear masks and stuff."

"Mrs. Nugent says all that sort of thing is tampering with the occult," said Wobbler. Mrs. Nugent was the Johnsons' next door neighbour, and known to be unreasonable on subjects like Madonna played at full volume at 3 a.m.

"Probably it is," said Johnny.

"She says witches are abroad on Halloween," said Wobbler.

"What?" Johnny's forehead wrinkled. "Like . . . Marjorca and places?"

"Suppose so," said Wobbler.

"Makes . . . sense, I suppose. They probably get special out-of-season bargains, being old ladies," said Johnny. "My aunt can go anywhere on the buses for almost nothing and she's not even a witch."

"Don't see why Mrs. Nugent is worried, then," said Wobbler. "It ort to be a lot safer round here, with all the witches on holiday."

They passed a very ornate mausoleum, which even had little stained-glass windows. It was hard to imagine who'd want to see in, but then, it was even harder to imagine who'd want to look out.

"Shouldn't like to be on the same plane as 'em," said Wobbler, who'd been thinking hard. "Just think, p'raps you can only afford to go on holiday in the autumn, and you get on the plane, and there's all these old witches going abroad."

"Singing 'Here we go, here we go, here we go'?" said Johnny. "And 'Viva a spanner'?"

"But I bet you'd get *really good* service in the hotel," said Johnny.

"Yeah."

"Funny, really," said Johnny.

"What?"

"I saw a thing in a book once," said Johnny, "about these people in Mexico or somewhere, where they all go down to the cemetery for a big fiesta at Halloween every year. Like, they don't see why people should be left out of things just because they're dead."

"Yuk. A picnic? In the actual cemetery?"

"Yes."

"Reckon you'd get green glowing hands pushing up through the earth and nicking the sarnies?"

"Don't think so. Anyway . . . they don't eat sarnies in Mexico. They eat tort . . . something."

"Tortoises."

"Yeah?"

"I bet," said Wobbler, looking around, "I bet . . . I bet you wouldn't dare knock on one of those doors. I bet you'd hear dead people lurchin' about inside."

"Why do they lurch?"

Wobbler thought about this.

"They always lurch," he said. "Dunno why. I've seen them in videos. And they can push their way through walls."

"Why?" said Johnny.

"Why what?"

"Why push their way through walls? I mean . . . living people can't do that. Why should dead people do it?"

Wobbler's mother was very easy-going in the matter of videos. According to him, he was allowed to watch ones which even people aged a hundred had to watch with their parents.

"Don't know," he said. "They're usually very angry about something."

"Being dead, you mean?"

"Probably," said Wobbler. "It can't be much of a life."

Johnny thought about this that evening, after meeting the Alderman. The only dead people he had known had been Mr. Page, who'd died in hospital of something, and his great-grandmother, who'd been ninety-six and had just generally died. Neither of them had been particularly angry people. His great-grandmother had been a bit confused about things, but never angry. He'd visited her in Sunshine Acres, when she watched a lot of television and waited for the next meal to turn up. And Mr. Page had walked around quietly, the only man in the street still at home in the middle of the day.

They didn't seem the sort of people who would get up after being dead just to dance with Michael Jackson. And the only thing his great-grandmother would have pushed her way through walls for would be a television that she could watch without having to fight fifteen other old ladies for the remote control.

It seemed to Johnny that a lot of people were getting things all wrong. He said this to Wobbler. Wobbler disagreed.

"It's prob'ly all different from a dead point of view," he said.

Now they were walking along West Avenue. The cemetery was laid out like a town, with streets. They weren't named very originally—North Drive and South Walk joined West Avenue, for example, at a little gravelled area with seats in. A kind of city centre. But the silence of the big Victorian mausoleums made the place look as though it was having the longest early-closing day in the world.

"My dad says this is all going to be built on," said Wobbler. "He said the Council sold it to some big company for fivepence because it was costing so much to keep it going."

"What, all of it?" said Johnny.

"That's what he said," said Wobbler. Even he looked a bit uncertain. "He said it was a scandal."

"Even the bit with the poplar trees?"

"All of it," said Wobbler. "It's going to be offices or something."

Johnny looked at the cemetery. It was the only open space for miles.

"I'd have given them at least a pound," he said.

"Yes, but you wouldn't have been able to build things on it," said Wobbler. "That's the important thing."

"I wouldn't want to build anything on it. I'd have given them a pound just to leave it as it is."

"Yes," said Wobbler, the voice of reason, "but people have got to work somewhere. We Need Jobs."

"I bet the people here won't be very happy about it," said Johnny. "If they knew."

"I think they get moved somewhere else," said Wobbler. "It's got to be something like that. Otherwise you'll never dare dig your garden."

Johnny looked up at the nearest tomb. It was one of the ones that looked like a shed built of marble. Bronze lettering over the door said:

ALDERMAN THOMAS BOWLER
1822–1906
Pro Bono Publico

There was a stone carving of—presumably—the Alderman himself, looking seriously into the distance as if he, too, was wondering what Pro Bono Publico meant.

"I bet *he'd* be pretty angry," said Johnny.

He hesitated for a moment, and then walked up the couple of broken steps to the metal door, and knocked on it. He never *did* know why he'd done that.

"Here, you mustn't!" hissed Wobbler. "Supposing he comes lurchin' out! Anyway," he said, lowering his voice a bit, "it's wrong to try to talk to the dead. It can lead to satanic practices, it said on television."

"Don't see why," said Johnny.

He knocked again.

And the door opened.

Alderman Thomas Bowler blinked in the sunlight, and then glared at Johnny.

"Yes?" he said.

Johnny turned and ran for it.

Wobbler caught him up halfway along North Drive. Wobbler wasn't normally the athletic type, and his speed would have surprised quite a lot of people who knew him.

"What happened? What happened?" he panted.

"Didn't you see?" said Johnny.

"I didn't see anything!"

"The door opened!"

"It never!"

"It did!"

Wobbler slowed down.

"No, it didn't," he muttered. "No one of 'em can open. I've looked at 'em. They've all got padlocks on."

"To keep people out or keep people in?" said Johnny.

A look of panic crossed Wobbler's face. Since he had a big face, this took some time. He started to run again.

"You're just trying to wind me up!" he yelled. "I'm not going to hang around practising being satanic! I'm going home!"

He turned the corner into East Way and sprinted towards the main gate.

Johnny slowed down.

He thought: padlocks.

It was true, actually. He'd noticed it in the past. All the mausoleums had locks on them, to stop vandals getting in.

And yet . . . and yet . . .

If he shut his eyes he could *see* Alderman Thomas Bowler. Not one of the lurchin' dead from out of Wobbler's videos, but a huge fat man in a fur-trimmed robe and a gold chain and a hat with corners on.

He stopped running and then, slowly, walked back the way he had come.

There was a padlock on the door of the Alderman's tomb. It had a rusty look.

It was the talking to Wobbler that did it, Johnny decided. It had given him silly ideas.

He knocked again, anyway.

"Yes?" said Alderman Thomas Bowler.

"Er . . . hah . . . sorry . . ."

"What do you want?"

"Are you *dead*?"

The Alderman raised his eyes to the bronze letters over the door. "See what it says up there?" he said.

"Er . . ."

"Nineteen hundred and six, it says. It was a very good funeral, I understand. I didn't attend, myself." The Alderman gave this some thought. "Rather, I *did*, but not in any position where I could observe events. I believe the vicar gave a very moving sermon. What was it you were wanting?"

"Er . . ." Johnny looked around desperately. "What . . . er . . . what does Pro Bono Publico *mean*?"

"For the Public Good," said the Alderman.

"Oh. Well . . . thank you." Johnny backed away. "Thank you very much."

"Was that all?"

"Er . . . yes."

The Alderman nodded sadly. "I didn't think it'd be anything important," he said. "I haven't had a visitor since nineteen twenty-three. And then they'd got the name wrong. They weren't even relatives. And they were *American*. Oh, well. Goodbye, then."

Johnny hesitated. I could turn around now, he thought, and go home.

And if I turn around, I'll never find out what happens next. I'll go away and I'll never know why it happened now and what would have happened next. I'll go away and grow up and get a job and get married and have children and become a grandad and retire and take up bowls and go into Sunshine Acres and watch daytime television until I die, and I'll never know.

And he thought: perhaps I did. Perhaps that all happened and then, just when I was dying, some kind of angel turned up and said would you like a wish? And I said, yes, I'd like to know what would have happened if I hadn't run away, and the angel said, OK, you can go back. And here I am, back again. I can't let myself down.

The world waited.

Johnny took a step forward.

"You're dead, right?" he said slowly.

"Oh, yes. It's one of those things one is pretty certain about."

"You don't *look* dead. I mean, I thought . . . you know . . . coffins and things . . ."

"Oh, there's *all that*," said the Alderman, airily, "and then there's this, too."

"You're a ghost?" Johnny was rather relieved. He could come to terms with a ghost.

"I should hope I've got more pride than that," said the Alderman.

"My friend Wobbler'll be really *amazed* to meet you," said Johnny. A thought crossed his mind. "You're no good at dancing, are you?" he said.

"I used to be able to waltz quite well," said the Alderman.

"I meant . . . sort of . . . like this," said Johnny. He gave the best impression he could remember of Michael Jackson dancing. "Sort of with your feet," he said apologetically.

"That looks grand," said Alderman Tom Bowler.

"Yes, and you have to have a glittery glove on one hand——"

"That's important, is it?"

"Yes, and you have to say '*Ow!*' "

"I should think anyone would, dancing like that," said the Alderman.

"No, I mean like '*Oooouwwwwweeeeeah*!,' with . . ."

Johnny stopped. He realized that he was getting a bit carried away.

"But, look," he said, stopping at the end of a groove in the gravel.

"I don't see how you can be dead and walking and talking at the same time . . ."

"That's probably all because of relativity," said the Alderman. He moonwalked stiffly across the path. "Like this, was it? *Ouch*!"

"A bit," said Johnny, kindly. "Um. What do you mean about relativity?"

"Einstein explains all that quite well," said the Alderman.

"What, *Albert* Einstein?" said Johnny.

"Who?"

"He was a famous scientist. He . . . invented the speed of light and things."

"Did he? I meant Solomon Einstein. He was a famous taxidermist in Cable Street. Stuffing dead animals, you know. I think he invented some kind of machine for making glass eyes. Got knocked down by a motor car in nineteen thirty-two. But a very keen thinker, all the same."

"I never knew that," said Johnny. He looked around.

It was getting darker.

"I think I'd better be getting home," he said, and began to back away.

"I think I'm getting the hang of this," said the Alderman, moonwalking back across the path.

"I'll . . . er . . . I'll see you again. Perhaps," said Johnny.

"Call any time you like," said the Alderman, as Johnny walked away as quickly yet politely as possible. "I'm always in."

"Always in," he added. "That's something you learn to be good at, when you're dead. Er. Eeeeyooowh, was it?"

2

Johnny raised the subject of the cemetery after tea.

"It's disgusting, what the Council are doing," said his grandfather.

"But the cemetery costs a lot to keep up," said his mother. "No-one visits most of the graves now, except old Mrs. Tachyon, and she's barmy."

"Not visiting graves has nothing to do with it, girl. Anyway, there's history in there."

"Alderman Thomas Bowler," said Johnny.

"Never heard of him. I was referring," said his grandfather, "to William Stickers. There was very nearly a monument to him. There *would* have been a monument to him. Everyone round here donated money, only someone ran off with it. *And* I'd given sixpence."

"Was he famous?"

"*Nearly* famous. *Nearly* famous. You've heard of Karl Marx?"

"He invented communism, didn't he?" said Johnny.

"Right. Well, William Stickers didn't. But he'd have been Karl Marx if Karl Marx hadn't beaten him to it. Tell you what . . . tomorrow, I'll show you." It was tomorrow.

It was raining softly out of a dark grey sky.

Grandad and Johnny stood in front of a large gravestone which read:

William Stickers
1897–1949
Workers of the
World Unit

"A great man," said Grandad. He had taken his cap off.

"What was the World Unit?" said Johnny.

"It should have been unite," said Grandad. "They ran out of money before they did the 'E.' It was a scandal. He was a hero of the working class. He would have fought in the Spanish Civil War except he got on the wrong boat and ended up in Hull."

Johnny looked around.

"Um," he said. "What sort of a man was he?"

"A hero of the proletariat, like I said."

"I mean, what did he look like?" said Johnny. "Was he quite big with a huge black beard and gold-rimmed spectacles?"

"That's right. Seen pictures, have you?"

"No," said Johnny. "Not exactly."

Grandad put his cap back on.

"I'm going down to the shops," he said. "Want to come?"

"No, thanks. Er . . . I'm going round to Wobbler's house."

"Righto."

Grandad wandered off towards the main gate.

Johnny took a deep breath.

"Hello," he said.

"It *was* a scandal, them not giving me the 'E,' " said William Stickers.

He stopped leaning against his memorial.

"What's your name, comrade?"

"John Maxwell," said Johnny.

"I knew you could see me," said William Stickers. "I could see you looking right at me while the old man was talking."

"I could tell you were you," said Johnny. "You look . . . um . . . thinner."

He wanted to say: not thin like in thick. Just . . . not all there. Transparent.

He *said*, "Um." And then he said, "I don't understand this. You are dead, right? Some kind of . . . ghost?"

"Ghost?" said dead William Stickers angrily.

"Well . . . spirit, then."

"There's no such thing. A relic of an outmoded belief system."

"Um, only . . . you're talking to me . . ."

"It's a perfectly understandable scientific phenomenon," said William Stickers. "Never let superstition get in the way of rational thought, boy. It's time for Mankind to put old cultural shibboleths aside and step into the bright socialist dawn. What year is it?"

"Nineteen ninety-three," said Johnny.

"Ah! And have the downtrodden masses risen up to overthrow the capitalist oppressors in the glorious name of communism?"

"Um. Sorry?" Johnny hesitated, and then a few vague memories slid into place. "You mean like . . . Russia and stuff? When they shot the Tsar? There was something on television about that."

"Oh, I know *that*. That was just the *start*. What's been happening since nineteen forty-nine? I expect the global revolution is well established, yes? No-one tells us anything in here."

"Well . . . there's been a lot of revolutions, I think," said Johnny. "All over the place . . ."

"Capital!"

"Um." It occurred to Johnny that people doing quite a lot of the revolutions recently had said they were overthrowing communist oppressors, but William Stickers looked so eager he didn't quite know how to say this. "Tell you what . . . can you read a newspaper if I bring you one?"

"Of course. But it's hard to turn the pages."

"Um. Are there a lot of you in here?"

"Hah! Most of them don't bother. They just aren't prepared to make the effort."

"Can you . . . you know . . . walk around? You could get into things for free."

William Stickers looked slightly panicky.

"It's hard to go far," he mumbled. "It's not really allowed."

"I read in a book once that ghosts can't move much," said Johnny.

"Ghost? I'm just . . . dead." He waved a transparent finger in the air. "Hah! But they're not getting me *that* way," he snapped. "Just because it turns out that I'm still . . . here after I'm dead, doesn't mean I'm prepared to *believe* in the whole stupid nonsense, you know. Oh, no. Logical, rational thought, boy. And don't forget the newspaper."

William Stickers faded away a bit at a time. The last thing to go was the finger, still demonstrating its total disbelief in life after death.

Johnny waited around a bit, but no other dead people seemed to be ready to make an appearance.

He felt he was being watched in some way that had nothing to do with eyes. It wasn't exactly creepy, but it *was* uncomfortable. You didn't dare scratch your bottom or pick your nose.

For the first time he really began to *notice* the cemetery. It had a leftover look, really.

Behind it there was the canal, which wasn't used any more, except as a rubbish dump; old prams and busted televisions and erupting settees lined its banks like monsters from the Garbage Age. Then on one side there was the crematorium and its Garden of Remembrance, which was all right in a gravel-pathed, keep-off-the-grass sort of way. In front was Cemetery Road, which had once had houses on the other side of it; now there was the back wall of the Bonanza Carpet (Save ££££!!) Warehouse. There was still an old phone box and a letter box, which suggested that once upon a time this had been a place that people thought of as home. But now it was just a road you cut through to get to the bypass from the industrial estate.

On the fourth side was nothing much except a wasteground of fallen brick and one tall chimney-all that remained of the Blackbury Rubber Boot Company ("If It's a Boot, It's a Blackbury" had been one of the most famously *stupid* slogans in the world.)

Johnny vaguely remembered there'd been something in the papers. People had been protesting about something—but then, they always were. There was always so much news going on you never had time to find out anything important.

He walked round to the old factory site. Bulldozers were parked around it now, although they were all empty. There was a wire fence which had been broken down here and there despite the notices about Guard Dogs on Patrol. Perhaps the guard dogs had broken out.

And there was a big sign, showing the office building that was going to be built on the site. It was beautiful. There were fountains in front of it, and quite old trees carefully placed here and there, and neat people standing chatting outside it. And the sky above it was a glorious blue, which was pretty unusual for Blackbury, where most of the time the sky was that odd, soapy colour you'd get if you lived in a Tupperware box.

Johnny stared at it for some time, while the rain fell in the real world and the blue sky glittered on the sign.

It was pretty obvious that the building was going to take up more room than the site of the old boot factory.

The words above the picture said, "An Exciting Development for United Amalagamated Consolidated Holdings: Forward to the Future!"

Johnny didn't feel very excited, but he did feel that "Forward to the Future" was even dafter than "If It's a Boot, It's a Blackbury."

Before school next day he pinched the newspaper and tucked it out of sight behind William Sticker's grave.

He felt more daft than afraid. He wished he could talk to someone about it.

He didn't have anyone to talk to. But he did have three people to talk *with*.

There were various gangs and alliances in the school, such as the sporty group, and the bright kids, and the Computer Club Nerds.

And then there was Johnny, and Wobbler, and Bigmac, who said he was the last of the well hard skinheads but was actually a skinny kid with short hair and flat feet and asthma who had difficulty even *walking* in Doc Martens, and there was Yo-less, who was technically black.

But at least they listened, during break, on the bit of wall between the school kitchens and the library. It was where they normally hung out—or at least, hung around.

"Ghosts," said Yo-less, when he'd finished.

"No-oo," said Johnny uncertainly. "They don't like being called ghosts. It upsets them, for some reason. They're just . . . dead. I suppose it's like not calling people handicapped or backward."

"Politically incorrect," said Yo-less. "I read about that."

"You mean they want to be called," Wobbler paused for thought, "*post-senior citizens*."

"Breathily challenged," said Yo-less.

"Vertically disadvantaged," said Wobbler.

"What? You mean they're short?" said Yo-less.

"Buried," said Wobbler.

"How about zombies?" said Bigmac.

"No, you've got to have a body to be a zombie," said Yo-less. "You're not really dead, you just get fed this secret voodoo mixture of fish and roots and you turn into a zombie."

"Wow. What mixture?"

"I don't know. How should I know? Just some kind of fish and some kind of root."

"I bet it's a real *adventure* going down the chippie in voodoo country," said Wobbler.

"Well, you ought to know about voodoo," said Bigmac.

"Why?" said Yo-less.

" 'Cos you're West Indian, right?"

"Do you know all about druids?"

"No."

"There you are, then."

"I 'spect your mum knows about it, though," said Bigmac.

"Shouldn't think so. My mum spends more time in church than the Pope," said Yo-less. "My mum spends more time in church than *God.*"

"You're not taking this seriously," said Johnny severely. "I *really saw them.*"

"It might be something wrong with your eyes," said Yo-less. "Perhaps there's a—"

"I saw this old film once, about a man with X-ray eyes," said Bigmac. "He could use 'em to see right through things."

"Women's clothes and stuff?" enquired Wobbler.

"There wasn't much of that," said Bigmac.

They discussed this waste of a useful talent.

"I don't see *through* anything," said Johnny, eventually. "I just see people who aren't ther—I mean, people other people don't see."

"My uncle used to see things other people couldn't see," said Wobbler. "Especially on a Saturday night."

"Don't be daft. I'm trying to be serious."

"Yeah, but once you said you'd seen a Loch Ness Monster in your goldfish pond," said Bigmac.

"All right, but—"

"Probably just a plesiosaur," said Yo-less. "Just some old dinosaur that ought to've been extinct seventy million years ago. Nothing special at all."

"Yes, but—"

"And then there was the Lost City of the Incas," said Wobbler.

"Well, I *found* it, didn't I?"

"Yes, but it wasn't that lost," said Yo-less. "Behind Tesco's isn't exactly *lost.*"

Bigmac sighed.

"You're all weird," he said.

"All right," said Johnny. "You all come down there after school, right?"

"Well—" Wobbler began, and shifted uneasily.

"Not *scared*, are you?" said Johnny. He knew that was unfair, but he was annoyed. "You ran away before," he said, "when the Alderman came out."

"I never saw no Alderman," said Wobbler. "Anyway, I wasn't scared. I ran away to wind you up."

"You certainly had *me* fooled," said Johnny.

"Me? Scared? I watched *Night of the Killer Zombies* three times—with *freeze frame*," said Wobbler.

"All right, then. You come. All three of you come. After school."

"After *Cobbers*," said Bigmac.

"Look, this is a lot more important than—"

"Yes, but tonight Janine is going to tell Mick that Doraleen took Ron's surfboard—"

Johnny hesitated.

"All right, then," he said. "After *Cobbers*."

"And then I promised to help my brother load up his van," said Bigmac. "Well, not exactly promised . . . he said he'd rip my arms off if I didn't."

"And I've got to do some Geography homework," said Yo-less.

"We haven't got any," said Johnny.

"No, but I thought if I did an extra essay on rainforests I could pull up my marks average," said Yo-less.

There was nothing odd about this, if you were used to Yo-less. Yo-less wore school uniform. Except that it wasn't really school uniform. Well, all right, *technically* it was school uniform, because everyone got these bits of paper at the start of every year saying what the school uniform was, but no-one ever wore it much, except for Yo-less, and so if hardly anyone else was wearing it, Wobbler said, how could it be a uniform? Whereas, said Wobbler, since at any one time nearly everyone was wearing jeans and a T-shirt, then really jeans and T-shirt *were* the *real* school uniform and Yo-less should be sent home for not wearing it.

"Tell you what," said Johnny. "Let's meet up later, then. Six o'clock. We can meet at Bigmac's place. That's right near the cemetery, anyway."

"But it'll be getting dark," said Wobbler.

"Well?" said Johnny. "You're not scared, are you?"

"Me? Scared? Huh! *Me?* Scared? Me? *Scared*?"

* * *

If you had to be somewhere frightening when it got dark, Johnny thought, the Joshua N'Clement block rated a lot higher on the *Aaargh* scale than any cemetery. At least the dead didn't mug you.

It was originally going to be the Sir Alec Douglas-Home block, and then it became the Harold Wilson block, and then finally the new Council named it the Joshua Che N'Clement block after a famous freedom fighter, who then became president of his country, and who was now being an ex-freedom fighter and president somewhere in Switzerland while some of his countrymen tried to find him and ask him questions like: What happened to the two hundred million dollars we thought we had, and how come your wife owned seven hundred hats?

The block had been described in 1965 as "an overwhelming and dynamic relationship of voids and solids, majestic in its uncompromising simplicity."

Often the *Blackbury Guardian* had pictures of people complaining about the damp, or the cold, or the way the windows fell out in high winds (it was always windy around the block, even on a calm day everywhere else), or the way gangs roamed its dank passageways and pushed shopping trolleys off the roof into the Great Lost Shopping Trolley Graveyard. The lifts hadn't worked properly since 1966. They lurked in the basement, too scared to go anywhere else.

The passages and walkways ("an excitingly brutal brushed concrete finish") had two smells, depending on whether or not the Council's ninja caretaker had been round in his van. The other one was disinfectant.

No-one liked the Joshua N'Clement block. There were two schools of thought about what should be done with it. The people who lived there thought everyone should be taken out and then the block should be blown up, and the people who lived *near* the block just wanted it blown up.

The odd thing was that although the block was cramped and fourteen storeys high, it had been built in the middle of a huge area of what was theoretically grass ("environmental open space"), but which was now the home of the Common Crisp Packet and Hardy-Perennial Burned-Out Car.

"Horrible place," said Wobbler.

"People've got to live somewhere," said Yo-less.

"Reckon the man who designed it lives here?" said Johnny.

"Shouldn't think so."

"I'm not going too near Bigmac's brother," said Wobbler. "He's a nutter. He's got tattoos and everything. And everyone knows he pinches stuff. Videos and things. Out of factories. And he killed Bigmac's hamster when he was little. And he chucks his stuff out of the window when he's angry. And if Clint's been let out—"

Clint was Bigmac's brother's dog, which had reputedly been banned from the Rottweiler/Pit Bull Terrier Crossbreed Club for being too nasty.

"Poor old Bigmac," said Johnny. "No wonder he's always sending off for martial arts stuff."

"I reckon he wants to join the Army so's he can bring his gun home one weekend," said Yo-less.

Wobbler looked up apprehensively at the huge towering bulk of the block.

"Huh! Bringing his tank home'd be favourite," he said.

Bigmac's brother's van was parked in what had been designed as the washing-drying area. Both the doors and the front wing were different colours. Clint was in the front seat, chained to the steering wheel. The van was the one vehicle that could be left unlocked anywhere near Joshua N'Clement.

"Weird, really," said Johnny. "When you think about it, I mean."

"What is?" said Yo-less.

"Well, there's a huge cemetery for dead people, and all the living people are crammed up in that thing," said Johnny. "I mean, it sounds like someone got something wrong . . ."

Bigmac emerged from the block, carrying a stack of cardboard boxes. He nodded hopelessly at Johnny, and put the boxes in the back of the van.

"Yo, duds," he said.

"Where's your brother?"

"He's upstairs. Come on, let's go."

"Before he comes down, you mean," said Wobbler.

"Shut up."

The breeze moved in the poplar trees, and whispered around the antique urns and broken stones.

"I don't know as this is right," said Wobbler, when the four of them had gathered by the gate.

"There's crosses all over the place," said Yo-less.

"Yes, but I'm an atheist," said Wobbler.

"Then you shouldn't believe in ghosts—"

"Post-living citizens," Bigmac corrected him.

"Bigmac?" said Johnny.

"Yeah?"

"What're you holding behind your back?"

"Nothing."

Wobbler craned to see.

"It's a bit of sharpened wood," he reported. "And a hammer."

"Bigmac!"

"Well, you never know—"

"Leave them here!"

"Oh, all *right*."

"Anyway, it's not stakes for ghosts. That's for vampires," said Yo-less.

"Oh, *thank you*," said Wobbler.

"Look, this is just the cemetery," said Johnny.

"It's got by-laws and things! It's not Transylvania! There's just dead people here! That doesn't make it scary, does it? Dead people are people who were living once! You wouldn't be so daft if there were living people buried here, would you?"

They set off along North Drive.

It was amazing how sounds died away in the cemetery. There was only a set of overgrown iron railings and some unpruned trees between them and the road, but noises were suddenly cut right down, as if they were being heard through a blanket. Instead, silence seemed to pour in—pour *up*, Johnny thought—like breathable water. It hissed. In the cemetery, silence made a noise.

The gravel crunched underfoot. Some of the more recent graves had a raised area in front of them which someone had thought would be a good idea to cover with little green stones. Now, tiny rockery plants were flourishing.

A crow cawed in one of the trees, unless it was a rook. It didn't really break the silence. It just underlined it.

"Peaceful, isn't it," said Yo-less.

"Quiet as the grave," said Bigmac. "Hah, hah."

"A lot of people come for walks here," said Johnny. "I mean, the park's miles away, and all there is there is *grass*. But this place has got tons of bushes and plants and trees and, and—"

"Environment," said Yo-less.

"And probably some ecology as well," said Johnny.

"Hey, look at this grave," said Wobbler.

They looked. It had a huge raised archway made of carved black marble, and a lot of angels wound around it, and a Madonna, and a faded photograph in a little glass window under the name: Antonio Vicenti (1897–1958). It looked like a kind of Rolls-Royce of a grave.

"Yeah. Dead impressive," said Bigmac.

"Why bother with such a big stone arch?" said Yo-less.

"It's just showing off," said Yo-less. "There's probably a sticker on the back saying 'My Other Grave Is A Porch.' "

"*Yo-less!*" said Johnny.

"Actually, I think that was very funny," said Mr. Vicenti. "He is a very funny boy."

Johnny turned, very slowly.

There was a man in black clothes leaning on the grave. He had neat black hair, plastered down, and a carnation in his buttonhole and a slightly grey look, as if the light wasn't quite right.

"Oh," said Johnny. "Hello."

"And what is the joke, exactly?" said Mr. Vicenti, in a very solemn voice. He stood very politely with his hands clasped in front of him, like an old-fashioned shop assistant.

"Well, you can get these stickers for cars, you see, and they say 'My Other Car is A Porsche,' " said Johnny. "It's not a very good joke," he added quickly.

"A Porsche is a kind of car?" said dead Mr. Vicenti.

"Yes. Sorry. I didn't think he should joke about things like that."

"Back in the old country I used to do magical entertainment for kiddies," said Mr. Vicenti. "With doves and similar items. On Saturdays. At parties. The Great Vicenti and Ethel. I like to laugh."

"The old country?" said Johnny.

"The alive country."

The three boys were watching Johnny carefully.

"You don't fool us," said Wobbler. "There's-there's no-one there."

"And I did escapology, too," said Mr. Vicenti, absent-mindedly pulling an egg from Yo-less's ear.

"You're just talking to the air," said Yo-less.

"Escapology?" said Johnny. Here we go again, he thought. The dead always want to *talk* about themselves . . .

"What?" said Bigmac.

"Escaping from things." Mr. Vicenti cracked the egg. The ghost of a dove flew away, and vanished as it reached the trees. "Sacks and chains and handcuffs and so on. Like the Great Houdini? Only in a semi-professional way, of course. My greatest trick involved getting out of a locked sack underwater while wearing twenty feet of chain and three pairs of handcuffs."

"Gosh, how often did you do that?" said Johnny.

"Nearly once," said Mr. Vicenti.

"Come on," said Wobbler. "Joke over. No-one's taken in. Come on. Time's getting on."

"Shut up, this is interesting," said Johnny.

He was aware of a rustling noise around him, like someone walking very slowly through dead leaves.

"And you're John Maxwell," said Mr. Vicenti. "The Alderman told us about you."

"Us?"

The rustling grew louder.

Johnny turned.

"He's not joking," said Yo-less. "Look at his face!"

I mustn't be frightened, Johnny told himself.

I mustn't be frightened!

Why *should* I be frightened? These are just . . . post-life citizens. A few years ago they were just mowing lawns and putting up Christmas decorations and being grandparents and things. They're nothing to be frightened of.

The sun was well behind the poplar trees. There was a bit of mist on the ground.

And, walking slowly towards him, through its coils, were the dead.

3

There was the Alderman, and William Stickers, and an old woman in a long dress and a hat covered in fruit, and some small children running on ahead, and dozens, *hundreds* of others. They didn't lurch. They didn't ooze any green. They just looked grey, and very slightly out of focus.

You notice things when you're terrified. Little details grow bigger.

He realized there were differences among the dead. Mr. Vicenti had looked almost . . . well, alive. William Stickers was slightly more colourless. The Alderman was definitely transparent around the edges. But many of the others, in Victorian clothes and odd assortments of coats and breeches from earlier ages, were almost completely without colour and almost without substance, so that they were little more than shaped air, but air that walked.

It wasn't that they had faded. It was just that they were further away, in some strange direction that had nothing much to do with the normal three.

Wobbler and the other two were still staring at him.

"Johnny? You all right?" said Wobbler.

Johnny remembered a piece about over population in a school Geography book. For everyone who was alive today, it said, there were twenty historical people, all the way back to when people had only just *become* people.

Or, to put it another way, behind every living person were twenty dead ones.

Quite a lot of them were behind Wobbler. Johnny didn't feel it would be a good idea to point this out, though.

"It's gone all cold," said Bigmac.

"We ought to be getting back," said Wobbler, his voice shaking. "I ought to be doing my homework."

Which showed he *was* frightened. It'd take zombies to make Wobbler prefer to do homework.

"You can't see them, can you," said Johnny. "They're all around us, but you can't see them."

"The living can't generally see the dead," said Mr. Vicenti. "It's for their own good, I expect."

The three boys had drawn closer together.

"Come on, stop mucking about," said Bigmac.

"Huh," said Wobbler. "He's just trying to spook us. Huh. Like Dead Man's Hand at parties. Huh. Well, it's not working. I'm off home. Come on, you lot."

He turned and walked a few steps.

"Hang on," said Yo-less. "There's something odd—"

He looked around at the empty cemetery. The rook had flown away, unless it was a crow.

"Something odd," he mumbled.

"Look," said Johnny. "They're here! They're all around us!"

"I'll tell my mum of you!" said Wobbler. "This is practising bein' satanic again!"

"John Maxwell!" boomed the Alderman. "We must talk to you!"

"That's right!" shouted William Stickers. "This is important!"

"What about?" said Johnny. He was balancing on his fear, and he felt oddly calm. The funny thing was, when you were on top of your fear you were a little bit taller.

"This!" said William Stickers, waving the newspaper.

Wobbler gasped. There was a rolled-up newspaper floating in the air.

"Poltergeist activity!" he said. He waved a shaking finger at Johnny. "You get that around adolescents! I read something in a magazine! Saucepans flying through the air and stuff! His head'll spin round in a minute!"

"What is the fat boy talking about?" said the Alderman.

"And what is Dead Man's Hand?" said Mr. Vicenti.

"There's probably a scientific explanation," said Yo-less, as the newspaper fluttered through the air.

"What?" said Bigmac.

"I'm trying to think of one!"

"It's holding itself open!"

William Stickers opened the paper.

"It's probably just a freak wind!" said Yo-less, backing away.

"I can't feel any wind!"

"That's why it's freaky!"

"What are you going to do about this?" the Alderman demanded.

"Excuse me, but this Dead Man's Hand. What is it?"

"Will everyone SHUT UP?" said Johnny.

Even the dead obeyed.

"Right," he said, settling down a bit. "Um. Look, um, you lot, these . . . people . . . want to talk to us. Me, anyway—"

Yo-less, Wobbler and Bigmac were staring intently at the newspaper. It hung, motionless, more than a metre above the ground.

"Are they . . . the breath-impaired?" said Wobbler.

"Don't be daft! That sounds like asthma," said Yo-less. "Come *on*. If you mean it, say it. Come right out with it. Are they . . ." He looked around at the darkening landscape, and hesitated. "Er . . . post-senior citizens?"

"Are they lurching?" said Wobbler. Now he and the other two were so close that they looked like one very wide person with six legs.

"You didn't tell us about this," said the Alderman.

"This what?" said Johnny.

"In the newspaper. Well, it is *called* a newspaper. But it has pictures of women in the altogether! Which may well be seen by respectable married women and young children!"

William Stickers was, with great effort, holding the paper open at the Entertainment Section. Johnny craned to read it. There was a rather poor photo of a couple of girls at Blackbury Swimming Pool and Leisure Centre.

"They've got swimsuits on," he said.

"Swimming suits? But I can see almost all of their legs!" the Alderman roared.

"Nothing wrong with that at all," snapped the elderly woman in the huge fruity hat. "Healthy bodies enjoying calisthenics in the God-given sunlight. And very practical clothing, I may say."

"Practical, madam? I dread to think for what!"

Mr. Vicenti leaned towards Johnny.

"The lady in the hat is Mrs. Sylvia Liberty," he whispered. "Died nineteen fourteen. Tireless suffragette."

"Suffragette?" said Johnny.

"Don't they teach you that sort of thing now? They campaigned for votes for women. They used to chain themselves to railings and chuck eggs at policemen and throw themselves under the Prince of Wales's horse on Derby days."

"Wow."

"But Mrs. Liberty got the instructions wrong and threw herself under the Prince of Wales."

"What?"

"Killed outright," said Mr. Vicenti. He clicked his disapproval. "He was a very heavy man, I believe."

"When you two have ceased this bourgeois arguing," shouted William Stickers, "perhaps we can get back to *important* matters?" He rustled the paper. Wobbler blinked.

"It says in this newspaper," said William Stickers, "that the cemetery is going to be closed. Going to be *built* on. Do you know about it?"

"Um. Yes. Yes. Um. Didn't *you* know?"

"Was anyone supposed to tell us?"

"What're they saying?" said Bigmac.

"They're annoyed about the cemetery being sold. There's a story in the paper."

"Hurry up!" said William Stickers. "I can't hold it much longer . . ."

The newspaper sagged. Then it fell *through* his hands and landed on the path.

"Not as alive as I was," he said.

"Definitely a freak whirlwind," said Yo-less. "I've heard about them. Nothing supernat—"

"This is our *home*," boomed the Alderman. "What will happen to *us*, young man?"

"Just a minute," said Johnny. "Hold on. Yo-less?"

"Yes?"

"They want to know what happens to people in graveyards if they get built on."

"The . . . dead want to know that?"

"Yes," said the Alderman and Johnny at the same time.

"I bet Michael Jackson didn't do this," said Bigmac. "He—"

"I saw this film," gabbled Wobbler, "where these houses were built on an old graveyard and someone dug a swimming pool and all these skeletons came out and tried to strangle people—"

"Why?" said the Alderman.

"He wants to know why," said Johnny.

"Search me," said Wobbler.

"I think," said Yo-less uncertainly, "that the . . . coffins and that get dug up and put somewhere else. I think there's special places."

"I'm not standing for that!" said dead Mrs. Sylvia Liberty. "I paid five pounds, seven shillings and sixpence for my plot! I remember the document Distinctly. Last Resting Place, it said. It didn't say After Eighty Years You'll Be Dug Up and Moved just so the living can build . . . what did it say?"

"Modern Purpose-Designed Offices," said William Stickers. "Whatever *they* are."

"I think it means they were designed on purpose," said Johnny.

"And how shameful to be sold for fivepence!" said dead Mrs. Liberty.

"That's the living for you," said William Stickers. "No thought for the downtrodden masses."

"Well, you see," said Johnny wretchedly, "the Council says it costs too much to keep up and the land was worth—"

"And what's this here about Blackbury Municipal Authority?" said the Alderman. "What happened to Blackbury City Council?"

"I don't know," said Johnny. "I've never heard of it. Look, it's not *my* fault. I like this place, too. I was only saying to Wobbler, I didn't like what's happening."

"So what are *you* going to do about it?" said the Alderman.

Johnny backed away, but came up against Mr. Vicenti's Rolls-Royce of a grave.

"Oh, no," he said. "Not me. It's not up to me!"

"I don't see why not," said dead Mrs. Sylvia Liberty. "After all, *you* can see and hear us."

"No-one else takes any notice," said Mr. Vicenti.

"We've been trying all day," said the Alderman.

"People walking their dogs. Hah! They just hurry away," said William Stickers.

"Not even old Mrs. Tachyon," said Mr. Vicenti.

"And *she's* mad," said the Alderman. "Poor soul."

"So there's only you," said William Stickers. "So you must go and tell this Municipal whateveritis that we aren't . . . going . . . to . . . move!"

"They won't listen to me! I'm twelve! I can't even vote!"

"Yes, but we can," said the Alderman.

"Can we?" said Mr. Vicenti.

The dead clustered around him, like an American football team.

"We're still over twenty-one, aren't we? I mean, technically."

"Yes, but we're dead," said Mr. Vicenti, in a reasonable tone of voice.

"You can vote at eighteen now," said Johnny.

"No wonder people have no respect," said the Alderman. "I said the rot'd set in if they gave the vote to women—"

Mrs. Liberty glared at him.

"Anyway, you can't use a dead person's vote," said William Stickers. "It's called Personation. I stood as Revolutionary Solidarity Fraternal Workers' Party Candidate. I know about this sort of thing."

"I'm not proposing to let anyone use my vote," said the Alderman. "I want to use it myself. No law against that."

"Good point."

"I served this city faithfully for more than fifty years," said the Alderman. "I do not see why I should lose my vote just because I'm dead. Democracy. That's the point."

"*People's* democracy," said William Stickers.

The dead fell silent.

"Well . . ." said Johnny miserably. "I'll see what I can do."

"Good man," said the Alderman. "And we'd also like a paper delivered every day."

"No, no," Mr. Vicenti shook his head. "It's so hard to turn the pages."

"Well, we must know what is happening," said Mrs. Liberty. "There's no telling what the living are getting up to out there while our backs are turned."

"I'll . . . think of something," said Johnny. "Something better than newspapers."

"Right," said William Stickers. "And then you get along to these Council people and tell them—"

"Tell them we're not going to take this lying down!" shouted the Alderman.

"Yes, right," said Johnny.

And the dead faded. Again there was the sensation of travelling, as if the dead people were going back into a different world . . .

"Have they gone?" said Wobbler.

"Not that they were here," said Yo-less, the scientific thinker.

"They were here, and they've gone," said Johnny.

"It definitely felt a bit weird," said Bigmac. "Very cold."

"Let's get out of here," said Johnny. "I need to think. They want me to stop this place being built on."

"How?"

Johnny led the way quickly towards the gates.

"Huh! They've left it up to me."

"We'll help," said Yo-less, promptly.

"Will we?" said Wobbler. "I mean, Johnny's OK, but . . . I mean . . . it's meddlin' with the occult. And your mum'll go *spare*."

"Yes, but if it's true then it's helping Christian souls," said Yo-less. "That's all right. They *are* Christian souls, aren't they?"

"I think there's a Jewish part of the cemetery," said Johnny.

"That's all right. Jewish is the same as Christian," said Bigmac.

"Not exactly," said Yo-less, very carefully. "But similar."

"Yeah, but . . ." said Wobbler, awkwardly. "I mean . . . dead people and that . . . I mean . . . he can see 'em, so it's up to him . . . I mean . . ."

"We all supported Bigmac when he was in juvenile court, didn't we?" said Yo-less.

"You said he was going to get hung," said Wobbler. "And I spent all morning doing that 'Free the Blackbury One' poster."

"It was a political crime," said Bigmac.

"You *stole* the Minister of Education's car when he was opening the school," said Yo-less.

"It wasn't stealing. I meant to give it back," said Bigmac.

"You *drove* it into a *wall*. You couldn't even give it back on a *shovel*."

"Oh, so it was my fault the brakes were faulty? I could have got badly hurt, right? I notice no-one worried about that. It was basically his fault, leaving cars around with Noddy locks and bad brakes—"

"I bet he doesn't have to repair his own brakes."

"It's society's fault, then—"

"*Anyway*," said Yo-less, "we were behind you that time, right?"

"Wouldn't like to be in front of him," said Wobbler.

"And we were right behind Wobbler when he got into trouble for complaining to the record shop about the messages from God he heard when he played Cliff Richard records backwards—"

"You said you heard it too," said Wobbler. "Hey, you said you heard it!"

"Only after you told me what it was," said Yo-less. "Before you told me what I was listening for, it just sounded like someone going ayip-ayeep-mwerp-ayeep."[1]

"They shouldn't do that sort of thing on records," said Wobbler defensively. "Gettin' at impressionable minds."

"The point I'm making," said Yo-less, "is that you've got to help your friends, right?" He turned to Johnny. "Now, *personally*, I think you're very nearly totally disturbed and suffering from psychosomatica and hearing voices and seeing delusions," he said, "and probably ought to be locked up in one of those white jackets with the stylish long sleeves. But that doesn't matter, 'cos we're friends."

"I'm touched," said Johnny.

"Probably," said Wobbler, "but we don't care, do we, guys?"

His mother was out, at her second job. Grandad was watching *Video Whoopsy*.

"Grandad?"

"Yes?"

"How famous was William Stickers?"

"Very famous. Very famous man," said the old man, without looking around.

"I can't find him in the encyclopedia."

"Very famous man, was William Stickers. Haha! Look, the man's just fallen off his bicycle! Right into the bush!"

Johnny took down the volume L-MIN, and was silent for a few minutes. Grandad had a complete set of huge encyclopedias. No-one really knew why. Somewhere in 1950 or something, Grandad had said to himself, "get educated," and had bought the massive books on hire purchase. He'd never opened them. He'd just built a bookcase for them. Grandad was superstitious about books. He thought that if you had enough of them around, education leaked out, like radioactivity.

"How about Mrs. Sylvia Liberty?"

---

[1]But according to Wobbler it was *really*: "Hey, kids! Go to school and get a good education! Listen to your parents! It's cool to go to church!"

"Who's she?"

"She was a suffragette, I think. Votes for women and things."

"Never heard of her."

"She's not in here under 'Liberty' or 'Suffragette.' "

"Never heard of her. Whoa, look here, the cat's fallen in the pond—!"

"All right . . . how about Mr. Antonio Vicenti?"

"What? Old Tony Vicenti? What's he up to now?"

"Was he famous for anything?"

For a moment, Grandad's eyes left the TV screen and focused on the past instead.

"He ran a joke shop in Alma Street where the multi-storey car park is now. You could buy stink bombs and itchy-powder. And he used to do conjuring tricks at kids' parties when your mum was a girl."

"Was he a famous man?"

"All the kids knew him. Only children's entertainer in these parts, see. They all knew his tricks. They used to shout out: 'It's in your pocket!' And things like that. Alma Street. And Paradise Street, that was there, too. And Balaclava Terrace. That's where I was born. Number Twelve, Balaclava Terrace. All under the car park now. Oh, dear . . . he's going to fall off that building . . ."

"So he wasn't really *famous*. Not like *really* famous."

"All the kids knew him. Prisoner of war in Germany, he was. But he escaped. And he married . . . Ethel Plover, that's right. Never had any kids. Used to do conjuring tricks and escaping from things. Always escaping from things, he was."

"He wore a carnation pinned to his coat," said Johnny.

"That's right! Every day. Never saw him without one. Always very smart, he was. He used to be a conjuror. Haven't seen him around for years."

"Grandad?"

"It's all changed around here now. I hardly see anywhere I recognize when I go into town these days. Someone told me they've pulled down the old boot factory."

"You know that little transistor radio?" said Johnny.

"What little transistor radio?"

"The one you've got."

"What about it?"

"You said it's too fiddly and not loud enough?"

"That's right."

"Can I have it?"

"I thought you'd got one of those ghetto-blowers."

"This is . . . for some friends." Johnny hesitated. He was by nature an honest person, because apart from anything else, lying was always too complicated.

"They're quite old," he added. "And a bit shut in."

"Oh, all right. You'll have to put some new batteries in—the old ones have gone all manky."

"I've got some batteries."

"You don't get proper wireless any more. We used to get *oscillation* when I was a boy. You never get it now. Hehe! There he goes—look, right through the ice—!"

Johnny went down to the cemetery before breakfast. The gates had been locked, but since there were holes all along the walls this didn't make a lot of difference.

He'd bought a plastic bag for the radio and had sorted out some new batteries, after scraping out the chemical porridge that was all that was left of the old ones.

The cemetery was deserted. There wasn't a soul there, living or dead. But there was the silence, the big *empty* silence. If ears could make a noise, they'd sound like that silence.

Johnny tried to fill it.

"Um," he said. "Anyone there?"

A fox leapt up from behind one of the stones and scurried away into the undergrowth.

"Hello? It's me?"

The absence of the dead was scarier than seeing them in the flesh—or at least, not in the flesh.

"I brought this radio. It's probably easier for you than newspapers. Um. I looked up radio in the encyclopedia and most of you ought to know what it is. Um. You twiddle the knobs and radio comes out. Um. So I'll just tuck it down behind Mr. Vicenti's slab, all right? Then you can find out what's going on."

He coughed.

"I . . . I did some thinking last night, and . . . and I thought maybe if people knew about all the . . . famous . . . people here, they'd be bound to leave it alone. I know it's not a very good idea," he said, hopelessly, "but it's the best I could come up with. I'm going to make a list of names. If you don't mind?"

He'd hoped Mr. Vicenti would be about. He quite liked him. Perhaps it was because he hadn't been dead as long as the others. He seemed friendlier. Less stiff.

Johnny walked from gravestone to gravestone, noting down names. Some of the older stones were quite ornate, with fat cherubs on them. But one had a pair of football boots carved on it. He made a special note of the name:

STANLEY "WRONG WAY" ROUNDWAY
1892–1936
The Last Whistle

He nearly missed the one under the trees. It had a flat stone in the grass, without even one of the ugly flower vases, and all it declared was that this was the last resting place of Eric Grimm (1885–1927). No "Just Resting," no "Deeply Missed," not even "Died," although probably he had. Johnny wrote the name down, anyway.

Mr. Grimm waited until after Johnny had gone before he emerged, and glared after him.

4

It was later that morning.

There was a new library in the Civic Centre. It was so new it didn't even have librarians. It had Assistant Information Officers. And it had computers. Wobbler was banned from the computers because of an incident involving a library terminal, the telephone connection to the main computer, another telephone line to the computer at East Slate Air Base ten miles away, *another* telephone line to a much bigger computer under a mountain somewhere in America, and almost World War Three.

At least, that's what Wobbler said. The Assistant Information Officers said it was because he got chocolate in the keyboard.

But he was allowed to use the microfiche readers. They couldn't think of a good reason to stop him.

"What're we looking for, anyway," said Bigmac.

"Nearly everyone that died here used to get buried in that cemetery," said Johnny. "So if we can find someone famous who lived here, and then we can find them in the cemetery, then it's a famous place. There's a cemetery in London with Karl Marx in it. It's famous for him being dead in it."

"Karl Marx?" said Bigmac. "What was he famous for?"

"You're ignorant, you are," said Wobbler. "He was the one who played the harp."

"No, Karl was the one who usedta talka lika dis," said Yo-less.

"Actually, he was the one with the cigar," said Wobbler.

"That's a very old joke," said Johnny severely. "The Marx Brothers. Hah, hah. Look, I've got the old newspaper files. The *Blackbury Guardian*. They go back nearly a hundred years. All we've got to do is look at the front pages. That's where famous people'd be."

"And the back pages," said Bigmac.

"Why the back pages?"

"Sports. Famous footballers and that."

"Yeah, right. Hadn't thought of that. All right, then. Let's get started . . ."

"Yeah, but . . ." said Bigmac.

"What?" said Johnny.

"So this Karl Marx, then," said Bigmac. "What films was he in?"

Johnny sighed. "Listen, he wasn't in any films. He was . . . he led the Russian Revolution."

"No he didn't," said Wobbler. "He just wrote a book called, oh, something like *It's About Time There Was a Revolution*, and the Russians just followed the instructions. The actual leaders were a lot of people with names ending in *ski*."

"Like Stalin," said Yo-less.

"Right."

"Stalin means Man Of Steel," said Yo-less. "I read where he didn't like his real name, so he changed it. It's Man of Steel in English."

"What was his real name?"

"His secret identity, you mean," said Yo-less.

"What are you talking about now?" said Bigmac.

"No, I get it. Man of Steel? Yo-less means he could leap Kremlins in a single bound," said Johnny.

"Don't see why not," said Wobbler. "I always thought it was unfair, the way the Americans got Superman. They've got all the superheroes. I don't see why we couldn't have had Superman round here."

They thought about it. Wobbler then spoke for them all.

"Mind you," he said, "round here he would have had trouble even being Clark Kent."

They disappeared under the hoods again.

"What did you say the Alderman was called?" said Wobbler, after a while.

"Alderman Thomas Bowler," said Johnny. "Why?"

"It says he got the Council to build a memorial horse trough in the square in nineteen hundred and five," said Wobbler. "It came in useful very quickly too, it says here."

"Why?"

"Well . . . it says here, the next day the first motor car ever to arrive in Blackbury crashed into it and caught fire. They used the water to put the fire out. Says here the Council praised Alderman Bowler for his forward thinking."

They looked at the microfilm viewer.

"What's a horse trough?" said Bigmac.

"It's that big stone trough thing that's outside Loggitt and Burnett's Building Society," said Johnny. "The one that's been filled with soil for a tasteful display of dead flowers and lager cans. They used to put water in those things for coach horses to drink out of."

"But if *cars* were just coming in," said Bigmac slowly, "then building things for horses to drink out of was a bit—"

"Yes," said Johnny. "I know. Come on. Let's keep going."

. . . *WHEEEsssh* . . . we built this city on . . . *ssshshhh* . . . on the phone right now . . . *wheeesshhh* . . . that was at Number Two . . . *ssshwupwup* . . . told a meeting in Kiev . . . *wsswssshsss* . . . Prime Minister . . . *shsss* . . . today . . . *shhssss* . . . scaramouche, can you . . . *shssssss* . . .

The tuning knob of the little radio behind Mr. Vicenti's grave turned back and forth very slowly, as if it was being moved with great effort. Occasionally it would stop on a programme, and then move again.

. . . *ssshhwwwss* . . . and the next caller . . . *shhwwsss* . . . Babylon . . .

And around it, for quite some distance, the air was cold.

In the library, the boys read on. Silence surrounded them. The Assistant Information Officers grew worried, and one of them went to find the cleaning fluid and the bent paperclip for getting chocolate out of keyboards.

"Let's face it," said Wobbler, eventually, "this is a town where famous people don't come from. It's famous for it."

"It says here," said Yo-less, from his viewer, "that Addison Vincent Fletcher of Alma Terrace invented a form of telephone in nineteen twenty-two."

"Oh, great," said Wobbler. "Telephones had been invented years before that."

"It says he said this one was better."

"Oh, yes," said Wobbler. He dialled an imaginary number. "Hello, is that—Who invented the real telephone, anyone?"

"Thomas Eddison," said Yo-less.

"Sir Humphrey Telephone," said Bigmac.

"Alexander Graham Bell," said Johnny. "Sir Humphrey *Telephone*?"

"Hello, Mr. Bell," said Wobbler, speaking into an imaginary mouthpiece, "You know that telephone you invented years ago? Well, mine's better. And I'm just off to discover America. Yes, I know Christopher Columbus discovered it first, but I'm discovering it *better*."

"It makes sense," said Bigmac. "If you're going to discover somewhere, you might as well wait until there's proper hotels and stuff."

"When did Columbus discover America, anyway?" said Wobbler.

"Fourteen ninety-two," said Johnny. "There's a rhyme: In fourteen hundred and ninety-two, Columbus sailed the ocean blue."

Wobbler and Bigmac looked at him.

"Actually, he could have got there in fourteen ninety-one," said Yo-less, without looking up, "but he had to sail around a bit because no-one could think up a rhyme for 'one.' "

"It *could* have been Sir Humphrey Telephone," said Bigmac. "Stuff gets named after inventors."

"They didn't name the telephone after Bell," said Wobbler.

"They named the *bell* after Bell, though," said Bigmac. "Telephone bells. Proves my point."

"Telephones haven't had bells on for years," said Wobbler.

"That," said Yo-less, "is due to the famous invention by Fred Buzzer."

"I think it's *impossible* for anyone famous to come from here," said Wobbler, "because *everyone* around here is mental."

"Got one," said Bigmac, turning the microfiche knob.

"Who? Which one?"

"The footballer. Stanley 'Wrong Way' Roundway. He played for Blackbury Wanderers. There's his obituary here. Amost half a page."

"Any good?"

"Says he scored a record number of goals."

"Sounds good," said Wobbler.

"Own goals."

"What?"

"Greatest number of own goals in the history of any sport, it says. It says he kept getting over-excited and losing his sense of direction."

"Oh."

"But he was a good footballer, it says. Apart from that. Not exactly a Hall of Fame, though—"

"Here, look at this," said Yo-less.

They clustered around his viewer. He'd found an ancient group photograph of about thirty soldiers, all beaming at the camera.

"Well?" said Wobbler.

"This is from nineteen sixteen," said Yo-less. "They're all going off to war."

"Which one?" said Wobbler.

"The first one, you nerd. World War One."

"I always wondered why they numbered it," said Bigmac. "Like they expected to have a few more. You know. Like Buy Two, Get One Free."

"Says here," Yo-less squinted, "it's the Blackbury Old Pals Battalion. They're just going off to fight. They all joined up at the same time . . ."

Johnny stared. He could hear people's voices, and the background noises of the library. But the picture looked as if it was at the bottom of a dark, square tunnel. And he was falling down it.

Things outside the picture were inky and slow. The picture was the centre of the world.

Johnny looked at the grinning faces, the terrible haircuts, the jug-handle ears, the thumbs all up.

Even today nearly everyone in the *Blackbury Guardian* had their photo taken with their thumb up, unless they'd won Super Bingo, in which case they were shown doing what the photographer thought was a high kick. The newspaper's one photographer was known as Jeremy the Thumb.

The people in the picture didn't look much older than Bigmac. Well, a couple of them did. There was a sergeant with a moustache like a scrubbing brush, and an officer in jodhpurs, but the rest of them looked like a school photo.

And now he was coming back from wherever he'd been. The picture dropped away again, became just an oblong on a page on a screen. He blinked.

There was a feeling, like—

—like on an aeroplane when it's about to land, and his ears went "pop." But it was happening with his brain, instead.

"Anyone know what the Somme is?" said Yo-less.

"No."

"That's where they went, anyway. Some place in France."

"Any of them win any medals?" said Johnny, struggling back into the real world. "That'd be famous. If there's someone in the cemetery with a lot of medals."

Yo-less spun the wheels of the viewer.

"I'll look ahead a few issues," he said. "There's bound to be something if—Hey . . . look at *this* . . ."

They all tried to get under the hood at once. Silence came back as they realized what he'd found.

I knew it was important, Johnny thought. What's happening to me?

"Wow," said Wobbler. "I mean—all those names . . . everyone killed in this big battle . . ."

Without saying anything, Johnny ducked into the other reader and wound it backward until he found the cheery photograph.

"Are they listed in alphabetical order?" he said.

"Yes," said Yo-less.

"I'll read out the names under the photo, then. Um . . . Armitage, K. . . . Atkins, T. . . ."

"Yes . . . no . . ." said Yo-less.

"Sergeant Atterbury, F. . . ."

"Yes."

"Hey, there's three from Canal Street," said Wobbler. "That's where my gran lives!"

"Blazer . . . Constantine . . . Fraser . . . Frobisher . . ."

"Yes . . . yes . . . yes . . . yes . . ."

They carried on to the end of the caption.

"They all died," said Johnny, eventually. "Four weeks after the picture was taken. All of them."

"Except for Atkins, T.," said Yo-less. "It says here what a Pals' Battalion was. It says, people all from one town or even one street could all join the Army together if they wanted, and all get sent to . . . the same place."

"I wonder if they all got there?" said Yo-less. "Eventually," he added.

"That's dreadful," said Bigmac.

"It probably sounded like a good idea at the time. Sort of . . . jolly."

"Yes, but . . . four weeks . . ." said Bigmac. "I mean . . ."

"You're always saying you can't wait to join the Army," said Wobbler. "*You* said you were sorry the Gulf War was over. And all the legs of your bed are off the ground because of all them copies of *Guns and Ammo* underneath it."

"Well . . . *yeah* . . . war, yeah," said Bigmac. "Proper fighting, with M16s and stuff. Not just all going off grinning and getting shot."

"They all marched off together because they were friends, and got killed," said Yo-less.

They stared at the little square of light with the names on it, and the long, long line of cheery thumbs.

"Except for Atkins, T.," said Johnny. "I wonder what happened to him?"

"It was nineteen sixteen," said Yo-less. "If he's still alive, he'll be dead."

"Any of them on your list?" said Wobbler.

Johnny checked.

"No-oo," he said, eventually. "There's one or two people with the same name but the wrong initial. Everyone round here used to get buried up there."

"Perhaps he came back from the war and moved away somewhere else," said Yo-less.

"It'd be a bit lonely around here, after all," said Bigmac.

They looked at him.

"Sorry," he said.

"I'm fed up with this," said Wobbler, pushing his chair back. "It's not *real*. There's no-one special in there. It's just people. And it's creepy. Come on, let's go down to the mall."

"I've found out what happens to dead bodies when old graveyards are built on," said Yo-less, as they stepped out into the Tupperware daylight. "My mum knows. They get taken to some kind of storage place called a necropolis. That's Latin for City of the Dead."

"Yuk," said Wobbler.

"Sounds like where Superman lives," said Bigmac.

"Necropolis!" said Wobbler, zooming his hands through the air. "By day, mild-mannered corpse—by night . . . duh duh duhduh DAH . . . ZombieMan!"

Johnny remembered the grinning young faces, not much older than Wobbler.

"Wobbler," he said, "If you make another joke like that—"

"What?"

". . . well . . . just don't. Right? I mean it."

. . . *ssshhhh* . . . mean, yo, youknowhatI'msayin' . . . *sipsipsip* . . . told the government that . . . *sswwwsss* . . . fact the whales *enjoy* being hunted, Bob, and . . . *wwwhhhhh* . . .

Click!

"So that's wireless telegraphy, is it? Hah! So much for Countess Alice Radioni!"

"I was an Ovalteenie when I was a little boy. That was during the war. The one against the Germans. Did I ever tell you? We used to sing along with the people on the wireless: 'We are the Ov—' WHAT? Who was Countess Alice Radioni?"

"Which war against the Germans?"

"What? How many have we had?"

"Two so far."

"Now, come ON! Radioni? It was *Marconi* who invented the radio!"

"Hah! And do you know who he stole the idea from?"

"Who cares who invented the wretched thing? Will you listen to what the living are doing?"

"Plotting to steal our cemetery, that is what they are doing!"

"Yes, but . . . I didn't know that all this was going on, did you? All this music and . . . the things they were talking about! Who *is* Shakespeare's Sister and why is she singing on the wireless? What is a Batman? And they said the last Prime Minister was a woman! That can't be possible. Women can't even vote."

"Yes, they can."

"Hurrah!"

"Well, they couldn't in MY time!"

"There's so much we don't know!"

"So why don't we find out?"

The dead fell silent—or rather, more silent than usual.

"How?"

"The man on the wireless said you can ring the wireless station on the telephone to Discuss Problems That Affect Us All Today. A Phone-Ing Program, he said."

"Well?"

"There's a phone box out in the street."

"Yes, but . . . that's . . . outside . . ."

"Not far outside."

"Yes, but . . ."

"The little boy stood in front of us and talked to us. And he was so frightened. And we can't walk six feet?"

The speaker was Mr. Vicenti. He looked through the crumbling railings to the street outside, with the eye of a man who'd spent much of his life escaping.

"But this is our PLACE! This is where we BELONG!"

"It's only a few steps . . ."

It wasn't really much of a mall. But it was all there was to hang out in.

Johnny had seen films of American shopping malls. They must have different sorts of people in America, he'd thought. They all looked cool, all the girls were beautiful, and the place wasn't crowded with little kamikaze grandmothers. Or mothers with seven children. Or Blackbury United football fans walking ten abreast singing the famous football song, *"URRRurrrURRR-UH!" (clapclapclap)*. You couldn't hang out properly in a place like that. All you could do was hang on.

The four of them hung on in the burger bar. Yo-less carefully read the pamphlet about how no rainforests were chopped down to make beef-burgers. Bigmac had his favourite Megajumbo Fries with fifteen packets of relish.

"Wonder if I could get a job here?" said Wobbler.

"No chance," said Bigmac. "The manager'd take one look at you and see where the profits would go."

"You saying I'm fat?" said Wobbler.

"Gravitationally challenged," said Yo-less, without looking up.

"Enhanced," said Bigmac.

Wobbler's lips moved as he tried these out.

"I'd rather be fat," he said. "Can I finish up your onion rings?"

"Anyway, there's loads of people want jobs here," said Bigmac. "You have to have three A-levels."

"What, just to make burgers?"

"No other jobs around," said Bigmac. "They're shutting all the factories around here. Nothing to do. No-one's making anything any more."

"Someone's making something," said Wobbler. "What about all the stuff in the shops?"

"That's all made in Taiwanaland or somewhere. Hah! What sort of future are *we* going to have, eh? That's right, eh? Johnny?"

"What?"

"You've just been staring at nothing the whole time, you know that?"

"Yeah, what's happened?" said Wobbler. "Some dead people come in for a takeaway?"

"No," said Johnny.

"What're you thinking about, then?"

"Thumbs," said Johnny, still staring at the wall.

"What?"

"What?" said Johnny, waking up.

"What about thumbs?"

"Oh . . . nothing."

"My mother said last night that there's a lot of people angry about the cemetery being sold," said Yo-less. "Everyone's moaning about it. And Pastor William says anyone who builds on there will be cursed unto the seventh generation."

"Yes, but he always says that kind of thing," said Wobbler. "Anyway, United Amalagamated Consolidated Holdings probably don't worry about that sort of thing. They've probably got a Vice-President in Charge of Being Cursed."

"And he probably gets his secretary to deal with it," said Bigmac.

"It won't stop anything, anyway," said Yo-less. "There's bulldozers just the other side of the fence."

"Anyone know what United Amalagamated Consolidated Holdings *do*?" said Wobbler.

"It said in the paper that they're a multinational information-retrieval and enhancement facility," said Yo-less. "It said on the news it'll provide three hundred jobs."

"For all the people who used to work at the old rubber boot factory?" said Bigmac.

Yo-less shrugged. "That's how it goes," he said. "You all right, Johnny?"

"What?"

"You OK? You're staring at the wall."

"What? Oh. Yeah. I'm OK."

"He's upset about the dead soldiers," said Wobbler.

Yo-less leaned across the table.

"Look . . . that's all in the past, right? It's just *gone*. It's a shame they died but . . . well . . . they'd be dead anyway, wouldn't they? It's just history. It's nothing to do with . . . well, with *now*."

Mrs. Ivy Witherslade was talking to her sister in the phone box on Cemetery Road when someone knocked impatiently on the glass, and that was odd, because there was no-one there. But she felt very cold and suddenly uneasy, as though she was walking on someone's grave. She stopped telling her sister about her legs and what the doctor said about them, and went home quickly.

If Johnny had been there, he would have heard what happened next. But he wasn't, so everyone else would have just heard the wind, and perhaps, just perhaps, the faintest of arguments:

"You should know, Mr. Fletcher. YOU invented it."

"Actually, that was Alexander Graham Bell, Mrs. Liberty. I just improved upon it."

"Well . . . make it work. Let me speak to the man on the wireless machine."

"Was it really Alexander Graham Bell?"

"Yes, Alderman."

"I thought it was Sir Humphrey Telephone."

The telephone stayed on its hook, but there were a few electric crackles and pops from somewhere in the machinery.

"I think I have mastered the intricacies, Mrs. Liberty—"

"Let ME do the talking. The people's voice must be heard!"

Frost was forming on the inside of the telephone box.

"Certainly not. You are a bolshevik!"

"What did Sir Humphrey Telephone invent, then?"

"Mr. Fletcher! Be so good as to expedite the electric communication!"

When there wasn't the burger bar to hang out in, and when they weren't allowed in J&J Software because of whatever Wobbler's latest crime was, there was only the fountain area with the sad, dying trees in it or Groovy Sounds record store, which was pretty much like any record store would be if it was called Groovy Sounds.

Anyway, Yo-less wanted to buy a tape for his collection.

"Famous British Brass Bands," said Wobbler, looking over his shoulder.

"Yes, but this is a good one," said Yo-less. "It's got the old Blackbury Rubber Boot Factory Band playing *The Floral Dance*. Very famous piece."

"You're just basically not black, are you," said Wobbler. "I'm going to report you to the Rastafarians."

"*You* like reggae and blues," said Yo-less.

"That's different."

Johnny listlessly shuffled through the tapes.

And froze.

There was a voice he recognized. It was crackly with static, but it sounded a lot like Mrs. Sylvia Liberty, and it was coming over the radio.

The radio was on the counter, turned to Wonderful Radio Blackbury's Mike Mikes Radio Show, which was as excellent and totally bodacious as two hours of phone-ins and traffic reports from the Blackbury bypass could be.

This time it was different. The phone-in had been about the Council's proposal to knock down the old Fish Market, which was going to happen no matter what anyone said, but it was a good subject for people to moan about.

"Well, what I say is *hello? Hello? This is Mrs. Sylvia Liberty speaking on the electric telephone! Hello?* not to be allowed, er, in my opinion, er, it is totally *hello*? (click . . . fizz . . . crackle) *I demand to be heard this INSTANT! The Fish Market is of NO importance whatsoever!* er . . . er . . . and . . ."

In his little studio on top of the Blackbury and Slate Insurance Society, Mike Mikes stared at his engineer, who stared at his switchboard. There was no way of cutting off the intrusive voice. It was coming in on all telephone lines at once.

"Er, hi," he said. "The caller on . . . er . . . all the lines . . ."

"Here, someone's *You listen to me, young man! And don't cut me off to start playing any more of your phonograph cylinders!* crossed line here, Mike, I *Do you realize that innocent citizens are being EVICTED* (click . . . garble . . . whirr . . . fizz) *many years of VALUED service to the community* (wheeeowwwwwh . . . crackle) *merely because of an ACCIDENT of birth* (fizzle . . . whipwhipwhip . . . crackle) *you listen to young Johnn* (snap . . . fizz . . .) *The People's Shroud is Deepest Black* (wheeeyooowwwww . . . pop) *We're Coming BACK . . . stop that this minute, William, you are nothing but a bolshevik agit . . .*"

But no-one heard the rest of the sentence because the engineer had pulled all the plugs and hit the switchboard with a hammer.

Johnny and his friends had gathered around the radio.

"You get some real loonies on these phone-ins," said Wobbler. "You ever listen to Mad Jim's Late Night Explosion?"

"He's not mad," said Yo-less. "He just says he is. And all he does is play old records and go 'yeah!' and 'yowsahyowsah!' a lot. That's not mad. That's just pathetic."

"Yes," said Wobbler.

"Yes," said Bigmac.

"Yes," said Yo-less.

They all looked at Johnny. They all looked like people with something on their minds.

"Ahem," said Wobbler.

"Er," said Bigmac.

"That was *them*, was it?" said Yo-less.

"Yes," said Johnny. "It was them."

"It didn't sound like normal radio. How can they use the phone?"

"I don't know. I suppose some of them knew how to use the phone when they were alive. And maybe being dead's a bit like . . . electricity or something."

"They nearly said your name," said Wobbler.

"Yes."

"Who was that one singing?"

"I think it was William Stickers. He's a bit of a communist."

"I didn't think there were any communists left these days," said Yo-less.

"There aren't. And he's one of them."

"You know, any minute now Rod Serling is going to come walking in here with a big book," said Bigmac. "You know. Like in *The Twilight Zone*."

"How come they know what's on the radio?" said Yo-less.

"I lent them Grandad's transistor."

"You know what I think?" said Yo-less. "I think you've started something."

"That's what I think, too."

"Nah!" said Wobbler. "Come *on*! Voices on the radio? I mean!

That's just mucking about. Could be anything. Kids ringing up and messing about. Oh, come *on*! Ghosts don't phone up radio stations!"

"I saw this film once where they came out of the telephone," said Bigmac, winner of the All-Blackbury Mr. Tactful Championship.

"Just you shut up! I don't believe you!"

It was very, very chilly inside the phone box.

"I must say, electricity is very easy to master when you're dead."

"What are you doing, Mr. Fletcher?"

"Very easy indeed. Who shall we talk to next?"

"We must speak to the Town Hall!"

"But it is a Saturday, Mrs. Liberty. There will be no-one there."

"Then try to find young Johnny. I don't know what he means about trying to find famous people buried in the cemetery. WE'RE here, after all."

"I'll keep trying. It's amazingly easy to understand."

"Where's Mr. Stickers gone?"

"He's trying to listen to Radio Moscow, whatever that is. On the wireless telegraphy apparatus."

"I say, this is rather invigorating, you know. I've never been out of the cemetery before."

"Yes. It's a new lease of life."

"You can escape from almost anything," said Mr. Vicenti.

There was a faint cough. They looked around.

Mr. Grimm was watching them through the railings.

The dead seemed to sober up. They always became more serious in front of Mr. Grimm.

They shuffled their spectral feet.

"You're outside," said Mr. Grimm. "You know that's wrong."

"Only a little way, Eric," said the Alderman. "That can't do any harm. It's for the good of the—"

"It's WRONG."

"We don't have to listen to him," said Mr. Vicenti.

"You'll get into terrible trouble," said Mr. Grimm.

"No we won't," said Mr. Vicenti.

"It's dabbling with the Known," said Mr. Grimm. "You'll get into dreadful trouble and it won't be my fault. You are bad people."

He turned, and walked back to his grave.

"Dial the number," said Mr. Vicenti. The others seemed to wake up.

"You know," said Mrs. Liberty, "he may have a point—"

"Forget about Mr. Grimm," said Mr. Vicenti. He opened his hands. A white dove shot out of his sleeve and perched on the phone box, blinking. "Dial the number, Mr. Fletcher."

"Hello, directory enquiries, what name please?"

"He's called Johnny Maxwell and he lives in Blackbury."

"I'm afraid that is not sufficient information—"

"That's all we—" (Listen, I can see how it works, there's a connection—) (How many of us are there in here?) (Can I try, please?) (This is a lot better than those seances) . . .

The operator rubbed her headset. For some reason, her ear had gone cold.

"Ow!"

She ripped it off.

The operator on her right leaned over.

"What's up, Dawn?"

"It went—it felt—"

They looked at the switchboard. Lights were coming on everywhere, and it was beginning to be covered in frost.

The point is—

—that all through history there have been people who couldn't invent things because the rest of the world wasn't ready. Leonardo da Vinci hadn't got the motors or materials to make his helicopter. Sir George Cayley invented the internal combustion engine before anyone else had invented petrol.[1]

And in his life Addison Vincent Fletcher had spent long hours with motors and relays and glowing valves and bits of wire, pursuing a dream the world didn't even have a name for yet.

In his phone box, dead Mr. Fletcher laughed. It had a name now. He knew *exactly* what a computer was when he saw one.

---

[1]So he ran it on pellets of gunpowder. Really. It was nearly the *external* combustion engine.

5

Johnny went home. He didn't dare go back to the cemetery.

It was Saturday evening. He'd forgotten about the Visit.

"You've got to come," said his mother. "You know she likes to see you."

"No she doesn't," said Johnny. "She forgets who I am. She calls me Peter. I mean, that's my dad's name. And the place smells of old ladies. Anyway, why doesn't Grandad ever come? She's his wife."

"He says he likes to remember her as she was," said his mother. "Besides, it's *Markie and Mo's Saturday Spectacular*. You know he doesn't like to miss it."

"Oh . . . all right."

"We don't have to stay long."

About ten minutes after Johnny had gone, the phone rang. Grandad dealt with it in his normal way, which was to shout "Phone!" while not taking his eyes off the screen. But it went on ringing. Eventually, grumbling and losing the remote control down the side of the cushion where it wouldn't be found for two days, he got up and shuffled out into the hall.

"Yes? He's not here. Gone out. Who? Well, I'll . . . is it? Never! Still doing the conjuring tricks, are you? Haven't seen you about the town much lately. No. Right. That's right. I don't get out much myself these days. How are you, in yourself? Dead. I see. But you've got out to use the telephone. It's wonderful, what they can do with science. You sound a long way off. Right. You *are* a long way off. I remember that trick you used to do with the handcuffs and the chains and—well, nearly did. Yes. Yes. Right. I'll tell him. Nice to hear from you. Goodbye."

He went back and settled down in front of the TV again.

After a few minutes a small worried frown crossed his face. He got up and went and glared at the telephone for a while.

It wasn't that Sunshine Acres was a *bad* place. As far as Johnny could see, it was clean enough and the staff seemed OK. There were bright murals on the walls and a big tank of goldfish in the TV room.

But it was more gloomy than the cemetery. It was the way everyone shuffled around quietly, and sat waiting at the table for the next meal hours before it was due, because there wasn't anything else to do. It was as if life had stopped and being dead hadn't started, so all there was to do was hang around.

His grandmother spent a lot of time watching TV in the main lounge, or watching her begonias in her room. At least, his grandmother's body did. He was never certain where her mind was, except that it was often far away and long ago.

After a while he got even more depressed at the conversation between his mother and his grandmother, which was exactly the same as the one last week and the week before that, and did what he always did, which was wander out into the corridor.

He mooched towards the door that led out into the garden, staring vaguely at nothing.

They never told you about this ghost stuff at school. Sometimes the world was so weird you didn't know where to start, and Social Education and GCSE Maths weren't a lot of help.

Why didn't this sort of thing happen to anyone else? It wasn't as if he went looking for it. He just tried to keep his head down, he just tried to be someone at the back of the crowd. But somehow everything was more complicated than it was for anyone else.

The thing was . . .

Mr. T. Atkins.

He probably wouldn't have noticed it, except that the name was in the back of his mind.

It was written on a little curling piece of paper stuck in a frame on one of the doors.

He stared at it.

It filled the whole world, just for a second or two.

Well, there could be lots of Atkinses . . .

He'd never find out unless he knocked, though . . . would he? . . .

"Open the door, will you, love? M'hands are full."

There was a large black woman behind him, her arms full of sheets. Johnny nodded mutely and turned the handle.

The room was more or less bare. There was certainly no-one else there.

"I see you come up here every week to see your gran," said the nurse, dumping the sheets on the bare bed. "You're a good boy to come see her."

"Uh. Yes."

"What was it you were wanting?"

"Uh. I thought I'd . . . you know . . . drop in to have a chat with Mr. Atkins? Uh." Inspiration seized him. "I'm doing a project at school. About the Blackbury Pals."

A project! You could get away with anything if you said you were doing a project.

"Who were they then, dear?"

"Oh . . . some soldiers. Mr. Atkins was one of them, I think. Uh . . . where . . . ?"

"Well, he passed away yesterday, dear. Nearly ninety-seven, I think he was. Did you know him?"

"Not . . . really."

"He was here for *years*. He was a nice old man. He used to say that when he died the war'd be over. It was his joke. He used to show us his old Army pay book. 'Tommy Atkins,' he'd say. 'I'm the one, I'm the boy, when I'm gone it's all over.' He used to laugh about that."

"What did he mean?"

"Don't know, dear. I just used to smile. You know how it is."

The nurse smoothed out the new sheets and pulled a cardboard box from under the bed.

"This was his stuff," she said. She gave him an odd look. "I expect it's all right for you to see. No-one ever visited him, except a man from the British Legion regular as clockwork every Christmas, God bless them. They've asked for his medals, you know. But I expect it's all right for you to have a look. If it's a project."

Johnny peered into the box while the nurse bustled around the room.

There were a few odds and ends—a pipe, a tobacco tin, a huge old penknife. There was a scrapbook, full of sepia postcards of flowers and fields of cabbages and simpering French ladies dressed in what someone must once have thought was a very daring way. Yellowing newspaper cuttings were stuck between the pages. And there was a small wooden box lined with toilet paper and containing several medals.

And there was a photograph of the Blackbury Pals, just like the one in the old newspaper.

Johnny lifted it out very carefully, and turned it over. It crackled.

Someone had written, in violet ink, a long time ago, the words: *Old Comrades!!! We're the Boys, Kaiser Bill! If You Know A Better 'ole, Go To IT!!* And there were thirty signatures underneath.

Beside twenty-nine of the signatures, in pencil, someone had made a small cross.

"They all signed it," he said, quietly. "He must have got a copy from the paper, and they all signed it."

"What was that, dear?"

"This photo."

"Oh, yes. He showed it to me once. That was him in the war, you know."

Johnny turned it over again and found Atkins, T. He looked a bit like Bigmac, with jughandle ears and a second-hand haircut. He was grinning. They all were. All the same kind of grin.

"He used to talk about them a lot," said the nurse.

"Yes."

"His funeral's on Monday. At the crem. One of us always goes, you know. Well, you have to, don't you? It's only right."

He dreamed, on Saturday night . . .

He dreamed of Rod Serling walking along Blackbury High Street, but as he was trying to speak impressively to the camera, Bigmac, Yoless and Wobbler started to peer over his shoulder and say things like, "What's this book about, then?" and "Turn over the page, I've read this bit" . . .

He dreamed of thumbs . . .

And woke up, and stared at the ceiling. He still hadn't replaced the bits of cotton that held up the plastic model of the Space Shuttle. It was forever doing a nosedive.

He was pretty sure other kids didn't have lives like this. It just kept on happening. Just when he thought he'd got a grip on the world, and saw how it all worked, it sprang something new on him, and what he thought was the whole thing, ticking away nicely, turned out to be just some kind of joke.

His grandad had mumbled a very odd message when Johnny had arrived home. As far as he could understand, Wobbler or someone had been making odd phone calls. His grandad had also muttered something about conjuring tricks.

He looked at his clock radio. It said 2.45. There was no chance of going back to sleep. He tried Radio Blackbury.

"—yowsahyowsahyowsah! And the next caller on Uncle Mad Jim's bodaaaacious Problem Corner iiiissss—"

Johnny froze. He had a feeling . . .

"William Stickers, Mad Jim."

"Hi, Bill. You sound a bit depressed, to *me*."

"It's worse than that. I'm dead, Jim."

"Wow! I can see that could be a real *downer*, Bill. Care to tell us about it?"

"You sound very understanding, comrade. Well . . ."

Of course he's understanding, thought Johnny as he struggled into his dressing gown. Everyone phones up Mad Jim in the middle of the night. Last week he talked for twenty minutes to a lady who thought she was a roll of wallpaper. You sound totally sane compared to most of them.

He snatched up his Walkman and switched on its radio so that he could go on listening as he ran down the stairs and out into the night.

"—and now I just heard there isn't even ANY *Soviet Union any more. What happened?"*

"Seems to me you haven't been keeping up with current events, Bill."

"I thought I explained about that."

"Oh, sure. You said. You've been dead. But you're alive again, right?" Mad Jim's voice had that little chuckle in it that it always got when he'd found a real dingdong on the line and could picture all his insomniac listeners turning up the volume.

"No. Still dead. It's not something you get better from, Jim. Now—"

Johnny pattered around the corner and sped along John Lennon Avenue.

Mad Jim was saying, in his special dealing-with-loonies velvet voice: "So tell us all out here in the land of the living, Bill—what's it *like*, being dead?"

"Like? LIKE? It is extremely DULL."

"I'm sure everyone out there would like to know, Bill . . . are there angels?"

Johnny groaned as he turned the corner into Eden Road.

"Angels? Certainly not!"

Johnny scurried past the silent houses and dodged between the bollards into Woodville Road.

"Oh, *dear*," said Mad Jim in his headset. "I hope there aren't any naughty men with pitchforks, then?"

"What on earth are you blathering about, man? There's just me and old Tom Bowler and Sylvia Liberty and all the rest of them—"

Johnny lost the thread of things when a sticking-out piece of laurel hedge knocked his headset off. When he managed to put it back on, it turned out that William Stickers had been invited to request a record.

"Don't think I know 'The Red Flag,' Bill. Who's it by?"

"It's the Internationale! The song of the downtrodden masses!"

"Doesn't fire a neuron, Bill. But for you and all the other dead people out there everywhere, tonight," the change in Mad Jim's tone suggested that William Stickers had been cut off, "and we're all dead sooner or later, ain't that the truth, here's one from the vaults by Michael Jackson . . . 'Thriller'—"

The streetlamp by the phone box was alight. And the little pool of light was all there was to see, unless you were Johnny . . .

The dead had spilled out on to the road. They'd managed to drag the radio with them. Quite a few of them were watching the Alderman.

"This is how you have to do it, apparently," he said, moonwalking backwards across the frosty street. "Johnny showed me."

"It is certainly a very interesting syncopated rhythm," said Mrs. Liberty. "Like this, you say?"

The ghostly wax cherries on her hat bounced up and down as she twirled.

"That's right. And apparently you spin around with your arms out and shout *'ow!,'* " said the Alderman, demonstrating.

Oh no, thought Johnny, hurrying towards them. On top of everything else, Michael Jackson's going to *sue* me—

"Get down and—what was it the man on the wireless said?" said the Alderman.

"Bogey, I believe."

They weren't actually very good at it, but they made up for being eighty years behind the times by sheer enthusiasm.

In fact, it was a party.

Johnny stuck his hands on his hips.

"You shouldn't be doing this!"

"Why not?" said a dancing dead.

"It's the middle of the night!"

"Well? We don't sleep!"

"I mean, what would your . . . your descendants think if they could see you acting like this?"

"Serve them right for not visiting us!"

"We're making carpets!" shouted Mrs. Liberty.

"Cutting a rung," corrected one of the dead.

"A rug," said the Alderman, slowing down a bit. "A rug. Cutting a rug. That's what Mr. Benbow, who died in nineteen thirty-one, says it is called. Getting down and bogeying."

"It's been like this all evening," said Mr. Vicenti. He was sitting on the pavement. In fact, he was sitting about half a metre *above* the pavement. "We've found some very interesting stations. What exactly *is* a DJ?"

"A disc jockey," said Johnny, giving up and sitting down. "He plays the discs and stuff."

"Is it some kind of punishment?"

"Quite a lot of people like to do it."

"How very strange. They are not mentally ill, or anything?"

The song finished. The dancers stopped twirling, but slowly and with great reluctance.

Mrs. Liberty pushed her hat back. It had tipped over her eyes.

"That was extremely enjoyable," she said. "Mr. Fletcher! Be so good as to instruct the man on the wireless to play something more!"

Interested despite himself, Johnny padded over to the phone box. Mr. Fletcher was actually kneeling down with his hands *inside* the telephone. A couple of other dead people were watching him. One of them was William Stickers, who didn't look very happy. The other was an old man with a mass of white hair in that dandelion-clock style known as Mad Scientist Afro.

"Oh, it's you," said William Stickers. "Call this a world, do you?"

"Me?" said Johnny. "I don't call it anything."

"Was that man on the radio making *fun* of me, do you think?"

"Oh, no," said Johnny, crossing his fingers.

"Mr. Sticker iz annoyed because he telephoned Moscow," said the white-haired man. "They said they've had enough revolutions to be going on wiz, but vould like some soap."

"They're nothing but dirty capitalists!" said William Stickers.

"But at least they want to be *clean* capitalists," said Mr. Fletcher. "Where shall we try next?"

"Don't you have to put money in?" said Johnny.

Mr. Fletcher laughed.

"I don't zink we've met," said the white-haired man, extending a slightly transparent hand. "Solomon Einstein (1869–1932)."

"Like Albert Einstein?" said Johnny.

"He vas my distant cousin," said Solomon Einstein. "Relatively speaking. Haha."

Johnny got the impression Mr. Einstein had said that line a million times, and still wasn't tired of it.

"Who're you ringing up?" said Johnny.

"We're just having a look at the world," said Mr. Fletcher. "What are those things that go round and round in the sky?"

"I don't know. Frisbees?"

"Mr. Vicenti just remembers them. They go round and round the world."

"Oh. You mean satellites?"

"Whee!"

"But how do you know how to—"

"I can't explain. Things are a lot simpler, I think. I can see it all laid out."

"All of what?"

"All the cables, all the . . . the satellites . . . Not having a body makes them a lot easier to use, too."

"What do you mean?"

"For one thing, you don't have to stay in one place."

"But I thought you—"

Mr. Fletcher vanished. He reappeared a few seconds later.

"Amazing things," he said. "My word, but we shall have fun."

"I don't underst—"

"Johnny?"

It was Mr. Vicenti.

Someone living had managed to get through to Mad Jim. The

dead, with much laughter, were trying to dance to a Country-and-Western number.

"What's going *on*?" said Johnny. "You said you couldn't leave the cemetery!"

"No-one has explained this to you? They do not teach you in schools?"

"Well, we don't get lessons in dealing with ghos— Sorry. Sorry. With dead people, I mean."

"We're not ghosts, Johnny. A ghost is a very sad thing. Oh, dear. It's hard to explain things to the living. *I* was alive once, and I know what I'm talking about."

Dead Mr. Vicenti looked at Johnny's blank face.

"We're . . . something else," he said. "But now you see us and hear us, you're making us free. You're giving us what we don't have."

"What's that?"

"I can't explain. But while you're thinking of us, we're free."

"My head doesn't have to spin round and round, does it?"

"That sounds like a good trick. Can you make it do that?"

"No."

"Then it won't."

"Only I'm a bit worried I'm dabblin' with the occult."

It seemed daft to say it, to Mr. Vicenti in his pinstripe trousers and little black tie and fresh ghostly carnation every day. Or Mrs. Liberty. Or the big bearded shape of William Stickers, who would have been Karl Marx if Karl Marx hadn't been Karl Marx first.

"Dear me, I hope you're not dabbling with the occult," said Mr. Vicenti. "Father Kearny (1891–1949) wouldn't like that at all."

"Who's Father Kearny?"

"A few moments ago he was dancing with Mrs. Liberty. Oh dear. We do mix things up, don't we?"

"Send him away."

Johnny turned.

One of the dead was still in the cemetery. He was standing right up against the railings, clasping them like a prisoner might hold the bars of his cell. He didn't look a lot different to Mr. Vicenti, except that he had a pair of glasses. It was amazing that they weren't melting; he had the strongest stare Johnny had ever seen. He seemed to be glaring at Johnny's left ear.

"Who's that?" he said.

"Mr. Grimm," said Mr. Vicenti, without looking around.

"Oh, yes. I couldn't find anything about him in the paper."

"I'm not surprised," said Mr. Vicenti, in a low and level voice. "In those days, there were things they didn't put in."

"You go away, boy. You're meddling with things you don't understand," said Mr. Grimm. "You're imperilling your immortal soul. And theirs. You go away, you bad boy."

Johnny stared. Then he looked back at the street, at the dancers, and the scientists around the telephone box. A bit further along there was Stanley Roundway, in shorts that came down to his knees, showing a group of somewhat older dead how to play football. He had "L" and "R" stencilled on his football boots.

Mr. Vicenti was staring straight ahead.

"Um—" said Johnny.

"I can't help you there," said Mr. Vicenti. "That sort of thing is up to you."

He must have walked home. He didn't really remember. But he woke up in bed.

Johnny wondered what the dead did on Sundays. Blackbury on Sundays went through some sort of boredom barrier and out the other side.

Most people did what people traditionally do on Sundays, which was dress up neatly and get in the car and go for family worship at the MegasuperSaver Garden Centre, just outside the town. There was a kind of tide of potted plants that were brought back to get killed off by the central heating in time for next week's visit.

And the mall was locked up. There wasn't even anywhere to hang around.

"The point about being dead in this town," said Wobbler, as they mooched along the towpath, "is that it's probably hard to tell the difference."

"Did anyone hear the radio last night?" said Johnny.

No-one had. He felt a bit relieved.

"When I grow up," said Wobbler, "I'm going to be out of here like a shot. Just you watch. That's what this place is. It's a place to come from. It's not a place to stay."

"Where're you going to go, then?" said Johnny.

"There's a huge big world out there!" said Wobbler. "Mountains! America! Australia! Tons of places!"

"You told me the other day you'd probably get a job working at your uncle's place over on the trading estate," said Bigmac.

"Yes . . . well . . . I mean, all those places'll be there, won't they, for when I get time to go," said Wobbler.

"I thought you were going to be a big man in computers," said Yo-less.

"I could be. I could be. If I *wanted*."

"If there's a miracle and you pass Maths and English, you mean," said Bigmac.

"I'm just more practically gifted," said Wobbler.

"You mean you just press keys until something happens."

"Well? Often things *do* happen."

"*I'm* going to join the Army," said Bigmac. "The SAS."

"Huh. The flat feet and the asthma will be a big help there, then," said Wobbler. "I can just see they'll want you to limp out and wheeze on terrorists."

"I'm pretty certain I want to get a law degree and a medical degree," said Yo-less, to keep the peace.

"That's good. That way they won't be able to sue you if you chop the wrong bits off," said Bigmac.

No-one really lost their temper. This was all part of hanging around.

"What about you?" said Wobbler. "What do you want to be?"

"Dunno," said Johnny.

"Didn't you go to the careers evening last week?"

Johnny nodded. It had been full of Great Futures. There was a Great Future in retail marketing. There was a Great Future in wholesale distribution. There was a Great Future in the armed forces, although probably not for Bigmac, who'd been allowed to hold a machine gun and had dropped it on his foot. But Johnny couldn't find a Great Future with any future in it.

"What I want to be," he said, "is something they haven't got a name for yet."

"Oh, yeah?" said Wobbler. "Like, in two years' time someone's going to invent the Vurglesplat, and when they start looking around for Vurglesplat operators, you're going to be first in the queue, right?"

They went through the cemetery. The others, without saying anything, bunched up slightly. But there were no dead people around.

"You can't just hang around waiting for Great Futures, that's the point," Johnny murmured.

"Hey," said Yo-less, in a dismally jolly voice, "my mum says why don't you guys come to church tonight?"

"It won't work," said Wobbler, after a while. "You say that every week."

"She says it'd be good for you. Especially Simon."

"Simon?" said Wobbler.

"Me," said Bigmac.

"She says you need looking after," said Yo-less.

"I didn't know you were called Simon," said Wobbler.

Bigmac sighed. He had "Blackbury Skins" on his T-shirt, a suede haircut, great big boots, great big braces and LOVE and HAT in Biro on his knuckles,[1] but for some reason Yo-less's mum thought he needed a proper home. Bigmac lived in dread that Bazza and Skazz, the only other Skins in Blackbury, would find out and confiscate his official braces.

"She said you're all growing up heathens," said Yo-less.

"Well, I'm going to a funeral at the crem tomorrow," said Johnny. "That's almost church."

"Anyone important?" said Wobbler.

"I'm not sure," said Johnny.

Johnny was amazed that so many people had come to Thomas Atkins's funeral, but that was because they'd really come to the one before it. All there was for Atkins's was himself and a stiff-looking old man in a blazer from the British Legion and the nurse from Sunshine Acres. And the vicar, who did his best, but had never met Tommy Atkins so had to put together his sermon out of a sort of kit of Proper Things to Say. And then some recorded organ music. And that was it.

The chapel smelled of new wood and floor polish.

The three others kept looking at Johnny in an embarrassed way, as if they felt he shouldn't be there but didn't know exactly how to put it.

---

[1]The "E" kept rubbing off.

He heard a faint sound behind him, just as the recorded music started up.

He turned around, and there were the dead, seated in rows. The Alderman had taken his hat off and was sitting stiffly at attention. Even William Stickers had tried to look respectable. Solomon Einstein's hair stood out like a halo.

The nurse was talking to the man in the blazer. Johnny leaned back so that he could speak to Mr. Fletcher.

"Why are you here?" he whispered.

"It's allowed," said Mr. Fletcher. "We used to go to all the funerals in the cemetery. Help them settle in. Make them welcome. It's always a bit of a shock."

"Oh."

"And . . . seeing as you were here . . . we thought we'd see if we could make it. Mr. Vicenti said it was worth a try. We're getting better at it!"

The nurse handed Tommy Atkins's box to the British Legion man and walked out, waving at Johnny uncertainly as she went past. And then the vicar ushered the man through another door, giving Johnny another funny look.

Outside, the October sun was shining weakly, but it was managing to shine. Johnny went outside and waited.

Eventually the man came out, holding two boxes this time.

"Uh," said Johnny, standing up. "Um."

"Yes, lad? The lady from the Home said you're doing a project for school."

Doing a project. It was amazing. If Saddam Hussein had said he was doing a school project on Kuwait, he'd have found life a lot easier . . .

"Um, yes. Uh. Can I ask you some stuff?"

"Of course, yes." The man sat down heavily on one of the benches. He walked with a limp, and sat with one leg stretched out straight in front of him. Johnny was surprised to see that he was probably as old as Grandad, but he had that dried-out, suntanned look of a man who keeps himself fit and is probably still going to be captain of the bowls club when he's eighty.

"Well . . . when Mr. Atkins said . . ." Johnny began. "I mean, he used to say that he was 'the one.' I know about the Blackbury Pals. I know they all got killed except him. But I don't think that's what he meant . . ."

"You know about the Pals, do you? How?"

"Read it in an old newspaper."

"Oh. But you don't know about Tommy Atkins?"

"Well, yes, he—"

"No, I mean *Tommy Atkins*. I meant, why he was so proud of the name. What the name *meant*?"

"I don't understand that," said Johnny.

"What do they teach you in school these days?"

Johnny didn't answer. He could tell it wasn't really a question.

"You see—in the Great War, the First World War . . . when a new recruit joined the Army he had to fill in his pay book, yes? You know? Name and address and that sort of thing? And to help them do it, the Army did a kind of guide to how to fill it in, and on the guide, where it said Name, they put: Thomas Atkins. It was just a name. Just to show them that's where their name should be. Like: John Smith. But it . . . well, it became a sort of joke. Tommy Atkins came to mean the average soldier—"

"Like The Man In The Street?"

"Yes . . . very much like that. It was a nickname for a soldier, I do know that. Tommy Atkins—the British Tommy."

"So . . . in a way . . . *all* soldiers were Tommy Atkins?"

"Yes. I suppose you could put it like that. Of course, that's a rather fanciful way of—"

"But he was a real person. He smoked a pipe and everything."

"Well, I suppose the Army used it because they thought it was a common sort of name. So there was bound to be a *real* Tommy Atkins somewhere. I know he was very proud of his name. I do know that."

"Was he the last man alive who fought in the war?"

"Oh, no. Good heavens, no. But he was the last one from around here, that's for certain. The last of the Pals."

Johnny felt a change in the air.

"He was a strange old boy. I used to go and see him every year at—"

There was a noise that might be made if a handful of silence was stretched thin and then plucked, like a guitar string.

Johnny looked around. Now there were three people sitting on the bench.

Tommy Atkins had his peaked hat on his knees. The uniform didn't really fit. He was still an old man, so his skinny neck stuck out of his collar like a tortoise's. He had an old-fashioned sort of face—one designed to wear a cloth cap and work in the rubber boot factory. He saw Johnny staring at him, and winked, and gave him the thumbs-up sign. Then he went back to gazing intently at the road leading into the car park.

Behind Johnny, the dead filed quietly out of the building, the older ones coming through the wall, the younger ones still using the door out of habit. They didn't say anything. They just stood and looked expectantly towards the main road.

Where, marching *through* the cars, were the Blackbury Pals.

6

The Pals swung up the road, keeping perfectly in step.

None of them were old. They all looked like their photograph.

But then, Tommy Atkins didn't look old any more. It was a young man who got to his feet, marched out into the car park, turned, and saluted Johnny and the dead.

Then, as the Pals strode past, he stepped neatly into the gap they'd left for him. All thirty men wheeled about, and marched away.

The dead streamed after them. They appeared to walk slowly while at the same time moved very fast, so that, in a few seconds, the car park was empty even of its ghosts.

"He's going back to France," said Johnny. Suddenly, he felt quite cheerful, even though he could feel the tears running down his face.

The British Legion man, who had been talking, stopped.

"What?" he said.

"Tommy Atkins. He's going back."

"How did you know that?"

Johnny realized he'd been talking aloud.

"Uh—"

The British Legion man relaxed.

"I expect the lady from the Home told you, did she? He mentioned it in his will. Would you like a handkerchief?"

"Uh. No. I'm all right," said Johnny. "Yes. She told me."

"Yes, we're taking him back this week. He gave us a map reference. Very precise, too." The man patted the second box he'd been given which, Johnny suddenly realized, probably contained all that was left in this world of Atkins, T., apart from a few medals and some faded photographs.

"What will you have to do?" he said.

"Just scatter his ashes. We'll have a little ceremony."

"Where . . . the Pals died?"

"That's right. He was always talking about them, I do know that."

"Sir?"

The man looked up.

"Yes?"

"My name's John Maxwell. What's yours?"

"Atterbury. Ronald Atterbury."

He extended a hand. They shook hands, solemnly.

"Are you Arthur Maxwell's grandson? He used to work for me at the boot factory."

"Yes. Sir?"

"Yes?"

Johnny knew what the answer was going to be. He could feel it looming ahead of him. But you had to ask the question, so that the answer could exist. He took a deep breath.

"Are you related to Sergeant Atterbury? He was one of the Pals."

"He was my father."

"Oh."

"I never saw him. He married my mother before he went off to the war. There was a lot of that sort of thing. There always is. Excuse me, young man, but shouldn't you be in school?"

"No," said Johnny.

"Really?"

"I should be here. I'm absolutely sure about that," said Johnny. "But I'd better be getting to school, anyway. Thanks for talking to me."

"I hope you haven't missed any important lessons."

"History."

"That's very important."

"Can I ask you one more question?"

"Yes?"

"Tommy Atkins's medals. Were they for anything special?"

"They were campaign medals. Soldiers got them, really, for just staying alive. And for being there. He went all the way through the war, you know. Right to the end. Didn't even get wounded."

Johnny walked back down the drive barely noticing the world around him. Something important had happened, and he alone of all the living had seen it, and it was *right*.

Getting medals for being there was right, too. Sometimes being there was all you could do.

He looked back when he reached the road. Mr. Atterbury was still sitting on the bench with the two boxes beside him, staring at the trees as if he'd never seen them before. Just staring, as if he could see right through them, all the way to France.

Johnny hesitated, and then started back.

"No," said Mr. Vicenti, right behind him.

He'd been waiting by the bus shelter. Haunting it, almost.

"I was only going to—"

"Yes, you were," said Mr. Vicenti. "And what would you say? That you'd seen them? What good would that do? Perhaps he's seeing them too, inside his head."

"Well—"

"It wouldn't work."

"But if I—"

"If you did something like that a few hundred years ago you'd probably be hung for witchcraft. Last century they'd lock you up. I don't know what they'd do now."

Johnny relaxed a little. The urge to run back up the driveway had faded.

"Put me on television, I expect," he said, walking along the road.

"Well, we don't want that," said Mr. Vicenti. He walked too, although his feet didn't always meet the ground.

"It's just that if I could make people see that—"

"Maybe," said Mr. Vicenti. "But making people see anything is a long, hard job—excuse me . . ."

He jerked his shoulder a bit, like a man trying to find a difficult itch, and then pulled a pair of doves from inside his jacket.

"They breed in there, I'm sure," he said, watching them fly away and disappear. "What are you going to do now?"

"School. And don't say it's very important."

"I said nothing."

They reached the entrance to the cemetery. Johnny could just see the big sign on the old factory site next door, its blue sky glowing again the dustier blue-grey of the real sky.

"They'll start taking us out the day after tomorrow," said Mr. Vicenti.

"I'm sorry. Like I said, I wish there was something I could do."

"You may have done it already."

Johnny sighed.

"If I ask you what you mean, you'll say it's hard to explain, right?"

"I think so. Come. You might enjoy this."

There wasn't even a dead soul in the cemetery. Even the rook had gone, unless it was a crow.

But there was a lot of noise coming from the canal.

The dead were swimming. Well, some of them were. Mrs. Liberty was. She was wearing a long swimming costume that reached from neck to knees, but she still kept her hat on.

The Alderman had stripped off his long robe and chain, and was sitting on the canal bank in his shirtsleeves and some braces that could have moored a ship. Johnny wondered how the dead changed clothes, or felt the heat, but he supposed it was all habit. If you thought your shirt was off, there it was . . . off.

As for swimming . . . there was no splash when they dived, just the faintest of shimmers, that spread out like ripples and vanished very quickly. And when they surfaced they didn't look wet. It dawned on Johnny that when a ghost (he had to use that word in his head) jumped into the water, the ghost didn't get wet, the water got ghostly.

Not all of them were having fun, though. At least, not the usual sort. Mr. Fletcher and Solomon Einstein and a few others were clustered around one of the dumped televisions.

"What are they doing?" said Johnny.

"Trying to make it work," said Mr. Vicenti.

Johnny laughed. The screen had been smashed. Rain had dripped into the case for years. There was even grass growing out of it.

"That'll never—" he began.

There was a crackle. A picture formed in the air, on a *screen that wasn't there any more*.

Mr. Fletcher stood up and solemnly shook Solomon Einstein's hand.

"Another successful marriage of advanced theoretics and practical know-how, Mr. Einstein."

"A shtep in the right direction, Mr. Fletcher."

Johnny stared at the flickering images. The picture was in beautiful colour.

Enlightenment dawned.

"It's the *ghost* of the television?" he said.

"Vot a clever boy!" said Solomon Einstein.

"But with *improvements*," said Mr. Fletcher.

Johnny peered inside the case. It was full of old leaves and stained, twisted metal. But over the top of it, shimmering gently, was the pearly outline of the ghost of the machine, purring away without electricity. At least, apparently without electricity. Who knew where the electricity went when the light was switched off?

"Oh, wow."

He stood up and pointed to the scummy green surface of the canal.

"Somewhere down there there's an old Ford Capri," he said. "Wobbler said he saw some men dump it in there once."

"I shall see to it directly," said Mr. Fletcher. "The internal combustion engine certainly could do with some improvements."

"But . . . look . . . machines aren't alive, so how can they have ghosts?"

"But zey have *existence*," said Einstein. "From moment to moment. Zo, we find the right moment, yes?"

"Sounds a bit occult," said Johnny.

"No! It is *physics*! It is *beyond* physics. It is—" he waved both hands excitedly, "*meta*physics. From the Greek *meta*, meaning 'beyond,' and *physika*, meaning . . . er . . ."

"Physics," said Mr. Vicenti.

"Exactly!"

"Nothing ever finishes. Nothing's ever really over."

It was Johnny who said that. He was surprised at himself.

"Correct! Are you a physicist?"

"Me?" said Johnny. "I don't know anything about science!"

"Marvellous! Ideal qualification!" said Einstein.

"What?"

"Ignorance is very important! It is an absolutely *essential* step in the learning process!"

Mr. Fletcher twiddled the ghost of a tuning knob.

"Well, we're all right now," he said, watching a programme in what sounded like Spanish. "Over here, everyone!"

"How very interesting," said Mrs. Liberty, dressing herself in the blink of an eye. "Miniature cinematography?"

When Johnny left they were all in front of the busted television, arguing over what to watch . . .

Except for Mr. Grimm. He stood a little apart, hands folded obediently, watching them.

"There will be trouble because of this," he said. "This is disobedience. Meddling with the physical."

He had a small moustache as well as glasses and, in daylight, Johnny saw that the lenses were those thick ones that seem to hide the person's eyes.

"There'll be trouble," he said again. "And it will be *your* fault, John Maxwell. You're getting them excited. Is this any way for the dead to behave?"

Two invisible eyes followed him.

"Mr. Grimm?" said Johnny.

"Yes?"

"Who are you?"

"That's none of your business."

"No, but it's just that everyone else always talks about—"

"*I* happen to believe in decency. I believe life should be taken seriously. There is a proper way to conduct oneself. *I* certainly don't intend to indulge in this foolish behaviour."

"I didn't mean to—"

Mr. Grimm turned around and walked stiffly to his little stone under the trees. He sat down with his arms folded, and glared at Johnny.

"No good will come of it," he said.

He said he'd been to see a specialist. That was always a good one. Teachers generally didn't ask any more questions.

At break, Wobbler had News.

"My mum said there's going to be a big meeting about it in the Civic Centre tonight, with television there and everything."

"It won't do any good," said Yo-less. "It's been going on for ages. It's too late. There's been all kinds of inquiries and stuff."

"I asked my mum about building things on old graveyards and she says they have to get a vicar in to desecrate the site first," said Wobbler. "That should be worth seeing."

"It's *de-consecrate*," said Yo-less. "Desecrate is all to do with sacrificing goats and things."

Wobbler looked wistful.

"I suppose there's no chance—"

"None!"

"I'm going to go along tonight," said Johnny. "And you lot ought to come."

"It won't do any good," said Yo-less.

"Yes it will," said Johnny.

"Look, the place has still been sold," said Yo-less. "I know you're sort of wound up about it, but it's all over."

"Going along will still do some good." He knew it, in the same way he'd known the Pals were important. Not for *reasons*. Just because it was.

"Will there be any . . . freak winds?" said Bigmac.

"How do *I* know? Shouldn't think so. They're all watching television."

The other three exchanged glances.

"The *dead* are watching television?" said Wobbler.

"That's right. And I know you're all trying to think of funny things to say. Just don't say them. They're watching television. They've made an old TV set work."

"Well, I suppose it passes the time," said Wobbler.

"I don't think they experience time like we do," said Johnny.

Yo-less slid down off the wall.

"Talking of time," he said, "I'm not sure tomorrow would be a good time to go hanging around cemeteries."

"Why not?" said Bigmac.

"You know what day it is?"

"Tuesday," said Johnny.

"Halloween," said Wobbler. "You're all coming to my party, remember?"

"Whoops," said Bigmac.

"The principle is astonishingly simple," said Mr. Fletcher. "A tiny point of light! That's all it is! Whizzing backwards and forwards inside a glass bottle. Basically it's a thermionic valve. *Much* easier to control than sound waves—"

"Excuse me," said Mrs. Liberty. "When you stand in front of the screen you make the picture go blurred."

"Sorry." Mr. Fletcher went back and sat down. "What's happening now?"

The dead were ranged in rows, fascinated.

"Mr. McKenzie has told Dawn that Janine can't go to Doraleen's party," said William Stickers, without taking his eyes off the screen.

"I must say," said the Alderman, "I thought Australia was a bit different. More kangaroos and fewer young women in unsuitable clothing."

"I'm quite happy with the young women," said William Stickers.

"Mr. Stickers! For shame! You're *dead*!"

"But I have a very good memory, Mrs. Liberty."

"Oh. Is it over?" said Solomon Einstein, as the credits rolled up the screen and the *Cobbers* theme tune rolled over the canal. "But there iss the mystery of who took the money from Mick's coat!"

"The man in the television just said there will be another performance tomorrow," said Mrs. Liberty. "We must be sure not to miss it."

"It is getting dark," said Mr. Vicenti, from the back of the group. "Time we were getting back."

The dead looked across at the cemetery.

"If we want to go, that is," he added. He was smiling faintly.

The dead were silent. Then the Alderman said, "Well, I'm blowed if I'm going back in there."

"Thomas Bowler!" snapped Mrs. Liberty.

"Well, if a man can't swear when he's dead, it's a poor lookout. Blowed, blowed, blowed. And damn," said the Alderman. "I mean, look, will you? There's radio and television and all sorts. There's things going on! I don't see why we should go back in there. It's dull. No way."

"No way?"

William Stickers nudged Mrs. Liberty. "That's Australian for 'certainly not,' " he whispered.

"But staying where we're put is *proper*," said Mrs. Liberty. "We have to stay, where we've been *put*—"

"Ahem."

It was Mr. Grimm. The dead looked at their feet.

"I entirely agree," he said.

"Oh. Hello, Eric," said the Alderman coldly.

Eric Grimm folded his hands on his chest and beamed at them. This worried even the dead. The thickness of his glasses somehow made his eyes get lost, so that all that was on the other side of them was pinkness.

"Will you listen to what you are saying?" he said.

"You're *dead*. Act your age. It's *over*." He waved a finger. "You know what will happen if you leave. You know what will happen if you're too long away. It's dreadful to think about, isn't it? You're letting this idiot child get you all upset."

The dead tried not to meet his gaze. When you were dead, there were some things that you knew, in the same way that when you were alive you knew about breathing. It was that *a day would come*. And you had to be prepared. There'd be a final sunrise, and you had to face it, and be ready.

A final sunrise. The day of judgement. It could be any day. You had to be ready.

"Not gallivanting off apeing your juniors," said Mr. Grimm, who seemed to read their thoughts. "We're dead. So we wait here, like decent people. Not go dabbling in the Ordinary."

The dead shuffled their feet.

"Well, I've waited eighty years," said the Alderman, at last. "If it happens tonight, it happens. I'm going to go and have a look around. Anyone else coming?"

"Yes. Me," said William Stickers, standing up.

"Anyone else?"

About half the dead stood up. A few more looked around and decided to join them. There was something about Mr. Grimm that made you want to be on the other side.

"You will get lost!" warned Mr. Grimm. "Something will go wrong, you know! And then you'll be wandering around forever, and you'll . . . forget."

"I've got descendants out there," said the Alderman.

"We've all got descendants," said Mrs. Liberty.

"And we know what the rules are. And so do you." She looked embarrassed.

There *were* rules. You were never told them, any more than you were told that things dropped when you let go of them. They were just *there*.

But the Alderman was unbudgeable in a sullen kind of way.

"At least I'm going to have a look around. Check out my old haunts," he muttered.

"Haunts?" said William Stickers.

"Check out?" said Mrs. Liberty.

"That's modern talk for—" William Stickers began.

"I'm *sure* I *don't* want to know!" Mrs. Liberty stood up. "The very idea!"

"There's a world out there, and we helped to make it, and now I want to find out what it's like," said the Alderman sulkily.

"Besides," said Mr. Vicenti, "if we stick together no-one will forget who they are, and we'll all go further."

Mrs. Liberty shook her head.

"Well, if you *insist* on going, then I suppose someone with some Sense should accompany you," she said.

The dead marched off in, as it were, a body, down the canal path and towards to the town centre. That left only Mr. Einstein and Mr. Fletcher, still sitting happily beside their television.

"What's got into them?" said Mr. Fletcher. "They're acting almost *alive*."

"It is disgusting," said Mr. Grimm, but somehow in a triumphant tone of voice, as if seeing people acting badly was very satisfying.

"Solomon here says that space is a delusion," said Mr. Fletcher. "Therefore, it is *impossible* to go anywhere. Or to be anywhere, either."

Einstein spat on his hands and tried to smooth down his hair.

"On ze other hand—" he said, "there *was* a nice little pub in Cable Street."

"You wouldn't get a drink, Solly," said Mr. Fletcher. "They don't serve spirits."

"I used to like it in there," said Einstein, wistfully. "After a hard day stuffing foxes, it wass nice to relax of an evenink."

"You *did* say space was a delusion," said Mr. Fletcher. "Anyway, I thought we were going to do some more work on the television. You said there was no theoretical reason why we shouldn't be able to make—"

"I zink," said Mr. Einstein carefully, "I would like to fool myself a little."

And then there was only Mr. Grimm.

He turned back, still smiling in a glassy kind of way, and settled down and waited for them to return.

7

The Frank W. Arnold Civic Centre meeting room was about half full.

It smelled of chlorine from the swimming baths, and of dust, and floor polish, and wooden chairs. Occasionally people would wander in thinking the meeting was the AGM of the bowls club, and then try to wander out again, pushing on the bar on the door marked "Pull" and then glaring at it as if only an idiot would put "Pull" on a door you pulled. The speakers spent a lot of the time asking people at the back if they could hear, and then holding the microphone too close to the loudspeakers, and then someone tried to make the PA system work properly, and blew a fuse, and went to find the caretaker, pushing on the door for a while like a hamster trying to find the way out of its treadmill.

In fact, it was like every other public meeting Johnny had ever attended. Probably on Jupiter seven-legged aliens had meetings in icy halls smelling of chlorine, he thought, with the microphones howling, and creatures frantically ▼Σσing at doors clearly marked "βΓπ."

There were one or two of his teachers in the audience. That was amazing. You never really thought of them doing anything after school. You never knew about people, like you never knew how deep a pond was because all you saw was the top. And he recognized one or two people he'd seen in the cemetery walking their dogs or just sitting on the seats. They looked out of place.

There were a couple of people from United Amalagamated Consolidated Holdings, and a man from the Council planning office, and the chairman of Blackbury Municipal Authority, who looked a lot like Mrs. Liberty and turned out to be a Miss Liberty. (Johnny wondered if Mrs. Liberty was her great-grandmother or something, but it would be hard to ask; you couldn't very well say, "Hey, you look like this dead lady, are you related?")

They didn't look out of place. They looked as though they were used to platforms.

Johnny found he couldn't listen to them properly. The pock-pock from the squash court on the other side of the wall punctuated the sentences like a rain of full stops, and the rattling of the door bar was a semi-colon.

"—better. Future. For the young; people of our city—"

Most of the people in the audience were middle aged. They listened to all the speakers very intently.

"—assure the good. People. of Blackbury; that. We. At United Consolidated; Holdings value. Public. Opinion most highly: and have no intention. Of—"

Words poured out. He could feel them filling up the hall.

And afterwards—he told himself, in the privacy of his own head—afterwards, the day after tomorrow, the cemetery would be shut, no matter what anyone said. It'd vanished into the past just like the old boot factory. And then the past would be rolled up and tucked away in old newspapers, just like the Pals. Unless someone did something.

Life was difficult enough already. Let someone else say something.

"—not even a *particularly* fine example. Of Edwardian funereal sculpture. With—"

The words would fill up the hall until they were higher than people's heads. They were smooth, soothing words. Soon they'd close over the top of all the trilbies and woolly hats, and everyone would be sitting there like sea anemones.

They'd come here with things to say, even if they didn't know how to say them.

The thing was to keep your head down.

But if you *did* keep your head down, you'd drown in other people's words.

"—fully taken into. Account; at every stage of the planning process—"

Johnny stood up, because it was that or drowning. He felt his head break through the tide of words, and he breathed in. And then out.

"Excuse me, please?" he said.

* * *

The White Swan in Cable Street, known for years as The Dirty Duck, was a traditional English pub, with a "Nuke the Gook" video machine that Shakespeare himself might have played. It was crowded, and noisy with electronic explosions and the jukebox.

In one corner, wedged between the video quiz game and the wall, in a black felt hat, nursing half a pint of Guinness, was mad old Mrs. Tachyon.

Mad is a word used about people who've either got no senses or several more than most other people.

Mrs. Tachyon was the only one who noticed the drop in temperature. She looked up, and grinned a one-toothed grin.

The patch of chilly air drifted across the crowded room until it came up against the jukebox. Frost steamed off it for a second.

The tune changed.

" 'Roses are Blooming in Piccardy,' " said Mrs. Tachyon happily. "Yes!"

She watched carefully as people clustered around the machine and started to thump it. Then they pulled the plug, which made no difference.

The barmaid screamed and dropped a tray of drinks when the games machine exploded and caught fire.

Then the lights fused.

A minute or two later, Mrs. Tachyon was left in the dark, listening to the barman cursing somewhere in a back room as fuses kept blowing.

It was quite pleasant, sitting in the warm glow of the melted machinery.

From the wreckage on the floor, the ghosts of two pints of beer detached themselves and floated across to the table.

"Cheers!" said Mrs. Tachyon.

The chairman of the Council looked over her glasses.

"Questions at the end, please."

Johnny wavered. But if he sat down, the words would close over his head again.

"When is the end, please?" he said.

Johnny felt everyone looking at him.

The chairman glanced at the other speakers. She had a habit, Johnny noticed, of closing her eyes when she started a sentence and opening them suddenly at the end, so that they'd leap out and surprise you.

"When *[close]* we've fully. Discussed. The situation. And then I will call for *[open!]* questions."

Johnny decided to swim for the shore.

"But I'll have to leave before the end," he said. "I have to be in bed by ten."

There was a general murmur of approval from the audience. It was clear that most of them approved of the idea of anyone under thirty being in bed by ten. It was almost true, anyway. He was generally in his room around ten, although there was no telling when the lights actually went off.

"Let the lad ask his question," said a voice from near the front.

"He's doing a project," said another voice. Johnny recognized Mr. Atterbury, sitting bolt upright.

"Oh . . . very well. What was it, young man?"

"Um." Johnny felt them all looking at him. "Well, the thing is . . . the thing I want to know *is* . . . is there anything that anyone can say here, tonight, that's going to make any difference?"

"That *[close]* hardly seems an appropriate sort of *[open!]* question," said the chairman severely.

"Seems damned good to me," said Mr. Atterbury. "Why doesn't the man from United Amalagamated Consolidated Holdings answer the boy? Just a simple answer would do."

The United man gave Johnny a frank, open smile.

"We shall, of course, take all views very *deeply* into consideration," he said. "And—"

"But there's a sign up saying that you're going to build anyway," said Johnny. "Only I don't think many people want the old cemetery built on. So you'll take the sign down, will you?"

"We have in fact bought the—"

"You paid fivepence," said Johnny. "I'll give you a pound."

People started to laugh.

"I've got a question too," said Yo-less, standing up.

The chairman, who had her mouth open, hesitated. Yo-less was beaming at her, defying her to tell *him* to sit down.

"We'll take the question from the other young man, the one in the shirt—no, not you, the—" she began.

"The black one," said Yo-less, helpfully. "Why did the Council sell the cemetery in the first place?"

The chairman brightened up at this one.

"I *[close]* think we have covered that very fully *[open!]*," she said. "The cost of upkeep—"

Bigmac nudged Johnny, pointed at a sheet of figures everyone had been given, and whispered in his ear.

"But I don't see how there's much upkeep in a cemetery," said Yo-less. "Sending someone in once or twice a year to cut the brambles down doesn't sound like much of a cost to me."

"We'd do it for nothing," said Johnny.

"Would we?" whispered Wobbler, who liked fresh air to be something that happened to other people, preferably a long way off.

People were turning round in their seats.

The chairman gave a loud sigh, to make it clear that Johnny was being just too stupid but that she was putting up with him nevertheless.

"The *fact*, young man, as I have explained time and again, is that it is simply too expensive to maintain a cemetery that is—"

As he listened, red with embarrassment, Johnny remembered about the chance to have another go. He could just put up with it and shut up, and for ever after he'd wonder what would have happened, and then when he died that angel—although, as things were going at the moment, angels were in short supply even after you were dead—would say, hey, would you have liked to have found out what happened? And he'd say yes, really, and the angel would send him back and maybe this *was*—

He pulled himself together.

"No," he said, "it isn't simply too expensive."

The woman stopped in mid-sentence.

"How dare you interrupt me!" she snapped.

Johnny ploughed on. "It says in your papers here that the cemetery makes a loss. But a cemetery can't make a loss. It's not like a business or something. It just *is*. My friend Bigmac here says what you're calling a loss is just the value of the land for building offices. It's the rates and taxes you'd get from United Amalagamated Consolidated Holdings. But the dead can't pay taxes so they're not worth anything."

The man from United Amalagamated Consolidated Holdings opened his mouth to say something, but the chairman stopped him.

"A democratically elected Council—" she began.

"I'd like to raise a few points concerning that," said Mr. Atterbury. "There are certain things about this sale which I should like to see more clearly explained in a democratic way."

"I've had a good look round the cemetery," said Johnny, plunging on. "I've been . . . doing a project. I've walked round it a lot. It's full of stuff. It doesn't matter that no-one in there is really famous. They were famous *here*. They lived and got on with things and died. They were *people*. It's wrong to think that the past is something that's just gone. It's still there. It's just that *you've* gone past. If you drive through a town, it's still there in the rear-view mirror. Time is a road, but it doesn't roll up behind you. Things aren't over just because they're *past*. Do you see that?"

People told one another that it was getting chilly for the time of year. Little points of coldness drifted around the town.

Screen K at the Blackbury Odeon was showing a 24-hour, non-stop Halloween Special, but people kept coming out. It was too cold in there, they said. And it was creepy. Armpit, the manager, who was one of Wobbler's mortal enemies, and who looked like two men in one dinner jacket, said it was *supposed* to be creepy. They said not *that* creepy. There were voices that you didn't exactly hear, and they—well, you kept getting the impression that people were sitting right beh—Well, let's go and get a burger. Somewhere brightly-lit.

Pretty soon there was hardly anyone in there at all except Mrs. Tachyon, who'd bought a ticket because it was somewhere in the warm, and spent most of the time asleep.

"Elm Street? Elm Street? Wasn't there an Elm Street down by Beech Lane?"

"I don't think it was this one. I don't remember this sort of thing going on."

She didn't mind the voices at all.

"Freddie. Now that's a NICE name."

They were company, in a way.

"And that's a nice jumper."

And a lot of people had left popcorn and things behind in their hurry to get out.

"But I don't think THAT'S very nice."

The next film was *Ghostbusters*, followed by *Wednesday of the Living Dead*.

It seemed to Mrs. Tachyon that the voices, which didn't exist anyway, had gone very quiet.

Everyone was staring at Johnny now.

"And . . . and," said Johnny, ". . . if we forget about them, we're just a lot of people living in . . . in buildings. We need them to tell us who we are. They built this city. They did all the daft human things that turn a lot of buildings into a place for people. It's wrong to throw all that away."

The chairman shuffled the papers in front of her.

"Nevertheless *[close]*, we have to deal with the *[open!]* present day," she said brusquely. "The dead are no longer here and I am afraid they do not vote."

"You're wrong. They are here and they have got a vote," said Johnny. "I've been working it out. In my head. It's called tradition. And they outvote us twenty to one."

Everyone went quiet. Nearly as quiet as the unseen audience in Screen K.

Then Mr. Atterbury started to clap. Someone else joined in—Johnny saw it was the nurse from Sunshine Acres. Pretty soon everyone was clapping, in a polite yet firm way.

Mr. Atterbury stood up again.

"Mr. Atterbury, sit down," said the chairman. "I am running this meeting, you know."

"I am afraid this does not appear to be the case," said Mr. Atterbury. "I'm standing up and I'm going to speak. The boy is right. Too much has been taken away, I do know that. You dug up the High Street. It had a lot of small shops. People lived there. Now it's all walkways and plastic signs and people are afraid of it at night. Afraid of the town where they live! I'd be ashamed of that, if I was you. And we had a coat of arms for the town, up on the Town Hall. Now we've got some kind of plastic logo thing. And you took the old allotments and built the Neil Armstrong Shopping Mall and all the little shops went out of business. And they were beautiful, those allotments."

"They were a mess!"

"Oh, yes. A beautiful mess. Home-made green-houses made of old window frames nailed together. Old men sitting out in front of their sheds in old chairs. Vegetables and dogs and children all over the place. I don't know where all those people went, do you? And then you knocked down a lot of houses and built the big tower block where no-one wants to live and named it after a crook."

"I didn't even live here in those days," said the chairman. "Besides, it's generally agreed that the Joshua N'Clement block was a . . . *misplaced* idea."

"A bad idea, you mean."

"Yes, if you must put it like that."

"So mistakes can be made, can they?"

"Nevertheless, the plain fact is that we have to build for the future—"

"I'm very glad to hear you say that, madam chairman, because I'm sure you'll agree that the most successful buildings have got very deep foundations."

There was another round of applause. The people on the platform looked at one another.

"I feel I have no alternative but to close the meeting," said the chairman stiffly. "This was supposed to be an informative occasion."

"I think it has been," said Mr. Atterbury.

"But you can't close the meeting," said Johnny.

"Indeed, I can!"

"You can't," said Johnny, "because this is a public hall, and we're all public, and no-one's done anything wrong."

"Then we shall leave, and there will really be *no* point in the meeting!" said the chairman. She swept up her papers and stalked across the platform, down the steps and across the hall. The rest of the platform party, with one or two helpless glances at the audience, followed her.

She led the way to the door.

Johnny offered up a silent prayer.

Someone, somewhere, heard it.

She pushed when she should have pulled. The rattling was the only noise, and it grew frantic as she began to lose her temper. Finally, one of the men from United Amalagamated Consolidated Holdings yanked the bar and the door jolted open.

Johnny risked looking behind him. He couldn't see anyone who looked dead.

A week ago that would have sounded really *odd*.

It didn't sound much better now.

"I thought I felt a draught," he said. "Just now?"

"They've left the windows open at the back," said Yo-less.

They're not here, Johnny thought. I'm going to have to do this by myself. Oh, well . . .

"Are we going to get into trouble?" said Wobbler. "This *was* supposed to be a public meeting."

"Well, we're public, aren't we?" said Johnny.

"Are we?"

"Why not?"

Everyone sat for a while looking at the empty platform. Then Mr. Atterbury got up and limped up the steps.

"Shall we have a meeting?" he said.

Cold air swirled out of the cinema.

"Well, THAT was an education."

"Some of those tricks must have been done with mirrors, if you want MY opinion."

"What shall we do now?"

"We should be getting back."

"Back where?"

"Back to the cemetery, of course."

"Madam, the night is young!"

"That's right! We've only just started enjoying ourselves."

"Yes! Anyway, you're a long time dead, that's what I always say."

"I want to get out there and enjoy life. I never enjoyed it much when I WAS alive."

"Thomas Bowler! That's no way for a respectable man to behave!"

The crowd queuing outside the burger bar drew closer together as the chilly wind drove past.

"Thomas Bowler? Do you know . . . I never really enjoyed being Thomas Bowler."

The audience in the Frank W. Arnold Civic Centre looked a bit sheepish, like a class after the teacher has stormed out. Democracy only works very well if people are told how to do it.

Someone raised a hand.

"*Can* we actually stop it happening?" she said. "It all sounded very . . . official."

"Officially, I don't think we can," said Mr. Atterbury. "There was a proper sale. United Amalagamated Consolidated Holdings could get unpleasant."

"There's plenty of other sites," said someone else. "There's the old jam works in Slate Road, and all that area where the old goods yard used to be."

"And we could give them their money back."

"We could give them *double* their money back," said Johnny.

There was more laughter at this.

"It seems to me," said Mr. Atterbury, "that a company like United Amalagamated Consolidated Holdings has to take notice of people. The boot factory never took notice of people, I do know that. It didn't have to. It made boots. That was all there was to it. But no-one's quite certain about what UACH does, so they have to be nice about it." He rubbed his chin. "Big companies like that don't like *fuss*. And they don't like being laughed at. If there was another site . . . and if they thought we were serious . . . and if we threaten to offer them, yes, double their money back . . ."

"And then we ought to do something about the High Street," said someone.

"And get some decent playgrounds and things again, instead of all these Amenities all over the place."

"And blow up Joshua N'Clement and get some proper houses built—"

"Yo!" said Bigmac.

"Here here," said Yo-less.

Mr. Atterbury waved his hands calmly.

"One thing at a time," he said. "Let's rebuild Blackbury first. We can see about Jerusalem tomorrow."

"And we ought to find a name for ourselves!"

"The Blackbury Preservation Society?"

"Sounds like something you put in a jar."

"All right, the Blackbury *Conservation* Society."

"Still sounds like jam to me."

"The Blackbury Pals," said Johnny.

Mr. Atterbury hesitated.

"It's a good name," he said eventually, while lots of people in the hall started asking one another who the Blackbury Pals were. "But . . . no. Not now. But they were officially the Blackbury Volunteers. That's a good name."

"But that doesn't say what we're going to do, does it?"

"If we start off not knowing what we're going to do, we could do anything," said Johnny. "Einstein said that," he added, proudly.

"What, Albert Einstein?" said Yo-less.

"No, Solomon Einstein," said Mr. Atterbury. "Hah! Know about him too, do you?"

"Er . . . yes."

"I remember him. He used to keep a taxidermist and fishing tackle shop in Cable Street when I was a lad. He was always saying that sort of thing. A bit of a philosopher, was Solomon Einstein."

"And all he did was stuff things?" said Yo-less.

"*And* think," said Johnny.

"Well, that kind of cogitation runs in the family, you might say," said Mr. Atterbury. "Besides, you've got a lot of time for abstract thought when you've got your hand stuck up a dead badger."

"Yes, you certainly wouldn't want to think about what you were doing," said Wobbler.

"Blackbury Volunteers it is, then," said Mr. Atterbury.

Frost formed on the receiver of the public phone in The White Swan.

"Ready, Mr. Einstein?"

"Let's go, Mr. Fletcher!"

The telephone clicked, and was silent. The air warmed up again.

Thirty seconds later, the air grew cold in the little wooden hut twenty miles away that housed the controls of Blackbury University's radio telescope.

"It works!"

"Off course. Off all the forces in the universe, the hardest to overcome is the force of habit. Gravity is easy-peasy by comparison."

"When did you think of that?"

"It came to me ven I was working on a particularly large trout."

"Really? Well . . . let's see what we can do . . ."

Mr. Fletcher looked around the little room. It was currently occupied only by Adrian "Nozzer" Miller, who'd wanted to be an astronomer because he thought it was all to do with staying up late looking through telescopes, and hadn't bargained on it being basically about adding columns of figures in a little shed in the middle of a windy field.

The figures the telescope was producing were all that was left of an exploding star twenty million years ago. A billion small rubbery things on two planets who had been getting on with life in a quiet sort of way had been totally destroyed, but they were certainly helping Adrian get his Ph.D. and, who knows, they might have thought it all worthwhile if anyone had asked them.

He looked up as the telescope motors ground into action. Lights flickered on the control panel.

He stared at the main switches, and then reached out for them. They were so cold they hurt.

"Ow!"

The big dish turned towards the moon, which was just over Blackbury.

There was a clattering from the printer beside him, and the endless stream of paper it was producing now read:

ololoolololoooloooloool lool loololo
HEREGOESNOTHINGGGGoooooooool1lol111
WELLIM*BACK*ooooloool . . .

Mr. Fletcher had just bounced off the moon.

"Vot was it like?"

"I didn't have time to see much, but I don't think I'd like to live there. It worked, though. The sky's the limit, Mr. Einstein!"

"Exactly, Mr. Fletcher! By the vay, where did that young man go?"

"I think he had to rush off somewhere."

"Oh. Well . . . we should go and tell the others, don't you think?"

It was a quiet night in Blackbury Central police station. Sergeant Comely had time to sit back and watch the little lights on the radio.

He'd never really been happy about the radio, even when he was younger. It was the bane of his life. He suffered from education, and he'd never been able to remember all that "Foxtrot Tango Piper" business—at least when he was, e.g., pelting down the street at 2 a.m. in puRsuit of miscreants. He'd end up sending messages about "Photograph Teapot Psychological." It had definitely blighted his promotion chances.

He especially hated radio on nights like this, when he was in charge. He hadn't joined the police to be good at technology.

Then the phones started to ring. There was the manager of the Odeon. Sergeant Comely couldn't quite make out what he was saying.

"Yes, yes, all right, Halloween Spectacular," he said. "What do you mean, it's all gone cold? What do you want me to do? Arrest a cinema for being cold? I'm a police officer, not a central heating specialist! I don't repair video machines, either!"

The phone rang again as soon as he put it down, but this time one of the young constables answered it.

"It's someone from the university," he said, putting his hand over the mouthpiece. "He says a strange alien force has invaded the radio telescope. You know, that big satellite dish thing over towards Slate?"

Sergeant Comely sighed. "Can you get a description?" he said.

"I saw a film about this, Sarge," said another policeman. "These aliens landed and replaced everyone in the town with giant vegetables."

"Really? Round here it'd be days before anyone noticed," said the sergeant.

The constable put the phone down.

"He just said it was like a strange alien force," he said. "Very cold, too."

"Oh, a *cold* strange alien force," said Sergeant Comely.

"And it was invisible, too."

"Right. Would he recognize it if he didn't see it again?"

The young policemen looked puzzled. I'm too good for this, the sergeant thought.

"All right," he said. "So we know the following. Strange invisible aliens have invaded Blackbury. They dropped in at The Dirty Duck, where they blew up the Space Invaders machine, which makes sense. And then they went to the pictures. Well, that makes sense too. It's probably *years* before new films get as far as Alfred Centuri . . ."

The phone rang again. The constable answered it.

"And what, we ask ourselves, is their next course of action?"

"It's the manager of Pizza Surprise, Sarge," said the constable. "He says—"

"Right!" said the sergeant. "That's right! They drop in for a Number Three with Extra Pepperoni! It probably looks like a friend of theirs."

"Wouldn't do any harm to go and chat to him," said the constable.

It had been a long time since dinner. "You know, just to show a bit of—"

"*I'll* go," said Sergeant Comely, picking up his hat. "But if I come back as a giant cucumber, there's going to be *trouble*."

"No anchovies on mine, Sarge," said the constable, as Sergeant Comely stepped out into the night.

There was something strange in the air. Sergeant Comely had lived in Blackbury all his life, and it had never felt like this. There was an electrical tingle to things, and the air tasted of tin.

It suddenly struck him.

What if it were real? Just because they made silly films about aliens and things didn't actually *mean*, did it, that it couldn't ever happen? He watched them on late night television. They always picked small towns to land near.

He shook his head. Nah . . .

William Stickers walked through him.

"You know, you really shouldn't have done that, William," said the Alderman, as Sergeant Comely hurried away.

"He's nothing but a symbol of the oppression of the proletariat," said William Stickers.

"You've got to have policemen," said Mrs. Liberty. "Otherwise people would simply do as they liked."

"Well, we can't have that, can we?" said Mr. Vicenti.

The Alderman looked around at the brightly lit street as they strolled along it. There weren't many living people around, but there were quite a lot of dead ones, looking in shop windows or, in the case of some of the older ones, looking *at* shop windows and wondering what they were.

"I certainly don't remember all these shopkeepers from *my* time," he said. "They must have moved in recently. Mr. Boots and Mr. Mothercare and Mr. Spudjulicay."

"Whom?" said Mrs. Liberty.

The Alderman pointed to the sign on the other side of the street.

"Spud-u-like," said Mr. Vicenti. "Hmm."

"Is that how you pronounce it?" said the Alderman. "I thought perhaps he was French. My word. And electric light all over the place. And no horse . . . manure in the streets at *all*."

"Really!" snapped Mrs. Liberty. "Please remember you are in company with a Lady."

"That's why he said manure," said William Stickers, happily.

"And the food!" said the Alderman. "Hindoo and Chinese! Chicken from Kentucky! And what did you say the stuff was that the clothes are made of?"

"Plastic, I think," said Mr. Vicenti.

"Very colourful and long-lasting," said Mrs. Liberty. "And many of the girls wear bloomers, too. Extremely practical and emancipated."

"And many of them are extremely handsome," said William Stickers.

"And everyone's taller and I haven't seen anyone on crutches," said the Alderman.

"It wasn't always like this," said Mr. Vicenti. "The nineteen thirties were rather gloomy."

"Yes, but now . . ." The Alderman spread his arms and turned around. "Shops full of cinematography televisions! Bright colours everywhere! Tall people with their own teeth! An age of miracles and wonders!"

"The people don't look very happy," said Mr. Vicenti.

"That's just a trick of the light," said the Alderman.

It was almost midnight. The dead met in the abandoned arcades of the shopping mall. The grilles were up and locked, but that doesn't matter when you're dead.

"Well, that was fun," said the Alderman.

"I have to agree," said Mrs. Sylvia Liberty. "I haven't enjoyed myself so much since I was alive. It's a shame we have to go back."

The Alderman crossed his arms.

"Go back?" he said.

"Now, then, Thomas," said Mrs. Liberty, but in a rather softer voice than she'd used earlier that evening, "I don't want to sound like Eric Grimm, but you know the rules. We have to return. *A day will come.*"

"I'm not going back. I've really enjoyed *myself*. I'm *not* going back!"

"Me neither," said William Stickers. "Down with tyranny!"

"We must be ready for Judgement Day," said Mrs. Liberty. "You never can tell. It could be tomorrow. Supposing it happened, and we missed it?"

"Hah!" said William Stickers.

"More than eighty years I've been sitting there," said Alderman Bowler. "You know, I wasn't expecting that. I thought things went dark for a moment and then there was a man handing out harps."

"For shame!"

"Well, isn't that what *you* expected?" he demanded.

"Not me," said William Stickers. "Belief in the survival of what is laughably called the soul after death is a primitive superstition which has no place in a dynamic socialist society!"

They looked at him.

"You don't tzink," said Solomon Einstein, carefully, "that it is worth reconsidering your opinions in the light of experimental evidence?"

"Don't think you can get round me just because you're accidentally right! Just because I happen to find myself still . . . basically here," said William Stickers, "does *not* invalidate the general theory!"

Mrs. Liberty banged her phantom umbrella on the floor.

"I won't say it hasn't been enjoyable," she said, "but the rules are that we must be back in our places at dawn. Supposing we stayed away too long and forgot who we were? Supposing tomorrow was Judgement Day?"

Thomas Bowler sighed.

"Well, supposing it is?" he said. "You know what I'd say? I'd say: I did the best I could for eighty-four years. And no-one ever told me that afterwards I'd still be this fat old man who gets out of breath. Why do I get out of breath? I don't *breathe*. I passed away, and next thing I knew I was sitting in a marble hut like a man waiting *an extremely long time* for an appointment with the doctor. For nearly ninety years! I'd say: you call this justice? Why are we waiting? *A day will come*. We all . . . arrive knowing it, but no-one says when!

"Just when I was beginning to enjoy life," he said. "I wish this night would never end."

Mr. Fletcher nudged Solomon Einstein.

"Shall we tell them?" he said.

"Tell us what?" said William Stickers.

"Vell, you see—" Einstein began.

"Times have changed," said Mr. Fletcher. "All that stuff about being home at dawn and not hearing the cock crow and stuff like that. That was all very well once upon a time, when people thought the Earth was flat. But no-one believes that now—"

"Er—" One of the dead raised a hand.

"Oh, yes," said Mr. Fletcher. "Thank you, Mr. Ronald Newton (1878–1934), former chairman of the Blackbury Flat Earth Society. I know you have Views. But the point I'm trying to make is—"

"—dawn is a place as well as a time," said Einstein, spreading his hands.

"What on earth do you mean?" said Mrs. Liberty.

"On Earth, and around earth," said Einstein, getting excited. "One night and one day, forever chasing one another."

"There is a night that never comes to an end," said Mr. Fletcher. "All you need is speed . . ."

"Relatively speaking," said Einstein.

8

There is a night that never comes to an end . . .

The clock of the world turns under its own shadow. Midnight is a moving place, hurtling around the planet at a thousand miles an hour like a dark knife, cutting slices of daily bread off the endless loaf of Time.

Time passes everywhere. But days and nights are little local things that happen only to people who stay in one place. If you go fast enough, you can overtake the clock . . .

"How many of us are in this phone box?" said Mr. Fletcher.

"Seventy-three," said the Alderman.

"Very well. Where shall we go? Iceland? It's not even midnight yet in Iceland."

"Can we have fun in Iceland?" said the Alderman.

"How do you feel about fish?"

"Can't abide fish."

"Not Iceland, then. I believe it's very hard to have fun in Iceland without fish being involved in some way. Well, now . . . it'll be early evening in New York."

"America?" said Mrs. Liberty. "Won't we get scalped?"

"Good grief, no!" said William Stickers, who was a bit more up to date about the world.

"*Probably* not," said Mr. Fletcher, who had been watching the news lately and was even more up to date than William Stickers.

"Look, we're *dead*," said the Alderman. "What else have we got to worry about?"

"Now, this may strike you as an unusual means of travel," said Mr. Fletcher, as something in the telephone began to click, "but all you have to do, really, is follow me. Incidentally, is Stanley Roundway here?"

The footballer raised his hand.

"We're going *west*, Stanley. For once in your death, try to get the directions right. And now . . ."

One by one, they vanished.

Johnny lay in bed, watching the stricken shuttle turning gently in the moonlight.

It had been quite busy after the meeting. Someone from the *Blackbury Guardian* had talked to him, and then Mid-Midlands TV had filmed him, and people had shaken his hand, and he hadn't got home until nearly eleven.

There hadn't been any trouble over that, at least. His mum hadn't come in yet and Grandad was watching a programme about bicycle racing in Germany.

He kept thinking about the Pals. They'd come all the way from France. Yet the dead in the cemetery were so frightened of moving. But they were all the same type of people, really. There had to be a reason for that.

The dead in the cemetery just hung around. Why? The Pals had marched from France, because it was the right thing to do. You didn't have to stay where you were put.

"New York, New York."

"Why did they name it twice?"

"Well, they ARE Americans. I suppose they wanted to be sure."

"The lights are extremely plentiful. What's that?"

"The Statue of Liberty."

"Looks a bit like you, Sylvia."

"Sauce!"

"Is everyone keeping a look out for those Ghost-breakers?"

"I think that was just cinematography, William."

"How long to morning?"

"Hours, yet! Follow me, everyone! Let's get a better view!"

No-one ever did work out why all the elevators in the World Trade Centre went up and down all by themselves for almost an hour . . .

October the 31st dawned foggy. Johnny wondered about having a one-day illness in preparation for what he suspected was going to be a busy evening, but decided to go to school instead. They always felt happier if you dropped in sometimes.

He went via the cemetery.

There wasn't a living soul. He hated it when it was like this. It was like the bits in the film when you were waiting for the aliens to jump out. Somehow, they were always more dreadful than the bits with the fangs in.

Then he found Mr. Grimm. Anyone else walking along the towpath would have just seen the busted set. But Johnny saw the little man in his neat suit, watching the ghost of the television.

"Ah, boy," he said. "You have been causing trouble, have you?" He pointed to the screen.

Johnny gasped. There was Mr. Atterbury, very calmly talking to a lady on a sofa. There was also one of the people from United Amalagamated Consolidated Holdings. And he was having some difficulty, was the Consolidated man. He'd come along with some prepared things to say and he was having problems getting his mind round the idea that they weren't working any more.

Mr. Grimm turned up the volume control.

"—at every stage, fully sensitive to public opinion in this matter, I can assure you, but there is no doubt that we entered into a proper and legal contract with the relevant Authority."

"But the Blackbury Volunteers say too much was decided behind closed doors," said the lady, who looked as though she was enjoying herself. "They say things were never fully discussed and that no-one listened to the local people."

"Of course, this is not the fault of United Amalagamated Consolidated Holdings," said Mr. Atterbury, smiling benevolently. "They have an enviable record of civic service and co-operation with the public. I think what we have here is a mistake rather than any *near-criminal activity*, and we in the Volunteers would be more than happy to assist them in any constructive way and, indeed, possibly even compensate them."

Probably no-one else but Johnny and the Consolidated man noticed Mr. Atterbury take a ten-pence piece out of his pocket. He turned it over and over in his fingers. The man from the company watched it like a mouse might watch a cat.

He's going to offer him double his money back, Johnny thought. Right there on television.

He didn't. He just kept turning the coin over and over, so that the man could see it.

"That seems a very diplomatic offer," said the interviewer. "Tell me, Mr.—er—"

"A spokesman," said the Consolidated man. He looked quite ill. There was a glint as light flashed off the coin.

"Tell me, Mr. Spokesman . . . what is it that United Amalagamated Consolidated Holdings actually *does*?"

Mr. Atterbury would probably have been a good man in the Spanish Inquisition, Johnny told himself.

Mr. Grimm turned the sound down again.

"Where's everyone else?" said Johnny.

"Haven't come back," said Mr. Grimm, with horrible satisfaction. "Their graves haven't been slept in. *That's* what happens when people don't *listen*. And do you know what's going to *happen* to them?"

"No."

"They're going to *fade away*. Oh, yes. You've put ideas in their heads. They think they can go gadding about. But people who go gadding about and not staying where they're put . . . they don't come back. And that's an *end* to it. It could be Judgement Day tomorrow, and they won't be here. Hah! Serves them right."

There was something about Mr. Grimm that made Johnny want to hit him, except that it wouldn't work anyway and, besides, hitting him would be like hitting mud. You'd get dirtier for doing it.

"I don't know where they've gone," he said, "but I don't think anything bad's happened to them."

"Think what you like," said Mr. Grimm, turning back to the television.

"Did you know it's Halloween?" said Johnny.

"Is it?" said Mr. Grimm, watching an advert for chocolate. "I shall have to be careful tonight, then."

When Johnny reached the bridge he looked back. Mr. Grimm was still there, all alone.

The dead rode a radio signal over Wyoming . . .

They were already changing. They were still recognizable, but only when they thought about it.

"*You see, I* told *you it was possible*," said the person who was occasionally Mr. Fletcher. *"We don't need wires!"*

They ran into an electric storm high over the Rocky Mountains. That was fun.

And then they surfed down the radio waves to California.

"What time is it?"

"Midnight!"

Johnny was a sort of hero in school. The *Blackbury Guardian* had a front page story headed: COUNCIL SLAMMED IN CEMETERY SALE RUMPUS. The *Guardian* often used words like "slammed" and "rumpus"; you wondered how the editor talked at home.

Johnny was in the story with his name spelled wrong, and there was a quote which ran: "War hero Arthur Atterbury, president of the newly formed 'Blackbury Volunteers,' told the *Guardian*: 'There are young people in this town with more sense of history in their little fingers than some adults have in their entire committee-bound bodies.' This is thought to be a reference to Cllr Miss Ethel Liberty, who was not available for comment last night."

Even one or two of the teachers mentioned it; it was unusual for people from the school to appear in the paper, except very close to headlines like TWO FINED AFTER JOYRIDE ESCAPADE.

Even the History master asked him about the Blackbury Pals. And then Johnny found himself telling the class about the Alderman and William Stickers and Mrs. Sylvia Liberty, although he said he'd got the information out of the library. One of the girls said she was definitely going to do a project on Mrs. Liberty, Champion of Women's Rights, and Wobbler said, yes, champion of women's right to get things wrong, and that started a good argument which lasted until the end of the lesson.

Even the headmaster took an interest—probably out of aforesaid relief that Johnny wasn't involved in one of those YOUTH GANG FINED FOR SHOPLIFTING stories. Johnny had to find his way to his office. The recommended method was to tie one end of a piece of string to somewhere you knew and get your friends to come and look for you if you were away more than two days. He got a short speech about "social awareness," and was out again a minute later.

He met the other three in the lunch break.

"Come on," he said.

"Where to?"

"The cemetery. I think something's gone wrong."

"I haven't had my lunch yet," said Wobbler. "It's very important for me to have regular meals. Otherwise my stomach acid plays up."

"Oh, shut up."

By the time they raced one another across the heart of Australia, they didn't even need the radio.

The dawn dragged its slow way across the Pacific after them, but they were running free.

"Do we ever need to stop?"

"No!"

"I always wanted to see the world before I died!"

"Well, then, it was just a matter of timing."

"What time is it?"

"Midnight!"

The cemetery wasn't empty now. There were a couple of photographers there, for one thing, including one from a Sunday newspaper. There was a film crew from Mid-Midlands Television. And the dog-walking people had been joined by others, just walking around and looking.

In a neglected corner, Mrs. Tachyon was industriously Vim-ing a gravestone.

"Never seen so many people here," said Johnny. He added, "At least, ones who're breathing."

Yo-less wandered over from where he'd been talking to a couple of enthusiastic people in woolly bobble hats, who were peering through the huge thicket behind Mrs. Liberty's grave.

"They say we've not only got environment and ecology, but some habitat as well," he said. "They think they've seen a rare Scandinavian thrush."

"Yeah, full of life, this place," said Bigmac.

A Council lorry had driven a little way up the towpath. Some men in donkey jackets were harvesting the old mattresses. The zombie television had already gone. Mr. Grimm was nowhere to be seen, even by Johnny.

And a police car was parked just outside the gates. Sergeant Comely was working on the general assumption that where you got lots of people gathered together, something illegal was bound to happen sooner or later.

The cemetery was alive.

"They've gone," said Johnny. "I can feel them . . . not here."

The other three found that, quite by accident, they'd all moved closer together.

A rare Scandinavian thrush, unless it was a rook, cawed in the elms.

"Gone where?" said Wobbler.

"I don't know!"

"I knew it! I *knew* it!" said Wobbler. "His eyes'll start to glow any minute, you watch. You've let 'em out! There'll be lurchin' goin' on before this day's over, you wait and see!"

"Mr. Grimm said that if they're away too long, they . . . they forget who they were . . ." said Johnny, uncertainly.

"See? See?" said Wobbler. "You laughed at me! Maybe they're OK when they're remembering who they were, but once they forget . . ."

"Night of the Killer Zombies?" said Bigmac.

"We've been through all that," said Johnny. "They're not zombies!"

"Yeah, but maybe they've been eating voodoo fish and chips," said Bigmac.

"They're just *not here*."

"Then where are they?"

"I *don't know*!"

"And it's Halloween, too," moaned Wobbler.

Johnny walked over to the fence around the old boot works. There were quite a few cars parked there. He could see the tall thin figure of Mr. Atterbury, talking to a group of men in grey suits.

"I wanted to tell them," he said. "I mean, we might *win*. Now. People are here. There's TV and everything. Last week it looked hopeless and now there's just a chance and last night I wanted to tell them and now they've gone! And this was their home!"

"Perhaps all these people have frightened them away," said Yoless.

"Day of the Living," said Bigmac.

"I should have had my lunch!" said Wobbler. "My stomach's definitely playing up!"

"They're probably waiting under your bed," said Bigmac.

"I'm not scared," said Wobbler. "I've just got a stomach upset."

"We ought to be getting back," said Yo-less. "I've got to do a project on projects."

"What?" said Johnny.

"It's for Maths," said Yo-less. "How many people in the school are doing projects. That kind of stuff. Statistics."

"I'm going to look for them," said Johnny.

"You'll get into trouble when they do the register."

"I'll say I've been doing something . . . social. That'll probably work. Anyone coming with me?"

Wobbler looked at his feet, or where his feet would be if Wobbler wasn't in the way.

"What about you, Bigmac? You've got your Everlasting Note, haven't you?"

"Yeah, but it's going a bit yellow now . . ."

No-one knew when it had been written. Rumour had it that it had been handed down through the generations in Bigmac's family. It was in three pieces. But it generally worked. Although Bigmac kept tropical fish and generally out of trouble, there was something about the way he looked and the way he lived in the Joshua N'Clement block that saw to it no teacher ever questioned the Note, which excused him from doing everything.

"Anyway, they could be anywhere," he said. "Anyway, I can't *look* for 'em, can I? Anyway, they're probably just inside your head."

"You heard them on the radio!"

"I heard *voices*. That's what radio's for, innit?"

It occurred to Johnny, not for the first time, that the human mind, of which each of his friends was in possession of one almost standard sample, was like a compass. No matter how much you shook it up, no matter what happened to it, sooner or later it'd carry on pointing the same way. If three-metre-tall green Martians landed on the shopping mall, bought some greetings cards and a bag of sugar cookies and then took off again, within a day or two people would believe it never happened.

"Not even Mr. Grimm's here, and he's *always* here," said Johnny.

He looked at Mr. Vicenti's ornate grave. Some people were taking photographs of it.

"Always here," he said.

"He's gone weird again," said Wobbler.

"You all go back," said Johnny, quietly. "I just thought of something."

They all looked round. Their *brains* don't believe in the dead, Johnny thought, but they keep getting outvoted by all the rest of them.

"I'm OK," said Johnny. "You go on back. I'll see you at Wobbler's party tonight, all right?"

"Remember not to bring any . . . you know . . . friends," said Wobbler, as the three of them left.

Johnny wandered down North Drive.

He'd never *tried* to talk to the dead. He'd said things when he knew they were listening, and sometimes they'd been clearly visible, but apart from that first time, when he'd knocked on the door of the Alderman's mausoleum for a joke . . .

"Will you look at this?"

One of the people who'd been examining the grave had picked up the radio, which had been lodged behind a tuft of grass.

"Honestly, people have no respect."

"Does it work?"

It didn't. A couple of days of damp grass had done for the batteries.

"No."

"Give it to the men dumping the rubbish on the lorry, then."

"I'll do it," said Johnny.

He hurried off with it, keeping a lookout, trying to find one dead person among the living.

"Ah, Johnny."

It was Mr. Atterbury, leaning over the wall of the old boot works. "Exciting day, isn't it? You started something, eh?"

"Didn't mean to," said Johnny, automatically. Things were generally his fault.

"It could go either way," said Mr. Atterbury. "The old railway site isn't so good, but . . . things look promising, I do know that. People have woken up."

"That's true. A *lot* of people."

"United Consolidated don't like fuss. The District Auditor is here, and a man from the Development Commission. It could go very well."

"Good. Um."

"Yes?"

"I saw you on television," said Johnny. "You called United Consolidated public-spirited and cooperative."

"Well, they might be. If they've got no choice. They're a bit shifty but we might win through. It's amazing what you can do with a kind word."

"Oh. Right. Well, then . . . I've got to go and find someone, if you don't mind . . ."

There was no sign of Mr. Grimm anywhere. Or any of the others. Johnny hung around for hours, with the birdwatchers and the people from the Blackbury Wildlife Trust, who'd found a fox's den behind William Stickers' memorial, and some Japanese tourists. No-one quite knew why the Japanese tourists were there, but Mrs. Liberty's grave was getting very well photographed.

Eventually, though, even Japanese tourists run out of film. They took one last shot of themselves in front of William Stickers' monument, and headed back towards their coach.

The cemetery emptied. The sun began to set over the carpet warehouse.

Mrs. Tachyon went past with her loaded shopping trolley to wherever it was she spent her nights.

The cars left the old boot works, and only the bulldozers were left, like prehistoric monsters surprised by a sudden cold snap.

Johnny sidled up to the forlorn little stone under the trees.

"I know you're here," he whispered. "You can't leave like the others. *You* have to stay. Because *you're* a ghost. A real ghost. You're still here, Mr. Grimm. You're not just hanging around like the rest of them. *You're* haunting."

There was no sound.

"What did you do? Were you a murderer or something?"

There was still no sound. In fact, there was even more silence than before.

"Sorry about the television," said Johnny nervously.

More silence, so heavy and deep it could have stuffed mattresses.

He walked away, as fast as he dared.

9

"This fuss over the cemetery's certainly breathed a bit of life into this town," said his mother. "Go and give your grandad his tray, will you? And tell him about it. You know he takes an interest."

Grandad was watching the News in Hindi. He didn't want to. But the thingy for controlling the set had got lost and everyone had forgotten how to change channels without it.

"Brought you your tray, Grandad."

"Right."

"You know the old cemetery? Where you showed me William Stickers' grave?"

"Right."

"Well, maybe it won't be built on now. There was a meeting last night."

"Right?"

"I spoke up at the meeting."

"Right."

"So it might be all right."

"Right."

Johnny sighed. He went back into the kitchen.

"Can I have an old sheet, Mum?"

"What on earth for?"

"Wobbler's Halloween party. I can't think of anything else."

"There's the one I used as a dustcover, if you're going to cut holes in it."

"Thanks, Mum."

"It's pink."

"Aaaaooow, Mum!"

"It's practically washed out. No-one'll notice."

It also, as it turned out, had the remains of some flowers embroidered on one end. Johnny did his best with a pair of scissors.

He'd promised he'd go. But he went the long way round, with the sheet in a bag, just in case the dead had come back and might see him. And there was Mr. Grimm to think about now.

After he'd been gone a few minutes, the TV started showing the News in English, which looked less interesting than the Hindi News.

Grandad watched it for a while, and then sat up.

"Hey, girl, it says they're trying to save the old cemetery."

"Yes, Dad."

"It looked like our Johnny on the stage there."

"Yes, Dad."

"No-one tells me anything around here. What's this?"

"Chicken, Dad."

"Right."

They were somewhere in the high plateaus of Asia, where once camel trains had traded silk across five thousand miles and now madmen with guns shot one another in the various names of God.

"How far to morning?"

"Nearly there . . ."

"What?"

The dead slowed down in a mountain pass, full of driving snow.

"We owe the boy something. He took an interest. He remembered us." "Zat's absolutely correct. Conservation of energy. Besides, he'll be worrying."

"Yes, but . . . if we go back now . . . we'll become like we were, won't we? I can feel the weight of that gravestone now."

"Sylvia Liberty! You said we shouldn't leave!"

"I've changed my mind, William."

"Yes. I spent half my life being frightened of dying, and now I'm dead I'm going to stop being frightened," said the Alderman. *"Besides . . . I'm remembering things . . ."*

There was a murmur from the rest of the dead.

"I think ve all are," said Solomon Einstein. *"All the zings we forgot when we were alive . . ."*

"That's the trouble with life," said the Alderman. *"It takes up your whole time. I mean, I won't say it wasn't fun. Bits of it. Quite a lot of it, really. In its own way. But it wasn't what you'd call* living . . ."

"We don't have to be fightened of the morning," said Mr. Vicenti. *"We don't have to be frightened of anything."*

A skeleton opened the door.

"It's me, Johnny."

"It's me, Bigmac. What're you, a gay ghost?"

"It's not that pink."

"The flowers are good."

"Come on, let me in, it's freezing out here."

"Can you float and mince at the same time?"

"Bigmac!"

"Come on, then."

Somehow, it looked as if Wobbler hadn't really put his heart into the decorations. There were a few streamers and some rubber spiders around the place, and a bowl of the dreadful punch you always get in these circumstances (the one with the brownish bits of orange in it) and bowls full of nibbles with names like Curly-Wigglies. And a vegetable marrow that looked as though it had walked into a combine harvester.

"It was *sposed* to be Jack-o'-Lantern," Wobbler kept telling everyone, "but I couldn't find a pumpkin."

"Met Hannibal Lecter in a dark alley, did it?" said Yo-less.

"The plastic bats are good, aren't they," said Wobbler. "They cost fifty-pence each. Have some more punch?"

There were other people there, too, although in the semi-darkness it was hard to make out who they thought they were. There was someone with a lot of stitches and a bolt through his neck, but that was only Nodj, who looked like that anyway. There were a bunch from Wobbler's computer group, who could get drunk on non-alcoholic alcohol and would then stagger around saying things like, "I'm totally *mad*!" There were a couple of girls Wobbler vaguely knew. It was that sort of party. You just knew someone would put something daft in the punch, and everyone would talk about school, and one of the girls' dads'd turn up at eleven o'clock and hang around looking determined and put a damper on things, as if they weren't soaking wet already.

"We could play a game," said Bigmac.

"Not Dead Man's Hand," said Wobbler. "Not after last year. You're supposed to pass around grapes and stuff, not just anything you find in the fridge."

"It wasn't what it *was*," said one of the girls. "It was what he said it was."

"All right," said Johnny to Yo-less, "I've been trying to work it out. Who are *you*?"

Yo-less had covered half his face with white make-up. He wasn't wearing a shirt, just his ordinary string vest, but he'd found a piece of fake leopard-skin-pattern material which he'd draped over his shoulders. And he had a black hat.

"Baron Samedi, the voodoo god," said Yo-less. "I got the idea out of James Bond."

"That's racial stereotyping," someone said.

"No, it's not," said Yo-less. "Not if *I'm* doing it."

"I'm pretty sure Baron Samedi didn't wear a bowler hat," said Johnny. "I'm pretty sure it was a top hat. A bowler hat makes you look a bit like you're going to an office somewhere."

"I can't help it, it was all I could get."

"Maybe he's Baron Samedi, the voodoo god of chartered accountancy," said Wobbler.

For a moment Johnny thought of Mr. Grimm; his face was all one colour, but he looked like a voodoo god of chartered accountancy if ever there was one.

"In the film he was all mixed up with tarot cards and stuff," said Bigmac.

"Not really," said Johnny, waking up. "Tarot cards are European occult. Voodoo is African occult."

"Don't be daft, it's American," said Wobbler.

"No, American occult is Elvis Presley not being dead and that sort of thing," said Yo-less. "Voodoo is basically West African with a bit of Christian influence. I looked it up."

"I've got some *ordinary* cards," said Wobbler.

"No messing around with cards," said Baron Yo-less severely. "My mum'd go spare."

"What about the thing with the letters and glasses?"

"The postman?"

"You know what I mean."

"No. That could lead to dark forces taking over," said Baron Yo-less. "It's as ouija boards."

Someone put on a tape and started to dance.

Johnny stared into his glass of horrible punch. There was an orange pip floating in it.

Cards and boards, he thought. And the dead. That's not dark forces. Making a fuss about cards and heavy metal and going on about Dungeons and Dragons stuff because it's got demon gods in it is like guarding the door when *it* is really coming up through the floorboards. Real dark forces . . . aren't dark. They're sort of grey, like Mr. Grimm. They take all the colour out of life; they take a town like Blackbury and turn it into frightened streets and plastic signs and Bright New Futures and towers where no-one wants to live and no-one really *does* live. The *dead* seem more alive than us. And everyone becomes grey and turns into numbers and then, somewhere, someone starts to do arithmetic . . .

The Demon God Yoth-Ziggurat might want to chop your soul up into little pieces, but at least he doesn't tell you that you haven't got one.

And at least you've got half a chance of finding a magic sword.

He kept thinking about Mr. Grimm. Even the dead kept away from him.

He woke up to hear Wobbler say, "We could go Trick or Treating."

"My mother says that's no better than begging," said Yo-less.

"Hah, it's worse than that around Joshua N'Clement," said Bigmac. "It's called, 'Giss five quid or kiss your tyres night-night.' "

"We could do it around here," said Wobbler. "Or we could go down the mall."

"That'll just be full of kids in costume running around screaming."

"A few more won't hurt, then," said Johnny.

"All right, then, everybody," Wobbler said. "Come on . . ."

In fact Neil Armstrong Mall was full of all the other people who'd run out of ideas at Halloween parties. They wandered around in groups looking at one another's clothes and talking, which was pretty much what people did normally in any case, except that tonight the mall looked like Transylvania on late-shopping night.

Zombies lurched under the sodium lights. Witches walked around in groups and giggled at the boys. Grinning pumpkins bobbed on the escalators. Vampires gibbered among the sad indoor trees, and kept fumbling their false fangs back in. Mrs. Tachyon rummaged for tins in the litter bins.

Johnny's pink ghost outfit caused a lot of interest.

"Seen any dead around lately?" said Baron Yo-less, when Wobbler and Bigmac had gone off to buy some snacks.

"Hundreds," said Johnny.

"You know what I mean."

"No. Not *them*."

"I'm worried something may have happened to them."

"They're *dead*. If they exist, that is," said Yo-less. "It's not as though they could get run over or something. If you've saved their cemetery for them, they probably just aren't bothering to talk to you any more. That's probably what it is. I think—"

"Anyone want a raspberry snake?" said Wobbler, rustling a large paper bag. "The skulls are good, too."

"I'm going home," said Johnny. "There's something wrong, and I don't know what it is."

A ten-year-old Bride of Dracula flapped past.

"I've got to admit, this isn't big fun," said Wobbler. "Tell you what . . . there's *Night of the Vampire Nerds* on TV. We could go and watch that."

"What about everyone else?" said Bigmac. The rest of the party had drifted off.

"Oh, well, they know where I live," said Wobbler philosophically, as a blood-streaked ghoul went by eating an ice cream.

"I don't believe in vampire nerds," said Bigmac, as they stepped into the night air. It was a lot colder now, and the mist was coming back.

"Oh, I dunno," said Wobbler. "It's the sort we'd have round here."

"They'd suck fruit juice," said Yo-less.

"Their mum'd make them go to bed late," said Bigmac, but they had to think about that.

"Why are we going this way?" said Wobbler. "This isn't the way back."

"It's foggy, too," said Bigmac.

"It's just the mist off the canal," said Johnny.

Wobbler stopped.

"Oh, no," he said.

"It's quicker this way," said Johnny.

"Oh, yes. *Quicker*. Oh, yes. Because I'm gonna *run*!"

"Don't be daft."

"It's Halloween!"

"So what? You're dressed up as Dracula—what're you worried about!"

"I'm not going past there tonight!"

"It's no different than going past during the day."

"All right, it's the same, but *I'm* different!"

"Scared?" said Bigmac.

"What? Me? Scared? Huh? Me? I'm not *scared*."

"Actually, it *is* a bit risky," said Baron Yo-less.

"Yes, risky," said Wobbler hurriedly.

"I mean, you never know," said Yo-less.

"Never know," Wobbler echoed.

"Look, it's a street in our town. There's lights and a phone box and everything," said Johnny. "I just . . . I won't be happy until I've checked, OK? Anyway, there's four of us, after all."

"That just means something bad can happen four times," said Wobbler.

But they'd been walking as they talked; now the little light in the phone box loomed in the fog like a blurred star.

The other three went quiet. The fog hushed all sounds.

Johnny listened. There wasn't even that blotting-paper silence that the dead made.

"See?" he whispered. "I said—"

Someone coughed, a long way off. All four boys suddenly tried to occupy the same spot.

"Dead people don't cough!" hissed Johnny.

"Then someone's in the cemetery!" said Yo-less.

"Body snatchers!" said Wobbler.

"Burke 'n Head!" said Bigmac.

"I've read about this in the papers!" whispered Wobbler. "People digging up graves for satanic rites!"

"Shutup!" said Johnny. They sagged. "Sounded to me like it came from the old boot factory," he said.

"But it's the middle of the night," said Yo-less.

They crept forward. There was a dim shape pulled on to the pavement where the streetlights barely shone.

"It's a van," said Johnny. "There. Count Dracula never drove a van."

Bigmac tried to grin. "Unless he was a Vanpire—"

There was a metallic *clink* somewhere in the fog.

"Wobbler?" said Johnny, in what he hoped was a calm voice.

"Yes?"

"You said you were going to run. Go round to Mr. Atterbury's house right now and tell him to come here."

"What? By myself?"

"You'll run faster if you're by yourself."

"Right!"

Wobbler gave them a frightened look and vanished.

"What, exactly, are we doing?" said Yo-less, as the other three peered into the fog.

There was no mistaking the noise this time. It was wrapped about with fog, but it was definitely the sound of a big diesel engine starting up.

"Someone's nicking a bulldozer!" said Bigmac.

"I wish that's what they were doing," said Johnny, "but I don't think they are. Come on, will you?"

"Listen, if someone's driving a bulldozer without lights in the fog, I'm not hanging around!" said Yo-less.

Lights came on, fifty metres away. They didn't show much. They just lit up two cones of fog.

"Is that better?" said Johnny.

"No."

The lights ground forward. The machine was bumping towards the cemetery railings. Old buddleia bushes and dead stinging nettles smashed under the treads, and there was a clang as the blade hit the low wall.

Johnny ran alongside the machine and shouted, "Oi!"

The engine stopped.

"Run away!" hissed Johnny to Yo-less. "Go on! Tell someone what's happening!"

A man unfolded himself from the cab and jumped down. He advanced towards the boys, waving a finger.

"You kids," he said, "are in *real* trouble."

Johnny backed away, and someone grabbed his shoulders.

"You heard the man," said a voice by his ear. "It's your fault, this.

So you'd better not have seen anything, right? Because we know where you live—Oh, no you don't." A hand shot out and grabbed Yo-less as he tried to back away.

"Know what I think?" said the man who had been driving the bulldozer. "*I* think it's lucky we happened to be passing and found 'em messing around, eh? Shame they'd driven it right through the place already, eh? Kids today, eh?"

A half-brick sailed past Johnny's face and hit the man beside him on the shoulder.

"What the—"

*"I'll smash your **** head in! I'll smash your **** head in!"*

Bigmac emerged from the fog. He looked terrifying. He reached beside him, yanked a railing from the broken wall and started to whirl it round his head as he advanced.

"You what? You what? You what? I'm MENTAL, me!"

Then he started to run forward.

"Aaaaaaarrrrrr—"

And it dawned on all four people at once that he wasn't going to stop.

10

Bigmac bounded over the rubble, an enraged skin-head skeleton.

"Get him!"

"*You* get him!"

The railing smacked into the side of the bulldozer, and Bigmac leapt.

Even fighting mad, he was still Bigmac, and the driver was a large man. But what Bigmac had going for him was that he was, just for a few seconds, unstoppable. If the man had managed to get one good punch in that would have been it, but there seemed to be too many arms and legs in the way, and also Bigmac was trying to bite his ear.

Even so—

But a pair of headlights appeared near the gate and started to bounce up and down in a way that suggested a car being driven at high speed across rough ground.

The man holding Johnny let go and vanished into the fog. The other one thumped Bigmac hard in the stomach and followed him.

The car skidded to a halt and a fat vampire leapt out, shouting "Make my night, make my night!"

Mr. Atterbury unfolded himself a little more sedately from the driver's seat.

"It's all right, they're gone," said Johnny. "We'll never find them in this fog."

There was the sound of an engine starting somewhere in the distance, and then wheels skidded out on to the unseen road.

"But I got the number!" shouted Wobbler, hopping from foot to foot. "I dint have a pen so I huffed on the window and wrote it in the huff!"

"They were going to drive the bulldozer into the cemetery!" said Yo-less.

"Right in the huff, look!"

"Dear me, I expect a bit more than this of United Consolidated," said Mr. Atterbury. "Hadn't we better see to your friend?"

Bigmac was kneeling on the ground, making small "oof, oof" noises.

"I'll have to keep huffing on it to keep them there, mind!"

"You all right, Bigmac?"

They knelt down beside him. He was wheezing with his asthma.

"I . . . I really frightened him . . . yeah?" he managed.

"Right, right," said Johnny. "Come on, we'll give you a hand up . . ."

"I jus' saw them there—"

"How do you feel?"

"Jus' winded."

"Hang on, I've got to go and huff on it again—"

"Help him into the car."

" 'S'all right—"

"I'll drive him to the hospital, just in case."

"No!"

Bigmac pushed them away, and rose unsteadily to his feet.

" 'm all right," he said. "Tough as old boots, me."

Red and blue lights bloomed in the fog and a police siren *dee-dahed* once or twice and then stopped out of embarrassment.

"Ah," said Mr. Atterbury. "I rather think my wife got a bit excited about things and phoned the police. Er . . . Bigmac, isn't it? Would you recognize those men if you saw them again?"

"Sure. One of 'em's got teethmarks in his ear." Bigmac suddenly had the hunted look of one who has never quite seen eye to eye with the constabulary. "But I ain't going in any police station. No way."

Mr. Atterbury straightened up as the police car crunched to a halt.

"I think it might be a good idea if I do most of the talking," he said, when Sergeant Comely stepped out into the night. "Ah, Ray," he said. "Glad you could drop by. Can I have a word?"

The boys stood in a huddle, watching as the men walked over to the bulldozer, and then inspected the remains of the wall.

"We're going to be in trouble," said Bigmac. "Old Comely's probably going to do me for ear-biting. Or pinching the bulldozer. You wait."

Wobbler tapped Johnny on the shoulder.

"You *knew* something was going to happen," he said.

"Yes. Don't know how."

They watched the policemen peer into Mr. Atterbury's car for a moment.

"He's reading my huff," said Wobbler. "That was lateral thinking, that was."

Then Comely went back to the police car. They heard him speaking into the radio.

"No! I say again. That's H for Hirsute, W for Wagner—Wagner! Wagner! No! W as in Westphalia, A for Aardvark—"

Mr. Atterbury appeared from the direction of the bulldozer, waving a pair of pliers.

"I don't think it's going to move again tonight," he said.

"What's going to happen?" said Johnny.

"Not sure. We can probably trace the van. I think I've persuaded Sergeant Comely that we ought to deal with this quietly, for now. He'll take statements from you, though. That might be enough."

"Were they from United Consolidated?"

The old man shrugged.

"Perhaps someone thought everything might be a lot simpler if the cemetery wasn't worth saving," he said. "Perhaps a couple of likely lads were slipped a handful of notes to do . . . er . . . a Halloween prank—"

There was a burst of noise from the police radio.

"We've stopped a van on the East Slate Road," the sergeant called out. "Sounds like our lads."

"Well Done, Said PC Plonk," said Yo-less, in a hollow voice. "You Have Captured The Whole Gang! Good Work, Fumbling Four! And They All Went Home For Tea And Cakes."

"It *would* help if you'd come along to the police station, Bigmac," said Mr. Atterbury.

"No way!"

"I'll come along with you. And one of your friends could come, too."

"It'd really help," said Johnny.

"I'll go with you," said Yo-less.

"And then," said Mr. Atterbury, "I'm going to take considerable pleasure in ringing up the chairman of United Consolidated. *Considerable* pleasure."

* * *

It was ten minutes later. Bigmac had gone to the police station, accompanied by Yo-less and Mr. Atterbury and an assurance that he wasn't going to be asked any questions about certain other minor matters relating to things like cars not being where the owners had expected them to be, and other things of that nature.

The sodium lights of Blackbury glowed in the fog, which was thinning out a bit now. They made the darkness beyond the carpet warehouse a lot deeper and much darker.

"Well, that's it, then," said Wobbler. "Game over. Let's go home."

The fog was being torn apart by the wind. It was even possible to see the moon through the flying streamers.

"Come on," he repeated.

"It's still not right," said Johnny. "It can't end like this."

"Best ending," said Wobbler. "Just like Yo-less said. Nasty men foiled. Kids save the day. Everyone gets a bun."

The abandoned bulldozer seemed a lot bigger in this pale light.

The air had a fizz to it.

"Something's going to happen," said Johnny, running towards the cemetery.

"Now, look—"

"Come on!"

"No! Not in there!"

Johnny turned around.

"And you're pretending to be a vampire?"

"But—"

"Come on, the railings have been knocked down."

"But it's nearly midnight! And there's dead people in there!"

"Well? We're all dead, sooner or later."

"Yeah, but *me*, I'd like it to be later, thank you!"

Johnny could feel it all around him—a squashed feel to things, like the air gets before a thunderstorm. It cracked off the buckled gravestones and tingled on the dusty shrubberies.

The fog was pouring away now, as if it was trying to escape from something. The moon shone out of a damp blue-black sky, casting darker shadows on the ground.

North Drive and East Way . . . they were still there, but they didn't look the same now. They belonged somewhere else—somewhere where people didn't take the roads of the dead and give them the names of the streets of the living . . .

"Wobbler?" said Johnny, without looking around.

"Yeah?"

"You there?"

"Yeah."

"Thanks."

He could feel something lifting off him, like a heavy blanket. He was amazed his feet still touched the ground.

He ran along North Drive, to the little area where all the dead roads met.

There was someone already there.

She spun around with her arms out and her eyes blissfully shut, the gravel crunching under her feet, the moonlight glinting off her ancient hat. All alone, twirling and twirling, Mrs. Tachyon danced in the night.

Not all alone . . .

The air sparkled. Glowing lines, blue as electricity, thin as smoke, poured out of the clear sky. Where they touched the fingers of the dancing woman they stretched out and broke, then re-formed.

They crawled over the grass. They whirred through the air. The whole cemetery was alive with pale blue comets.

Alive . . .

Mrs. Tachyon's feet *were* off the ground.

Johnny looked at his own fingers. There was a blue glow crackling over his right hand, like St Elmo's Fire. It sparkled as he waved it towards the stars and felt his feet leave the gravel path.

"Ooowwwwwah!"

The lights spun him around and let him drift gently back down.

"Who *are* you?"

A line of fire screamed across the night and then exploded. Sparks flew out and traced lines in the air, which took on, as though it was outlined in neon, a familiar shape.

"Well, until tonight," it said, blue fire sizzling in his beard, "I thought I was William Stickers. Watch this!"

Blue glows arched over the gravestones again and clustered around the dark bulk of the bulldozer, flowing across it so that it glowed.

The engine started.

There was a clash of gears.

It moved forward. The railings clanged and cart-wheeled away. The brick wall crumbled.

Lights orbited around the bulldozed as it ploughed onward.

"Hey! Stop!"

Metal groaned. The engine note dropped to a dull, insistent throbbing.

The lights turned to look at Johnny. He could feel their attention.

"What are you *doing*?"

A light burst into a glittering diagram of the Alderman.

"Isn't this what people wanted?" he said. "We don't need it any more. So if anyone's going to do it, it should be us. That's only right."

"But you said this was your place!" said Johnny.

Mrs. Sylvia Liberty outlined herself in the air.

"We have left Nothing there," she said, "of any Importance."

"Force of habit," said William Stickers, "is what has subjugated the working man for too long. I was right about that, anyway."

"The disgusting bolshevik, although he needs a shave, is Quite correct," said Mrs. Liberty. And then she laughed. "It seems to me we've spent Far too long moping around because of what we're not, without any Consideration of what we might *be*."

"Chronologically gifted," said Mr. Einstein, crackling into existence.

"Dimensionally advantaged," said Mr. Fletcher, sparkling like a flashbulb.

"Bodily unencumbered," said the Alderman.

"Into Extra Time," said Stanley Roundway.

"Enhanced," said Mr. Vicenti.

"We had to find it out," said Mr. Fletcher. "You have to find it out. You have to forget who you were. That's the first step. And stop being frightened of old ghosts. Then you've got room to find out what you *are*. What you can *be*."

"So we're off," said the Alderman.

"Where to?"

"We don't know. It iss going to be very interesting to find out," said Solomon Einstein.

"But . . . but . . . we've saved the cemetery!" said Johnny. "We had a meeting! And Bigmac . . . and I spoke up and . . . there's been things on the television and people have really been *talking* about this place!

No-one's going to build anything on it! There's been birdwatchers here and everything! Turn the machine off! We've saved the cemetery."

"But we don't need it any more," said the Alderman.

"We do!"

The dead looked at him.

"We do," Johnny repeated. "We . . . need it to be there."

The diesel engine chugged. The machine vibrated. The dead, if that's what they still were, seemed to be thinking.

Then Solomon Einstein nodded.

"This iss of course very true," he said, in his excited squeaky voice. "It all balances, you see. The living have to remember, the dead have to forget. Conservation of energy."

The bulldozer's engine stuttered into silence.

Mr. Vicenti held up a hand. It glowed like a firework.

"We came back to say goodbye. And thank you," he said.

"I hardly did anything."

"You listened. You tried. You were there. You can get medals just for being there. People forget the people who were just there."

"Yes. I know."

"But, now . . . we must be somewhere else."

"No . . . don't go yet," said Johnny. "I have to ask you—"

Mr. Vicenti turned.

"Yes?"

"Um . . ."

"Yes?"

"Are there . . . angels involved? You know? Or . . . devils and things? A lot of people would like to know."

"Oh, no. I don't think so. That sort of thing . . . no. That's for the living. No."

The Alderman rubbed his spectral hands. "I rather think it's going to be a lot more interesting than that."

The dead were walking away, some of them fading back into shining smoke as they moved.

Some were heading for the canal. There was a boat there. It looked vaguely like a gondola. A dark figure stood at one end, leaning on a pole that vanished into the water.

"This is my lift," said William Stickers.

"It looks a bit . . . spooky. No offence meant," said Johnny.

"Well, I thought I'd give it a try. If I don't like it, I'll go somewhere else," said William Stickers, stepping aboard. "Off we go, comrade."

RIGHT said the ferryman.

The boat moved away from the bank. The canal was only a few metres wide, but the boat seemed to be drifting off a long, long way . . .

Voices came back over the waters.

"You know, an outboard motor on this and it'd go like a bird."

I LIKE IT THE WAY IT IS, MR. STICKERS.

"What's the pay like?"

SHOCKING.

"I wouldn't stand for it, if I was you—"

"I'm not sure where he's going," said the Alderman, "but he's certainly going to reorganize things when he gets there. Bit of a traditional thinker, our William."

There was a click and hum from further along the bank. Einstein and Fletcher were sitting proudly in some sort of-well, it looked partly like an electronic circuit diagram, and partly like a machine, and partly like mathematics would look if it was solid. It glowed and fizzled.

"Good, isn't it," said Mr. Fletcher. "You've heard of a train of thought?"

"This is a flight of the imagination," said Solomon Einstein.

"We're going to have a good look at some things."

"That's right. Starting with everything."

Mr. Fletcher thumped the machine happily.

"Right! The sky's the limit, Mr. Einstein!"

"Not even that, Mr. Fletcher!"

The lines grew bright, drew together, became more like a diagram. And vanished. Just before they vanished, though, they seemed to be accelerating.

And then there were three.

"Did I see them waving?" said Mrs. Liberty.

"And particling, I shouldn't wonder," said the Alderman. "Come, Sylvia. I feel a more down-to-earth mode of transport would be suitable for us."

He took her hand. They ignored Johnny and stepped on to the black waters of the canal.

And sank, slowly, leaving a pearly sheen on the water which gradually faded away.

Then there was the sound of a motor starting up.

Out of the water, transparent as a bubble, the spirit of the dead Ford Capri rose gently towards the sky.

The Alderman wound down an invisible window.

"Mrs. Liberty thinks we ought to tell you something," he said. "But . . . it's hard to explain, you know."

"What is?" said Johnny.

"By the way, why are you wearing a pink sheet?"

"Um—"

"I expect it's not important."

"Yes."

"Well—" The car turned slowly; Johnny could see the moon through it. "You know those games where this ball runs up and bounces around and ends up in a slot at the bottom?"

"Pinball machines?"

"Is that what they're called now?"

"I think so."

"Oh. Right." The Alderman nodded. "Well . . . when you're bouncing around from pin to pin, it is probably very difficult to know that outside the game there's a room and outside the room there's a town and outside the town there's a country and outside the country there's a world and outside the world there's a billion trillion stars and that's only the start of it . . . but it's there, d'you see? Once you know about it, you can stop worrying about the slot at the bottom. And you might bounce around a good deal longer."

"I'll . . . try to remember it."

"Good man. Well, we'd better be going . . ."

Ghostly gears went crunch. The car juddered.

"Drat the thing. Ah . . . Be seeing you . . ."

It rose gently, turned towards the east, and sped away and up . . .

And then there was one.

"Well, I think I might as well be off," said Mr. Vicenti. He produced a top hat and an old-fashioned walking cane out of thin air.

"Why are you all leaving?" said Johnny.

"Oh, yes. It's Judgement Day," said Mr. Vicenti. "We decided."

"I thought that was chariots and things."

"I think you'll have to use your own judgement on that one. No point in waiting for what you've already got. It's different for everybody, you see. Enjoy looking after the cemetery. They're places for the living, after all."

Mr. Vicenti pulled on a pair of white gloves and pressed an invisible lift button. He began to rise. White feathers cascaded out of his sleeves.

"Dear me," he said, and opened his jacket. "Go on, away with you! All of you! Shoo!"

Half a dozen ghostly pigeons untangled themselves and rocketed off into the dawn.

"There. That proves it. You can escape from anything, eventually," he called down. Johnny just managed to hear him add, ". . . although I will admit that three sets of manacles, twenty feet of chain and a canvas sack can present a considerable amount of difficulty in certain circumstances . . ."

The light glinted off his hat.

And then there was . . . one.

Johnny turned around.

Mr. Grimm was standing neatly in the middle of the path, with his neat hands neatly folded. Darkness surrounded him like a fog. He was watching the sky. Johnny had never seen such an expression . . .

He remembered the time, many years ago, when Bigmac had a party and hadn't invited him. He'd said afterwards, "Well, of course not. I knew you'd come, you didn't have to be asked, you didn't need to be asked, you could just have turned up." But everyone else was going to go, and was talking about going, and he'd felt like a pit had opened up in his life. That sort of thing was pretty awful when you were seven.

It looked much, much worse when you were dead.

Mr. Grimm saw Johnny staring at him.

"Huh," he said, pulling himself together. "They'll be sorry."

"I'm going to find out about you, Mr. Grimm," said Johnny.

"Nothing to find out," snapped the ghost.

Johnny walked through him. There was a chilly moment, and then Mr. Grimm was gone.

And then there were none.

Real night flowed back in. The sounds of the town, the distant hum of the traffic, filled the space taken up by the silence.

Johnny walked back along the gravel path.

"Wobbler?" he whispered. "Wobbler?"

He found him crouched behind a gravestone with his eyes shut.

"Come on," said Johnny.

"Look, I—"

"Everything's OK."

"It was fireworks, right?" said Wobbler. His Count Dracula make-up was streaked and smudged, and he'd lost his fangs. "Someone was letting some fireworks off, yes?"

"That's right."

"Of course, I wasn't scared."

"No."

"But those things can be dangerous . . ."

"Oh, that's right."

They turned as a rattling sound started up behind them. Mrs. Tachyon appeared, pushing her shopping trolley; the wheels bounced and skidded on the gravel.

She ignored both of them. They stepped aside hurriedly as the trolley, one wheel squeaking, vanished into the gloom.

Then they walked home, through the morning mists.

11

As Tommy Atkins had once said, things aren't necessarily over just because they've stopped.

There was Bigmac, for a start. Yo-less had gone home with him, and Bigmac's brother had been waiting up and had started on at him and Bigmac had looked at him strangely for a few seconds and then hit him so hard that he knocked him out. Yo-less said, with awe in his voice, that it'd been so hard that the word "TAH" was printed in Biro on the brother's chin. And then he'd growled at Clint and the dog had hid under the sofa. So Yo-less had to get his mother out of bed to bring her car round to carry Bigmac's suitcase, three tropical fish tanks and two hundred copies of *Guns and Ammo* back to her spare room.

And there was the generous donation to the Blackbury Volunteers by United Amalagamated Consolidated Holdings. As Mr. Atterbury said, it's amazing what you can do with a kind word, provided you've also got a big stick.

The cemetery was already looking more lived-in. There were endless arguments between the Volunteers who wanted it to be habitat and the ones who wanted it to be ecology and a middle group who just wanted it to be clean and tidy, but at least it was wanted, which seemed to Johnny to be the most important thing.

It took Johnny a week to find what *he* wanted, and when he found it he took it along to the cemetery after school, when no-one was about. There was frost on the ground.

"Mr. Grimm?"

He found him by the canal, sitting staring at the water.

"Mr. Grimm?"

"Go away. You're dangerous."

"I thought you'd be a bit . . . lonely. So I bought you this."

He opened the bag.

"Mr. Atterbury helped," he said. "He phoned around some of his friends who've got electrical shops. It's been repaired. It'll work until the batteries die, and then I thought maybe it'd work on ghost batteries."

"What *is* it?"

"A very small television," said Johnny. "I thought I could put it right in a bush or somewhere and no-one'll know it's there except you."

"What are you doing this for?" said Mr. Grimm, suspiciously.

"Because I looked you up in the newspaper. May the twenty-first, nineteen twenty-seven. There wasn't very much. Just the bit about them finding . . . you in the canal, and the coroner's inquest."

"Oh? Poking around, eh? And what do you think you know about *anything*?"

"Nothing."

"I don't have to explain."

"Is that why you couldn't leave with the others?"

"What? I can leave whenever I like," said the ghost of Mr. Grimm, very quickly. "If I'm staying here, it's because I want to be here. I know my place. I know how to do the right thing. I could leave whenever I want. But I've got more pride than that. People like you don't understand that. You don't take life seriously."

It hadn't been a long report in the paper. Mr. Vicenti was right. In those days, some things didn't get a lot of reporting. Mr. Grimm had been a respectable citizen, keeping his head down, a man at the back of the crowd, and then his business had failed and there'd been some other trouble involving money, and then there'd been the canal. Mr. Grimm had taken life very seriously, starting with his own.

People didn't talk much about that sort of thing in those days. Suicide was against the law. Johnny had wondered why. It meant that if you missed, or the gas ran out, or the rope broke, you could get locked up in prison to show you that life was really very jolly and thoroughly worth living.

Mr. Grimm sat with his hands clasped around his knees.

Johnny realized that he could think of nothing to say, so he said nothing.

Instead, he wedged the little pocket television deep in a bush, where no-one, not even the keenest birdwatcher, would find it.

"Can you turn it on with your mind?" he said.

"Who says I shall want to?"

The picture came on, and there was the faint tinkly sound of the familiar signature tune.

"Let's see," said Johnny. "You've missed a week . . . Mrs. Swede has just found out Janine didn't go to the party . . . Mr. Hatt has sacked Jason from the shop because he thinks he took the money . . . and . . ."

"I see."

"So . . . I'll be off, then, shall I?"

"Right."

Johnny backed away.

"I'm sure the hours'll just fly by."

"Right."

"So . . . cheerio, then."

"Right."

"Mr. Grimm?" Johnny wanted to say: you can leave any time you want. But there seemed to be no point.

"Right."

Johnny watched for a while, and then turned and walked away. The other three were waiting for him by the phone box.

"Was he there?" said Yo-less.

"Yes."

"What's he doing now?"

"Watching television," said Johnny.

"I expect ghosts do that a lot," said Wobbler.

" 'Spect so."

"You all right?"

"Just thinking about the difference between heaven and hell."

"That doesn't sound like 'all right' to me."

Johnny blinked. And looked around at the world.

It was, not to put too fine a point on it, wonderful. Which wasn't the same as nice. It wasn't even the same as good. But it was full of . . . stuff. You'd never get to the end of it. It was always springing new things on you . . .

"Yeah," he said. "All right. What shall we do now?"

JOHNNY AND THE BOMB

I would like to thank the Meteorological Office, the Royal Mint and my old friend Bernard Pearson—who, if he doesn't know something, always knows a man who does—for their help in the research for this book. When historical details are wrong, it's my fault for not listening. But who knows what really happened in the other leg of the Trousers of Time?

1

After the Bombs

It was nine o'clock in the evening, in Blackbury High Street.

It was dark, with occasional light from the full moon behind streamers of worn-out cloud. The wind was from the south-west and there had been another thunderstorm, which freshened the air and made the cobbles slippery.

A policeman moved, very slowly and sedately, along the street.

Here and there, if someone was very close, they might have seen the faintest line of light around a blacked-out window. From within came the quiet sounds of people living their lives—the muffled notes of a piano as someone practiced scales, over and over again, and the murmur and occasional burst of laughter from the wireless.

Some of the shop windows had sandbags piled in front of them. A poster outside one shop urged people to Dig For Victory, as if it were some kind of turnip.

On the horizon, in the direction of Slate, the thin beams of searchlights tried to pry bombers out of the clouds.

The policeman turned the corner, and walked up the next street, his boots seeming very loud in the stillness.

The beat took him up as far as the Methodist chapel, and in theory would then take him down Paradise Street, but it didn't do that tonight because there was no Paradise Street any more. Not since last night.

There was a lorry parked by the chapel. Light leaked out from the tarpaulin that covered the back.

He banged on it.

"You can't park that 'ere, gents," he said. "I fine you one mug of tea and we shall say no more about it, eh?"

The tarpaulin was pushed back and a soldier jumped out. There was a brief vision of the interior—a warm tent of orange light, with a few soldiers sitting around a little stove, and the air thick with cigarette smoke.

The soldier grinned.

"Gi'us a mug and a wad for the sergeant," he said, to someone in the lorry.

A tin mug of scalding black tea and a brick-thick sandwich were handed out.

"Much obliged," said the policeman, taking them. He leaned against the lorry.

"How's it going, then?" he said. "Haven't heard a bang."

"It's a 25-pounder," said the soldier. "Went right down through the cellar floor. You lot took a real pounding last night, eh? Want a look?"

"Is it safe?"

" 'Course not," said the soldier cheerfully. "That's why we're here, right? Come on." He pinched out his cigarette and put it behind his ear.

"I thought you lot'd be guarding it," said the policeman.

"It's two in the morning and it's been pissing down," said the soldier. "Who's going to steal an unexploded bomb?"

"Yes, but . . ." The sergeant looked in the direction of the ruined street.

There was the sound of bricks sliding.

"Someone is, by the sound of it," he said.

"What? We've got warning signs up!" said the soldier. "We only knocked off for a brew-up! Oi!"

Their boots crunched on the rubble that had been strewn across the road.

"It *is* safe, isn't it?" said the sergeant.

"Not if someone drops a dirty great heap of bricks on it, no! Oi! You!"

The moon came out from behind the clouds. They could make out a figure at the other end of what remained of the street, near the wall of the pickle factory.

The sergeant skidded to a halt.

"Oh, no," he whispered. "It's Mrs. Tachyon."

The soldier stared at the small figure that was dragging some sort of cart through the rubble.

"Who's she?"

"Let's just take it quietly, shall we?" said the policeman, grabbing his arm.

He shone his torch and set his face into a sort of mad friendly grin.

"That you, Mrs. Tachyon?" he said. "It's me, Sergeant Bourke. Bit chilly to be out at this time of night, eh? Got a nice warm cell back at the station, yes? I daresay there could be a big hot mug of cocoa for you if you just come along with me, how about that?"

"Can't she read all them warning signs? Is she mental?" said the soldier, under his breath. "She's right by the house with the bomb in the cellar!"

"Yes . . . no . . . she's just different," said the sergeant. "Bit . . . touched." He raised his voice. "You just stay where you are, love, and we'll come and get you. Don't want you hurting yourself on all this junk, do we?"

"Here, has she been looting?" said the soldier. "She could get shot for that, pinching stuff from bombed-out houses!"

"No-one's going to shoot Mrs. Tachyon," said the sergeant. "We *know* her, see? She was in the cells the other night."

"What'd she done?"

"Nothing. We let her kip in a spare cell in the station if it's a nippy night. I gave her a tanner and pair of ole boots what belong to me mum only yesterday. Well, look at her. She's old enough to be your granny, poor old biddy."

Mrs. Tachyon stood and watched them owlishly as they walked, very cautiously, towards her.

The soldier saw a wizened little woman wearing what looked like a party dress with layers of other clothes on top, and a woolly hat with a bobble on it. She was pushing a wire cart on wheels. It had a metal label on it.

"Tes-co," he said. "What's that?"

"Dunno where she gets half her stuff," muttered the sergeant.

The trolley seemed to be full of black bags. But there were other things, which glittered in the moonlight.

"I know where she got *that* stuff," muttered the soldier. "That's been pinched from the pickle factory!"

"Oh, half the town was in there this morning," said the sergeant. "A few jars of gherkins won't hurt."

"Yeah, but you can't have this sort of thing. 'Ere, you! Missus! You just let me have a look at—"

He reached towards the trolley.

Some sort of demon, all teeth and glowing eyes, erupted from it and clawed the skin off the back of his hand.

"Blast! 'Ere, help me get hold of—"

But the sergeant had backed away.

"That's Guilty, that is," he said. "I should come away if I was you!"

Mrs. Tachyon cackled.

"Thunderbirds Are Go!" she chortled. "Wot, no bananas? That's what *you* think, my old dollypot!"

She hauled the trolley round and trotted off, dragging it behind her.

"Hey, don't go in *there*—" the soldier shouted.

The old woman hauled the trolley over a pile of bricks. A piece of wall collapsed behind her.

The last brick hit something far below, which went *boink*.

The soldier and the policeman froze in mid-run.

The moon went behind a cloud again.

In the darkness, there was a ticking sound. It was far off, and a bit muffled, but in that pool of silence both men heard it all the way up their spines.

The sergeant's foot, which had been in the air, came down slowly.

"How long've you got if it starts to tick?" he whispered.

There was no-one there. The soldier was accelerating away.

The policeman ran after him and was halfway up the ruins of Paradise Street before the world behind him suddenly became full of excitement.

It was nine o'clock in the evening, in Blackbury High Street.

In the window of the electrical shop, nine TVs showed the same picture. Nine televisions projected their flickering screens at the empty air.

A newspaper blew along the deserted pavement until it wrapped around the stalks in an ornamental flowerbed. The wind caught an empty lager tin and bowled it across the pavement until it hit a drain.

The High Street was what Blackbury District Council called a Pedestrian Precinct and Amenity Area, although no-one was quite sure what the amenities were, or even what an amenity *was*. Perhaps it was the benches, cunningly designed so that people wouldn't sit on them for too long and make the place untidy. Or maybe it was the flower-beds, which sprouted a regular crop of the hardy perennial Crisp Packet. It couldn't have been the ornamental trees. They'd looked quite big and leafy on the original drawings a few years ago, but what with cutbacks and one thing and another, no-one had actually got around to planting any.

The sodium lights made the night cold as ice.

The newspaper blew on again, and wrapped itself around a yellow litter bin in the shape of a fat dog with its mouth open.

Something landed in an alleyway and groaned.

"Tick tick tick! Tickety Boo! Ow! National . . . Health . . . Service . . ."

The interesting thing about worrying about things, thought Johnny Maxwell, was the way there was always something new to worry about.

His friend Kirsty said it was because he was a natural worrier, but that was because she didn't worry about *anything*. She got angry instead, and did things about it, whatever *it* was. He really envied the way she decided what *it* was and knew exactly what to do about *it* almost instantly. Currently she was saving the planet most evenings, and foxes at weekends.

Johnny just worried. Usually they were the same old worries—school, money, whether you could get AIDS from watching television, and so on. But occasionally one would come out of nowhere like a Christmas Number One and knock all the others down a whole division.

Right now, it was his mind.

"It's not exactly the same as being ill," said Yo-less, who'd read all the way through his mother's medical encyclopedia.

"It's not being ill at all. If lots of bad things have happened to you it's healthy to be depressed," said Johnny. "That's sense, isn't it? What with the business going down the drain, and Dad pushing off, and Mum just sitting around smoking all the time and everything. I mean, going around smiling and saying, 'Oh, it's not so bad'—that *would* be mental."

"That's right," said Yo-less, who'd read a bit about psychology as well.

"My gran went mental," said Bigmac. "She—ow!"

"Sorry," said Yo-less. "I wasn't looking where I put my foot but, fair's fair, you weren't either."

"It's just dreams," said Johnny. "It's nothing *mad*."

Although, he had to admit, it was dreams during the day, too. Dreams so real that they filled his eyes and ears.

The planes . . .

The bombs . . .

And the fossil fly. Why that? There'd be these nightmares, and in the middle of it, there'd be the fly. It was a tiny one, in a piece of amber. He'd saved up for it and done a science project on it. But it wasn't even scary-looking. It was just a fly from millions of years ago. Why was *that* in a nightmare?

Huh. *School teachers?* Why couldn't they be like they were supposed to be and just chuck things at you if you weren't paying attention? Instead they all seemed to have been worrying about him and sending notes home and getting him to see a specialist, although the specialist wasn't too bad and at least it got him out of Maths.

One of the notes had said he was "disturbed." Well, who wasn't disturbed? He hadn't shown it to his mum. Things were bad enough as it was.

"You getting on all right at your grandad's?" said Yo-less.

"It's not too bad. Grandad does the housework most of the time anyway. He's good at fried bread. And Surprise Surprise."

"What's that?"

"You know that stall on the market that sells tins that've got the labels off?"

"Yes?"

"Well, he buys loads of those. And you've got to eat them once they're opened."

"Yuk."

"Oh, pineapple and meatballs isn't too bad."

They walked on through the evening street.

The thing about all of us, Johnny thought, the *sad* thing is that we're not very good. Actually that's not the worst part. The worst part is we're not even much good at being not much good.

Take Yo-less. When you looked at Yo-less you might think he had possibilities. He was black. Technically. But he never said "Yo," and only said "check it out" in the supermarket, and the only person he ever called a mother was his mother. Yo-less said it was racial stereotyping to say all black kids acted like that but, however you looked at it, Yo-less had been born with a defective cool. *Trainspotters* were cooler than Yo-less. If you gave Yo-less a baseball cap he'd put it on the right way round. That's how, well, *yo-less* Yo-less was. Sometimes he actually wore a tie.

Now, Bigmac . . . Bigmac *was* good. He was good at Maths. Sort of. It made the teachers wild. You could show Bigmac some sort of horrible equation and he'd say "x=2.75" and he'd be right. But he never knew *why*. "It's just what it is," he'd say. And that was *no* good. Knowing the answers wasn't what Maths was about. Maths was about showing how you worked them out, even if you got them wrong. Bigmac was also a skinhead. Bigmac and Bazza and Skazz were the last three skinheads in Blackbury. At least, the last three who weren't someone's dad. And he had LOVE and HAT on his knuckles, but only in Biro because when he'd gone to get tattooed he fainted. And he bred tropical fish.

As for Wobbler . . . Wobbler wasn't even a nerd. He *wanted* to be a nerd but they wouldn't let him join. He had a Nerd Pride badge and he messed around with computers. What Wobbler wanted was to be a kid in milk-bottle-bottom glasses and a deformed anorak, who could write amazing software and be a millionaire by the time he was twenty, but he'd probably settle for just being someone whose computer didn't keep smelling of burning plastic every time he touched it.

And as for Johnny . . .

. . . if you go mad, do you know you've gone mad? If you don't, how do you know you're *not* mad?

"It wasn't a bad film," Wobbler was saying. They'd been to Screen W at the Blackbury Odeon. They generally went to see any film that promised to have laser beams in it somewhere.

"But you can't travel in time without messing things up," said Yo-less.

"That's the whole point," said Bigmac. "That's what you *want* to do. I wouldn't mind joining the police if they were *time* police. You'd go back and say, 'Hey, are you Adolf Hitler?' and when he said, 'Achtung, that's me, ja' . . . *Kablooeee!* With the pump-action shotgun. End of problem."

"Yes, but supposing you accidentally shot your own grandfather," said Yo-less patiently.

"I wouldn't. He doesn't look a bit like Adolf Hitler."

"Anyway, you're not that good a shot," said Wobbler. "You got kicked out of the Paintball Club, didn't you?"

"Only 'cos they were jealous that they hadn't thought of a paintball hand grenade before I showed them how."

"It was a *tin* of *paint*, Bigmac. A two-litre tin."

"Well, yeah, but in *contex'* it was a hand grenade."

"They said you might at least have loosened the lid a bit. Sean Stevens needed stitches."

"I didn't mean *actually* shooting your *actual* grandfather," said Yo-less, loudly. "I mean messing things up so maybe you're not actually born or your time machine never gets invented. Like in that film where the robot is sent back to kill the mother of the boy who's going to beat the robots when he grows up."

"Good one, that," said Bigmac, strafing the silent shops with an invisible machine gun.

"But if he never got born how did they know he'd existed?" said Yo-less. "Didn't make any sense to me."

"How come you're such an expert?" said Wobbler.

"Well, I've got three shelves of Star Trek videos," said Yo-less.

"Anorak alert!"

"Nerd!"

"Trainspotter!"

"*Anyway*," said Yo-less, "if you changed things, maybe you'd end up not going back in time, and there you would be, back in time, I mean, except you never went in the first place, so you wouldn't be able to come back on account of not having gone. *Or*, even if you could get back, you'd get back to another time, like a sort of parallel dimension, because if the thing you changed hadn't happened then you wouldn't've gone, so you could only come back to somewhere you never went. And there you'd be—stuck."

They tried to work this out.

"Huh, you'd have to be mad even to understand time travel," said Wobbler eventually.

"Job opportunity for you there, Johnny," said Bigmac.

"*Bigmac*," said Yo-less, in a warning voice.

"It's all right," said Johnny. "The doctor said I just worry about things too much."

"What kind of loony tests did you have?" said Bigmac. "Big needles and electric shocks and that?"

"No, Bigmac," sighed Johnny. "They don't do that. They just ask you questions."

"What, like 'are you a loony?' "

"It'd be sound to go a *long* way back in time," said Wobbler. "Back to the dinosaurs. No chance of killing your grandad then, unless he's *really* old. Dinosaurs'd be all right."

"Great!" said Bigmac. "Then I could wipe 'em out with my plasma rifle! Oh, yes!"

"Yeah," said Wobbler, rolling his eyes. "That'd explain a lot. Why did the dinosaurs die out sixty-five million years ago? Because Bigmac couldn't get there any earlier."

"But you haven't *got* a plasma rifle," said Johnny.

"If Wobbler can have a time machine, then I can have a plasma rifle."

"Oh, all right."

"And a rocket launcher."

A time machine, thought Johnny. That *would* be something. You could get your life exactly as you wanted it. If something nasty turned up, you could just go back and make sure that it didn't. You could go wherever you wanted and nothing bad would ever have to happen.

Around him, the boys' conversation, as their conversations did, took on its own peculiar style.

"Anyway, no-one's proved the dinosaurs *did* die out."

"Oh, yeah, right, sure, they're still around, are they?"

"I mean p'raps they only come out at night, or are camouflaged or something . . ."

"A brick-finished stegosaurus? A bright red Number 9 brontosaurus?"

"Hey, neat idea. They'd go round pretending to be a bus, right, and people could get on—but they wouldn't get off again. Oooo-Eee-Oooo . . ."

"Nah. False noses. False noses and beards. Then just when people aren't expecting it—UNK! Nothing on the pavement but a pair of shoes and a really big bloke in a mac, shuffling away . . ."

Paradise Street, thought Johnny. Paradise Street was on his mind a lot, these days. Especially at night.

I bet if you asked the people *there* if time travel was a good idea they'd say yes. I mean, no-one knows what happened to the dinosaurs, but we know what happened to Paradise Street.

I wish I could go back to Paradise Street.

Something hissed.

They looked around. There was an alleyway between the charity clothes shop and the video library. The hissing came from there, except now it had changed into a snarl.

It wasn't at all pleasant. It went right into his ears and right through Johnny's modern brain and right down into the memories built into his very bones. When an early ape had cautiously got down out of its tree and wobbled awkwardly along the ground, trying out this new "standing upright" idea all the younger apes were talking about, this was exactly the kind of snarl it hated to hear.

It said to every muscle in the body: run away and climb something. And possibly throw down some coconuts, too.

"There's something in the alley," said Wobbler, looking around in case there were any trees handy.

"A werewolf?" said Bigmac.

Wobbler stopped. "Why should it be a werewolf?" he said.

"I saw this film, *Curse of the Revenge of the Werewolf*," said Bigmac, "and someone heard a snarl like that and went into a dark alley, and next thing, he was lying there with all his special effects spilling out on the pavement."

"Huh," quavered Wobbler. "There's no such things as werewolves."

"You go and tell it, then."

Johnny stepped forward.

There was a shopping trolley lying on its side just inside the alley, but that wasn't unusual. Herds of shopping trolleys roamed the streets of Blackbury. While he'd never seen one actually moving, he sometimes suspected that they trundled off as soon as his back was turned.

Bulging carrier bags and black plastic dustbin liners lay around it, and there was a number of jars. One of them had broken open, and there was a smell of vinegar.

One of the bundles was wearing trainers.

You didn't see that very often.

A terrible monster pulled itself over the top of the trolley and spat at Johnny.

It was white, but with bits of brown and black as well. It was scrawny. It had three and a half legs but only one ear. Its face was a mask of absolute, determined evil. Its teeth were jagged and yellow, its breath as nasty as a pepper spray.

Johnny knew it well. So did practically everyone else in Blackbury.

"Hello, Guilty," he said, taking care to keep his hands by his sides.

If Guilty was here, and the shopping trolley was here . . .

He looked down at the bundle with the trainers.

"I think something's happened to Mrs. Tachyon," he said.

The others hurried up.

It only looked like a bundle, because Mrs. Tachyon tended to wear everything she owned, all at once. This was a woolly hat, about twelve jerseys and a pink ra-ra skirt, then bare pipe-cleaner legs down to several pairs of football socks and the huge trainers.

"Is that *blood?*" said Wobbler.

"Ur," said Bigmac. "Yuk."

"I think she's alive," said Johnny. "I'm sure I heard a groan."

"Er . . . I know first aid," said Yo-less, uncertainly. "Kiss of life and stuff."

"Kiss of life? *Mrs. Tachyon?* Yuk," said Bigmac.

Yo-less looked very worried. What seemed simple when you did it in a nice warm hall with the instructor watching seemed a lot more complicated in an alleyway, especially with all the woolly jumpers involved. Whoever invented first aid hadn't had Mrs. Tachyon in mind.

Yo-less knelt down gingerly. He patted Mrs. Tachyon vaguely, and something fell out of one of her many pockets. It was fish and chips, wrapped in a piece of newspaper.

"She's always eating chips," said Bigmac. "My brother says she picks thrown-away papers out of the bin to see if there's any chips still in 'em. Yuk."

"Er . . ." said Yo-less desperately, as he tried to find a way of administering first aid without actually touching anything.

Finally Johnny came to his rescue and said, "I know how to dial 999."

Yo-less sagged with relief. "Yes, yes, that's right," he said. "I'm pretty sure you mustn't move people, on account of breaking bones."

"Or the crust," said Wobbler.

2

Mrs. Tachyon

Mrs. Tachyon had always been there, as long as Johnny could remember. She was a bag lady before people knew what bag ladies were, although strictly speaking she was a trolley woman.

It wasn't a *normal* supermarket trolley, either. It looked bigger, the wires looked thicker. And it hurt like mad when Mrs. Tachyon pushed it into the small of your back, which she did quite a lot. It wasn't that she did it out of nastiness—well, it *probably* wasn't—but other people just didn't exist on Planet Tachyon.

Fortunately, one wheel squeaked. And if you didn't get accustomed to moving away quickly when you heard the *squee . . . squee . . . squee* coming, the monologue was another warning.

Mrs. Tachyon talked all the time. You could never be quite certain who she was talking to.

". . . I sez, that's what you sez, is it? That's what *you* think. An' I could get both hands in yer mouth and still wind wool, I sez. Oh, yes. Tell Sid! Yer so skinny yer can close one eye and yer'd look like a needle, I sez. Oh, yes. They done me out of it! Tell that to the boys in khaki! That's a pelter or I don't know what is!"

But quite often it was just a mumble, with occasional triumphant shouts of "I *told* 'em!" and "That's what *you* think!"

The trolley with its squeaky wheel could turn up behind you at any hour of the day or night. No-one knew when to expect it. Nor did anyone know what was in all those bags. Mrs. Tachyon tended to rummage a lot, in bins and things. So no-one wanted to find out.

Sometimes she'd disappear for weeks on end. No-one knew where she went. Then, just when everyone was beginning to relax, there'd be the *squee . . . squee . . . squee* behind them and the stabbing pain in the small of the back.

Mrs. Tachyon picked things out of the gutter. That was probably how she'd acquired Guilty, with his fur like carpet underlay, broken teeth, and boomerang-shaped backbone. When Guilty walked, which wasn't often since he preferred to ride in the trolley, he tended to go around in circles. When he ran, usually because he was trying to fight something, the fact that he only had one and a half legs in front meant that sooner or later his back legs would overtake him, and by then he was always in such a rage that he'd bite his own tail.

Even DSS, the rabid dog owned by Syd the Crusty, which once ate a police Alsatian, would run away at the sight of Guilty spinning towards him, frantically biting himself.

The ambulance drove off, blue light flashing.

Guilty watched Johnny from the trolley, going cross-eyed with hatred.

"The ambulance man said she looked as if she'd been hit by something," said Wobbler, who was also watching the cat. It was never a good idea to take your eye off Guilty.

"What're we going to do with all this stuff?" said Johnny.

"Yeah, can't leave it," said Bigmac. "That'd be littering."

"But it's her stuff," said Johnny.

"Don't look at *me*," said Bigmac. "Some of those bags *squelch*."

"And there's the cat," said Johnny.

"Yeah, we ought to kill the cat," said Bigmac. "It took all the skin off my hand last week."

Johnny cautiously pulled the trolley upright. Guilty clung to it, hissing.

"He likes you," said Bigmac.

"How can you tell?"

"You've still got both eyes."

"You could take it along to the RSPCA in the morning," said Yoless.

"I suppose so," said Johnny, "but what about the trolley? We can't just leave it here."

"Yeah, let's push it off the top of the multistorey," said Bigmac.

Johnny prodded a bag. It moved a bit, and then flowed back, with an unpleasant oozing noise.

"Y'know, my brother said Mrs. Tachyon killed her husband years ago and then went mental and they never found his body," said Bigmac.

They looked at the bags.

"None of them is big enough for a dead body," said Yo-less, who wasn't allowed to watch horror movies.

"Not a *whole* one, no," said Bigmac.

Yo-less took a step back.

"*I* heard she stuck his head in the oven," said Wobbler. "Very messy."

"Messy?" said Yo-less.

"It was a microwave oven. Get it? If you put a—"

"Shut up," said Yo-less.

"I heard she's really, really rich," said Bigmac.

"Stinking rich," said Wobbler.

"Look, I'll just . . . I'll just put in it in my grandad's garage," said Johnny.

"I don't see why we have to do it," said Yo-less. "There's supposed to be Care in the Community or something."

"He doesn't keep much in there now. And then in the morning . . ."

Oh, well. The morning was another day.

"And while you've got it you could have a rummage to see if there's any money," said Bigmac.

Johnny glanced at Guilty, who snarled.

"No, I like a hand with all its fingers on," he said. "You lot come with me. I'd feel a right clod pushing this by myself."

The fourth wheel squeaked and bounced as he pushed the trolley down the street.

"Looks heavy," said Yo-less.

There was a snigger from beside him.

"Well, they say *Mr.* Tachyon was a very big man—"

"Just shut up, Bigmac."

It's me, he thought, as the procession went down the street. It's like on the Lottery, only it's the *opposite*. There's this big finger in the sky and it comes through your window and flicks you on the ear and says "It's YOU—har har har." And you get up and think you're going to have a normal day and suddenly you're in charge of a trolley with one squeaky wheel and an insane cat.

"Here," said Wobbler. "These fish and chips are still warm."

"What?" said Johnny. "You picked up her actual fish and chips?"

Wobbler backed away. "Well, yeah, why not, shame to let them go to waste—"

"They might have got her spit on 'em," said Bigmac. "Yuk."

"They haven't even been unwrapped, actually," said Wobbler, but he did stop unwrapping them.

"Put them in the trolley, Wobbler," said Johnny.

"Dunno who wraps fish and chips in newspaper round here," said Wobbler, tossing the package onto the pile in the trolley. "Hong Kong Henry doesn't. Where'd she get them?"

Sir John was normally awakened at half past eight every morning by a butler who brought him his breakfast, another butler who brought him his clothes, a third butler whose job it was to feed Adolf and Stalin if necessary, and a fourth butler who was basically a spare.

At nine o'clock his secretary came and read him his appointments for today.

When he did so this morning, though, he found him still staring at his plate with a strange expression. Adolf and Stalin swam contentedly in the tank by his desk.

"Five different kinds of pill, some biscuits made of cardboard and a glass of orange juice with all the excitement removed," said Sir John. "What's the point of being the richest man in the world—I am still the richest man in the world, aren't I?"

"Yes, Sir John."

"Well, what's the point if it all boils down to pills for breakfast?" He drummed his fingers on the table. "Well . . . I've had enough, d'y'hear? Tell Hickson to get the car out."

"Which car, Sir John?"

"The Bentley."

"Which Bentley, Sir John?"

"Oh, one I haven't used lately. He can choose. And find Blackbury on the map. We own a burger bar there, don't we?"

"Er . . . I think so, Sir John. Wasn't that the one where you personally chose the site? You said you just knew it would be a good one. Er . . . but today you've got appointments to see the chairman of—"

"Cancel 'em all. I'm going to Blackbury. Don't tell 'em I'm coming. Call it . . . a lightning inspection. The secret of success in business is to pay attention to the little details, am I right? People get underdone burgers or the fries turn out to be too soggy and before you know where you are the entire business is down around your ears."

"Er . . . if you say so, Sir John."

"Right. I'll be ready in twenty minutes."

"Er . . . you could, perhaps, leave it until tomorrow? Only the committee did ask that—"

"No!" The old man slapped the table. "It's got to be today! Today's when it all happens, you see. Mrs. Tachyon. The trolley. Johnny and the rest of them. It's got to be today. Otherwise . . ." He pushed away the dull yet healthy breakfast. "Otherwise it's this for the rest of my life."

The secretary was used to Sir John's moods, and tried to lighten things a little.

"Blackbury . . ." he said. "That's where you were evacuated during the war, wasn't it? And you were the only person to escape when one of the streets got bombed?"

"Me and two goldfish called Adolf and Stalin. That's right. That's where it all started," said Sir John, getting up and going over to the window. "Go on, jump to it."

The secretary didn't go straightaway. One of his jobs was to keep an eye on Sir John. The old boy was acting a bit odd, people had said. He'd taken to reading very old newspapers and books with words like "Time" and "Physics" in the title, and sometimes he even wrote angry letters to very important scientists. When you're the richest man in the world, people watch you very closely.

"Adolf and Stalin," said Sir John, to the whole world in general. "Of course, these two are only their descendants. It turned out that Adolf was female. Or was it Stalin?"

Outside the window, the gardens stretched all the way to some rolling hills that Sir John's landscape gardener had imported specially.

"Blackbury," said Sir John, staring at them. "That's where it all started. The whole thing. There was a boy called Johnny Maxwell. And Mrs. Tachyon. And a cat, I think."

He turned.

"Are you still here?"

"Sorry, Sir John," said the secretary, backing out and shutting the door behind him.

"That's where it all started," said Sir John. "And that's where it's all going to end."

Johnny always enjoyed those first few moments in the morning before the day leapt out at him. His head was peacefully full of flowers, clouds, kittens—

His hand still *hurt*.

Horrible bits of last night rushed out from hiding and bounced and gibbered in front of him.

There was a shopping trolley full of unspeakable bags in the garage. There was also a spray of milk across the wall and ceiling where Guilty had showed what he thought of people who tried to give him an unprovoked meal. Johnny had had to use the biggest Elastoplast in the medicine tin afterwards.

He got up, dressed, and went downstairs. His mother wouldn't be up yet and his grandad was definitely in the front room watching Saturday morning TV.

Johnny opened the garage door and stepped back hurriedly, in case a ball of maddened fur came spinning out.

Nothing happened.

The dreadful trolley stood in the middle of the floor. There was no sign of Guilty.

It was, Johnny thought, just like those scenes in films where you know the monster is in the room somewhere . . .

He jumped sideways, just in case Guilty was about to drop out of the ceiling.

It was bad enough seeing the wretched cat. *Not* seeing it was worse.

He scurried out and shut the door quickly, then went back into the house.

He probably ought to tell someone official. The trolley belonged to Mrs. Tachyon (actually, it probably belonged to Mr. Tesco or Mr. Safeway) so it might be stealing if he kept it.

As he went back inside, the phone rang. There were two ways he could tell. Firstly, the phone rang. Then his grandfather shouted "Phone!," because he never answered the phone if he thought there was a chance it could be answered by someone else.

Johnny picked it up.

"Can I speak to—" said Yo-less, in his Speaking to Parents voice.

"It's me, Yo-less," said Johnny.

"Hey, you know Mrs. Tachyon?"

"Of course I—"

"Well, my mum was on duty at the hospital last night. She's got horrible bruises and everything. Mrs. Tachyon, I mean, not my mum. Someone really had a go at her, she said. My mum, not Mrs. Tachyon. She said we ought to tell the police."

"What for?"

"We might have seen something. Anyway . . . er . . . someone might think it was . . . us . . ."

"*Us?* But we called the ambulance!"

"*I* know that. Er . . . and you've got her stuff . . ."

"Well, we couldn't just leave it there!"

"*I* know that. But . . . well, we did have Bigmac with us . . ."

And that was it, really. It wasn't that Bigmac was actually *evil*. He'd happily fire imaginary nuclear missiles at people but he wouldn't hurt a fly, unless perhaps it was a real hard biker fly which'd given him serious grief. However, he did have a problem with cars, especially big fast ones with the keys still in the ignition. And he *was* a skinhead. His boots were so big that it was quite hard for him to fall over.

According to Sergeant Comely of Blackbury police station, Bigmac was guilty of every unsolved crime in the town, whereas in real life he was probably only guilty of ten per cent, maximum. He *looked* like trouble. No-one looking at Bigmac would think he was innocent of *anything*.

"And Wobbler, too," Yo-less added.

And Wobbler would admit to anything if you got him frightened enough. All the great unsolved mysteries of the world—the Bermuda Triangle, the Marie Celeste, the Loch Ness Monster—could be sorted out in about half an hour if you leaned a bit on Wobbler.

"I'll go by myself, then," said Johnny. "Simpler that way."

Yo-less sighed with relief. "Thanks."

The phone rang just as Johnny put it down again.

It started saying "Hello? Hello?" before he got it to his ear.

"Er . . . hello?" he said.

"Is that *you?*" said a female voice. It wasn't exactly an unpleasant one, but it had a sharp, penetrating quality. It seemed to be saying that if you *weren't* you, then it was *your* fault. Johnny recognized it instantly. It was the voice of someone who dialled wrong numbers and then complained that the phone was answered by people she didn't want to speak to.

"Yes. Er . . . yes. Hello, Kirsty."

"It's Kasandra, actually."

"Oh. Right," said Johnny. He'd have to make a note. Kirsty changed her name about as often as she changed her clothes, although at least these days she was sticking to ones beginning with K.

"Have you heard about old Mrs. Tachyon?"

"I *think* so," said Johnny, guardedly.

"Apparently a gang of yobs beat her up last night. She looked as though a bomb'd hit her. Hello? Hello? Hello?"

"I'm still here," said Johnny. Someone had filled his stomach with ice.

"Don't you think that's shameful?"

"Er. Yes."

"One of them was black."

Johnny nodded dismally at the phone. Yo-less had explained about this sort of thing. He'd said that if one of his ancestors had joined Attila the Hun's huge horde of millions of barbarians and helped them raid Ancient Rome, people would've definitely remembered that one of them was black. And this was Yo-less, who collected brass bands, had a matchbox collection and was a known spod.

"Er," he said, "it was us. I mean, *we* didn't beat her up, but we found her. I got the ambulance and Yo-less tried—Yo-less was definitely *thinking* about first aid . . ."

"Didn't you tell the police?"

"No—"

"Honestly, I don't know what would happen if I wasn't around! You've got to tell them now. I'll meet you at the police station in half an hour. You know how to tell the time? The big hand is—"

"Yes," said Johnny, miserably.

"It's only two stops on the bus from your house. You know about catching buses?"

"Yes, yes, yes, of course I—"

"You need money. That's the round stuff you find in your pockets. *Ciao.*"

Actually, after he'd been to the toilet, he felt a bit better about it all. Kirs—Kasandra took charge of things. She was the most organized person Johnny knew. In fact she was so organized that she had too much organization for one person, and it overflowed in every direction.

He was her friend. More or less, anyway. He wasn't sure he'd ever been given a choice in the matter. Kirs—*Kasandra* wasn't good at friends. She told him so herself. She'd said it was because of a character flaw, only because she was Ki—Kasandra, she thought it was a character flaw in everyone else.

The more she tried to help people by explaining to them how stupid they were, the more they just wandered off for no reason at all. The only reason Johnny hadn't was that he *knew* how stupid he was.

But sometimes—not often—when the light was right and she wasn't organizing anything, he'd look at Ki—Kasandra and wonder if there weren't two kinds of stupidity: the basic El Thicko kind that he had, and a highly specialized sort that you only got when you were stuffed too full of intelligence.

He'd better tell Grandad where he was going, he thought, just in case the power went off or the TV broke down and he wondered where Johnny had gone.

"I'm just off to—" he began, and then said, "I'm just off out."

"Right," said Grandad, without taking his eyes off the set. "Hah! Look, there he goes! Right in the gunge tank!"

Nothing much was going on in the garage.

After a while, Guilty crawled out from his nest among the black plastic sacks and took up his usual position in the front of the cart, where he was wont to travel on the offchance that he could claw somebody.

A fly banged on the window pane for a while and then went back to sleep.

And the bags moved.

They moved like frogs in oil, slithering very slowly around each other. They made a rubbery, squeaky noise, like a clever conjurer trying to twist an animal out of balloons.

There were other noises, too. Guilty didn't pay them much attention because you couldn't attack noises and, besides, he was pretty well used to them by now.

They weren't very clear. They might have been snatches of music. They might have been voices. They might have been a radio left on, but slightly off station and two rooms away, or the distant roar of a crowd.

Johnny met Kasandra outside the police station.

"You're lucky I've got some spare time," she said. "Come on."

Sergeant Comely was on the desk. He looked up as Johnny and Kasandra came in, then looked back at the book he was writing in, and then looked up again slowly.

"You?"

"Er, hello, Sergeant Comely," said Johnny.

"What is it this time? Seen any aliens lately?"

"We've come about Mrs. Tachyon, Sergeant," said Kasandra.

"Oh yes?"

Kasandra turned to Johnny.

"Go on," she said. "Tell him."

"Er . . ." said Johnny. "Well . . . me and Wobbler and Yo-less and Bigmac . . ."

"Wobbler and Yo-less and Bigmac and I," said Kasandra.

Sergeant Comely looked at her.

"All five of you?" he said.

"I was just correcting his grammar," said Kasandra.

"Do you do that a lot?" said the sergeant. He looked at Johnny. "Does she do that a lot?"

"All the time," said Johnny.

"Good grief. Well, go on. You, not her."

When Sergeant Comely had been merely PC Comely he'd visited Johnny's school to show everyone how nice the police were, and had accidentally locked himself into his own handcuffs. He was also a member of the Blackbury Morris Men. Johnny had actually seen him wearing bells around his knees and waving two hankies in the air. These were important things to remember at a time like this.

"Well . . . we were proceeding along . . ." he began.

"And no jokes."

Twenty minutes later, they walked slowly down the steps of the police station.

"Well, that wasn't too bad," said Kasandra. "It's not as though you were arrested or anything. Have you really got her trolley?"

"Oh, yes."

"I liked the look on his face when you said you'd bring Guilty in. He went quite pale, I thought."

"What's next-of-kin mean? He said she'd got no next-of-kin."

"Relatives," said Kasandra. "Basically, it means relatives."

"None at all?"

"That isn't unusual."

"Yes," said Johnny, "but generally there's a cousin in Australia you don't know about."

"Is there?"

"Well, apparently *I've* got a cousin in Australia, and I didn't know about her till last month, so it can't be that unusual."

"The state of Mrs. Tachyon is a terrible Indictment on Society," said Kasandra.

"What's indictment mean?"

"It means it's wrong."

"That she's got no relatives? I don't think you can get them from the Governm—"

"No, that she's got no home and just wanders around the place living on what she can find. Something Ought to be Done."

"Well, I suppose we could go and see her," said Johnny. "She's only in St Mark's."

"What good would that do?"

"Well, it might cheer *her* up a bit."

"Do you know, you start almost every sentence with 'Well'?"

"Well—"

"Going hospital visiting won't do anything about the disgusting neglect of street people and the mentally ill, will it?"

"Probably not. She just might be a bit cheered up, I suppose."

Kasandra walked in silence for a moment.

"It's just that . . . I've got a thing about hospitals, if you must know. They're full of sick people."

"We could take her something she likes. And she'd probably be glad to know that Guilty is OK."

"They smell bad, too," said Kasandra, not listening to him. "That horrible disinfectant smell."

"When you're up close to Mrs. Tachyon you won't notice."

"You're just going on about it because you know I hate hospitals, aren't you?"

"I . . . just think we ought to do it. Anyway, I thought you did things like this for your Duke of Edinburgh award or whatever it was."

"Yes, but there was some *point* in that."

"We could go towards the end of visiting time so we won't be there very long. That's what everyone else does."

"Oh, all *right*," said Kasandra.

"We'd better take her something, too. You have to."

"Like grapes, you mean?"

Johnny tried to picture Mrs. Tachyon eating grapes. It didn't work. "I'll think about it."

The garage door swung back and forth, slowly.

Inside the garage there was:

A concrete floor. It was old and cracked and soaked in oil. Animal footprints crossed it, embedded in the concrete, suggesting that a dog had run across it when it was being laid. This happens in every patch of wet concrete, everywhere. There were also a couple of human footprints, fossilized in time, and now filled with black grease and dust. In other words, it was more or less like any piece of concrete. There was also:

A tool bench.

Most of a bicycle, upside down, and surrounded by tools and bits of bike in a haphazard manner which suggested that someone had mastered the art of taking a bike to bits without succeeding in the craft of putting it back together again.

A lawnmower entangled in a garden hosepipe, which is what always happens in garages, and isn't at all relevant.

A trolley, overflowing with plastic bags of all kinds, but most particularly six large black ones.

A small pile of jars of pickles, where Johnny had carefully stacked them last night.

The remains of some fish and chips. As far as Guilty was concerned, catfood only happened to other cats.

A pair of yellow eyes, watching intently from the shadows under the bench.

And that was all.

3

Bags of Time

To be honest about it, Johnny didn't much like hospitals either. Mostly, the people he'd gone to visit in them were not going to come out again. And no matter how they tried to cheer the place up with plants and pictures, it never looked friendly. After all, no-one was there because they wanted to be.

But Kirsty was good at finding out things and getting harassed people to give her answers, and it didn't take long to find Mrs. Tachyon's ward.

"That's her, isn't it?" she said.

Kasandra pointed along the line of beds. One or two of them didn't have visitors around them, but there was no mistaking the one belonging to Mrs. Tachyon.

She was sitting up in bed in a hospital night-gown and her woolly hat, over which she had a pair of hospital headphones.

Mrs. Tachyon stared intently in front of her, and jigged happily among the pillows.

"She looks happy enough," said Kasandra. "What's she listening to?"

"I couldn't say for sure," said the nurse. "All I know is the headphones aren't plugged in. Are you relatives?"

"No. We're—" Kasandra began.

"It's a sort of project," said Johnny. "You know . . . like weeding old people's gardens and that sort of thing."

The nurse gave him an odd look, but the magic "project" word did its usual helpful stuff.

She sniffed. "Can I smell vinegar?" she said.

Kasandra glared at Johnny. He tried to look innocent.

"We've just brought some grapes," he said, showing her the bag.

Mrs. Tachyon didn't look up as they dragged chairs over to her bed.

Johnny had never spoken to her in his life, except to say "sorry" when she rammed him with her trolley. He wasn't sure how to start now.

Kasandra leaned over and pulled one earphone aside.

"Hello, Mrs. Tachyon!" she said

Mrs. Tachyon stopped jigging. She turned a beady eye on Kasandra, and then on Johnny. She had a black eye, and her stained white hair looked frizzled at the front, but there was something horribly *unstoppable* about Mrs. Tachyon.

"Indeed? That's what *you* think!" she said. "Call again tomorrow, baker, and we'll take a crusty one! Poor old biddy, is it? That's what *you* think! Millennium hand and shrimp? Free teeth and corsets? Maybe, for them as likes it, but not me, thank you so much. Wot, no bananas? I had a house, oh yes, but it's all black men now. Hats."

"Are they treating you all right?" said Kasandra.

"Don't you worry! Right as rain and twice as ninepence. Hah! Tick tick bang! I'd like to see them try. There's puddings. Of course, I remember when it was all fields, but would they listen?"

Kasandra looked at Johnny.

"I think she's a bit . . . confused," she said. "She doesn't understand anything I'm saying."

"But we don't understand anything she's saying, either," said Johnny, who felt confused all the time in any case.

Mrs. Tachyon adjusted her headphones and started to boogie again.

"I don't believe this," said Kasandra. "Excuse *me*."

She pulled the headphones off the woolly hat and listened to them.

"The nurse was right," she said. "There's nothing at all."

Mrs. Tachyon bounced up and down happily.

"One born every minute!" she chortled.

Then she winked at Johnny. It was a bright, knowing wink, from Planet Tachyon to Planet Johnny.

"We've brought you some grapes, Mrs. Tachyon," he said.

"That's what *you* think."

"Grapes," said Johnny firmly. He opened the bag, exposing the steaming greaseproof fish and chip paper inside. Her eyes widened. A scrawny hand shot out from under the covers, grabbed the packet, and disappeared under the blanket again.

"Him and his coat," she said.

"Don't mention it. Er. I'm keeping your trolley safe. And Guilty is all right, although I don't think he's eaten anything apart from some chips and my hand."

"I blame Mr. Chamberlain," said Mrs. Tachyon.

A bell tinkled.

"Oh dear that's the end of visiting time my word don't the hours just fly past what a shame," said Kasandra, standing up quickly. "Nice to have met you Mrs. Tachyon sorry we have to be going come on Johnny."

"Lady Muck," said Mrs. Tachyon.

She nodded at Johnny.

"What's the word on the street, mister man?"

Johnny tried to think like Mrs. Tachyon.

"Er . . . 'No Parking'?" he suggested.

"That's what *you* think. Them's bags of time, mister man. Mind me bike! Where your mind goes, the rest of you's bound to follow. Here today and gone yesterday! Doing it's the trick! Eh?"

Johnny stared. It was as though he had been listening to a lot of static on the radio and then, just for a second, there was this one clear signal.

The other Mrs. Tachyon came back.

"He's mixing sugar with the sand, Mr. McPhee!" she said. "That's what *you* think."

"What did you have to go and give her them for?" Kasandra hissed, as she strode out of the ward. "She needs a proper healthy balanced diet! Not hot chips! What did you give her them for?"

"Well, I thought hot chips would be exactly what someone'd like who'd got used to cold chips. Anyway, she didn't get any supper last night. Hey, there was something very odd about—"

"She *is* very odd."

"You don't like her much, do you?"

"Well, she didn't even say thank you."

"But *I* thought she was an unfortunate victim of a repressive political system," said Johnny. "That's what you said when we were coming here."

"Yes, all right, but courtesy doesn't cost anything, *actually*. Come on, let's get out of here."

"Hello?" said someone behind them.

"They've found out about the chips," muttered Kirsty, as she and Johnny turned around.

But it wasn't a nurse bearing down on them, unless the hospital had a plain clothes division.

It was a young woman in glasses and a worried hairstyle. She also had boots that would have impressed Bigmac, and a clipboard.

"Um . . . do you two *know* Mrs. . . . er . . . Tachyon?" she said. "Is that her name?"

"I suppose so," said Johnny. "I mean, that's what everyone calls her."

"It's a very odd name," said the woman. "I suppose it's foreign."

"We don't actually *know* her," said Kasandra. "We were just visiting her out of social concern."

The woman looked at her. "Good grief," she said. She glanced at her clipboard.

"Do you know anything about her?" she said. "Anything at all?"

"Like what?" said Johnny.

"Anything. Where she lives. Where she comes from. How old she is. Anything."

"Not really," said Johnny. "She's just around. You know."

"She must *sleep* somewhere."

"Don't know."

"There's no records of her *anywhere*. There's no records of *anyone* called Tachyon anywhere," said the woman, her voice suggesting that this was a major criminal offence.

"Are you a social worker?" said Kasandra.

"Yes. I'm Ms. Partridge."

"I think I've seen you talking to Bigmac," said Johnny.

"Bigmac? Who's Bigmac?"

"Er . . . Simon . . . Wrigley, I think."

"Oh, yes," said Ms. Partridge darkly. "Simon. The one who wanted to know how many cars he had to steal to get a free holiday in Africa."

"And *he* and *you* said you'd only send him if cannibalism was still—"

"Yes, yes," said Ms. Partridge, hurriedly. When she'd started the job, less than a year ago, she'd firmly believed that everything that was wrong with the world was the fault of Big Business and the Government. She believed even more firmly now that it was all the fault of Bigmac.

"He was dead impressed, he said—"

"But you don't actually *know* anything about Mrs. Tachyon, do you?" said the social worker. "She had a trolley full of junk, but no-one seems to know where it is."

"Actually—" Kasandra began.

"I don't know where it is either," said Johnny firmly.

"It'd be very helpful if we could find it. It's amazing what they hoard," said Ms. Partridge. "When I was in Bolton there was an old lady who'd saved every—"

"We'll miss the bus," said Kasandra. "Sorry we can't help, Miss Partridge. Come on, Johnny."

She pulled him out of the building and down the steps.

"You *have* got the trolley, haven't you," she said. "You *told* me."

"Yes, but I don't see why people should take it away from her or poke around in it. You wouldn't want people poking around in your stuff."

"My mother said she was married to an airman in the Second World War and he never came back and she went a bit strange."

"My grandad said he and his friends used to tip up her trolley when *he* was a boy. He said they did it just to hear her swear."

Kasandra hesitated.

"What? How old is your grandad?"

"Dunno. About sixty-five."

"And how old is Mrs. Tachyon, would you say?"

"It's hard to tell under all those wrinkles. Sixty?"

"Doesn't that strike you as odd?"

"What?"

"Are you dense or something? She's *younger* than your grandfather!"

"Oh . . . well . . . perhaps there was another Mrs. Tachyon?"

"That isn't very likely, is it?"

"So you're saying she's a hundred years old?"

"Of course not. There's bound to be a sensible explanation. What's your grandfather's memory like?"

"He's good at television programmes. You'll be watching, and then he'll say something like, 'Hey, him . . . the one in the suit . . . he was the policeman in that programme, *you* know, the one with the man with the curly hair, couple of years ago, *you* know.' And if you buy anything, he can always tell you that you could get it for sixpence and still have change when he was a lad."

"Everyone's grandad does that," said Kasandra severely.

"Sorry."

"Haven't you looked in the bags?"

"No . . . but she's got some odd stuff."

"How do you mean?"

"Well . . . there are these jars of pickles . . ."

"Well? Old people like pickles."

"Yes, but these are . . . kind of new and old at the same time. And there was fish and chips wrapped up in a newspaper."

"Well?"

"No-one wraps up fish and chips in newspaper these days. But they all looked fresh. I had a look because I thought I might as well give the fish to the cat, and the newspaper . . ."

Johnny stopped.

What could he say? That he *knew* that front page? He knew every word of it. He'd found the same one on the microfiche in the library and the librarian had given him a copy to help him with his history project. He'd never seen it apart from the copy and the fuzzy image on the screen and suddenly there it was, unfolded in front of him, greasy and vinegary but undoubtedly . . .

. . . *new*.

"Well, let's have a *look* at them, at least. That can't hurt."

Kasandra was like that. When all else failed, she tried being reasonable.

The big black car sped up the motorway. There were two motorcyclists in front and two more behind, and another car trailing behind them containing some serious men in suits who listened to little radios a lot and wouldn't even trust their mothers.

Sir John sat by himself in the back of the black car, with his hands crossed on his silver-topped walking stick and his chin on his hands.

There were two screens in front of him, which showed him various facts and figures to do with his companies around the world, beamed down to him from a satellite, which he also owned. There were also two fax machines and three telephones.

Sir John sat and stared at them.

Then he reached over and pressed the button that operated the driver's intercom.

He'd never liked Hickson much. The man had a red neck. On the other hand, he was the only person there was to talk to right now.

"Do you believe it's possible to travel in time, Hickson?"

"Couldn't say, sir," said the chauffeur, without turning his head.

"It's been done, you know."

"If you say so, sir."

"Time's been changed."

"Yes, sir."

"Of course, you wouldn't know about it, because you were in the time that it changed into."

"Good thing for me then, sir."

"Did you know that when you change time you get two futures heading off side by side?"

"Must have missed that in school, sir."

"Like a pair of trousers."

"Definitely something to think about, Sir John."

Sir John stared at the back of the man's neck. It really was very red, and had unpleasant little patches of hair on it. He hadn't hired the man, of course. He had people who had people who had people who did things like that. It had never occurred to them to employ a chauffeur with an interest in something else besides what the car in front was doing.

"Take the next left turn," he snapped.

"We're still twenty miles from Blackbury, sir."

"Do what you're told! Right now!"

The car skidded, spun half around, and headed up the off-ramp with smoke coming from its tyres.

"Turn left!"

"But there's traffic coming, Sir John!"

"If they haven't got good brakes they shouldn't be on the road! Good! You see? Turn right!"

"That's just a lane! I'll lose my job, Sir John!"

Sir John sighed.

"Hickson, I'd like to lose all our little helpers. If you can get me to Blackbury by myself I will personally give you a million pounds. I'm serious."

The chauffeur glanced at his mirror.

"Why didn't you say, sir? Hold on to something, sir!"

As the car plunged down between high hedges, all three of the telephones started to ring.

Sir John stared at them for a while. Then he pressed the button that wound down the nearest window and, one by one, threw them out.

The fax machine followed.

After some effort he managed to detach the two screens, and they went out too, exploding very satisfactorily when they hit the ground.

He felt a lot better for that.

4

Men in Black

The bus rumbled along the road towards Johnny's house.

"There's no sense in getting *excited* about Mrs. Tachyon," said Kasandra. "If she's really been a bag lady here for years and years, then there's a whole range of perfectly acceptable explanations without having to resort to far-fetched ones."

"What's an acceptable explanation?" said Johnny. He was still wrapped up in the puzzle of the newspaper.

"She's an alien, possibly."

"That's acceptable?"

"Or she could be an Atlantean. From Atlantis. You know? The continent that sank under the sea thousands of years ago. The inhabitants were said to be very long-lived."

"They could breathe underwater?"

"Don't be silly. They sailed away just before it sank, and built Stonehenge and the Pyramids and so on. They were scientifically very advanced, actually."

Johnny looked at her with his mouth open. You expected this sort of thing from Bigmac and the others, but not from Ki—Kasandra, who was already doing A-levels at fourteen years old.

"I didn't know that," he said.

"It was hushed up by the government."

"Ah." Kasandra was good at knowing things that were hushed up by the government, especially considering that they had been, well, hushed up. They were always slightly occult. When giant footprints had appeared around the town centre during some snow last year there had been two theories. There was Kir—Kasandra's, which was that it was Bigfoot, and Johnny's, which was that it was a combination of Bigmac and two "Giant Rubber Feet, A Wow at Parties!!!!" from the Joke Emporium in Penny Street. Ki—Kasandra's theory had the backing of so many official sources in the books she'd read that it practically outweighed Johnny's, which was merely based on watching him do it.

Johnny thought about the Atlanteans, who'd all be two metres tall in Greek togas and golden hair, leaving the sinking continent in their amazing golden ships. And on the deck of one of them, Mrs. Tachyon, ferociously wheeling her trolley.

Or you could imagine Attila the Hun's barbarians galloping across the plain and, in the middle of the line of horsemen, Mrs. Tachyon on her trolley. Off her trolley, too.

"What happens," said Kasandra, "is that if you see a UFO or a yeti or something like that, you get a visit from the Men in Black. They drive around in big black cars and menace people who've seen strange things. They say they're working for the government but they're really working for the secret society that runs everything."

"How d'you know all this?"

"Everyone knows. It's a well-known fact. I've been waiting for something like this, ever since the mysterious rain of fish we had in September," said Kasandra.

"You mean, when there was that gas leak under the tropical fish shop?"

"Yes, we were *told* it was a leak under the tropical fish shop," said Kasandra darkly.

"What? Of course it was the gas leak! They found the shopkeeper's wig in the telephone wires in the High Street! Everyone had guppies in their gutters!"

"The two might have been coincidentally connected," said Kasandra reluctantly.

"And you still believe that those crop circles last year weren't made by Bigmac even though he swears they were?"

"All right, perhaps *some* of them might have been made by Bigmac, but who made the first ones, eh?"

"Bazza and Skazz, of course. They read about 'em in the paper and decided we should have some, too."

"They didn't necessarily make *all* of them."

Johnny sighed. As if life wasn't complicated enough, people had to set out to make it worse. It had been difficult enough before he'd heard about spontaneous combustion. You could be sitting peacefully in your chair, minding your own business, and next minute, *whoosh*, you were just a pair of shoes with smoke coming out. He'd taken to keeping a bucket of water in his bedroom for some weeks after reading about that.

And then there were all these programmes about aliens swooping down on people and taking them away for serious medical examinations in their flying saucers. If you were captured and taken away by aliens, but then they messed around with your brain so you forgot about them *and* they had time travel, so they could put you back exactly where you were before they'd taken you away . . . how would you know? It was a bit of a worry.

Kasandra seemed to think all this sort of thing was interesting, instead of some kind of a nuisance.

"Kasandra," he said.

"Yes? What?"

"I wish you'd go back to Kirsty."

"Horrible name. Sounds like someone who makes scones."

". . . I didn't mind Kimberly . . ."

"Hah! I now realize that was a name with 'trainee hairdresser' written all over it."

". . . although Klymenystra was a bit over the top."

"When was that?"

"About a fortnight ago."

"I was probably feeling a bit gothy at the time."

The bus pulled up at the end of Johnny's road, and they got off.

The garages were in a little cul-de-sac around the back of the houses. They weren't used much, at least for cars. Most of Grandad's neighbours parked in the street, so that they could enjoy complaining about stealing one another's parking spaces.

"You haven't even peeked in the bags?" said Kasandra, as Johnny fished in his pockets for the garage key.

"No. I mean, supposing they were full of old knickers or something?"

He pushed open the door.

The trolley was where he left it.

There was something odd about it that he couldn't quite put his finger on. It was clearly standing in the middle of the floor but managed to give the impression of moving very fast at the same time, as though it were a still frame from a movie.

Kasandra-formerly-Kirsty looked around.

"Bit of a dump," she said. "Why's that bike upside down over there?"

"It's mine," said Johnny. "It got a puncture yesterday. I haven't managed to repair it yet."

Kasandra picked up one of the jars of pickle from the bench. The label was sooty. She wiped it and turned it towards the light.

" 'Blackbury Preserves Ltd Gold-Medal Empire Brand Mustard Pickle,' " she read. " 'Six Premier Awards. Grand Prix de Foire Internationale des Conichons Nancy 1933. Festival of Pickles, Manchester, 1929. Danzig Pökelnfest 1928. Supreme Prize, Michigan State Fair, 1933. Gold Medal, Madras, 1931. Bonza Feed Award, Sydney, 1932. Made from the Finest Ingredients.' And then there's a picture of some sort of crazed street kid jumping about, and it says underneath, 'Up In The Air Leaps Little Tim, Blackbury Pickles Have Bitten Him.' Very clever. Well, they're pickles. So what?"

"They're from the old pickle factory," said Johnny. "It got blown up during the war. At the same time as Paradise Street. Pickles haven't been made here for more than fifty years!"

"Oh, no!" said Kasandra. "You don't mean . . . we're in a town where no pickles are made? That's creepy, that is."

"You don't have to be sarcastic. It's just odd, was all I meant."

Kasandra shook the jar. Then she picked up another sooty jar of gherkins, which sloshed as she turned it over.

"They've kept well, then," she said.

"I tried one this morning," said Johnny. "It was nice and crunchy. And what about *this*?"

Out of his pocket came the newspaper that had wrapped Mrs. Tachyon's fish and chips. He spread it out.

"It's an old newspaper," said Johnny. "I mean . . . it's very old, but not *old*. That's all stuff about the Second World War. But . . . it doesn't look old or feel old or smell old. It's . . ."

"Yes, I know, it's probably one of those reprinted newspapers you can get for the day you were born, my father got *me* one for—"

"Wrapping fish and chips?" said Johnny.

"It's odd, I must admit," said Kasandra.

She turned and looked at him as though seeing him for the first time.

"I've waited *years* for something like this," she said. "Haven't you?"

"For something like Mrs. Tachyon's trolley?"

"Try to pay attention, will you?"

"Sorry."

"Haven't you ever wondered what'd happen if a flying saucer landed in your garden? Or you found some sort of magical item that let you travel in time? Or some old cave with a wizard that'd been asleep for a thousand years?"

"Well, as a matter of fact I *did* once find an old cave with—"

"I've read books and books about that sort of thing, and they're full of unintelligent children who go around saying 'gosh.' They just drift along having an *adventure*, for goodness' sake. They never seem to think of it as any kind of opportunity. They're never prepared. Well, I *am*."

Johnny tried to imagine what'd happen if Kirsty was ever kidnapped by aliens. You'd probably end up with a galactic empire where everyone had sharp pencils and always carried a small torch in case of emergencies. Or they'd make a million robot copies who'd fly around the universe telling everyone not to be stupid and forcing them to be sensible.

"This is *obviously* something very odd," she said. "Possibly mystic. Possibly a time machine of some sort."

And that was the thing about her. She arrived at an explanation. She didn't mess around with uncertainty.

"Didn't *you* think that?" she said.

"A time machine? A time shopping trolley?"

"Well, what other explanation fits the facts? Apart from possibly she was kidnapped by aliens and brought here at the speed of light, which is something they do a lot for some reason. But there might be something else, I'm sure you've thought of it." She glanced at her watch. "No hurry," she added sarcastically. "Take your time."

"Well . . ."

"No rush."

"Well . . . a time machine'd have flashing lights . . ."

"Why?"

"You've *got* to have flashing lights."

"What for?"

Johnny wasn't going to give in.

"To flash," he said.

"Really? Well, who says a time machine has to look like anything?" said Kasandra in a superior tone of voice, or at least an even more superior voice than the one she usually used. "Or has to be powered by electricity?"

"Yo-less says you can't have time machines because everyone'd keep changing the future," said Johnny.

"Oh? So what's the alternative? How come she turned up with this new old newspaper and all these new old pickle jars?"

"All right, but I don't go leaping to great big conclusions!"

In fact he did. He knew he did. All the time. But there was something about the way Kasandra argued that automatically made you take the other side.

He waved a hand at the trolley.

"I mean," he said, "do you really think something could just press the . . . oh, the handle, or the bags or something, and suddenly it's hello, Norman the Conqueror?"

He thumped his hand down on a black bag.

The world flashed in front of his eyes.

There was concrete under his feet, but there were no walls. At least, not much in the way of walls. They were one brick high.

A man cementing the new row looked up very slowly.

"Blimey," he said, "how did you get there?" Then he seemed to get a grip on himself. "Hey, that concrete's still—Fred! You come here!"

A spaniel sitting by the man barked at Johnny and rushed forward, jumping up at Johnny and knocking him back against the trolley.

There was another flash. It was red and blue and it seemed to Johnny that he was squashed very flat and then pulled out again.

There were walls, and the shopping trolley was still in the middle of the floor, as was Kasandra, staring at him.

"You vanished for a moment," she said, as if he'd done something wrong. "What happened?"

"I . . . I don't know, how should I know?" said Johnny.

"Move your feet," she said. "Very slowly."

He did. They met a very slight obstacle, a tiny ridge in the floor. He looked down.

"Oh, they're just the footprints in the cement," he said. "They've been . . . there . . . ages . . ."

Kasandra knelt down to look at the footprints he'd been standing in. They were ingrained with dust and dirt, but she made him take off his trainer and held it upside down by the print.

It matched exactly.

"See?" she said triumphantly. "You're standing in your *own* footprints."

Johnny stepped gingerly aside and looked at the footprints where he'd been standing. There was no doubt they'd been there a long time.

"Where did you go?"

"Back in time . . . I think. There was a man building this place, and a dog."

"A dog," said Kasandra. Her voice suggested that she would have seen something *much* more interesting. "Oh, well. It's a start."

She shifted the trolley. It was standing in four small grooves in the concrete. They were dirty and oily. They'd been there a long time, too.

"This," said Kirsty, "is no ordinary shopping trolley."

"It's got Tesco written on it," Johnny pointed out, hopping up and down as he replaced his shoe. "*And* a squeaky wheel."

"Obviously it's still switched on or something," Kirsty went on, ignoring him.

"And that's time travel, is it?" said Johnny. "I thought it'd be more exciting. You know—battles and monsters and things? And it's not much fun if all we can do is—*don't touch it*!"

Kasandra prodded a bag.

The air flickered and changed.

Kasandra looked around her. The garage hadn't changed in any way. Except—

"Who repaired your bike?" she said.

Johnny turned. His bike was no longer upside down with a wheel off, but leaning against the wall, both tyres quite full.

"You see, I notice things," said Kasandra. "I am remarkably observant. We must have gone into the future, when you've mended it."

Johnny wasn't sure. He'd torn three inner tubes already, plus he'd also lost the thingy from the inside of the valve. Probably no time machine could ever go *so* far into the future that he'd be good at cycle repair.

"Let's have a look round," said Kirsty. "Obviously where we go is controlled by some factor I haven't discovered yet. If we're in the future, the important thing is to find out which horses are going to win races, and so on."

"Why?"

"So we can bet money on them and become rich, of course."

"I don't know how to bet!"

"One problem at a time."

Johnny looked though the grimy window. The weather didn't look very different. There were no flying cars or other definite signs of futurosity. But Guilty was no longer under the bench.

"Grandad has a racing paper," he said, feeling a bit light-headed.

"Let's go, then."

"What? Into my house?"

"Of course."

"Supposing I meet me?"

"Well, you've always been good at making friends."

Reluctantly, Johnny led the way out of the garage. Garden paths in the future, he noted, were made of some gritty grey substance which was amazingly like cracked concrete. Back doors were an excitingly futuristic faded blue colour, with little dried flakes where the paint had bubbled up. It was locked, but his ancient key still fitted.

There was a rectangle on the floor consisting of spiky brown hairs. He wiped his feet on it, and looked at the time measurement module on the wall. It said ten past three.

The future was amazingly like the present.

"Now we've got to find a newspaper," said Kirsty.

"It won't be a lot of help," said Johnny. "Grandad keeps them around until he's got time to read them. They go back months. Anyway, everything's *normal*. This doesn't look very futuristic to *me*."

"Don't you even have a calendar?"

"Yes. There's one on my bedside clock. I just hope I'm at school, that's all."

According to the clock, it was the third of October.

"The day before yesterday," said Johnny. "Mind you, it could be the clock. It doesn't work very well."

"Yuk. You *sleep* in here?" said Kirsty, looking around with an expression like a vegetarian in a sausage factory.

"Yes. It's my room."

Kirsty ran her hand over his desk, which was fairly crowded at the moment.

"What're all these photocopies and photos and things?"

"*That's* the project I'm doing in History. We're doing the Second World War. So I'm doing Blackbury in the war."

He tried to get between her and the desk, but Kirsty was always interested in things people didn't want her to see.

"Hey, this is you, isn't it?" she said, grabbing a sepia photograph. "Since when did *you* wear a uniform and a pudding-basin haircut?"

Johnny tried to grab it. "And that's Grandad when he was a bit older than me," he mumbled. "I tried to get him to talk about the war like the teacher said but he tells me to shut up about it."

"You're so *local*, aren't you," said Kirsty. "I can't imagine much happening here—"

"Something did happen," said Johnny. He pulled out Mrs. Tachyon's chip paper and jabbed at the front page with his finger. "At 11.07 pm on May 21, 1941. Bombs! Real bombs! They called it the Blackbury Blitz. And this is the paper from the day after. Look." He rummaged among the stuff on his desk and pulled out a photocopy. "See? I got a copy of the same page out of the library! But *this* paper's real, it's new!"

"If she *is* . . . from the past . . . why does she wear an old ra-ra skirt and trainers?" said Kirsty.

Johnny glared angrily at her. She had no *right* not to care about Paradise Street!

"Nineteen people got killed! In one night!" he said. "There wasn't any warning! The only bombs that fell on Blackbury in the whole of the war! The only survivors were two goldfish in a bowl! It got blown into a tree and still had water in it! All the people got killed!"

Kirsty picked up a felt-tipped pen, but it didn't write because it had dried up. Johnny had a world-class collection of pens that didn't work.

She had this infuriating habit of appearing not to notice him when he was excited about something.

"You know you've still got Thomas the Tank Engine on your wallpaper?" she said.

"*What?* Have I? Gosh, I hadn't realized," said Johnny, with what he hoped was sarcasm.

"It's OK to have Thomas the Tank Engine when you're seven,

and it's quite cool to have it when you're nineteen, but it's not cool at thirteen. Honestly, if I wasn't here to help from time to time, you just wouldn't have a clue."

"Grandad put it up a couple of years ago," said Johnny. "This was my room when I stayed with them. You know grandparents. It's Thomas the Tank Engine until you die."

Then there was the click of the front door opening.

"Your grandad?" hissed Kirsty.

"He always goes shopping in town on Thursdays!" whispered Johnny. "And Mum's at work!"

"Who else has got a key?"

"Only me!"

Someone started to climb the stairs.

"But I can't meet *me*!" said Johnny. "I'd remember, wouldn't I? Yo-less says if you meet yourself the whole universe explodes! I'd remember that happening!"

Kirsty picked up the bedside lamp, and glanced at the design on it.

"Good grief, the Mr. Men, you've still got Mr.—"

"Shutupshutupshutup. What're you going to *do* with it?"

"Don't worry, you won't feel a thing, I learned how to do this in self-defence classes—"

The doorhandle turned. The door opened a fraction.

Downstairs, the phone rang.

The handle clicked back. Footsteps went downstairs again.

Johnny heard the phone picked up. A distant voice said: "Oh, hi, Wobbler."

Kirsty looked at Johnny and raised her eyebrows.

"Wobbler phoned," said Johnny. "About going to the movies yest—tomorrow. I just remembered."

"Were you on the phone long?"

"Don't . . . think so. And I went to get a sandwich afterwards."

"Where's your phone?"

"In the front room."

"Let's go, then!"

Kirsty opened the door and darted down the stairs, with Johnny trailing behind her.

His coat was on the coat rack. He was *also* wearing it. He stood and stared.

"Come *on*," hissed Kirsty.

She was almost at the bottom when the door started to open.

Johnny opened his mouth to say: oh, yes, I remember, I had to go and get my wallet to see if I'd got any money.

He desperately wanted not to meet himself. If the entire universe exploded, people would be bound to blame him afterwards . . .

. . . and there was a flash in front of his eyes.

The black car slid surreptitiously out of a side road just before a sign indicating that it was about to enter BLACKBURY (twinned with Aix-et-Pains).

"Nearly there, Sir John."

"Good. What time are we in?"

"Er . . . quarter past eleven, sir."

"That wasn't what I meant. If time was a pair of trousers, what leg would we be in?"

It occurred to Hickson the chauffeur that this might be quite a difficult million pounds to earn.

"They all got mixed up today, you see," said a voice from the seat behind him.

"Right, sir. If I see any trousers, sir, you just tell me what leg to drive down."

5

The Truth Is Out of Here

Johnny was still on the stairs. Kirsty was still in front of him. The door was shut. His coat wasn't on the coat rack. The Blackbury Shopper, which was delivered on Fridays and stayed on the hall table until someone threw it away, was indeed on the table.

"We've time travelled again, haven't we," said Kirsty, calmly. "I think we're back to where we started. Possibly . . ."

"I saw the back of my own head!" whispered Johnny. "My actual own back of my own head! Without mirrors or anything! No-one's ever done that since the Spanish Inquisition! How can you be so calm about this?"

"I'm just acting calm," said Kirsty. "This is even worse wallpaper, isn't it? Looks like an Indian restaurant."

She opened the front door, and slammed it again.

"You know I said that if you started getting too interested in mysterious occult things these men in black cars turn up?"

"Yes? Well?"

"Look through the letterbox, will you?"

Johnny levered it open with a finger.

There was a car pulling up outside. It was black. Utterly. Black. Black tyres, black wheels, black headlights. Even the windows were darker than a pair of Mafia sunglasses. Here and there were bits of chrome, but they only made the blackness blacker by comparison.

It stopped. Johnny could just make out the shadow of the driver behind the tinted glass.

" 'S . . . just . . . coincidence," he said.

"Your grandad often gets visitors like this, does he?" Kasandra demanded.

"Well . . ." He didn't. Someone came round on Thursday to collect his football pools coupon and that was about it. Grandad was not one for the social whirl.

The car door opened. A man got out. He was wearing a black chauffeur's uniform. The car door shut. It shut with the kind of final, heavy *thonk* that only the most expensive car doors can achieve, because they are lined with money.

Johnny let go of the letterbox and jumped back.

A few seconds later, someone banged heavily on the door.

"Run!" whispered Kasandra.

"Where?"

"The back door? Come *on!*"

"We haven't done anything wrong!"

"How do you know?"

Kasandra opened the back door and hurried down the path and into the garage, dragging Johnny behind her. The trolley was still in the middle of the floor.

"Get ready to open the big doors and don't stop for anything!"

"Why?"

"Open the doors now!"

Johnny opened them, because practically anything was better than arguing with Kirsty.

The little garage area was empty, except for someone washing their car.

Johnny was nearly knocked aside as the trolley rattled out, with Kasandra pushing determinedly on the handle. It rattled across the concrete and lurched uncertainly into the alleyway that led to the next road.

"Didn't you see that programme about the flying saucer that crashed and these mysterious men turned up and hushed it all up?" said Kasandra.

"No!"

"Well, did you even *hear* about the flying saucer crashing?"

"No!"

"See?"

"All right, but in that case how come there was a TV programme about it, then?"

A car edged around the corner into the road.

"I can't waste time answering silly questions," said Kasandra. "Come *on*."

She shoved the trolley as hard as she could. It rolled down the sloping pavement, the squeaky wheel bouncing and juddering over the slabs.

The car turned the corner very slowly, as though driven by someone who didn't know the area very well.

Johnny caught up with Kir-Kasandra and clung to the handle because the trolley was rocking all over the pavement.

The trolley, under its heavy load, began to pick up speed.

"Try to hold it back!"

"*I'm* trying! Are *you?*"

Johnny risked a look behind. The car seemed to be catching up.

He jumped onto the trolley.

"What are you playing at?" said Kirsty, who was far too worried to remember any new names now.

"Come on!"

He grabbed her hand and pulled her up on the other side of the cart. Now she was no longer holding the handle, it surged forward.

"Do you think this is *really* a time machine?" he said, as the rushing wind made the bags flutter.

"It must be!"

"D'you see that film where the car travelled in time when it went at eighty-eight miles an hour?"

They looked down. The wheels were screaming. Smoke was coming out of the axles. They looked up the hill. The car was catching them up. They looked down the hill. There were the traffic lights. The Blackbury by-pass was a solid wall of thundering traffic.

Then they looked up into each other's frightened faces.

"The lights are red! The lights are red! I don't want to die!" said Kirsty. "I haven't even been to university!"

One hundred metres ahead, sixteen-wheeled lorries barrelled onwards, taking a million English razor blades from Sheffield to Italy and, coming the other way, a million Italian razor blades from Rome to England.

The trolley was, without a shadow of a doubt, going to smash right into the middle of them.

The air flickered.

And there were no lorries, or, rather, there *were* lorries, snorting and hissing and waiting at the lights. The lights ahead of Johnny were green.

The trolley rolled through, wheels screaming. Johnny looked up into the puzzled faces of the drivers.

Then he risked a look behind.

The black car had vanished.

There were no other turnings off the hill. Wherever it had gone, it hadn't got there by any means known to normal cars.

He met Kirsty's eyes.

"Where did it go?" she said. "And what happened with the lights? Did we travel in time again?"

"You're wearing your mac!" said Johnny. "You *were* wearing your old coat but now you're wearing your mac! Something's changed!"

She looked down, and then back up at him.

Beside the crossroads was the Neil Armstrong Shopping Mall. Johnny pointed to it.

"We can make this go into the car park!" he shouted.

The big black Bentley jerked to a halt at the side of the road.

"They just vanished!" said Hickson, staring over the top of the wheel. "That wasn't . . . this time travel stuff, was it? I mean, they just vanished!"

"I think they went from one now *to another* now,*" said Sir John.*

"Is that . . . like . . . these trousers you were going on about, sir?"

"I suppose you could say they went from one knee to the other. One 1996 to another 1996."

Hickson turned around in his seat.

"Are you serious, *sir? I saw this scientist on TV . . . you know, the one in the wheelchair . . . and there was all this stuff about other universes all crammed in, and—"*

"He'd know the proper way of talking about it," said Sir John. "For the rest of us, it's easier to think about trousers."

"What shall we do now, sir?"

"Oh, I think we wait until they come back to our now.*"*

"How long's that going to be?"

"About two seconds, I think . . ."

* * *

In the shopping mall, a joke was going wrong.

"Make me . . . er," said Bigmac, "make me one with pickle and onion rings and fries."

"Make me one with extra salad and fries, please," said Yo-less.

Wobbler took a long look at the girl in the cardboard hat.

"Make me one with everything," he said. "Because . . . I'm going to become a Muslim!"

Bigmac and Yo-less exchanged glances.

"Buddhist," said Yo-less, patiently. "It's *Buddhist!* Make me one with everything because I'm going to become a Buddhist! It's Buddhists that want to be one with everything. Singing 'om' and all that. You mucked it up! You were practising all the way down here and you still mucked it up!"

"Buddhists wouldn't have the burger," said the girl. "They'd have the Jumbo Beanburger. Or just fries and a salad."

They stared at her.

"Vegetarianism," said the girl. "I may have to wear a paper hat but I haven't got a cardboard brain, thank you." She glared at Wobbler. "You want a bun with everything. You want fries with that?"

"Er . . . yes."

"There you go. Have a day."

The boys took their burgers and wandered back out into the mall.

"We do this every Saturday," said Bigmac.

"Yes," said Wobbler.

"And every Saturday we work out a joke."

"Yes."

"And you always mess up the punchline."

"Well . . . it's something to do."

And there wasn't much else to do at the mall. Sometimes there were displays and things. At Christmas there'd been a nice tableau of reindeer and Dolls of Many Countries that really moved (jerkily) to music, but Bigmac had found out where the controls were and speeded up everything four times, and a Norwegian's head had gone through the window of the cookie shop on the second floor.

All there was today in the way of entertainment were the people selling plastic window frames and someone else trying to get people to try a new artificial baked potato mix.

The boys sat down by the ornamental pond, and watched out for the security guards. You could always tell where Bigmac was in the mall by watching the flow of the security guards, several of whom had been hit by bits of disintegrating Scandinavian and bore a grudge. As far as anyone knew, Bigmac had never been guilty of anything other than the occasional confused approach to the ownership of other people's cars, but he had an amazing way of looking as though he was thinking about committing some rather daft crime, probably with a can of spray paint. His camouflage jacket didn't help. It might have worked in a jungle, but it tended to stand out when the background was the Olde Card and Cookie Shoppe.

"Old Johnny may be a bit of a nerd but it's always interesting when he's around," said Wobbler. "Stuff happens."

"Yeah, but he hangs around with Kimberly or Kirsty or whoever she is today and she gives me the creeps," said Yo-less. "She's weird. She always looks at me as if I haven't answered a question properly."

"Her brother told me everyone expects her to go to university next year," said Bigmac.

Yo-less shrugged. "You don't have to be dumb to be weird," he said. "If you're brainy you can be even weirder. It's all that intelligence looking for something to do. That's what I think."

"Well, Johnny's weird," said Bigmac. "Well, he is. It's amazing the stuff that goes on in his head. Maybe he *is* a bit mental."

"It's amazing the stuff that goes on *outside* his head," said Wobbler. "He's just—"

There was a crash somewhere in the mall, and people started to shout.

A shopping trolley rolled at high speed up the aisle, with shoppers running to get out of the way. It had a plastic window frame hanging on the front and was splashed with artificial potato. Johnny and Kirsty were hanging on either side.

He waved at them as he drifted past.

"Help us get this out of the back door!"

"That's old Mrs. Tachyon's trolley, isn't it?" said Yo-less.

"Who cares?" said Bigmac. He put his burger down on the edge of the pond, where it was surreptitiously picked up by Wobbler, and ran after the trolley.

"Someone's chasing us," Johnny panted, as they caught up.

"Brilliant!" said Bigmac. "Who?"

"Some people in a big black car," said Johnny. "Only . . . they've vanished . . ."

"Oh, an *invisible* big black car," said Yo-less.

"I see *them* all the time," said Bigmac.

"Are you going to stand around all *day*?" Kirsty demanded. "It's probably got some kind of special shield! Come *on*!"

The trolley wasn't massively heavy, although the piles of bags did weigh it down. But it did need a lot of steering. Even with all of them helping—or, Johnny thought later, perhaps *because* of all of them helping—it skidded and wobbled as they tried to keep it in a straight line.

"If we can get out of the other doors, we're in the High Street," said Johnny. "And it can't go in there because there's bollards and things."

"I wish I had my five-megawatt laser cannon," said Bigmac, as they fought the trolley round a corner.

"You haven't got a laser cannon," said Yo-less.

"I know, that's why I wish I had one."

"Ow!"

Wobbler leapt back.

"It bit me!" he screamed.

Guilty stuck his head out of the heap of bags and hissed at Johnny.

Security guards were strolling towards them. There were five kids arguing around a trolley, Bigmac was among them and, as Yo-less would have pointed out, one of them was black. This sort of thing attracts attention.

"This trolley might be a time machine," said Johnny. "And that car . . . Kirsty thinks someone's after it. I mean me. I mean us."

"Great, how do we make it work?" said Bigmac.

"A time machine," said Yo-less. "Ah. Yes?"

"Where's this invisible car got to?" said Wobbler.

"We can't go out of the other doors," said Kirsty, flatly. "There's a couple of guards there."

Johnny stared at the black dustbin liners. Then he picked one up and undid the string. For a moment his fingers felt cold and the air was full of faint whispers—

The mall vanished.

It vanished above them, and around them.

And below them.

They landed in a heap on the grass, about a metre below where they'd been standing. The trolley landed on top of them, one wheel slamming into the small of Johnny's back. Bags bounced out, and Guilty took the opportunity to scratch Bigmac's ear.

And then there was silence, except for Bigmac swearing.

Johnny opened his eyes. The ground sloped up all around him. There were low bushes at the top.

"If I asked what happened," said Yo-less, from somewhere under Bigmac, "what'd you say?"

"I *think* we may have travelled in time," said Johnny.

"D'you get an electric feeling?" said Wobbler, clutching his jaw. "Like . . . all your teeth standing on end?"

"Which way did we go?" said Yo-less, still talking in his deliberate voice. "Are we talking dinosaurs, or mutant robots? I want to know this before I open my eyes."

Kirsty groaned.

"Oh dear, it's going to be *that* kind of adventure after all," she hissed, sitting up. "It's just the sort of thing I didn't want to happen. Me, and four token boys. Oh, dear. Oh, dear. It's only a mercy we haven't got a dog." She sat up and brushed some grass off her coat. "Anyone got the least idea of where we are?"

"Ah," said Yo-less. "I see there's grass. That means no dinosaurs. I saw that in a film. Grass didn't evolve until after there were dinosaurs."

Johnny stood up. His head was aching. He walked to the edge of the little hollow they'd landed in, and looked out.

"Really. Someone's been paying attention," said Kirsty. "Well, that narrows it down to some time in the last sixty million years."

"*Proper* time travellers have proper digital read-outs," Wobbler grumbled. "No grass? What did dinosaurs eat, then?"

"You only get digital time machine clocks in America," said Bigmac. "I saw a film about a time machine in Victorian England and it just had light bulbs. They ate other dinosaurs, didn't they?"

"You're not allowed to call them dinosaurs any more," said Yo-less. "It's speciesist. You have to call them pre-petroleum persons."

"Yeah," said Bigmac. "One Million Years PC. Get it? 'Cos there was this film called One Million Years BC, but—"

Kirsty's mouth was open.

"Do you lot go on like this all the time?" she said. "Yes, you do. I've noticed it before, actually. Rather than face up to facts, you start yakking on about weird things. When *are* we?"

"May the twenty-first," said Johnny, sitting down next to her. "Just gone half past three."

"Oh yes?" said Kirsty. "And how come you're so sure?"

"I went and asked a man who was walking his dog," said Johnny.

"Did he say what year?"

Johnny met Kirsty's gaze. "No," he said. "But I *know* what year."

They climbed out of the hollow and pushed their way through the bushes.

A scrubby field stretched away below them. There were some allotment gardens at the bottom end of the field, and then a river, and then the town of Blackbury.

It was definitely Blackbury. There was the familiar rubber boot factory chimney. There were a few other tall chimneys as well. He'd never seen those before. The man with the dog was watching them from some way off. So was the dog. Neither of them seemed particularly Jurassic, although the dog looked somewhat suspicious.

"Wha . . ?" said Wobbler. "Here, what's been happening? What have you done?"

"I told you we'd travelled in time," said Kirsty. "Weren't you listening?"

"I thought it was just some trick! I thought you were just messing about!" He gave Johnny a very worried look. "This *is* just messing about, isn't it?"

"Yes."

Wobbler relaxed.

"It's messing about with time travel," said Johnny.

Wobbler looked scared again.

"Sorry. But that's Blackbury all right. It's just smaller. I think we're where the mall is *going* to be."

"How do we get back?" said Yo-less.

"It just sort of happens, I think."

"You're just doing it with hallucinations, aren't you," said Wobbler, never a boy to let go of hope. "It's probably the smell from the trolley. We'll come round in a minute and have a headache and it'll all be all right."

"It just sort of happens?" said Yo-less. He was using his careful voice again, the voice that said there was something nasty on his mind. "How do you get back?"

"There's a flash, and there you are," said Kirsty.

"And you're back where you left?"

"Of course not. Only if you didn't move. Otherwise you go back to wherever where you are now is going to be then."

There was silence while they all worked this out.

"You mean," said Bigmac, "that if you walk a couple of metres, you'll be a couple of metres away from where you started when you get back?"

"Yes."

"Even if there's been something *built* there?" said Yo-less.

"Yes . . . no . . . I don't know."

"So," said Yo-less, still speaking very slowly, "if there's a lot of concrete, what happens?"

They all looked at Kirsty. She looked at Johnny.

"I don't know," he said. "Probably you kind of . . . get lumped together."

"Yuk," said Bigmac.

There was a wail from Wobbler. Sometimes, when it involved something horrible, his mind worked very fast.

"I don't want to end up with just my arms sticking out of a concrete wall!"

"Oh, I don't think it'd happen like that," said Yo-less.

Wobbler relaxed, but not much. "How *would* it happen, then?" he said.

"What I *think* would happen is, see, all the atoms in your body, right, and all the atoms in the wall would be trying to be in the same place at the same time and they'd all smash together suddenly and—"

"And what?" said Kirsty.

"—and . . . er . . . bang, good night, Europe," said Yo-less. "You can't argue with nuclear physics, sorry."

"My arms *wouldn't* end up sticking out of a wall?" said Wobbler, who hadn't quite caught up.

"No," said Yo-less.

"Not a wall near here, anyway," said Bigmac, grinning.

"Don't wind him up," said Yo-less severely. "This is serious. It could happen to *any* of us. We dropped when we landed, right? Does that mean that if we suddenly go back now we'll be sticking out of the floor of the mall, causing an instant atomic explosion?"

"They make enough fuss when you drop a Coke tin," said Johnny.

"Where's Wobbler gone?" said Kirsty.

Wobbler was a disappearing shape, heading for the allotments. He shouted something.

"What'd he say?" she said.

"He said 'I'm off home!' " said Johnny.

"Yeah, but," said Bigmac, ". . . where he's running now . . . if we're where the mall is . . . *will* be . . . then over there's the shopping estate. That field he's running across." He squinted. "That's where Currys is going to be."

"How will we know we're about to go back?" said Yo-less.

"There's a sort of flicker for a moment," said Johnny. "Then . . . zap. Er . . . what'll happen if he comes out where there's a fridge or something? Is that as bad as a concrete wall?"

"I don't know much about fridge atoms," said Yo-less. "They might not be as bad as concrete atoms. But I shouldn't think anyone around here would need new wallpaper ever again."

"Wow! An atomic Wobbler!" said Bigmac.

"Let's get the trolley and go after him," said Johnny.

"We don't need it. Leave it here," said Kirsty.

"No. It's Mrs. Tachyon's."

"There's just one thing I don't understand," said Yo-less, as they hauled the trolley across the field.

"There's *millions* of things *I* don't understand," said Johnny.

"What? *What?* What are you going on about now?"

"Televisions. Algebra. How skinless sausages hold together. Chinese," said Johnny. "I don't understand any of them."

"The trolley's got no works," said Yo-less. "There's no time machinery."

"Maybe the time is in the bags," said Johnny.

"Oh, right! Bags of time? You can't just shove time in a bag!"

"Maybe Mrs. Tachyon didn't know that. She's always picking up odds and ends of stuff."

"You can't pick up time, *actually*. Time's what you pick things up *in*," said Kirsty.

"My granny saves string," said Bigmac, in the manner of someone who wants to make a contribution.

"Really? Well, you can't pick up the odd half-hour and knot it on to another ten minutes you've got spare, in case you haven't noticed," said Kirsty. "Honestly, don't they teach you any physics at your school? Fridge atoms was bad enough! What on earth's a fridge atom?"

"The smallest possible particle of fridge," said Yo-less.

Perhaps you *could* save time, Johnny thought rebelliously. You could waste it, it could run through your fingers and you could put a stitch in it. Of course, perhaps that was only a manner of speaking and it all depended on how you looked at it, but Mrs. Tachyon looked at things in a corkscrew kind of way.

He remembered touching a bag. Had time leaked out? *Something* had hissed through his fingers.

"You can't have the smallest possible particle of fridge! It'd just be iron atoms and so on!"

"A fridge molecule, then. One atom of everything you need to make a fridge," said Yo-less.

"You couldn't ha—well, all right, you *could* have one atom of everything you need to make a fridge but that wouldn't make it a fridge molecule because—" She rolled her eyes. "What am I saying? You've got *me* thinking like that now!"

The rest of the universe said that time wasn't an object, it was just Nature's way of preventing everything from happening at once, and Mrs. Tachyon had said: that's what *you* think . . .

The path across the field led through the allotments. They looked like allotments everywhere, with the occasional old man who looked exactly like the old men who worked on allotments. They wore the special old man's allotment trousers.

One by one, they stopped digging as the trolley bumped along the path. They turned and watched in a silent allotment way.

"It's probably Yo-less's coat they're looking at," Kirsty hissed. "Purple, green and yellow. It's plastic, right? Plastic hasn't been around for long. Of course, it might be Bigmac's *Heavy Mental* T-shirt."

They're planting beans and hoeing potatoes, thought Johnny. And tonight there's going to be a crop of great big bomb craters . . .

"I can't see the by-pass," said Bigmac. "And there's no TV tower on Blackdown."

"There's all those extra factory chimneys, though," said Yo-less. "I don't remember any of those. And where's the traffic noise?"

It's May 21, 1941, thought Johnny. I *know* it.

There was a very narrow stone bridge over the river. Johnny stopped in the middle of it and looked back the way they'd come. A couple of the allotment men were still watching them. Beyond them was the sloping field they'd arrived in. It wasn't particularly pretty. It had that slightly grey tint that fields get when they're right next to a town and know that it's only a matter of time before they're under concrete.

"I remember when all this was buildings," he said to himself.

"What're you going on about now?"

"Oh, nothing."

"I recognize *some* of this," said Bigmac. "This is River Street. That's old Patel's shop on the corner, isn't it?"

But the sign over the window said: *SMOKE WOODBINES* J. Wilkinson (prop.).

"Woodbines?" said Bigmac.

"It's a kind of cigarette, obviously," said Kirsty.

A car went past. It was black, but not the dire black of the one on the hill. It had mud and rust marks on it. It looked as though someone had started out with the idea of making a very large mobile jelly mould and had changed their mind about halfway through, when it was slightly too late. Johnny saw the driver crane his head to stare at them.

It was hard to tell much from the people on the streets. There were a lot of overcoats and hats, in a hundred shades of boredom.

"We shouldn't hang around," said Kirsty. "People are looking at us. Let's go and see if we can get a newspaper. I want to know when we are. It's so *gloomy*."

"Perhaps it's the Depression," said Johnny. "My grandad's always going on about when he was growing up in the Depression."

"No TV, everyone wearing old-fashioned clothes, no decent cars," said Bigmac. "No wonder everyone was depressed."

"Oh, God," said Kirsty. "Look, try to be careful, will you? Any little thing you do could seriously affect the future. Understand?"

They entered the corner shop, leaving Bigmac outside to guard the trolley.

It was dark inside, and smelled of floorboards.

Johnny had been on a school visit once, to a sort of theme park that showed you what things had been like in the all-purpose Olden Days. It had been quite interesting, although everyone had been careful not to show it, because if you weren't careful they'd sneak education up on you while your guard was down. The shop was a bit like that, only it had things the school one hadn't shown, like the cat asleep in the sack of dog biscuits. And the smell. It wasn't only floorboards in it. There was paraffin in it, and cooking, and candles.

A small lady in glasses looked at them carefully.

"Yes. What can I do for you?" she said. She nodded at Yo-less. "Sambo's with you, dear, is he?" she added.

6

The Olden Days

Guilty lay on top of the bags and purred.

Bigmac watched the traffic. There wasn't a lot. A couple of women met one another as they were both crossing the street, and stood there chatting in the middle of the road, although occasionally one of them would turn to look at Bigmac.

He folded his arms over HEAVY MENTAL.

And then a car pulled up, right in front of him. The driver got out, glanced at Bigmac, and walked off down the street.

Bigmac stared at the car. He'd seen ones like it on television, normally in those costume dramas where one car and two women with a selection of different hats keep going up and down the same street to try to fool people that this isn't really the present day.

The keys were still in the ignition.

Bigmac wasn't a criminal, he was just around when crimes happened. This was because of stupidity. That is, *other people's* stupidity. Mainly other people's stupidity in designing cars that could go from 0–120mph in ten seconds and then selling them to even more stupid people who were only interested in dull things like fuel consumption and what colour the seats were. What was the point in that? That wasn't what a car was *for*.

The keys were still in the ignition.

As far as Bigmac was concerned, he was practically doing people a favour by really seeing what their cars could do, and no way was that stealing, because he always put the cars back if he could and they were often nearly the same shape. You'd think people'd be *proud* to know their car could do 130mph along the Blackbury by-pass instead of complaining all the time.

The keys were still in the ignition. There were a million places in the world where the keys could have been, but in the ignition was where they were.

Old cars like this probably couldn't go at any speed at all.

The keys were still in the ignition. Firmly, invitingly, in the ignition.

Bigmac shifted uncomfortably.

He was aware that there were people in the world who considered it wrong to take cars that didn't belong to them but, however you looked at it . . .

. . . the keys were still in the ignition.

Johnny heard Kirsty's indrawn breath. It sounded like Concorde taking off in reverse.

He felt the room grow bigger, rushing away on every side, with Yo-less all by himself in the middle of it.

Then Yo-less said, "Yes, indeed. I'm with them. Lawdy, lawdy."

The old lady looked surprised.

"My word, you speak English very well," she said.

"I learned it from my grandfather," said Yo-less, his voice as sharp as a knife. "He ate only very educated missionaries."

Sometimes Johnny's mind worked fast. Normally it worked so slowly that it embarrassed him, but just occasionally it had a burst of speed.

"He's a prince," he said.

"Prince Sega," said Yo-less.

"All the way from Nintendo," said Johnny.

"He's here to buy a newspaper," said Kirsty, who in some ways did not have a lot of imagination.

Johnny reached into his own pocket, and then hesitated.

"Only we haven't got any money," he said.

"Yes we have, I've got a least two pou—" Kirsty began.

"We haven't got the *right* money," said Johnny meaningfully. "It was pounds and shillings and pence in those days, not pounds and pee—"

"Pee?" said the woman. She looked from one to the other like someone who hopes that it'll all make sense if they pay enough attention.

Johnny craned his head. There were a few newspapers still on the counter, even though it was the afternoon. One was *The Times*. He could just make out the date.

May 21, 1941.

"Oh, you have a paper, dear," said the old woman, giving up, "I don't suppose I shall sell any more today."

"Thank you very much," said Johnny, grabbing a paper and hurrying the other two out of the shop.

"Sambo," said Yo-less, when they were outside.

"What?" said Kirsty. "Oh, that. Never mind about that. Give me that newspaper."

"My grandad came here in 1952," said Yo-less, in the same plonking, hollow voice. "He said little kids thought his colour'd come off if he washed."

"Yes, well, I can see you're upset, but that's just how things were, it's all changed since then," said Kirsty, turning the pages.

"*Then* hasn't even happened yet," said Yo-less. "I'm not stupid. I've read old books. We're back in golliwog history. Plucky niggers are hooray for the Empire. She called me *Sambo*."

"Look," said Kirsty, still reading the newspaper. "This is the olden days. She didn't mean it . . . you know, nastily. It's just how she was brought up. You people can't expect us to rewrite history, you know."

Johnny suddenly felt as though he'd stepped into a deep freeze. It was almost certainly the *you people*. Sambo had been an insult, but *you people* was worse, because it wasn't even personal.

He had never seen Yo-less so angry. It was a kind of rigid, brittle anger. How could someone as intelligent as Kirsty be so dumb? What she needed to do now was say something sensible.

"Well, I'm certainly glad you're here," said Yo-less, sarcasm gleaming on his words. "So's you can explain all this to me."

"All right, don't go on about it," she said, without looking up. "It's not *that* important."

It was amazing, Johnny thought. Kirsty had a sort of talent for striking matches in a firework factory.

Yo-less took a deep breath.

Johnny patted him on the arm.

"She didn't mean it . . . you know, nastily," he said. "It's just how she was brought up."

Yo-less sagged, and nodded coldly.

"You know we're in the middle of a war, don't you," said Kirsty. "That's what we've ended up in. World War Two. It was very popular around this time."

Johnny nodded.

May the twenty-first, 1941.

Not many people cared or even knew about it now. Just him, and the librarian at the public library who'd helped him find the stuff for the project, and a few old people. It was ancient history, after all. The olden days. And here he was.

And so was Paradise Street.

Until tonight.

"Are you all right?" said Yo-less.

He hadn't even known about it until he'd found the old newspapers in the library. It was—it was as if it hadn't *counted*. It had happened, but it wasn't a proper part of the war. And worse things had happened in a lot of other places. Nineteen people hardly mattered.

But he'd imagined it happening in *his* town. It was horribly easy.

The old men would go home from their allotments. The shops would shut. There wouldn't be many lights in any case, because of the blackout, but bit by bit the town would go to sleep.

And then, a few hours later, it'd happen.

It'd happen tonight.

Wobbler wheezed along the road. And he *did* wobble. It wasn't his fault he was fat, he'd always said, it was just his genetics. He had too many of them.

He was trying to run but most of the energy was getting lost in the wobbling.

He was trying to think, too, but it wasn't happening very clearly.

They hadn't gone time travelling! It was just a windup! They were always trying to wind him up! He'd get home and have a sit down, and it'd all be all right . . .

And this *was* home.

Sort of.

Everything was . . . smaller, somehow. The trees in the street were the wrong size and the cars were wrong. The houses looked . . . newer.

And this was Gregory Road. He'd been along it millions of times. You went along halfway and turned into . . .

. . . into . . .

A man was clipping a hedge. He wore a high collar and tie *and* a pullover with a zig-zag pattern. He was also smoking a pipe. When he saw Wobbler he stopped clipping and took his pipe out of his mouth.

"Can I help you, son?" he said.

"I . . . er . . . I was looking for Seeley Crescent," whispered Wobbler.

The man smiled.

"Well, I'm Councillor Edward Seeley," he said, "but I've never heard of a Seeley Crescent." He called over his shoulder to a woman who was weeding a flowerbed. "Have you heard of a Seeley Crescent, Mildred?"

"There's a big chestnut tree on the corner—" Wobbler began.

"We've got a chestnut tree," said Mr. Seeley, pointing to what looked like a stick with a couple of leaves on it. He smiled. "It doesn't look much at the moment, but just you come back in fifty years' time, eh?"

Wobbler stared at it, and then at him.

It was a wide garden here, with a field beyond it. It struck him that it was quite wide enough for a road, if . . . one day . . . someone wanted to build a road . . .

"I will," he said.

"Are you all right, young man?" said Mrs. Seeley.

Wobbler realized that he wasn't panicking any more. He'd run out of panic. It was like being in a dream. *Afterwards*, it all sounded daft, but while you were in the dream you just got on with it.

It was like a rocket taking off. There was a lot of noise and worry and then you were in orbit, floating free, and able to look down on everything as if it weren't real.

It was an amazing feeling. Wobbler had spent a large part of his life being frightened of things, in a vague kind of way. There were always things he should have been doing, or shouldn't have done. But here it all didn't seem to matter. He wasn't even born yet—in a way, anyway—so absolutely nothing could be his fault.

"I'm fine," he said. "Thank you very much for asking. I'll . . . just be off back into town."

He could feel them watching him as he wandered back down the road.

This *was* his home town. There were all sorts of clues that told him so. But all sorts of other things were . . . strange. There were more trees and fewer houses, more factory chimneys and fewer cars. A lot less colour, too. It didn't look much fun. He was pretty certain no-one here would even know what a pizza *was*—

" 'Ere, mister," said a hoarse voice.

He looked down.

A boy was sitting by the side of the road.

It was almost certainly a boy. But its short trousers reached almost to its ankles, it had a pair of glasses with one lens blanked out with brown paper, its hair had been cut apparently with a lawnmower, and its nose was running. And its ears stuck out.

No-one had ever called Wobbler "mister" before, except teachers when they wanted to be sarcastic.

"Yes?" he said.

"Which way's London?" said the boy. There was a cardboard suitcase next to him, held together with string.

Wobbler thought for a moment. "Back that way," he said, pointing. "Dunno why there's no road signs."

"Our Ron says they took 'em all down so Jerry wun't know where he was," said the boy. He had a line of small stones on the kerb beside him. Every so often he'd pick one up and throw it with great accuracy at a tin can on the other side of the road.

"Who's Jerry?"

One eye looked at him with deep suspicion.

"The *Germans*," said the boy. "Only I wants 'em to come here and blow up Mrs. Density a bit."

"Why? Are we fighting the Germans?" said Wobbler.

"Are you 'n American? Our dad says the Americans ought to fight, only they're waitin' to see who's winnin'."

"Er . . ." Wobbler decided it might be best to be American for a bit. "Yes. Sure."

"Garn! Say something American!"

"Er . . . right on. Republican. Microsoft. Spiderman. Have a nice day."

This demonstration of transatlantic origins seemed to satisfy the small boy. He threw another stone at the tin can.

"Our mam said I've got to stop along of Mrs. Density's and the food's all *rubbish*," said the boy. "You know what, she makes me drink *milk*! I dint mind the proper *milk* at home but round here, you know what, it comes out of a cow's *bum*. I seen it. They took us to a farm with all muck all over the place and, you know what, you know how eggs come out? Urrr! And she makes us go to bed at seven o'clock and I miss our mam and I'm going home. I've had enough of being 'vacuated!"

"It can really make your arm ache," said Wobbler. "I had it done for tetanus."

"Our Ron says it's good fun, going down the Underground station when the siren goes off," the boy went on. "Our Ron says the school got hit an' none of the kids has to go any more."

It seemed to Wobbler that it didn't matter what he said. The boy was really talking to himself Another stone turned the can upside down.

"Huh," said the boy. "Like to see 'em hit the school *here*. They just pick on us just 'cos we're from London and, you know what, that Atterbury kid pinched my piece of shrapnel! Our Ron give it me. Our Ron's a copper, he gets a chance to pick up really good stuff for me. You don't get shrapnel round here, huh!"

"What's shrapnel?" said Wobbler.

"Are you a loony? It's bits of bomb! Our Ron says Alf Harvey got a whole collection *an'* a bit off 'f a Heinkel. Our Ron said Alf Harvey found a real Nazi ring with an actual finger still in it." The boy looked wistful, as though unfairly shut off from untold treasures. "Huh! Our Ron says other kids down our street have gone back home and I reckon I'm old enough, too, so I'm gain'."

Wobbler had never bothered much with history. As far as he was concerned it was something that had happened to other people.

He vaguely remembered a TV programme with some film shot back in the days when people were so poor they could only afford to be in black and white.

Kids with labels round their necks, waiting at railway stations. Every single adult wearing a hat . . .

Evacuees, that was it. Sent out from the big cities so's they wouldn't get bombed, it said.

"What year's this?" he said.

The boy looked at him sideways.

"You're a spy, incha," he said, standing up. "You don't know anyfink about nuffink. You ain't American 'cos I seen 'em on the pictures. If you're'n American, where's your gun?"

"Don't be daft, Americans don't all have guns," said Wobbler. "Lots of them don't have guns. Well . . . some don't, anyway."

"Our Ron said there was something in the paper about German parachuters landing disguised as nuns," said the boy, backing away. "Seems to *me* you could've been a parachuter, if it was a big parachute."

"All right, I'm English," said Wobbler.

"Oh, yeah? Who's the Prime Minster, then?"

Wobbler hesitated.

"I don't think we've done that at school," he said.

"You don't get no lessons in knowing about Winston Churchill," said the boy dismissively.

"Hah, you're just trying to mess me around," said Wobbler. " 'Cos I know for a *fact* we've never had a black Prime Minister."

"You don't know *nuffink*," said the boy, grabbing his battered suitcase. "*And* you're fat."

"I don't have to stand here listening to you," said Wobbler, heading off down the road.

"Spy spy spy," said the boy.

"Oh, shut up."

"*An'* you wobble. I saw that Goering on the newsreels. You look *jus'* like him. *An'* you're dressed up all funny. Spy spy spy!"

Wobbler sighed. He was fairly used to this, only not so much these days because once he'd just been fat and now he was *big* and fat.

"And *you're* stupid," he said. "But at least *I* could get slimmer."

Biting sarcasm didn't work.

"Spy spy spy! Nasty nasty Nazi!"

Wobbler tried walking faster.

"I'm goin' to tell Mrs. Density an' she can telephone our Ron and he can come an' arrest you!" shouted the boy, jumping along behind him.

Wobbler tried walking faster still.

"He's got a *gun*, our Ron."

A man went by slowly on his bike.

"He's a spy," said the boy, pointing at Wobbler. "I'm arresting him for our Ron."

The man just grinned at Wobbler and pedalled onwards.

"Our Ron says you spies send Morse code messages to Nazi submarines by flashing torches," said the boy.

"We're twenty miles from the sea," said Wobbler, who'd almost broken into a run.

"You could stand on something high. Nyer nyer nyer. Spy spy spy."

It was just plain stupid, thought Bigmac, as he watched the two plumes of steam in front of him.

What kind of idiots built a car without power steering or synchromesh gears and put in brakes apparently operated by string? He was practically doing the world a favour by taking the car off the road.

Not just off the road, in fact, but over the pavement and across a flowerbed and into the Alderman Bowler Memorial Horsetrough.

The plumes of steam were quite pretty, really. There were little rainbows in them.

"Well, now," said a voice, as someone opened a car door, "what do we have here?"

"I think I banged my head," said Bigmac.

A large hand encircled his arm and pulled him out of the car. Bigmac looked up into two round faces that had "policeman" written all over them. There was room for quite a lot of things to be written all over them. They were very large faces.

"That is Dr. Roberts' car," they said, "and you, my lad, are in for it. What's your name?"

"Simon Wrigley," mumbled Bigmac. "Ms. Partridge knows all about me . . ."

"She does, does she? And who's she?"

Bigmac blinked at the two faces which miraculously flowed together and became one.

He'd quite liked Ms. Partridge. She was nasty. The two social workers he'd had before had made out that he was wet, whereas Ms. Partridge made it clear that if she had her way Bigmac would have been strangled at birth. You could *respect* someone like that. They didn't make you feel like some kind of a useless nerd.

Something prodded at his memory.

"When is this?" he said, rubbing his head.

"You can start by telling me where you live—" The policeman leaned closer. There was something about Bigmac that bothered him.

"What do you mean, when is this?" he said.

"What year?"

The policeman had fairly fixed ideas about what should happen to car thieves, but they usually knew what year it was.

"It's 1941," he said, and straightened up. His eyes narrowed.

"Who's the captain of the England cricket team?" he said.

Bigmac blinked.

"What? How should I know?"

"Who won the Boat Race last year?"

"What boat race?"

The policeman looked again.

"And what's that on your belt?"

Bigmac blinked again, and looked down.

"I didn't nick it," he said quickly. "It's only a transistor, anyway."

"What's that wire going into your ear?"

"Don't be daft. It's only the earphone—"

The policeman's hand landed on his shoulder with the kind of thud that suggested it wasn't going to let go in a hurry.

"You come along with me, Fritz," he said. "I wasn't born yesterday."

Bigmac's brain drifted into focus. He looked at the uniform, and at the crowd behind it, and it began to dawn on him that he was all alone and a long, long way from home.

"I wasn't born yesterday, either," he said. "Does that help?"

Johnny, Kirsty and Yo-less sat in a little garden. As far as Johnny could tell, it was where part of the ring road and a traffic island were going to be one day. Now it contained a bench and some geraniums.

"They'll blow up Paradise Street tonight," said Johnny.

"Where's that?" said Yo-less.

"Here. It's where the sports centre was. . . . will be, I mean."

"Never heard of it."

"Yes. I did *say*. It got blown up. And you know the funny thing about it?"

"There's something funny about it?" said Kirsty.

"It was by accident! The Germans had meant to bomb the big goods yard at Slate! But they got a bit lost and the weather turned bad and they saw the railway yards here and dropped all their bombs and went home. Everyone was in bed because the air raid sirens didn't go off in time!"

"All right, all right, I know, you've told me before, and all about Adolf and Stalin. It's very sad but you shouldn't get worked up about it," said Kirsty. "It's history. That sort of thing happens in history."

"Aren't you listening? It hasn't happened *yet*. This is *now*. It's going to happen *tonight*."

They stared at the geraniums.

"Why haven't we gone back yet?" said Kirsty. "We've been here *ages*."

"How should I know?" said Johnny. "Maybe the further you go, the longer you stay."

"*And* we just happened to go to somewhere you know all about," said Yo-less. "That's a bit strange, in my opinion."

It had worried Johnny, too. Everything *felt* real, but maybe he'd just gone mad and taken everyone else with him.

"I don't want to stay here, that's definite," said Yo-less. "Being Little Black Sambo wasn't my idea of a full life."

Johnny stood up and grasped the handles of the trolley.

"I'm going to see Paradise Street," he said.

"That's a very bad idea," said Kirsty. "I told you, anything you do affects the future."

"I'm only going to have a look."

"Oh yes? I find that very hard to believe, actually."

"She's right," said Yo-less, trying to keep up. "You shouldn't mess around with Time. I read this book where a man went right back in time and trod on . . . on a dinosaur, and changed the whole future."

"A dinosaur?" said Kirsty.

"I think it was a dinosaur. Maybe they had small ones."

"Huh. Or he was a very big man, perhaps," said Kirsty.

The trolley bumped off the pavement, rattled across a road, and clanked up the pavement on the other side.

"What're you going to do?" said Kirsty. "Knock on people's doors and say, 'Excuse me, some bombers are going to bomb this street tonight'?"

"Why not?"

"Because they'll lock you up, that's why," said Yo-less.

"Right," said Kirsty. "It'll be just like the man who trod on Yo-less's dinosaur."

"It may have been some sort of insect, now I come to think of it," said Yo-less. "Anyway, there's nothing you can do. It's already happened, otherwise how come you know about it? You can't mess up history."

The trolley stopped so quickly that they ran into the back of Johnny.

"Why does everyone always talk like that?" he said. "It's *stupid*. You would really watch someone run over by a car because that's what was supposed to happen, would you? Everything we do changes the future, all the time. So we ought to do what's *right*."

"Don't shout, people are looking at us," said Kirsty.

The trolley bumped over the kerb and started to bounce on some cobbles. They were already out of the town centre.

And there was Paradise Street.

It wasn't very long. There were only ten terraced houses on either side, and some of them were boarded up. The far end was a pair of double wooden gates to a factory. They'd once been painted green, but time and the weather had turned the colour into a sort of mossy grey.

Someone had chalked a set of goalposts on the doors, and half a dozen small boys in knee-length shorts were kicking a ball about.

Johnny watched them as they scuffled and perpetrated fouls that would have gladdened the heart of any football manager.

About halfway along the street a young man was repairing a motorcycle. Tools lay on a piece of sacking on the pavement. The football emerged from a complicated tackle, hit the spanners, and almost knocked the bike over.

"Turn it up, you little devils," said the man, pushing the ball away.

"You never said anything about children," said Kirsty, so quietly that Johnny nearly didn't hear her.

Johnny shrugged.

"It's *all* going to get blown up?" said Yo-less.

Johnny nodded.

"There wasn't very much detail in the local paper," he said. "They didn't used to put very much in, in case the enemy read it. It was all to do with something they called the war effort. You know . . . not wanting to let the enemy know you'd been hurt. There was a photo of a lady with her thumb up saying 'Blackbury can take it, Mister

Hitler!' but there was hardly anything else about the raid until a couple of years afterwards."

"You mean the government hushed it up?" said Kirsty.

"Makes sense, I suppose," said Yo-less gloomily. "I mean, you don't want to say to the enemy, 'Hey, you missed your target, have another go.' "

The football slammed against the factory gates, rattling them. There didn't seem to be any teams. The ball just went everywhere, surrounded by a mob of small boys.

"I don't see what we could *do*," said Kirsty. Her voice sounded uneasy, now.

"What? Just now you were telling me I *shouldn't* do anything," said Johnny.

"It's different when you see people, isn't it?"

"Yes."

"I suppose it *wouldn't* work if we just told someone?"

"They'd say 'how do you know?' and then you'd probably get shot as a spy," said Yo-less. "They used to shoot spies."

7

Heavy Mental

The man in the khaki uniform turned Bigmac's transistor radio over and over in his hands.

Bigmac watched nervously. There was a police sergeant in the room, and Bigmac was familiar with policemen. But there was a soldier standing by the door, and he had a gun in a holster. And the one sitting down looked tired but had a very sharp expression. Bigmac was not the fastest of thinkers, but it had dawned on him that this was unlikely to be the kind of situation where you got let off with a caution.

"Let's start again," said the seated soldier, who had introduced himself as Captain Harris. "Your name is . . . ?"

Bigmac hesitated. He wanted to say, "You get Ms. Partridge, she'll sort it all out, it's not my fault, she says I'm socially dysfunctional," but there was an expression on the captain's face that suggested that this might be a very unfortunate move.

"Simon Wrigley."

"And you say you are fourteen years old and live in—" Captain Harris glanced at his notes, "the Joshua Che N'Clement 'block' which is near here, you say."

"You can see it easily," said Bigmac, trying to be helpful. "Or you could do, if it was here."

The captain and the police sergeant glanced at one another.

"It's not here?" said the captain.

"Yes. I don't know why," said Bigmac.

"Tell me again what Heavy Mental is," said the captain.

"They're a neo-punk thrash band," said Bigmac.

"A music band?"

"Er, yes."

"And we would have heard them on the wireless, perhaps?"

"I shouldn't think so," said Bigmac. "Their last single was 'I'm going to rip off your head and spit down the hole.' "

" 'Rip off your head—' " said the policeman, who was taking notes.

" '—and spit down the hole,' " said Bigmac helpfully.

"This watch of yours with the numbers on it," said the captain. "I see it's got little buttons, too. What happens if I press them?"

The policeman tried to move away a little.

"The one on the left lights it up so you can see it in the dark," said Bigmac.

"Really? And why would you want to do that?"

"When you wake up in the night and want to know what time it is?" Bigmac suggested, after some deep thought.

"I see. And the other button?"

"Oh, that's to tell you what time it is in another country."

Everyone suddenly seemed very interested.

"What other country?" said the captain sharply.

"It's stuck on Singapore," said Bigmac.

The captain laid it down very carefully. The sergeant wrote out a label and tied it to the watch strap. Then the captain picked up Bigmac's jacket.

"What is this made of?" he said.

"I dunno. Some kind of plastic," said Bigmac. "They sell them down the market."

The captain pulled it this way and that.

"How is it made?"

"Ah, I know that," said Bigmac. "I read about it. You mix some chemicals together, and you get plastic. Easy."

"In camouflage colours," said the captain.

Bigmac licked his lips. He was sure that he was in deep trouble, so there was no sense in pretending.

"That's just to make you look hard," he said.

"Hard. I see," said the captain, and his eyes didn't give away whether he really saw or not. He held up the back of the jacket and pointed to two words done rather badly in biro.

"What exactly are BLACKBURY SKINS?" he said.

"Er. That's me and Bazza and Skazz. Er. Skinheads. A . . . kind of gang . . ."

"Gang," said the captain.

"Er. Yes."

"Skinheads?"

"Er . . . the haircut," said Bigmac.

"Looks like an ordinary military haircut to me," said the sergeant.

"And these," said the captain, pointing to the swastikas on either side of the name. "Gang badges, are they? Also to make you look . . . hard?"

"Er . . . it's just . . . you know . . . Adolf Hitler and that," said Bigmac.

All the men were staring at him.

"It's just decoration," said Bigmac.

The captain put the coat down very slowly.

"It's nothing to get *excited* about," said Bigmac. "Where I come from, you can buy badges and things down the market, you can get Gestapo knives—"

"That's enough!" said the captain. "Now listen to me. You'll make it easier on yourself if you tell me the truth right now. I want your name, the names of your contacts . . . everything. A unit is coming from headquarters and they aren't as patient as I am, do you understand?"

He stood up and started to put Bigmac's labelled belongings into a sack.

"Hey, that's my stuff—" mumbled Bigmac.

"Lock him up."

"You can't lock me up just for some old car—"

"We can for spying," said Captain Harris. "Oh, yes, we can."

He strode out of the room.

"Spying?" said Bigmac. "Me?"

"Are you one of them Hitler Youths?" said the sergeant, conversationally. "I saw you lot on the newsreel. Waving all them torches. Nasty pieces of work, I thought. Like Boy Scouts gone bad."

"I haven't spied for anyone!" shouted Bigmac. "don't know how to spy! I don't even like Germany! My brother got sent home from Munich for stitching up one of their football supporters with a scaffolding pole even though it wasn't his fault!"

Such rock-solid evidence of anti-Germanic feeling did not seem to impress the sergeant.

"You can get shot, you know," he said. "For the first offence"

The door was still open. Bigmac could hear noises in the corridor. Someone was talking on the phone, somewhere in the distance.

Bigmac wasn't an athlete. If there was an Olympic Sick Note event, he would have been in the British team. He would've won the 100 metres I've Got Asthma, the half-marathon Lurk in the Changing Rooms, and the freestyle Got to Go to the Doctor.

But his boots dug into the floor and he rose out of his chair like a missile going off. His feet barely touched the table top. He went past the policeman's shoulder with his legs already making running motions. Fear gave him superhuman acceleration. Ms. Partridge might make cutting remarks but she wasn't allowed to use bullets however much she wanted to.

Bigmac landed in the doorway, turned at random, put his head down and charged. It was a hard head. It hit someone around belt level. There was a shout and a crash.

He saw another gap and headed for it. There was another crash, and the sound of a telephone smashing on the floor. Someone yelled at him to halt or they'd fire.

Bigmac didn't stop to find out what'd happened. He just hoped that a pair of 1990s Doc Martens that had been practically bought legally by his brother off a man with a lorry full of them were *much* better for dodging and running than huge police boots.

Whoever had been shouting stop or they'd fire . . . fired.

There was a *crack* and a clang somewhere ahead of Bigmac, but he turned down a corridor, ran under the outstretched arms of another policeman, and out into a yard.

A policeman was standing next to a Jurassic bicycle, a huge machine that looked as if it were made of drainpipes welded together.

Bigmac went past him in a blur, grabbed the handlebars, swung onto the saddle and rammed his feet onto the pedals.

" 'Ere, what're you doin'—"

The policeman's voice faded behind him.

The bike swung out into the lane behind the station.

It was a cobbled street. The saddle was solid leather. Bigmac's trousers were very thin.

"No wonder everyone was very depressed," he thought, trying to cycle standing up.

"Nyer nyer nyer. Spy spy spy."

"Shut up!" said Wobbler. "Why don't you run away to London?"

"Ain't gonna run away to London *now*," said the boy. " 'S'lot more fun catchin' spies *here*."

They were back in the heart of the town now. The boy trailed behind Wobbler, pointing him out to passers-by. Admittedly, no-one seemed to be about to arrest him, but he was getting some odd looks.

"My brother Ron's a *policeman*," said the boy. "He'll come up from London and shoot you with his *gun*."

"Go away!"

"Sharn't!"

Opposite the entrance to Paradise Street was a small church. It was a non-conformist chapel, according to Yo-less. It had a shut-up, wet Sunday look. A couple of elderly evergreen trees on either side of the door looked as though it'd take a shovel just to get the soot off their leaves.

The three of them sat on the steps, watching the street. A woman had come out and was industriously scrubbing her doorstep.

"Did this chapel get hit?" said Kirsty.

"You mean *will*. I don't think so."

"Pity."

"It's still here . . . I mean, in 1996," said Yo-less. "Only it's just used as a social hall. You know, for keep-fit classes and stuff. I know, 'cos I come here for Morris Dance practice every Wednesday. Will, I mean."

"You?" said Kirsty. "*You* do Morris Dancing? With sticks and hankies and stuff? *You?*"

"There's something wrong?" said Yo-less coldly.

"Well . . . no . . . no, of course not . . . but . . . it's just an unusual interest for someone of—your—"

Yo-less let her squirm for a bit and then said, "Height?" He dropped the word like a weight. Kirsty shut her mouth.

"Yes," she said.

Another woman appeared, next door to the one scrubbing her front doorstep, and started scrubbing *her* doorstep.

"What are we going to *do*?" said Kirsty.

"I'm thinking," said Yo-less.

Somewhere in the distance a bell went off, and kept on going off.

"I'm thinking, too," said Johnny. "I'm thinking: we haven't seen Bigmac for ages."

"Good," said Kirsty.

"He might be in some trouble, I mean," said Johnny.

"What do you mean, *might* be?" said Yo-less.

"And we haven't seen Wobbler, either," said Johnny.

"Oh, you know Wobbler. He's probably hiding somewhere."

Another woman opened the door on the other side of the street and entered the doorstep-scrubbing competition.

Kirsty straightened up.

"Why're we acting so miserable?" she said. "We're Nineties people. We should be able to think of something. We could . . . we could . . ."

"We could ring up Adolf Hitler," Yo-less suggested. "Can't remember his phone number, sorry, but directory inquiries in Germany're *bound* to know."

Johnny stared glumly at the shopping trolley. He hadn't expected time travel to be this hard. He thought of all those wasted lessons when they could have been telling him what to do if some mad woman left him a trolley full of time. School never taught you anything that was useful in real life. There probably wasn't a single text book that told you what to do if it turned out you were living next door to Elvis Presley.

He looked down the length of Paradise Street, and felt Time streaming past him. Yo-less and Kirsty faded away. He could *feel* them there, though, as insubstantial as dreams, as the light faded from the sky and the footballers went indoors and the wind got up and the clouds rolled in from the south-west and the town went to sleep and the bombers came out of the east and fire rained down on the houses and the allotments and the people and the goalposts chalked on the wall and all the nice, clean, white doorsteps . . .

Captain Harris turned Bigmac's watch over.

"Amazing," he said. "And it says 'Made In Japan'."

"Fiendishly cunning," said the police sergeant.

The captain picked up the radio.

"Japanese again," he said. "Why? Why put it on the back? See here. Made in Japan."

"I thought it was all rice," said the sergeant. "That's what my dad said. He was out there."

Captain Harris fiddled one of the tiny headphones into his ear and moved a switch. He listened to the hiss that was due to be replaced by Radio Blackbury in forty-eight years' time, and nodded.

"It's doing *something*," he said. His thumb touched the wave-change switch, and he blinked.

"It's the Home Service," he said. "Clear as a bell!"

"We could have the back off it in no time," said the sergeant.

"No," said Sergeant Harris. "This has got to go to the Ministry. The men in white coats can have a look at it. How can you get valves to fit in this? Where's the aerial?"

"Very small feet," said the sergeant.

"Sorry, sergeant?"

"That's what my dad said. Japanese. The women. Very small feet, he said. So maybe they've got small hands, too. Just a thought." The sergeant tried to extend his line of technological speculation. "Good for making small things? You know. Like ships in bottles?"

The captain put the tiny radio back in the box.

"I've seen people do them," said the sergeant, still anxious to be of assistance. "You get a bottle, then you get a lot of very thin thread—"

"He's the best actor I've ever seen, I know that," said Captain Harris. "You could really think he was just a stupid boy. But this stuff . . . I just can't believe it. It's all very . . . odd."

"We've got every man out after him," said the sergeant. "And the inspector has called out the army from West Underton. We'll have him in no time."

The captain sealed the box with sticky tape.

"I want this guarded," he said.

"We'll keep an eye on it in the main office."

"No. I want it secure."

"Well, there's an empty cell. Actually there's someone in it but I'll soon have 'em out."

"More secure than that."

The sergeant scratched an ear.

"There's the Lost Property cupboard," he said. "But there's important stuff in it—"

"Lost Property cupboard! Haven't you got a safe?"

"No."

"What'd happen if the Crown Jewels were found in the gutter, then?"

"We'd put 'em in the Lost Property cupboard," said the sergeant promptly. "And then ring up the King. If his name was in them, of course. Look, it's a good thick door and there's only one key and I've got it."

"All right, take out what's in there and put it in your cell and put the box in the cupboard," said the captain.

"Chief Inspector won't like that. Very important stuff, Lost Property."

"Tell him we can co-operate in a very friendly fashion now or if he prefers he can take a call from the Chief Constable in two minutes," said Captain Harris, putting his hand on the phone. "One way or the other, hmm?"

The sergeant looked worried. "You serious about this, sir?" he said.

"Oh, yes."

"That stuff's not going to go off bang or anything, is it?"

"I'm not sure. I don't think so."

Five minutes later the sergeant walked down to the cells with his arms full of the contents of the cupboard, and a put-upon expression on his face. He put them on a bench in the corridor and fished out his keys. Then he pulled aside the hatch in a cell door.

"You all right, old girl?"

"That's what *you* think. Talk about a blue pencil! You can tell he's a lad, can't yer, Mister Shadwell?"

"Yes, yes," said the sergeant, opening the door.

The old lady sat on the bed. She was so short that her feet swung several inches above the floor. And there was a cat on her lap. It growled when it saw the sergeant—a slow, rising growl which suggested that, if there was any attempt to pick the cat up, it was all going to end in claws.

The sergeant had long ago stopped worrying about how the cat could get into the cells. It happened every time. There wasn't room via the windows and it certainly couldn't have got in through the door, but every night the old lady was in the cells, the cat would be in there, too, in the morning.

"Finished your breakfast, have you?"

"Millennium hand and shrimp," said Mrs. Tachyon happily.

"Good. Then you just come along with me. It's a nice day outside," said the sergeant.

"Beam me up, Scotty," said Mrs. Tachyon, standing up and following him obediently. The sergeant shook his head sadly.

She trailed behind him into the station yard where, under a bit of canvas the sergeant had thrown over it the night before, there was a wire trolley loaded down with bags.

Mrs. Tachyon looked at it.

"No-one nicked anything?" she said.

She was like that, the sergeant thought. Mad as a hatter most of the time and then suddenly a sentence'd come out at you like a razor blade in candy floss.

"Now then, old love, as if anyone'd touch that lot," he said, as kindly as possible.

"Points win prizes. Hats."

The sergeant reached under the trolley and produced a pair of boots.

"These belonged to my mum," he said. "She was going to throw 'em out, but I said, there's still some good leather on them—"

Mrs. Tachyon snatched them out of his hand. In seconds they were somewhere in the pile of bags on the trolley.

"It's a small step for a man," said Mrs. Tachyon.

"Yes, they're size sixes," said the sergeant.

"Ah, Bisto. It's a great life if yer don't weaken, but of course they've put a bridge there now."

The sergeant looked down at the trolley.

"Dunno where you get this stuff from," he said. "What're these bags made of, love? Looks like rubber or something."

"Obbly Obbly Ob. Weeeed!" said Mrs. Tachyon. "I told them, but no-one listens to a teapot. Fab!"

The sergeant sighed, put his hand in his pocket and produced a sixpence.

"Get yourself a cup of tea and a bun," he said.

"Hats. That's what *you* think," said Mrs. Tachyon, taking it.

"Don't mention it."

The sergeant headed back into the police station.

He was *used* to Mrs. Tachyon. When nights were cold you'd sometimes hear a milk bottle smash on the step outside. This was technically a crime, and it meant that Mrs. Tachyon was looking for somewhere warm for the night.

Not on *every* cold night, though. That was a puzzler, and no mistake. Last winter it had been very nippy indeed for quite a long time and the lads had got a bit worried. It came as quite a relief when they'd heard the crash of breaking glass and the cry of "I *told* 'em! That's what *you* think!" Mrs. Tachyon came and went, and no-one knew where she came from, and you never found out where she'd gone . . .

Beam me up, Snotty? Mad as a hatter, of course.

But . . . strange, too. Like, after you'd given her something you ended up feeling as if she'd done you a favour.

He heard the rattle of the trolley behind him, and then a sudden silence.

He turned around. The trolley, and Mrs. Tachyon, had gone.

Johnny felt the *hereness* of here. It'd happen *here*, not in some far-off country full of odd names and foreign people with thick moustaches shouting slogans.

It'd happen *here*, where there were public libraries and zebra crossings and people who did the football pools.

Bombs would come crashing through roofs and ceilings and down to the cellars, and turn the world white.

And it would happen, because as Yo-less said, it *had* happened. It was going to have happened, and he couldn't possibly stop it, because if he *did* find some way of stopping it, then he wouldn't know about it happening, would he?

Maybe Mrs. Tachyon collected Time. Johnny felt in a way that he couldn't quite put into words that Time wasn't just something that was on clocks and calendars but lived in people's heads, too. And if that meant you had to think like this, no wonder she sounded mad.

"Are you all right?" said a voice, a long way away.

Miraculously, the rubble became houses again, the light came up, the football rattled against the goal in the warm afternoon air.

Kirsty waved a hand in front of his face.

"Are you OK?"

"I was just . . . thinking," said Johnny.

"I hate it when you switch off like that."

"Sorry."

Johnny stood up.

"We didn't come back here by accident," he said. "I was thinking a lot about tonight, and we ended up coming here just in time. I don't know why. But we've got to do something, even if there's nothing we can do. So I'm going to—"

A bicycle came around the corner. It was bouncing up and down on the cobbles and the skinny figure riding it was a mere blur. It clanked to a halt in front of them.

They stared at the cyclist. He was shaking so much he looked slightly out of focus.

"Bigmac?"

"Ur-ur-ur—" shuddered Bigmac.

"How many fingers am I holding up?" said Kirsty.

"Ur-ur-ur-n-n-nineteen? H-h-hide the bike!"

"Why?" said Kirsty.

"I didn't do anything!"

"Ah," said Yo-less, knowingly. "It's like that, is it?"

He picked up the bike and wheeled it into the sooty shrubs.

"Like what?" said Kirsty, looking bewildered.

"Bigmac *always* never does anything," said Johnny.

"That's right," said Yo-less. "There can't be anyone in the whole universe who's got into so much trouble for things he didn't do in places he wasn't at that weren't his fault."

"Th-th-they *shot* at me!"

"Wow!" said Yo-less. "You must've not done anything really *big* this time!"

"Th-there was th-this c-car—"

The ringing Johnny had heard before started again, somewhere behind the buildings.

"Th-that's a police car!" said Bigmac. "I tried to give them the slip down Harold Wilson Drive and—it wasn't there! And one of them shot at me! With an actual gun! Soldiers aren't supposed to shoot people!"

They dragged the trembling Bigmac into the horrible bushes. Kirsty gave him her mac to stop him shivering.

"All right, game over. I said game over!" he moaned. "Let's pack it in, all right? Let's go home!"

"I think we should try to tell people about the bombs," Johnny said. "Someone might listen."

"And if they ask how do you know, you'll say you're from 1996, will you?"

"Maybe you could . . . you know . . . write a note," said Yo-less. "Slip it into someone's letterbox?"

"Oh, yes?" said Kirsty, hotly. "What should we write? 'Go for a long walk' perhaps? Or 'Wear a very hard hat'?"

She stopped when she saw Johnny's expression.

"Sorry," she said. "I didn't mean that."

"Wobbler!" said Yo-less.

They turned. Wobbler was toiling along the street. It took some effort for Wobbler to manage a run, but when he did so, there was also something terribly unstoppable about him.

He spotted them, and changed direction.

"Am I glad to see you," he panted. "Let's get out of here! Some loony kid chased me all the way down the hill. He kept shouting out that I was a spy!"

"Did he try to shoot you?" said Bigmac.

"He threw stones!"

"Hah! *I* got shot at!" said Bigmac, with a sort of pride.

"All right," said Kirsty. "We're all here. Let's go."

"You *know* I don't know how!" said Johnny.

The bags lay there in the trolley. There were the words "Shop At Tescos" on a piece of metal on the front of the wire. Probably Mr. Tesco just owned a tiny grocery shop or something back here, Johnny thought wildly. Or hadn't been born yet.

"It's your mind that works it," said Kirsty. "It must be. You go where you're thinking."

"Oh, come *on*," said Yo-less. "That's like *magic*."

Johnny stared at the trolley again. "I could . . . try," he said.

A police car went by, a street away.

"Let's get somewhere more hidden," said Yo-less.

"Good idea," muttered Bigmac.

A cinder path went around the back of the little church, to an area with dustbins and a heap of dead flowers. There was a small green door. It opened easily.

"In those—in these days, they didn't lock churches," said Yo-less.

"But there's silver candlesticks and stuff, isn't there?" said Bigmac. "Anyone could walk right in and nick 'em."

"Don't," said Johnny.

They manhandled the trolley into a back room. It contained a tea urn on a trestle table, a pile of battered hymnbooks, and not much else except the smell of old embroidery, furniture polish and stale air, which is known as the odour of sanctity. There was no sign of any silver candlesticks anywhere—

"Bigmac! Shut that cupboard!" said Yo-less.

"I was only *looking*."

Johnny stared at the sacks. All right, he thought. Let's say they're full of time. It's a daft idea. After all, they're quite small sacks—

On the other hand, how much space does time take up?

Perhaps it's compressed . . . folded up . . .

Mrs. Tachyon collects time like other old ladies collect string?

This is daft.

But . . .

There was a deep, rumbling sound. Guilty had sat up in the trolley and was purring happily.

Johnny took a sack and held it carefully by the neck. It felt warm, and he was sure it moved slightly under his grip.

"This probably won't work," he said.

"Should we hold on to the trolley?" said Yo-less.

"I don't think so. I don't know! Look, are you all sure? I really don't know what I'm doing!"

"Yes, but you've never really known what you're doing, have you?" said Kirsty.

"That's right," said Yo-less. "So you've had a lot of practice."

Johnny shut his eyes and tried to think of . . . 1996.

The thought crept into his mind from somewhere outside. It's not a time, it's a *place*.

It's a place where the model of the Space Shuttle on the ceiling hangs by a bit of red wool because you ran out of black thread.

And the model's got streaks of glue on it because you always get it wrong somewhere.

It's a place where your mum just smokes a lot and looks out of the window.

It's a place where your grandad watches TV all day.

It's *where you want to be.*

His mind began to go fuzzy at the edges. He thought of Thomas the Tank Engine wallpaper and the Mr. Men lamp, until they were so close he could almost taste them. He could *hear* the place where Grandad had hung the wallpaper wrong so that there was an engine that was half Thomas and half James. It hung like a beacon in his head.

He opened his eyes. The images were still around him; the others looked like ghosts. They were staring at him.

He opened the bag, just a fraction.

Wobbler swallowed.

"Er . . ." he said.

He turned around. And then, just in case, he looked behind the table.

"Er . . . guys? Johnny? Bigmac? Yo-less?" He swallowed again, but sometimes you just had to face up to unpleasant facts, and so he bravely said: "Er . . . *Kirsty*?"

No-one answered. There was no-one *there* to answer.

He was all alone with the tea urn.

"Hey, I was even holding on!" he said. "Oi! I'm still here! Very funny, ha ha, now joke over, all right? Guys? Johnny? You've left me *behind*! All right? It worked, yes. Joke over, ha ha ha, all right? Please?"

He opened the door and looked out into the shadowy yard.

"I know you're only doing this to wind me up, well, it hasn't worked," he moaned.

Then he went back and sat on a bench with his hands on his lap.

After a while he fished out a grubby paper handkerchief and blew his nose. He was about to throw it away when he stopped and glared at it. It was probably the only paper handkerchief in the *world*.

"I can see you peering out at me," he said, but his heart wasn't in it. "You're going to jump out any minute, I know. Well, it's not working. 'Cos I'm not worried, see. Let's all go home and get a burger, eh? Good idea, eh? Tell you what, I've got some money, I don't mind buyin' 'em, eh? Hey? Or we could go down the Chinese and get a take-away—"

He stopped, and looked exactly like someone who'd realized that it was going to be a long, long time before there were any beansprouts in this town. Or burgers, come to that. All there probably was to eat was meat and fish and stuff.

"All right, fair enough, you can come out now . . ."

A fly stirred on the windowsill, and started to bang itself absent-mindedly on the glass.

"Look, it's not funny any m . . . more, all right?"

There was a movement of air behind him, and a definite sensation that, where there had been no one, there was now someone.

Wobbler turned around, a huge relieved grin on his face.

"Ha, I bet you thought you'd got me going—*what*?"

The Over-50s' Keep-Fit class was in full wheeze. The tutor had long ago given up expecting everyone to keep up, so she just pressed on in the hope that people would do what they could manage and, if possible, not actually die while on the premises.

"And *bend* and *bend* and *bend* and—do the best you can, Miss Windex—*step* and *step* and—what?"

She blinked.

Johnny looked around.

The keep-fit class, after ten minutes of aerobics, were not the most observant people. One or two of them actually made space for the newcomers.

The tutor hesitated. She'd been brought up to believe in a healthy mind in a healthy body, and, since she was pretty sure she had a healthy body, it was not possible, she reasoned, that a group of people and an overloaded shopping trolley could have suddenly appeared at the back of the old church hall. They must have just come in, she reasoned. Admittedly, there was no actual door there, but people certainly didn't just appear out of thin air.

"Where are we?" Kirsty hissed.

"Same place," whispered Yo-less. "Different time!"

Even some of the slower fitness fans had caught up by now. The whole class had stopped and turned around and were watching them with interest.

"Well, *say* something!" said Kirsty. "Everyone's *looking*."

"Er . . . is this Pottery?" said Johnny.

"What?" said the tutor.

"We're looking for Beginners' Pottery," said Johnny. It was a wild stab, but every hall and hut and spare room in Blackbury seemed to have its time filled up with people doing weird hobbies or industriously learning Russian.

A small light went on behind the tutor's eyes. She grabbed at the familiar words like a singer snatching a microphone.

"That's Thursdays," she said. "In the Red Cross Hall."

"Oh. Is it? Tch. We're *always* getting it wrong," said Johnny.

"And after we've lugged all this clay up here, too," said Yo-less. "That's a nuisance, isn't it, Bigmac?"

"Don't look at *me*," said Bigmac. "They *shot* at me!"

The tutor was staring from one to the other.

"Er. Yes. Well, it can get pretty nasty in Beginners' Pottery," said Johnny. "Come on, everyone."

They all grabbed hold of the trolley. Tracksuited figures limped politely out of the way as it squeaked its way across the floor, bumped down the step and landed in the damp yard outside.

Johnny pushed the door shut behind them, and listened for a moment.

". . . well, then . . . *bend* and *stretch* and *wheeze* and *bend* . . ."

He straightened up. It was *amazing* what you could get away with. Ten-legged aliens would be immediately accepted in Blackbury if they were bright enough to ask the way to the Post Office and complain about the weather. People had a way of just not seeing anything that common sense said they shouldn't see.

"I bet something's gone wrong," said Bigmac.

"Er . . ." said Yo-less.

"No, this has *got* to be the 1990s," said Kirsty. "It's the only period in history when you wouldn't be burned at the stake for wearing a green and purple tracksuit, isn't it?"

The bulk of the sports centre loomed opposite them. Five minutes ago, thought Johnny, five of *my* minutes ago, that was a street. Get your head round that.

"Er . . ." said Yo-less again.

"They *shot* at me," said Bigmac. "A *real* bullet! I heard it hit the actual wall!"

"Er . . ." said Yo-less.

"Oh, what's the *matter* with you?" said Kirsty.

"Er . . . where's Wobbler?"

They looked around.

"Oh, *no* . . ." said Johnny.

They were Wobblerless.

"I ain't going back!" said Bigmac, backing away. "Not to get shot at!"

"He wouldn't have wandered off again, would he?" said Kirsty.

"No," said Johnny. "He must still be there!"

"Look, get a grip, will you?" said Kirsty. "You said the church doesn't get hit! He's *OK*."

"Yes . . . but he's OK in 1941!"

"S'posing something goes wrong?" said Bigmac. "*He* didn't come back this time, s'posing we go back and *all* get stuck? I'll get shot!"

"You think *you've* got problems?" said Yo-less. "*I'd* have to learn to play the banjo."

"Will you all stop panicking and *think* for a moment?" said Kirsty. "This is *time* travel. He's always going to be there, *whenever* we go back! Of *course* we ought to go and get him! But we don't have to *rush*."

Of course, it was true. He'd always be there, thought Johnny. They could go back in ten years' time and he'd still be there. Just like something on a tape—you could play it, and fast forward, and rewind, and it would always be there. And later that night, the bombs would land in Paradise Street—and *that* night would always be there. For ever. Every second, always there. Like little fossils.

Kirsty hauled the trolley away and pushed it down the steps towards the pavement.

"His mum 'n dad'll worry," said Yo-less, uncertainly.

"No, they won't," said Kirsty. "Because we can bring him back to right *here*."

"Really? Why can't we see us doing it, then?" said Yo-less. "You mean any minute we're just going to pop up with Wobbler and say 'hi, us, here's Wobbler, see you later'?"

"Oh, good grief," said Kirsty. "I can't think about that. You can't think about time travel with a logical mind."

Yo-less turned and looked at Johnny's face.

"Oh, no," he said, "He's off again . . ."

Everything's there waiting, Johnny thought. That's the thing about time. It doesn't matter how long it takes to build a time machine. We could all die out and evolution could start again with moles or something, it could take millions of years, but sooner or later someone will find out how to do it. It might not even be a machine. It might just be a way of understanding what time *is*, like everyone was scared of lightning and then one day someone said, look, you can store it in little bottles and then it was just electricity. But it wouldn't actually matter, because once you'd worked out how to use it, everything would be there. If someone ever finds a way of travelling in time, *ever*, in the entire history of the universe, then they could be here today.

And then he thought of the bombers, nosing through the clouds over the houses and the footballers and all those clean doorsteps . . .

"Uh?" he said.

"You all right?" said Yo-less.

"Let's get a drink, at least," said Kirsty, shoving the trolley firmly towards the town centre.

And then she stopped.

Johnny hadn't often seen her shocked. Kirsty normally dealt with the terrible and the unexpected by getting angry with it. But now she stopped, and went pale.

"Oh, no . . ." she said.

The road from the old church led down the hill towards traffic lights at the bottom.

An overloaded shopping trolley, with a boy and a girl clinging to it, was hurtling down the other road.

As they watched, it heeled over like a yacht tacking against the wind, turned a full ninety degrees, and plunged into the car park of the Neil Armstrong Shopping Mall.

A long black car followed it.

He'd forgotten all about the car. Maybe there *were* secret societies. Maybe there were men in black in long black cars who said things like, "The truth is out there" and came and found you if you got your hand trapped in the occult.

Johnny could see a map in his head. But it was a map of time.

They'd moved in time at his house. But Yo-less was right, you probably could move in time like a train on a track, so you flipped over onto another track just a little bit further along. You moved in space, really.

And he'd done it again, when he thought they were going to die at the traffic lights. And the black car had vanished . . . because it didn't exist in *this* time. He definitely hadn't seen it when he'd looked behind him.

They'd come back to a time when it existed.

The car pulled to a halt outside the mall.

A feeling of absolute certainty stole over Johnny. He knew the answer. Later on, with any luck, he'd find out what the question was, but right now he was sure of the answer.

Forget about secret societies. Forget about time police. Policemen had to have nice logical minds, and to deal with time you needed a mind like Mrs. Tachyon.

But there was someone else who'd *know* where they'd be today, wasn't there . . .

Because . . . supposing we *didn't* go back? Supposing . . . maybe we went back and did things wrong?

He started to run.

Johnny dodged across the road. A car hooted at him.

Across in the car park, a man in black, with black sunglasses and a peaked black hat, got out of the car and hurried into the mall.

Johnny leapt over the low wall into the car park and weaved between shoppers and their trolleys . . .

. . . And panted to a halt in front of the car.

It had stopped right in front of the entrance, where no-one was ever allowed to park.

In the bright sunlight it looked even blacker than Johnny remembered. Its engine ticked occasionally as it cooled down. On the hood was a silver ornament.

It looked very much like a hamburger.

If he squinted, Johnny could just make out a figure in the rear seat, a mere shadow behind the darkness of the glass.

He ran around and snatched at the handle of the back door, yanking it open.

"All right! I know you're in there! Who are you, really?"

Most of the figure was in deep shade, but there was a pair of hands visible, resting on a black cane with a silver tip.

Then the figure moved. It unfolded slowly, and became a large man in a coat that was half coat, half cloak. He emerged carefully, making sure both feet were firmly on the ground before easing the rest of his body out of the car.

He was quite tall, tall enough so that he was big rather than fat. He wore a large black hat and had a short, silvery beard.

He smiled at Johnny, and nodded at the others as they hurried up.

"Who am I?" he said. "Well, now . . . why don't you guess? You were always good at this sort of thing."

Johnny looked at him, and then at the car, and then back up the hill to where the old church was just visible.

"I think . . ." he said.

"Yes?" said the old man. "Yes? Go on?"

"I think that . . . I mean, I don't know . . . but I know I'm going to know . . . I mean, I think I know why you've come to find us . . ."

"Yes?"

Johnny swallowed. "But we were—" he began.

The old man patted him on the shoulder.

"Call me Sir John," he said.

8

Trousers of Time

There were differences in the mall. One big difference, certainly. The burger bar had changed. There were different-shaped paper hats, and the colour scheme was blue and white instead of red and yellow.

The old man led the way.

"Who *is* he?" hissed Kirsty.

"You'll laugh if I tell you! This is *time* travel! I'm still trying to work out the rules!"

Sir John sat down heavily in a seat, motioned them to sit down as well, and then did the second-worst thing anyone could do in a fast-food restaurant.

He snapped his fingers at a waitress.

All the staff were watching them anxiously.

"Young lady," said Sir John, wheezing slightly, "these people will have whatever they want. I will have a glass of water. Thank you."

"Yes, Sir John," said the waitress, and hurried away.

"You're not s'posed to do that," said Bigmac hoarsely. "You're s'posed to queue up."

"No, *you're* supposed to queue up," said Sir John. "I don't have to."

"Have you always been called Sir John?" said Johnny.

The man winked at him.

"You know, don't you," he said. "You've worked it out. You're right. Names are easily changed, especially in wartime. I thought it might be better. I got the knighthood in 1964 for services to making huge amounts of money."

The waitress hurried back with the water, and then produced a notebook and looked expectantly at them all with the bright, brittle smile of someone who is expecting to be sacked at any moment.

"I'll have . . . well, I'll have everything," said Yo-less.

"Me too," said Bigmac.

"Cheeseburger?" said Johnny.

"Chilli beanburger," said Kirsty. "And I want to know what's going on, OK?"

Sir John beamed at her in a slightly distracting way. Then he nodded at the waitress.

"Make me one with everything," he said, slowly and carefully, as if quoting something he'd heard a long time ago, "because I want to become a Muslim."

"A *Buddhist*," said Yo-less, without thinking. "You *always* muck up the punchl—" Then his mouth dropped open.

"Do I?" said Wobbler.

"Well . . . I hung around for a while and you didn't come back," said Wobbler. "And then—"

"But we did! I mean, we will!" said Kirsty.

"This is where it gets difficult," said Wobbler, patiently. "Johnny knows. Supposing you didn't go back? Supposing you were scared to, or you found that you couldn't? The possibility exists, and that means the future forks off in two different ways. In one you went back, in one you didn't. Now you've ended up in the future where you didn't go back. I've been here since 1941. Don't try to think too hard about this, because it'll make your brain hurt.

"Anyway . . . *first* I stayed with Mr. and Mrs. Seeley," he continued. "I'd met them that first day. Their son was away in the Navy and everyone thought I was an evacuee who was a bit daft and, what with one thing and another, there's too much to worry about in a big war for people to ask too many questions about one fat boy. They were very nice people. They sort of . . . adopted me, I suppose, because their son got torpedoed. But I moved away after a few years."

"Why?" said Kirsty.

"I didn't want to meet my own parents or anything like that," said Wobbler. He still seemed out of breath. "History is full of patches as it is, without causing any more trouble, eh? Changing my name wasn't hard, either. In a war . . . well, records go missing, people get killed, everything gets shaken up. A person can duck down and pop up somewhere else as *someone* else. I was in the Army for a few years, after the war."

"*You?*" said Bigmac.

"Oh, everyone had to be. National Service, it was called. Out in Berlin. And then I came back and had to make a living. Would you like another milkshake? I personally wouldn't, if I were you. I know how they're made."

"You could've invented computers!" said Bigmac.

"Really? You think so?" The old man laughed. "Who'd have listened to a boy who hadn't even been to university? Besides . . . well, look at this . . ."

He picked up a plastic fork and tapped it on the table.

"See this?" he said. "We throw away millions of them every day. After five minutes' use they're in the trash, right?"

"Yes, of course," said Kirsty. Behind Wobbler, the staff were watching nervously, like monks in some quiet monastery somewhere who've just had St. Peter drop in for tea.

"A hundred years ago it'd have been a marvel. And now we throw them away without a second thought. So . . . how do you make one?"

"Well . . . you get some oil, and . . . I think there's something about it in a book I've got—"

"Right," said Wobbler, leaning back. "You don't know. I don't know, either."

"But I wouldn't bother with that. *I'd* write science fiction," said Kirsty. "Moon landings and stuff."

"You probably could," said Wobbler. A tired expression crossed his face, and he started to pat the pockets of his coat as if looking for something. "But I've never had much of a way with words, I'm afraid. No. I opened a hamburger bar."

Johnny looked around, and then started to grin.

"That's right," said Wobbler. "In 1952. I knew it all, you see. Thick shakes, Double Smashers with Cheese'n Egg, paper hats for the staff, red sauce in those little round plastic bottles that look like tomatoes . . . oh, yes. I had three bars in the first year, and ten the year after that. There's thousands, now. Other people just couldn't keep up.

I *knew* what would work, you see. Birthday treats for the kids, the Willie Wobbler clown—"

"*Willie Wobbler*?" said Kirsty.

"Sorry. They were more innocent times," said Wobbler. "And then I started . . . other things. Soft toilet paper, for a start. Honestly, the stuff they had back in the 1940s you could use as roofing felt! And when that was going well, I started to listen to people. People with bright ideas. Like 'I think I could make a tape recorder *really small* so that people could carry it around' and I'd say 'That might just catch on, you know, here's some money to get started.' Or 'You know, I think I know a way of making a machine to record television signals on tape so that people could watch them later' and I'd say 'Amazing! Whatever will they think of next! Here's some money, why don't we form a company and build some? And while we're about it, why don't we see if movies can be put on these tape thingies too?' "

"That's dishonest," said Kirsty. "That's *cheating*."

"I don't see why," said Wobbler. "People were amazed that I'd listen to them, because everyone else thought they were crazy. I made money, but so did they."

"Are you a millionaire?" said Bigmac.

"Oh, no. I was a millionaire back in 1955. I'm a billionaire now, I think." He snapped his fingers again. The chauffeur in black, who had silently appeared behind them, stepped forward.

"I *am* a billionaire, aren't I, Hickson?"

"Yes, Sir John. Many times."

"Thought so. And I think I own some island somewhere. What was it called now . . . Tasmania, I think."

Wobbler patted his pockets again, and finally brought out a slim silver case. He flicked it open and took out two white pills, which he swallowed. He grimaced, and sipped from his glass of water.

"You haven't touched your One with Everything," said Johnny, watching him.

"Oh, I asked for it just to make the point," said Wobbler. "I'm not allowed to eat them. Good heavens. I have a diet. No sodium, no cholesterol, low starch, no sugar." He sighed. "Even a glass of water is probably too exciting."

The manager of the burger bar had at last plucked up the courage to approach the table.

"Sir John!" he said, "This is a such an honour—"

"Yes, yes, thank you, please go away, I'm talking to my friends—" Wobbler stopped, and smiled evilly. "Fries all right, Bigmac? Properly crisp?" he said. "What about that milkshake, Yo-less? Right sort of texture, is it?"

The boys glanced up at the manager, who suddenly looked like a man praying to the god of everyone who has to work while wearing a namebadge saying "My name is KEITH."

"Er . . . they're fine," said Bigmac.

"Great," said Yo-less.

KEITH gave them a relieved grin.

"They're always good," said Yo-less.

"I expect," said Bigmac, "that they'll go *on* being good."

KEITH nodded hurriedly.

"We're gen'rally in most Saturdays," added Bigmac, helpfully. "If you want us to make sure."

"Thank you, Keith, you may go," said Wobbler. He winked at Bigmac as the man almost ran away.

"I know I shouldn't do it," he said, "but it's about the only fun I get these days."

"Why did you come here?" said Johnny quietly.

"You know, I couldn't resist doing a *little* checking," said Wobbler, ignoring him. "I thought it might be . . . interesting . . . to watch myself growing up. Not interfering, of course." He stopped smiling. "And then I found I wasn't born. I'd never been born. Nor was my father. My mother lived in London and was married to someone else. That's one thing about money. You can buy any amount of private detectives."

"That's nonsense," said Kirsty. "You're *alive*."

"Oh, yes," said Wobbler. "I was born. In another time. In the leg of the trousers of time that we were all born in. And then I went back in time with you all, and . . . something went wrong. I'm not sure what. So . . . I had to come back the long way. You could say I had to walk home."

"I'm sure that's not logical," said Kirsty.

Wobbler shrugged. "I don't think time is all that logical," he said. "It bends itself around humans. It's probably full of loose ends. Whoever said it shouldn't be? Sometimes loose ends are necessary. If they weren't, spaghetti would be merely an embarrassing experience." He chuckled. "Spoke to a lot of scientists about this. Damn fools. Idiots! Time's in our heads. Any fool can see that—"

"You're ill, aren't you," said Johnny.

"Is it obvious?"

"You keep taking pills, and your breathing doesn't sound right."

Wobbler smiled again. But this time there was no humour in it.

"I'm suffering from life," he said. "However, I'm nearly cured."

"Look," said Kirsty, in the voice of one who is trying to be reasonable against the odds, "we weren't going to leave you there. We were going to go back. We *will* go back."

"Good," said Wobbler.

"You don't mind? Because surely, if we *do*, you won't exist, will you?"

"Oh, I will. Somewhere," said Wobbler.

"That's right," said Johnny. "Everything that happens . . . stays happened. Somewhere. There's lots of times side by side."

"You always were a bit of an odd thinker," said Wobbler. "I remember that. An imagination so big it's outside your head. Now . . . what was the other thing? Oh, yes. I think I have to give you this."

The chauffeur stepped forward.

"Er . . . Sir John, you know the Board did want—"

There was a blur in the air. Wobbler's silverheaded cane hit the table so hard that Bigmac's fries flew into the air. The *crack* echoed around the restaurant.

"God damn it, man, I'm paying you, and you will do what I say! The Board can wait! I'm not dead *yet*! I didn't get where I am today by listening to a lot of lawyers whining! I'm having some time off! Go away!"

Wobbler reached into his jacket and took out an envelope. He handed it to Johnny.

"I'm not telling you to go back," he said. "I've got no right. I've had a pretty good life, one way and the other—"

"But," said Johnny. Through the glass doors of the mall he could see a car and four motorcycles pull up.

"I'm sorry?" said Wobbler.

"The next word you were going to say was 'but,' " said Johnny. Men were hurrying up the steps.

"Oh, yes. But . . ." Wobbler leaned forward, and began speaking quickly. "If you go back, I've written a letter to . . . well, you'll know what to do with it. I know I really shouldn't do it, but who could pass up an opportunity like this?"

He stood up, or at least attempted to. Hickson rushed up as Wobbler caught the edge of his chair, but was waved away.

"I never had any children," said Wobbler. "Never got married. Don't know why, really. It just didn't seem right."

He leaned heavily on his stick and turned back to them.

"I want to be young again," he said. "Somewhere."

"We were going to go back," said Johnny. "Honestly."

"Good. But, you see . . . it's not just a case of going back. It's going back and doing the right things."

And then he was gone, walking heavily towards the men with the suits, who closed in behind him.

Bigmac was staring so much that a long rivulet of mustard, tomato sauce, special chilli relish and vivid green chutney had dripped out of his burger and down his sleeve without him noticing.

"Wow," said Yo-less, under his breath. "Will *we* be like that one day?"

"What? Old? Probably," said Johnny.

"I just can't get my head around old Wobbler being old," said Bigmac, sucking at his sleeve.

"We've got to go and get him," said Johnny. "We can't let him get . . ."

"Rich?" said Yo-less. "I don't think we can do anything about the 'old' bit."

"If we bring him back, then he—the old one—won't exist here," said Kirsty.

"No, he'll exist in *this* here, but not in the *other* here. I don't think he'll be existing anywhere for very long anyway," said Johnny. "Come on."

"What's in the envelope?" said Kirsty, as they left.

Johnny was surprised. Usually she'd say something like "Let's see what's in this, then," while snatching it out of his hand.

"It's for Wobbler," said Johnny.

"He's written a letter to *himself*? What's he say?"

"How do I know? I don't open other people's letters!"

Johnny shoved the envelope back into his inside pocket.

"The keep-fit club should have finished by now," he said. "Come on."

"Wait," said Kirsty. "If we're going back to 1941, let's go *prepared* this time, shall we?"

"Yeah," said Bigmac. "Armed."

"No. Properly dressed, I mean."

9

"Every Little Girl . . ."

It was an hour later. They met behind the church, in the damp little yard where they'd left the trolley.

"All *right*," said Kirsty. "Where did you get that outfit, Johnny?"

"Grandad's got loads of stuff in the attic. These are his old football shorts. And he always wears old pullovers, so I thought that was probably OK, too. And I've got my project stuff in this box in case it helps. It's genuine 1940s. It's what they carried gasmasks in."

"Oh, is *that* what they are?" said Bigmac. "I *thought* people had rather big Walkmans."

"At least take the cap off, you look like Just William," said Kirsty. "What's this, Yo-less?"

"Me and Bigmac went along to that theatre shop in Wallace Street," said Yo-less. "What do you think?" he added uncertainly.

He shuffled round nervously. He was wearing a broad-brimmed hat, shoes with soles like two bumper cars parked side by side, and tight trousers. At least, what could be seen of the trousers looked tight.

"Is that an overcoat?" said Johnny critically.

"It's called a drape jacket," said Yo-less.

"Bright red," said Kirsty. "Yes, I can see no-one will notice you at all. And those trousers . . . you must have had to grease your feet to get them on."

"It looks a bit . . . stylish," said Johnny. "You know . . . jazzy."

"The man in the shop said it's about right for the period," said Yo-less defensively.

"You look like you're about to play the saxophone," said Johnny. "I mean . . . well, I've never seen you looking so . . . you know . . . cool."

"That's why it's a disguise," said Yo-less.

Kirsty turned to Bigmac, and sighed.

"Bigmac, why is it I get this feeling you've missed the point?"

"I *told* him," said Yo-less. "But he wouldn't listen."

"The man said they wore this in 1941," said Bigmac defensively.

"Yes, but don't you think that people might notice it's a *German* uniform?"

Bigmac looked panicky.

"Is it? I thought Yo-less was trying to wind me up! I thought they had all swastikas and stuff!"

"That's the Gestapo. You're dressed up like an ordinary German soldier."

"I can't help it, it's the only one they had left, it was this or chain mail!"

"At least leave the jacket and helmet off, all right? Then it'll probably look like any other uniform."

"Why're you wearing that fur coat, Kirsty?" said Johnny. "You always say that wearing the skins of dead animals is murder."

"Yeah, but she only says it to old ladies in fur coats," muttered Bigmac under his breath. "Bet she never says it to Hell's Angels in leather jackets."

"*I* took some care," said Kirsty, ignoring him. She adjusted her hat and shoulder bag. "This is pretty accurate."

"What, even the shoulders?"

"Yes. Shoulders were being worn wide."

"Do you have to go through doors sideways?" said Yo-less.

"Let's get on with it, shall we?"

"What's worrying me is when old Wobb . . . I mean, *old* old Wobbler . . . said we've got to do the right things to bring him back," said Yo-less. "What things?"

"We'll have to find out," said Johnny. "He didn't say it was easy."

"Come on," said Bigmac, opening the door. "I miss old Wobbler."

"Why?" said Kirsty.

" 'Cos I don't throw straight."

The keep-fit people had long ago staggered home. Johnny shoved the trolley into the middle of the floor, and stared at the sacks. Guilty was still asleep on a couple of them.

"Er . . ." said Yo-less. "This isn't *magic*, is it?"

"I don't think so," said Johnny. "It's probably just very, very, very strange science."

"Oh, good," said Yo-less. "Er . . . what's the difference?"

"Who cares?" said Kirsty. "Get on with it."

Guilty started to purr.

Johnny picked up a bag. It seemed to wriggle in his grasp. With great care, he loosened the string.

And concentrated.

It was easier this time. Before, he'd just been dragged along like a cork in a current. This time he knew where he was going. He could *feel* the time.

Minds moved in time all the time. All the sacks did was let your body come too, just like Mrs. Tachyon had said.

Years spiralled into the bag like water down a plughole. Time sucked out of the room.

And then there were the pews, and the scent of highly-polished holiness.

And Wobbler, turning around with his mouth open.

"*What—?*"

"It's all right, it's us," said Johnny.

"Are you all right?" said Yo-less.

Wobbler might not have been the winner of the All-Europe Uptake Speed Trials, but an expression of deep suspicion spread across his face as he looked at them.

"What's up?" he said. "You're all looking at me as if I'd gone weird! And what're you all dressed up for? Why's Bigmac wearing a German uniform?"

"See?" said Yo-less triumphantly. "I *said* so, and does anyone listen?"

"We've just come back to fetch you," said Johnny. "There's no problem."

"That's right. No problem at all," said Yo-less. "Everything's fine."

"Yeah, fine. Everything's fine," said Bigmac. "Er . . . you're not feeling . . . *old*, are you?"

"What? After five minutes?" said Wobbler.

"I've brung you something," said Bigmac. He took a square, flat shape from his pocket. It was rather battered, but it was nevertheless the only styrofoam box currently existing on the planet.

It was a BigWob . . . One with Everything.

"Did you nick that?" said Yo-less.

"Well, the old bloke said he wasn't going to eat it," said Bigmac. "So it'd only get chucked away, all right? It's not stealing if it'd only get chucked away. Anyway, it *is* his, isn't it, because—"

"You're not going to *eat* that, are you?" said Kirsty quickly. "It's cold and greasy and it's been in Bigmac's pocket, for heaven's sake."

Wobbler lifted out the bun.

"I could eat it even if a giraffe'd licked it," he said, and bit into the cold bread. "Hey, this isn't bad! Whose is it?" He looked at the face printed on the box. "Who's the old fart with the beard?"

"Just some old fart," said Johnny.

"Yeah, we don't know anything about him at all," said Bigmac.

Wobbler gave them a suspicious look.

"What's going on here?" he said.

"Look, I can't explain now," said Johnny. "You're . . . stuck here. Er. Apparently, er, something's gone wrong. Er. There's been a snag."

"What kind of snag?"

"Er. Quite a big one."

Wobbler stopped eating. It was *that* serious.

"How big?" he said.

"Er. You're not going to be born . . . er."

Wobbler stared at him. Then he stared at the half-eaten burger.

"Am I eating this burger? Are these my teeth marks?" he demanded.

"Look, it's perfectly *simple*," said Kirsty. "You're alive here, yes, but when we first came back, something must have happened which changed history. Everything anyone does changes history. So there's two histories. You were born in one, but things have been changed and when we got back it was into a different history where you weren't. All we have to do is put things back the way they should be, and then everything will be all right."

"Hah! You haven't got a shelf of Star Trek videos as well, have you?" said Wobbler.

Kirsty looked as though someone had hit her.

"Well, er, I don't, er, what?" she said. "Er . . . one or two . . . a few . . . not many . . . so what, anyway? I hardly ever look at them!"

"Hey," said Yo-less, brightening up, "have you got that one where a mysterious force—"

"Just shut up! Just shut up right now! Just because the programme happens to be an accurate reflection of late 20th century social concerns, *actually*, it doesn't mean you can go around winding people up just because they've been taking an academic interest!"

"Have you got a Star Trek uniform?" said Yo-less.

Kirsty started to go red.

"If any of you tell *anybody* else there'll be big trouble," said Kirsty. "I mean it!"

Johnny opened the door of the church. Outside, Wednesday afternoon was turning into Wednesday evening. It was raining gently. He took a deep breath of 1941 air. It smelled of coal and pickles and jam, with a hint of hot rubber. People were *making* things. All those chimneys . . .

No-one made anything in Blackbury in 1996. There was a factory that put together computers, and some big warehouses, and the Department of Road Signs regional headquarters. People just moved things around, or added up numbers.

"So I watch some science fiction films," said a plaintive voice behind him. "At least I do it in a spirit of intelligent deconstruction. I don't just sit there saying 'Cor, lasers, brill!' "

"No-one said you did," said Yo-less, managing to sound infuriatingly reasonable.

"You're not going to let me forget this, are you?" said Kirsty.

"Won't mention it ever again," said Yo-less.

"If we do, may we be pulled apart by wild Vegans," said Bigmac, smirking.

"No, vegans are the people who don't eat animal products," said Yo-less. "You mean Vulcans. Vulcans are the ones with green blood—"

"Will you lot shut up? Here's me not even being born and you're goin' on about daft aliens!" said Wobbler.

"What did we do here that changed the future?" said Johnny, turning around.

"Practically everything, I suppose," said Kirsty. "And Bigmac left all his stuff at the police station."

"They shot at me—"

"Let's face it," said Yo-less, "*anything* we do changes the future. Maybe we bumped into someone so he was five seconds late crossing the road and got hit by a car or something. Like treading on a dinosaur. Any little thing changes the whole of history."

"That's daft," said Bigmac. "I mean, rivers still flow the same way no matter how the little fish swim."

"Er . . ." said Wobbler. "There was this . . . kid . . ."

He said it in the slow, plonking tones of someone who is afraid that he might have come up with an important piece of evidence.

"What kid?" said Johnny.

"Just some kid," said Wobbler. "He was running away from home or something. *To* home, I mean. All long shorts and bogeys up the nose."

"What do you mean, running to home?"

"Oh, he was goin' on about being evacuated here and being fed up and running off back to London. But he followed me back into town throwing stones at me 'cos he said I was a spy. He's probably still outside, 's'matter of fact. He ran off down that road there."

"Paradise Street?" said Johnny.

"What about it?" said Wobbler, looking worried.

"It's going to be bombed tonight," said Kirsty. "Johnny's got a thing about it."

"Hah, can't see any Germans wanting to bomb *him*, he was practically on their side," said Wobbler.

"Are you sure it was Paradise Street?" said Johnny. "Are you *sure*? Did you have any relatives there? Grandparents? *Great*-grandparents?"

"How should I know? That was ages ago!"

Johnny took a deep breath. "It's right now!"

"I-I-I don't know! One of my grandads lives in Spain and the other one died before I was born!"

"How?" said Kirsty.

"Fell off a motorbike, I think. In 1971." Wobbler brightened up. "See? So that's all right."

"Oh, Wobbler, Wobbler, it's *not* all right!" said Johnny. "Get it into your head! Where did he live?"

Wobbler was trembling, as he always did when life was getting too exciting.

"I dunno! London, I think! My dad said he came up here in the war! And then later on he came back on a visit and met my grandma! Er! Er!"

"Go on! Go on!" said Johnny.

"Er! Er!" Wobbler stuttered.

"How old was he when he died?" said Yo-less.

"Er! Forty, my dad said! Er! He'd bought the bike for his birthday!"

"So he's . . ." Johnny subtracted in his head, ". . . ten now?"

"Er! Er!"

"You don't think he was that boy, do you?" said Yo-less.

"Oh, yes," said Wobbler, finally giving up panic for anger. "I should have asked him, should I? 'Hello, are you going to be my grandad? PS don't buy a motorbike'?"

Johnny fished in his gas mask box and pulled out a crumpled folder stuffed with bits of paper.

"Did he mention any names?" he said, flicking through the pages.

"Er! Er! Someone called Mrs. Density!" said Wobbler, desperation throwing up a memory.

"Number Eleven," said Johnny, pulling out a photocopy of a newspaper clipping. "Lived there with her daughter Gladys. I got all the names for my project."

"My gran's name was Gladys!" said Wobbler. "You mean, because he *didn't* run off back to London, he's going to die tonight and I'm not going to be born?"

"Could be," said Yo-less.

"What'll happen to me?"

"You'll just have to stay here," said Johnny.

"No way! This is the *olden days*! It's awful! I went past a cinema and it's all old movies! In black and white! And there was this cafe and you know what they'd got chalked on a board in front? 'Meat and two veg'! What kind of food is that? Even Hong Kong Henry's takeaway tells you what *kind* of meat! Everyone dresses like someone out of Eastern Europe! I'd go round the bend here!"

"*My* grandad always goes on about how they used to have so much fun when he was a kid even though they didn't have anything," said Bigmac.

"Yes, but everyone's grandad says that," said Kirsty. "It's compulsory. It's like where they say '50p for a chocolate bar? When I was young you could get one and still have change out of sixpence.' "

"I think they had fun," said Johnny, "because they didn't *know* they didn't have anything."

"Well, *I* know," said Wobbler. "I know about food that's more than two colours, and stereo systems, and decent music and . . . and all kinds of stuff! I want to go *home*!"

They all looked at Johnny.

"You got us into this," said Yo-less.

"Me?"

"It's your imagination," said Kirsty. "It's too big for your head, just like Sir J . . ." She stopped. "Just like I've always said," she corrected herself, "and it drags everyone else along with it. I don't know how, but it does. You got all worked up about Paradise Street, and now here we are."

"You said it didn't make any difference if the street got bombed or not," said Johnny. "*You* said it was just history!"

"*I* don't want to be history!" moaned Wobbler.

"All *right*, you *win*," said Kirsty. "What do you want us to do?"

Johnny shuffled the papers.

"Well . . . what I found out for my project was that . . . there was a big storm, you see. The weather got very bad. And the bombers must've seen Blackbury and dropped their bombs *anyway* and turned around. That used to happen. There was . . . there *is* an air-raid siren. It was supposed to go off if bombers were near," he said. "Only it didn't."

"Why not?"

The folder shut with a snap.

"Let's start by finding out," said Johnny.

It was on a pole on the roof in the High Street. It didn't look very big.

"That's all it is?" said Yo-less. "Looks like a giant yo-yo."

"That's an air-raid siren all right," said Kirsty. "I saw a picture in a book."

"How d'they work? Set off by radar or something?"

"I'm sure that's not been invented yet," said Johnny.

"Well, how then?"

"Maybe there's a switch somewhere?"

"It'd be somewhere safe, then," said Yo-less. "Somewhere where people wouldn't be able to set it off for a laugh."

Their joint gaze travelled down the pole, across the roof, down the wall, past the blue lamp, and stopped when it met the words: "Police Station."

"Oh, dear," said Yo-less.

They sat down on a bench by a civic flowerbed, opposite the door. A policeman came out and stood in the sunshine, watching them back.

"It's a good job we left Bigmac to guard the trolley," said Yo-less.

"Yes," said Johnny. "He's always been allergic to policemen."

Kirsty sighed. "Honestly, you boys haven't got a clue."

She stood up, crossed the road and began to talk to the policeman. They could hear the conversation. It went like this:

"Excuse me, officer—"

He gave her a friendly smile.

"Yes, little lady? Out in your mum's clothes, are you?"

Kirsty's eyes narrowed.

"Oh, dear," said Johnny, under his breath.

"What's the matter?" said Yo-less.

"Well, you know you and 'Sambo'? That's Kirsty and words like 'little lady'."

"I was just wondering," said the little lady, through clenched teeth, "how that big siren works."

"Oh, I shouldn't worry your head about that, love," said the policeman. "It's very complicated. You wouldn't understand."

"Look for something to hide behind," said Johnny. "Like another planet."

Then his mouth dropped open as Kirsty won a medal.

"It's just that I get *so* worried," she said, and managed a simper, or what she probably thought was a simper. "I'm *sure* Mr. Hitler's bombers are going to come one night and the siren won't go off. I can't get to sleep for worrying!"

The policeman laid a hand on the shoulder of the girl who had left Blackbury Karate Club because no boy would dare come within two metres of her.

"Oh, we can't have that, love," he said. He pointed. "See up there on Blackdown? Well, Mr. Hodder and his very brave men are up there every night, keeping a look-out. If any planes come near here tonight he'll ring the station in a brace of shakes, don't you worry."

"But supposing the phone doesn't work?"

"Oh, then he'll be down here on his bike in no time."

"Bike? A bike? That's *all*?"

"It's a *motor*bike," said the policeman, giving her the nervous looks everyone eventually gave Kirsty.

She just stared at him.

"It's a Blackbury Phantom," he added still further, in a tone of voice that suggested this should impress even a girl.

"Oh? Really? Oh, that's a relief," said Kirsty. "I feel a lot better for knowing that. Really."

"That's right. There's nothing for you to worry about, love," said the policeman happily.

"I'll just go off and play with my dolls, I expect," said Kirsty.

"That's a good idea. Have a tea party," said the policeman, who apparently didn't know withering scorn when he heard it.

Kirsty crossed the road and sat down on the seat. "Yes, I expect I should have a party with all my dollies," she said, glaring at the flowers.

Yo-less looked at Johnny over her head.

"What?" he said.

"Did you hear what that ridiculous policeman said?" said Kirsty. "Honestly, it's obvious that the stupid man thinks that just because I'm female I've got the brains of a baby. I mean, good grief! Imagine living in a time when people could even *think* like that without being prosecuted!"

"Imagine living in a time when a bomb could come through your ceiling," said Johnny.

"Mind you, my father said he lived in the shadow of the atomic bomb all through the Sixties," said Kirsty. "I think that was why he wore flares. Hah! Dollies! Pink dresses and pink ribbons. 'Don't worry your head about that, girlie.' This is the *dark ages*."

Yo-less patted her on the arm.

"He didn't mean it . . . you know, nastily," he said. "It's just how he was brought up. You people can't expect us to rewrite history, you know—"

Kirsty frowned at him.

"Is that sarcasm?" she said.

"Who? Me?" said Yo-less innocently.

"All right, all right, you've made your point. What's so special about a Blackbury Phantom, anyway?"

"They used to make them here," said Johnny. "They were quite famous, I think. Grandad used to have one."

They raised their eyes to the dark shape of Blackdown. It had loomed over the town even back in 1996, but then it had a TV mast.

"That's *it*?" said Kirsty. "Men just sitting on hills and listening?"

"Well, Blackbury wasn't very important," said Johnny. "We made jam and pickles and rubber boots and that was about it."

"I wonder what's going to go wrong tonight?" said Yo-less.

"We could climb up there and find out," said Johnny. "Let's go and get the others—"

"Hang on," said Kirsty. "*Think*, will you? How do you know we might not *cause* what's going to go wrong tonight?"

Johnny hesitated. For a moment he looked like a statue. Then he said:

"No. If we start thinking like that we'll never do anything."

"We've already messed up the future once! *Everything* we do affects the future!"

"It always has. It always will. So what? Let's get the others."

10

Running Into Time

There was no question of using the roads, not with the police still looking for a Bigmac who, with a wardrobe of costumes to chose from, had chosen to go back in time wearing a German soldier's uniform.

They'd have to use the fields and footpaths. Which meant—

"We'll have to leave the trolley," said Yo-less. "We can shove it in the bushes here."

"That means we'll be stuck here if anything goes wrong!" said Bigmac.

"Well, I'm not lugging it through mud and stuff."

"What if someone finds it?"

"There's Guilty," said Kirsty. "He's better than a guard dog."

The cat that was better than a guard dog opened one eye and yawned. It was true. No-one would want to be bitten by that mouth. It would be like being savaged by a plague laboratory.

Then he curled into a more comfortable ball.

"Yes, but it belongs to Mrs. Tachyon," said Johnny, weakly.

"Hey, we're not thinking sensibly—again," said Kirsty. "All we have to do is go back to 1996, go up to Blackdown on the bus, then come back in time again and we'll be up there—"

"No!" shouted Wobbler.

His face was bright red with terror.

"I'm not stopping here by myself again! I'm stuck here, remember? Supposing you don't come back?"

"Of course we'll come back," said Johnny. "We came back this time, didn't we?"

"Yes, but supposing you don't? Supposing you get run over by a lorry or something? What'll happen to me?"

Johnny thought about the long envelope in his inside pocket. Yo-less and Bigmac were looking at their feet. Even Kirsty was looking away.

"Here," said Wobbler suspiciously. "This is time travel, right? Do you know something horrible?"

"We don't know anything," said Bigmac.

"Absolutely right," said Kirsty.

"What, us? We don't know a thing," said Johnny miserably.

"Especially about burgers," said Bigmac.

Kirsty groaned. "*Bigmac!*"

Wobbler glared at them.

"Oh, yes," he muttered. "It's 'wind up ole Wobbler' time again, right? Well, I'm going to stay with the trolley, right? It's not going anywhere without me, rights?"

He stared from one to the other, daring them to disagree.

"All right, I'll stay with you," said Bigmac. "I'll probably only get shot anyway, if I go anywhere."

"What're you going to do up on Blackdown, anyway?" said Wobbler. "Find this Mr. Hodder and tell him to listen really carefully? Wash out his ears? Eat plenty of carrots?"

"They're for good eyesight," said Yo-less helpfully. "My granny said they used to believe carrots helped you see in—"

"Who cares!"

"I don't know *what* we can do," said Johnny. "But . . . something must have gone wrong, right? Maybe the message didn't get through. We'll have to make sure it does."

"Look," said Kirsty.

The sun had already set, leaving an afterglow in the sky. And there were clouds over Blackdown. Dark clouds.

"Thunderstorm," she said. "They always start up there."

There was a growl in the distance.

Blackbury was a lot smaller once they were in the hills. A lot of it wasn't there at all.

"Wouldn't it be great if we could tell everyone what they're going to do wrong," said Johnny, when they paused for breath.

"No-one'd listen," said Yo-less. "Supposing someone turned up in 1996 and said they were from 2040 and started telling everyone what to do? They'd get arrested, wouldn't they?"

Johnny looked ahead of them. The sunset sky lurked behind bars of angry cloud.

"The listeners'll be up at the Tumps," said Kirsty. "There's an old windmill up there. It was some kind of look-out post during the war. Is, I mean."

"Why didn't you say so before?" said Johnny.

"It's different when it's now."

The Tumps were five mounds on top of the down. They grew heather and wortleberries. It was said that dead kings were buried there in the days when your enemy was at arm's length rather than ten thousand feet above your head.

The clouds were getting lower. It was going to be one of those Blackbury storms, a sort of angry fog that hugged the hills.

"You know what I'm thinking?" said Kirsty.

"Telephone lines," said Johnny. "They go out in thunderstorms."

"Right."

"But the policeman said there was a motorbike," said Yo-less.

"Starts first time, does it?" said Johnny. "I remember my grandad said that before you were qualified to ride a Blackbury Phantom you had to learn to push it fifty metres, cursing all the way. He said they were great bikes when they got started."

"How long is it till . . . you know . . . the bombs?"

"About an hour."

Which means they're already on the way, Johnny thought. Men have walked out onto airfields and loaded bombs onto planes with names like Dorniers and Heinkels. And other men have sat round in front of a big map of England, only it'd be in German, and there'd be crayon marks around Slate. Blackbury probably wasn't even on the map. And then they'd get up and walk out and get into the planes and take off. And men on the planes would get out *their* maps and draw lines on them; lines which crossed at Slate. Your mission for tonight: bomb the goods yard at Slate.

And then the roar filled his ears. The drone of the engines came up through his legs. He could taste the oil and the sweat and the stale rubber smell of the oxygen mask. His body shook with the throb of the engines and also with the thump of distant explosions. One was very close and the whole aircraft seemed to slide sideways. And he knew what the mission for tonight was. Your mission for tonight is *to get home safely*. It always was.

Another explosion shook the plane, and someone grabbed him.

"What?"

"It's weird when you do that!" shouted Kirsty, above the thunder. "Come on! It's *dangerous* out here! Haven't you got enough sense to get out of the rain?"

"It's starting to happen," Johnny whispered, while the storm broke around him.

"What is?"

"The future!"

He blinked as the rain started to plaster his hair against his head. He could *feel* time stretching out around him. He could feel its slow movement as it carried forward all those grey bombs and those white doorsteps, pulling them together like bubbles being swirled around a whirlpool. They were all carried along by it. You couldn't break out of it because you were *part* of it. You couldn't steer a train.

"We'd better get him under cover!" shouted Yo-less as lightning hit something a little way off. "He doesn't look well at *all*!"

They staggered on, occasionally lurking under a wind-bent tree to get their breath back.

There was a windmill among the Tumps. It had been built on one of the mounds, although the sails had long gone. The others put their arms around Johnny and ran through the soaking heather until they reached it and climbed the steps.

Yo-less hammered on the door. It opened a fraction.

"Good lord!" said a voice. It sounded like the voice of a young man. "What're you? A circus?"

"You've got to let us in!" said Kirsty. "He's ill!"

"Can't do that," said the voice. "Not allowed, see?"

"Do we look like spies?" shouted Yo-less.

"Please!" said Kirsty.

The door started to close, and then stopped.

"Well . . . all right," said the voice, as unseen hands pulled the door open. "But Mr. Hodder says to stand where we can see you, OK? Come on in."

"It's happening," said Johnny, who still had his eyes closed. "The telephone won't work."

"What's he going on about?"

"Can you try the telephone?" said Kirsty.

"Why? What's wrong with it?" said the boy. "We tested it out at the beginning of the shift just now. Has anyone been mucking about with it?"

There was an older man sitting at a table. He gave them a suspicious look, which lingered for a while on Yo-less.

"I reckon you'd better try the station," he said. "I don't like the sound of all this. Seems altogether a bit suspicious to me."

The first man reached out towards the phone.

There was a sound outside as lightning struck somewhere close. It wasn't a *zzzippp*—it was almost a gentle silken hiss, as the sky was cut in half.

Then the phone exploded. Bits of bakelite and copper clattered off the walls.

Kirsty's hand flew to her head.

"My hair stood on end!"

"So did mine," said Yo-less. "And that doesn't often happen, believe me," he added.

"Lightning hit the wire," said Johnny. "I knew that. Not just here. Other stations on the hills, too. And now he'll have trouble with the motorbike."

"What's he going on about?"

"You've got a motorbike, haven't you?" said Kirsty.

"So what?"

"Good grief, man, you've lost your telephone! Aren't you supposed to do something about that?"

The men looked at one another. Girls weren't supposed to shout like Kirsty.

"Tom, nip down to Doctor Atkinson's and use his phone and tell the station ours has gone for a burton," said Mr. Hodder, not taking his eyes off the three. "Tell them about these kids, too."

"It won't start," said Johnny. "It's the carburettor, I think. That . . . always gives trouble."

The one called Tom looked at him sideways. There was a change in the air. Up until now the men had just been suspicious. Now they were uneasy, too.

"How did you know that?" he said.

Johnny opened his mouth. And shut it again.

He couldn't tell them about the feel of the *time* around him. He felt that if he could only focus his eyes properly, he could even see it. The past and future were there, just around some kind of corner, bound up to the ever-travelling *now* by a billion connections. He felt that he could almost reach out and point, not there or over there or up there but *there*, at right angles to everywhere else.

"They're on their way," he said. "They'll be here in half an hour."

"What will? What's he going on about?"

"Blackbury's going to be bombed tonight," said Kirsty. Thunder rolled again.

"We think," said Yo-less.

"Five planes," said Johnny.

He opened his eyes. Everything overlapped like a scene in a kaleidoscope. Everyone was staring at him, but they were surrounded by something like fog. When they moved, images followed them like some kind of special effect.

"It's the storm and the clouds," he managed to say. "They think they're going to Slate but they'll drop their bombs over Blackbury."

"Oh, yes? And how d'you know this, then? They told you, did they?"

"Listen, you stupid man," said Kirsty. "We're not spies! Why would we *tell* you if we were?"

Mr. Hodder pulled open the door.

"I'm going down to use the doctor's phone," he said. "Then maybe we can sort out what's going on."

"What about the bombers?" said Kirsty.

The older man opened the door. The thunder had rolled away to the north-east, and there was no sound but the hiss of the rain.

"What bombers?" he said, and shut it behind him.

Johnny sat down with his head in his hands, blinking his eyes again to shut out the flickering images.

"You lot'd better get out," said Tom. "It's against the rules, having people in here . . ."

Johnny blinked. There were more bombers in front of his eyes, and they *didn't* go away.

He scrabbled at the playing cards on the table.

"What're these for?" he said urgently. "Playing cards with bombers on them?"

"Eh? What? Oh . . . that's for learning aircraft recognition," said Tom, who'd been careful to keep the table between him and Johnny. "You plays cards with 'em and you sort of picks up the shapes, like."

"You learn subliminally?" said Kirsty.

"Oh, no, you learn from playing with these here cards," said Tom desperately. Outside, there was the sound of someone trying to start a motorbike.

Johnny stood up.

"All right," he said. "I can *prove* it. The next card . . . the next card you show me . . . the next card . . ."

Images filled his eyes. If this is how Mrs. Tachyon sees the world, he thought, no wonder she never seems all there—because she's *everywhere*.

Outside, there was the sound of someone trying to start a motorbike even harder.

". . . the next card . . . will be the five of diamonds."

"I don't see why I should have to play games—" The man glanced nervously at Kirsty, who had that effect on people.

"Scared?" she said.

He grabbed a card at random and held it up.

"It's the five of diamonds all right," said Yo-less.

Johnny nodded. "The next one . . . the next one . . . the next one will be the knave of hearts."

It was.

Outside, there was the sound of someone trying to start a motorbike very hard and swearing.

"It's a trick," said the man. "One of you messed around with the pack."

"Shuffle them all you like," said Johnny. "And the next one you show me will be . . . the ten of clubs."

"How did you do that?" said Yo-less, as the boy turned the card over and stared at it.

"Er . . ." It had *felt* like memory, he told himself. "I remembered seeing it," said Johnny.

"You remembered seeing it before you actually saw it?" said Kirsty.

Outside, there was the sound of someone trying to start a motorbike very hard and swearing even harder.

"Er . . . yes."

"Oh, wow," she said. "Precognition. You're probably a natural medium."

"Er, I'm a size eleven," said Johnny, but they weren't listening.

Kirsty had turned to Tom.

"You see?" she said. "Now do you believe us?"

"I don't like this. This isn't right," he said. "Anyway . . . anyway, there's no phone—"

The door burst open.

"All right!" roared Mr. Hodder. "What did you kids do to my bike?"

"It's the carburettor," said Johnny. "I told you."

"Here, Arthur, you ought to listen to this, this boy knows things—"

Kirsty glanced at her watch.

"Twenty minutes," she said. "It's more than two miles down to the town. Even if we ran I'm not sure we could do it."

"What're you talking about now?" said Mr. Hodder.

"There must be some kind of code," said Kirsty. "If you have to ring up and tell them to sound the siren, what do you say?"

"Don't tell them!" snapped Mr. Hodder.

" 'This is station BD3,' " said Johnny, his eyes looking unfocused.

"How did you know that? Did he tell you? Did you tell them?"

"No, Arthur!"

"Come on," said Kirsty, hurrying towards the door. "I got a county medal in athletics!"

She elbowed the older man aside.

The thunder was growling away in the east. The storm had settled down to a steady, grey rain.

"We'll never make it," said Yo-less.

"I thought you people were good at running," said Kirsty, stepping out.

"People of my height, you mean?"

"You were right," said the young man, as Johnny was dragged out into the night. "This *is* station BD3!"

"I know," said Johnny. "I remembered you just telling me."

He staggered and grabbed at Yo-less to stay upright. The world was spinning around him. He hadn't felt like this since that business with the cider at Christmas. The voices around him seemed to be muffled, and he couldn't be sure whether they were really there, or voices he was remembering, or words that hadn't even been spoken yet.

He felt that his mind was being shaken loose in time, and it was only still here because his body was a huge great anchor.

"It's downhill all the way," said Kirsty, and sped off. Yo-less followed her.

Far away, down in the town, a church clock began to strike eleven.

Johnny tried to lumber into a run, but the ground kept shifting under his feet.

Why are we doing this? he thought. We *know* it happened, I've got a copy of the paper in my pocket, the bombs *will* land and the siren *won't* go off.

You can't steer a train!

That's what *you* think, said a voice in his head . . .

He wished he'd been better at this. He wished he'd been a hero.

From up ahead, he heard Yo-less's desperate cry.

"I've tripped over a sheep! I've tripped over a sheep!"

The lights of Blackbury spread out below them. There weren't many of them—the occasional smudge from a car, the tiny gleam from a window where the moths had got at the blackout curtain.

A wind had followed the storm. Streamers of cloud blew across the sky. Here and there a star shone through.

They ran on. Yo-less ran into another sheep in the blackness.

There was the crunch of heavy boots on the road behind them and Tom caught them up.

"If you're wrong there's going to be big trouble!" he panted.

"What if we're right?" said Kirsty.

"I hope you're wrong!"

Thunder rumbled again, but the four runners plunged on in a bubble of desperate silence.

They were leaving the moor behind. There were hedges on either side of the road now.

Tom's boots skidded to a halt.

"Listen!"

They stopped. There was the grumbling of the thunder and the hiss of the rain.

And, behind the noises of the weather, a faint and distant droning.

Gravel flew up as the young man started to run again. He'd been moving fast before but now he flew down the road.

A large house loomed up against the night. He leapt over the fence, pounded across the lawns, and started to hammer on the front door.

"Open up! Open up! It's an emergency!"

Johnny and the others reached the gate. The droning was louder now.

We could have done something, Johnny thought. *I* could have done something. I could've . . . well, there *must* have been *something*. We thought it would be so easy. Just because we're from the future. What do we know about anything? And now the bombers are nearly here and there's nothing we can do.

"Come on! Open up!"

Yo-less found a gate and hurried through it. There was a splash in the darkness.

"I think I've stepped into some sort of pond," said a damp voice.

Tom stepped away from the house and groped on the ground for something.

"Maybe I can smash a window," he mumbled.

"Er . . . it's quite deep," said Yo-less, damply. "And I'm caught up on some kind of fountain thing . . ."

Glass tinkled. Tom reached through the window beside the door. There was a click, and the door opened.

They heard him trip over something inside, and then a weak light went on. Another click and—

"This phone's dead too! The lightning must've got the exchange!"

"Where's the next house?" said Kirsty, as Tom hurtled down the path.

"Not till Roberts Road!"

They ran after him, Yo-less squelching slightly.

The drone was much louder now. Johnny could hear it above the sound of his own breath.

Someone *must* notice it in the town, he thought. It fills the whole sky!

Without saying anything, they all began to run faster—

And, at last, the siren began to wail.

But the clouds were parting and the moon shone through and there were shadows nosing through the rags of cloud and Johnny could feel the unseen shapes turning over and over as they drifted towards the ground.

First there was the allotment, and then the pickle factory, and then Paradise Street exploded gently, like a row of roses opening. The petals were orange tinged with black and unfolded one after another, as the bombs fell along the street.

Then the sounds arrived. They weren't bangs but crunches, punches, great wads of noise hammered into the head.

Finally they died away, leaving only a distant crackling and the rising sound of a fire bell.

"Oh, no!" said Kirsty.

Tom had stopped. He stood and stared at the distant flames.

"The phone wasn't working," he whispered. "I tried to get here but the phone wasn't working."

"We're *time* travellers!" said Yo-less. "This *isn't* supposed to happen!"

Johnny swayed slightly. The feeling was like flu, but much worse. He felt as if he were outside his own body, watching himself.

It was the *hereness* of here, the *nowness* of now . . . People survived by not paying any attention to feelings like this. If you stopped, and opened your head to them, the world would roll over you like a tank . . .

Paradise Street was always going to be bombed. It was being bombed. It would *have been* bombed. Tonight was a fossil in time. It was a *thing*. Somewhere, it would always have happened. You couldn't steer a train!

That's what you *think* . . .

Somewhere . . .

Flames flickered over the housetops. More bells were ringing.

"The bike wouldn't start!" mumbled Tom. "The phone wouldn't work! There was a storm! I tried to get down here in time! How could it have been my fault?"

Somewhere . . .

Johnny felt it again . . . the sense that he could reach out and go in directions not found on any map or compass but only on a clock. It poured up from inside him until he felt that it was leaking out of his fingers. He hadn't got the trolley or the bags but . . . maybe he could remember how it felt . . .

"We've got time," he said.

"Are you *mad*?" said Kirsty.

"Are you going to come or not?" said Johnny.

"Where?"

Johnny took her hand, and reached out for Yo-less with his other hand.

Then he nodded towards Tom, who was still staring at the flames.

"Grab him, too," he said. "We'll need him when we get there."

"Where?"

Johnny tried to grin.

"Trust me," he said. "Someone has to."

He started to walk. Tom was dragged along with them like a sleepwalker.

"Faster," said Johnny. "Or we'll never get there."

"Look, the bombs have *fallen*," said Kirsty, wearily. "It's happened."

"Right. It had to," said Johnny. "Otherwise we couldn't get there before it did. Faster. Run."

He pushed forward, dragging them after him.

"I suppose we might be able to . . . help," panted Yo-less. "I know . . . first aid."

"*First* aid?" said Kirsty. "You saw the explosions!"

Beside her, the young man suddenly seemed to wake up. He stared at the fire in the town and lurched forward. And then they were all running, all trying to keep up, all causing the others to go faster.

And there was *the* road, in *that* direction.

Johnny took it.

The dark landscape lit up in shades of grey, like a very old film. The sky went from black to an inky purple. And everything around them looked cold, like crystal; all the leaves and bushes glittering as if they were covered in frost.

He couldn't *feel* cold. He couldn't feel anything.

Johnny ran. The road under his feet was sticky, as though he was trying to sprint in treacle.

And the air filled with the noise he'd last heard from the bags, a great whispering rush of sound, like a million radio stations slightly out of tune.

Beside him Yo-less tried to say something, but no words came out. He pointed with his free hand, instead.

Blackbury lay ahead of them. It wasn't the town he knew in 1996, and it wasn't the one from 1941 either. It glowed.

Johnny had never seen the Northern Lights. He'd read about them, though. The book said that on very cold nights sometimes the lights would come marching down from the North Pole, hanging in the sky like curtains of frozen blue fire.

That was how the town looked. It gleamed, as cold as starlight on a winter night.

He risked a glance behind.

There, the sky was red, a deep crimson that brightened to a ruby glow at its centre.

And he knew that if he stopped running it would all end. The road would be a road again, the sky would be the sky . . . but if he just kept going in *this* direction . . .

He forced his legs to move onward, pedalling in slow motion through the thick, cold, silent air. The town got closer, brighter.

Now the others were pulling on his arms. Kirsty was trying to shout too, but there was no sound here except the roar of all the tiny noises.

He snatched at their fingers, trying to hold on . . .

And then the blue rushed towards him and met the red coming the other way and he was toppling forward onto the road.

He heard Kirsty say, "I'm covered in ice!"

Johnny pushed himself to his feet and stared at his own arms. Ice crackled and fell off his sleeves as he moved.

Yo-less looked white. Frost steamed off his face.

"What did we do? What did we *do*?" said Kirsty.

"Listen, will you?" said Yo-less. "Listen!"

There was a whirring somewhere in the darkness, and a clock began to strike.

Johnny listened. They were on the edge of town. There was no traffic in the dark streets. But there were no fires, either. There was the muffled sound of laughter from a nearby pub, and the chink of glasses.

The clock went on striking. The last note died away. A cat yowled.

"Eleven o'clock?" said Kirsty. "But we *heard* eleven o'clock when we . . . were . . . on the downs . . ."

She turned and stared at Johnny.

"*You* took us *back* in *time*?"

"Not . . . back, I think," said Johnny. "I think . . . behind. Outside. Around. Across. I don't know!"

Tom had managed to get to his knees. What they could see of his face in the dusk said that here was a man to whom too much had happened, and whose brain was floating loose.

"We've got seven minutes," said Johnny.

"Huh?" said Tom.

"To get them to sound the siren!" shouted Kirsty.

"Huh? The bombs . . . I saw the fires . . . it wasn't my fault, the phone—"

"They didn't! But they will! Unless you do something! Right now! On your feet right now!" shouted Kirsty.

No-one could resist a voice like that. It went right through the brain and gave its commands directly to the muscles. Tom rose like a lift.

"Good! Now *come on*!"

The police station was at the end of the street. They reached the door in a group and fought one another to get through it.

There was an office inside, with a counter running across it to separate the public from the forces of Law and Order. A policeman was standing behind it. He had been writing in a large book, but now he was looking up with his mouth open.

"Hello, Tom," he said. "What's going on?"

"You've got to sound the siren!" said Johnny.

"Right now!" said Kirsty.

The sergeant looked from one to the other and then at Yo-less, where his gaze lingered for a while. Then he turned and glanced at a man in military uniform who was sitting writing at a desk in the office. The sergeant was the sort of man who liked an audience if he thought he was going to be funny.

"Oh, yes?" he said. "And why should I do that, then?"

"They're right, sergeant," said Tom. "You've got to do it! We . . . ran all the way!"

"What, off the down?" said the sergeant. "That's two miles, that is. Sounds a bit fishy to me, young man. Been round the back of the pub again, have you? Hah . . . remember that Dornier 111 bomber you heard last week?" He turned and smirked at the officer again. "A lorry on the Slate road, that was!"

Kirsty's patience, which in any case was only visible with special scientific equipment, came to an end.

"Don't you patronize us, you ridiculous buffoon!" she screamed.

The sergeant went red and took a deep breath. Then it was let out suddenly.

"Hey, where do you think *you're* going?"

Tom had scrambled over the desk. The soldier stood up but was pushed out of the way.

The young man reached the switch, and pulled it down.

11

You Want Fries With That?

Wobbler and Bigmac skulked behind the church.

"They've been gone a long time," said Bigmac.

"It's a long way up there," said Wobbler.

"I bet something's happened. They've been shot or something."

"Huh, I thought you *liked* guns," said Wobbler.

"I don't mind guns. I don't like bullets," said Bigmac. "And I don't want to get stuck here with you!"

"We've got the time trolley," said Wobbler. "But do you know how to work it? I reckon you've got to be half mental like Johnny to work it. I don't want to end up fighting Romans or something."

"You won't," said Bigmac.

He froze as he realized what he'd said. Wobbler homed in.

"What do you mean, stuck here with you? What *does* happen if I don't go home?" he said. "You lot went back to 1996. I wasn't there, right?"

"Oh, you don't want to know any stuff like that," said Bigmac.

"Oh, yeah?"

"You come in here and act cheeky—" the sergeant began.

"Be quiet!" snapped Captain Harris, standing up. "Why doesn't your siren work?"

"We tests it every Tuesday and Friday, reg'lar—" said the sergeant.

"There's a hole in the ceiling," said Yo-less.

Tom stood looking at the switch. He was certain he'd done his bit. He wasn't sure how, but he'd done it. And things that should be happening next weren't happening.

"It wasn't my fault," he mumbled.

"Your man fired a gun," said the sergeant. "We never did know where the bullet went."

"We know now," said the captain grimly. "It's hit a wire somewhere."

"There's got to be some other way," said Johnny. "It *mustn't* end like this! Not after everything! Look!"

He pulled a crumpled piece of paper out of his pocket and held it up.

"What's that?" said the captain.

"It's tomorrow's newspaper," said Johnny. "If the siren doesn't go off."

The captain stared at it.

"Oh, trying to pull our leg, eh?" said the police sergeant nervously.

The captain turned his eyes from the paper to Johnny's wrist. He grabbed it.

"Where did you get this watch?" he snapped. "I've seen one like it before! Where do you come from, boy?"

"Here," said Johnny. "Sort of. But not . . . now."

There was a moment's silence. Then the captain nodded at the sergeant.

"Ring up the local newspaper, will you?" he said. "It's a morning paper, isn't it? Someone should still be there."

"You're not seriously—"

"Please do it."

Seconds ticked by as the policeman huddled over the big black phone. He muttered a few words.

"I've got Mr. Stickers, the chief compositor," he said. "He says they're just clearing the front page and what do we want?"

The captain glanced at the paper, and sniffed at it.

"Fish? Never mind . . . is there an advertisement for Johnson's Cocoa in the bottom left hand corner of the page? Don't stare. Ask him."

There was some mumbling.

"He says yes, but—"

The captain turned the page over.

"On page two, is there a single column story headed 'Fined 2/6d for Bike Offence'? On the crossword, is One Down 'Bird of Stone, We Hear' with three letters? Next to an advertisement for Plant's Brushless Shaving Creams? *Ask him.*"

The sergeant glared at him, but spoke to the distant Stickers.

"Roc," said Kirsty, in an absentminded way.

The captain raised an eyebrow.

"It's a mythical bird, I think," said Yo-less, in the same hypnotized voice. "Spelled like 'rock' but without a K. 'We hear' means it sounds the same."

"He says yes," said the sergeant. "He says—"

"Thank you. Tell him to be ready in case . . . no, let's not be hasty . . . just thank him."

There was a click when the sergeant put the phone down.

Then the captain said, "Do you know how long we've got?"

"Three minutes," said Johnny.

"Can we get on the roof, sergeant?" said the captain.

"Dunno, but—"

"Is there some other siren in the town?"

"There's a manky old wind-up thing we used to use, but—"

"Where is it?"

"It's under the bench in the Lost Property cupboard but—"

There was a leathery noise and suddenly the captain was holding a pistol.

"You can argue with me afterwards," he said. "You can report me to whomever you like. But right now you can give me the keys or unlock the blasted cupboard, or I'll shoot the lock off. And I've always wanted to try that, believe me."

"You don't *believe* these kids, do—"

"Sergeant!"

In a sudden panic, the sergeant fumbled in his pockets and trotted across the room.

"You *do* believe us?" said Kirsty.

"I'm not sure," said the captain, as the sergeant dragged out something big and heavy. "Thank you, sergeant. Let's get it outside. No. I'm not sure at all, young lady. But I might believe that watch. Besides

. . . if I'm wrong, then all that will happen is that I'll look foolish, and I daresay the sergeant will give you all a thick ear. If I'm right then . . . this won't happen?" He waved the paper.

"I . . . think so," said Johnny. "I don't even know if *any* of this will happen . . ."

Bigmac was on the floor with Wobbler on top of him. Wobbler might not know how to fight, but he did know how to weigh.

"Get off!" said Bigmac, flailing around. Trying vicious street-fight punches on Wobbler was like hitting a pillow.

"I'm still alive in 1996, aren't I?" said Wobbler. " 'Cos I've been *born*, right? So even if I never time travel back *I* ought to still be alive in 1996, right? I bet you know something about me!"

"No, no, we never met you!"

"I'm alive, then? You *do* know something, right?"

"Get off, I can't breathe!"

"Come on, tell me!"

"You're not supposed to know what's going to happen!"

"Who says? Who says?"

There was a yowl behind him. Wobbler turned his head. Bigmac looked up.

Guilty the cat stretched lazily, yawned, and hopped down off the bags. He padded confidently alongside the mossy wall, moving in his lurching diagonal fashion, and disappeared around the building.

"Where's it going?" said Wobbler.

"How should I know? Get off'f me!"

The boys followed the cat, who didn't seem at all bothered by their presence.

He stopped at the church door and lay down with his front paws outstretched.

"First time I've seen him go away from the trolley," said Bigmac.

And then they heard it.

Nothing.

The faint noises of the town didn't stop. There was the sound of a piano from a pub somewhere. A door opened, and there was laughter. A car went by slowly, in the distance. But suddenly the sounds were coming from *a long way off*, as if there was some sort of thick invisible wall.

"You know those bombs . . ." said Wobbler, not taking his eyes off the cat.

"What bombs?" said Bigmac.

"The bombs Johnny's been going on about."

"Yeah?" said Bigmac.

"Can you remember what time he said? It was pretty soon, I think."

"Brilliant! I've never seen anywhere bombed," said Bigmac.

Guilty started to purr, very loudly.

"Er . . . you know my sister lives in Canada," said Wobbler, in a worried voice.

"What about her? What's she got to do with anything?"

"Well . . . she sent me a postcard once. There's this cliff there, right, where the Indians used to drive herds of buffalo over to kill them . . ."

"Isn't geography *wonderful*."

"Yeah, only . . . there was this Indian, right, and he wondered what the drive would look like from underneath . . . and that's why it's called Head-Bashed-In Jump. Really."

They both turned and looked at the chapel.

"This is still here in 1996," said Bigmac. "I mean, it's not going to get bombed . . ."

"Yeah, but don't you think it'd be better to be sort of behind it—"

The wail of a siren rose and fell.

There were faint noises in Paradise Street. Someone must have moved a blackout curtain, because light showed for a moment. Someone else shouted, in a back garden somewhere.

"Great!" said Bigmac. "All we need is popcorn."

"But it's going to happen to real people!" said Wobbler, aware that real people could include him.

"No, 'cos the siren's gone off. They'll all be down their bomb shelters. That's the whole point. Anyway, it'd happen *anyway*, right? It's history, OK? It'd be like going back to 1066 and watching the Battle of . . . whatever it was. It's not often you get to see an entire pickled onion factory blow up, either."

People were certainly moving. Wobbler could hear them in the night. A sound from this end of the street was exactly like someone walking into a tin bath in the darkness.

And then . . .

"Listen," said Bigmac, uncertainly.

Guilty sat up and looked alert.

There was a faint droning noise in the east.

"Brilliant," said Bigmac.

Wobbler edged towards the side of the church.

"This isn't television," he mumbled.

The droning got closer.

"Wish I'd brought my camera," said Bigmac.

A door opened. An avenue of yellow light spilled out into the night and a small figure dashed along it and came to a halt in the middle street.

It shouted: "Our Ron'll get *you*!"

The drone filled the sky.

Bigmac and Wobbler started running together. They cleared the churchyard steps in one jump and pounded towards the boy, who was dancing around waving a fist at the sky.

The aircraft were right overhead.

Bigmac got to him first and lifted him off his feet. Then he skidded on the cobbles as he turned and headed back towards the church.

They were halfway there when they heard the whistling.

They were at the top of the steps when the first bomb hit the allotments.

They were jumping behind the wall when the second and third bombs hit the pickle factory.

They were landing on the grass as the bombs marched up the street and filled the air with a noise so loud it couldn't be heard and a light so white it came right through the eyelids, and then the roar picked up the ground and shook it like a blanket.

That was the worst part, Wobbler said later. And it was hard to find the worst part because all the others were so bad. But the ground should be the ground, there, solid, dependably under you. It shouldn't drop away and then come back up and hit you so hard.

Then there was a sound like a swarm of angry bees.

And then there was just the clink of collapsing brickwork and the crackle of fires.

Wobbler raised his head, very slowly.

"Ugh," he said.

There were no leaves on the trees behind them. And the trunks *sparkled*.

He got up very slowly, and reached out.

It was glass. Bits of glass studded the whole trunk of the tree. There were no leaves any more. Just glass.

Beside him, Bigmac got to his feet like someone in a dream.

A frying pan had hit the church door so hard that it had been driven in halfway, like a very domesticated martial arts weapon. A stone doorstep had smashed a chunk out of the brickwork.

And everywhere there was glass, crunching underfoot like permanent hail. It glittered on the walls, reflecting the fires in the ruins. There seemed far too much to be from just a few house windows.

And then it began to rain.

First it rained vinegar.

And then it rained pickles.

There was red liquid all over Bigmac. He licked a finger and then held it up.

"Tomato sauce!"

A gherkin bounced off Wobbler's head.

Bigmac started to laugh. People can start laughing for all sorts of reasons. But sometimes they laugh because, against all expectations, they're still alive and have a mouth left to laugh with.

"You—" he tried to say, "You—you—you want fries with that?"

It was the funniest thing Wobbler had ever heard. Right now it was the funniest thing anyone had ever said anywhere. He laughed until the tears ran down his face and mingled with the mustard pickle.

From somewhere in the shadows by the wall a small voice said, " 'Ere, did anyone get any shrapnel?"

Bigmac started to laugh on top of the laugh he was already laughing, which caused a sound like a boiler trying not to burst.

"What, what, what's shrapnel anyway?" he managed to say.

"It's . . . it's . . . it's bits of bomb!"

"*You want fries with that?*" said Bigmac, and almost collapsed with laughing.

The siren sang out again. But this time it wasn't the rising and falling wail but one long tone, which eventually died away.

"They're coming back!" said Wobbler. The laughter drained out of him as though a trapdoor had been opened.

"Nah, that's the All Clear," said the voice by the wall. "Don't you know nuffin'?"

Wobbler's grandfather stood up and looked down the length of what had once been Paradise Street.

"Cor!" he said, obviously impressed.

There wasn't a whole house left standing. Roofs had gone, windows had blown out. Half of the buildings had simply vanished into rubble, which spilled across the street.

Bells rang in the distance. Two fire engines skidded to a halt right outside the church. An ambulance pulled up behind them.

"You want—" Bigmac began.

"Shut up, will you?" said Wobbler.

There were fires everywhere. Big fires, little fires. The pickle factory was well alight and smelled like the biggest fish and chip shop in the world.

People were running from every direction. Some of them were pulling at the rubble. There was a lot of shouting.

"I suppose everyone . . . would've got out, right?" said Wobbler. "They *would* have got out, wouldn't they?"

The siren's wail slowed to a growl and then a clicking noise, and then stopped.

Johnny felt as though his feet weren't exactly on the ground. If he were any lighter he'd float away.

"They must have got out. They had nearly a whole minute," he said.

The sergeant had already headed toward Paradise Street. The three of them had been left with Tom and the captain, who was watching Johnny thoughtfully.

Things pattered onto the roof of the police station and bounced down into the street. Yo-less picked one up.

"Pickled onions?" he said.

They could see the flames over the rooftops.

"So . . ." said the captain. "You were right. A bit of an adventure, yes? And this is where I say 'Well done, chums,' isn't it . . ."

He walked to the yard door and shut it. Then he turned.

"I can't let you go," he said. "You must know that. You were with that other boy, weren't you. The one with the strange devices."

There seemed no point in denying it.

"Yes," said Johnny.

"I think you might know a lot of things. Things that we need. And we certainly need them. Perhaps you know that?" He sighed. "I don't like this. You may have saved some lives tonight. But it's possible that you could save a lot more. Do you understand?"

"We won't tell you anything," said Kirsty.

"Just name, rank and serial number, eh?" said the captain.

"Supposing we . . . did know things," said Johnny. "It wouldn't do you any good. And those things won't help, either. They won't make the war better, they'll just make it different. Everything happens somewhere."

"Right now, I think we'd settle for different. We've got some very clever men," said the captain.

"Please, captain." It was Tom.

"Yes?"

"They didn't have to do all this, sir. I mean, they came and told us about the bombing, didn't they? And . . . I don't know how they got me down here, sir, but they did. 'S not right to put them in prison, sir."

"Oh, not prison," said the captain. "A country house somewhere. Three square meals a day. And lots of people who'll want to talk to them."

Kirsty burst into tears.

"Now, no-one's going to *hurt* you, little girl," said the captain. He moved over and put his arm around her shaking shoulders.

Johnny and Yo-less looked at one another, and took a few steps backwards.

"It's all *right*," said the captain. "We just need to know some things, that's all. Things that may be going to happen."

"Well, one thing . . ." sobbed Kirsty, "one thing . . . one thing that's going to happen is . . . one thing is . . ."

"Yes?" said the captain.

Kirsty reached out and took his hand. Then her leg shot out and she pivoted, hauling on the man's arm. He somersaulted over her shoulder and landed on his back on the cobbles. Even as he tried to struggle upright she was spinning around again, and caught him full in the chest with a foot. He slumped backwards.

Kirsty straightened her hat and nodded at the others.

"Chauvinist. Honestly, it's like being back with the dinosaurs. Shall we go?" she said.

Tom backed away.

"Where do girls learn to do *that*?" he said.

"At school," said Johnny. "You'd be amazed."

Kirsty reached down and took the captain's pistol.

"Oh, no," said Yo-less. "Not guns! You can get into real trouble with guns!"

"I happen to be the under-18 county champion," said Kirsty, unloading the gun. "But I'm not intending to use it. I just don't want him to get excited." She threw the pistol behind some dustbins. "Now, are we going, or what?"

Johnny looked around at Tom.

"Sorry about this," he said. "Can you, er, explain things to him when he wakes up?"

"I wouldn't know how to start! I don't know what happened myself!"

"Good," said Kirsty firmly.

"I mean, did I run down here or not?" said Tom. "I thought I saw the bombing but—I must've imagined it, because it didn't happen until after we got here!"

"It was probably the excitement," said Yo-less.

"The mind plays strange tricks," said Kirsty.

They both glared at Johnny.

"Don't look at *me*," he said. "I don't know anything about *anything*."

12

Up Another Leg

What Bigmac said afterwards was that he'd never *intended* to help. It had been like watching a film until he'd seen people scrabbling at the wreckage. Then he'd stepped through the screen.

Firemen were pouring water on the flames. People were pulling at fallen timbers, or moving gingerly through each stricken house, calling out names—in a strange, polite way, in the circumstances.

"Yoo-hoo, Mr. Johnson?"

"Excuse me, Mrs. Density, are you there?"

"Mrs. Williams? Anyone?"

And Wobbler said afterwards that he could remember three things. One was the strange metallic clinking sound bricks make as piles of them slide around. One was the smell of wet burnt wood. And one was the bed. The blast had taken off the roof and half the walls of a house but there was a double bed hanging out over the road. It even still had the sheets on it. It creaked up and down in the wind.

The two boys scrambled over the sliding rubble until they reached a back garden. Glass and bricks covered everything.

An elderly man wearing a nightshirt tucked into his trousers was standing and staring at the wreckage on his garden.

"Well, that's my potatoes gone," he said. "It was late frost last year, and now this."

"Still," said Bigmac, in a mad cheerful voice, "you've got a nice crop of pickled cucumbers."

"Can't abide 'em. Pickles give me wind."

Fences had been laid flat. Sheds had been lifted up and dealt like cards across the gardens.

And, as though the All Clear had been the Last Trump, people were rising out of the ground.

"I just hope the others are still there," said Kirsty, as they ran through the streets.

"What do *you* think?" said Yo-less.

"Sorry?"

"I mean, maybe they're sitting quietly waiting for us *or* they've got into some kind of trouble. Bets?"

Kirsty slowed down.

"Hang on a minute," she said. "There's something I've got to know. Johnny?"

"Yes?" he said. He'd been dreading this moment. Kirsty asked such penetrating questions.

"What did we do? Back there? I *saw* the bombs drop! And I'm a very good observer! But we got down to the police station *before* it happened! So either I'm mad—and I'm not mad—or we—"

"Ran through time," said Yo-less.

"Look, it was just a direction," said Johnny. "I just saw the way to go . . ."

Kirsty rolled her eyes. "Can you do it again?"

"I . . . don't think so. I can't remember how I did it."

"He was probably in a state of heightened awareness," said Yo-less. "I've read about them."

"What . . . drugs?" said Kirsty suspiciously.

"Me? I don't even like coffee!" said Johnny. The world had always seemed so strange in any case that he'd never dared try anything that'd make it even weirder.

"But it's an amazing talent! Think of the things you—"

Johnny shook his head. He could remember seeing the way, and he could remember the feelings, but he couldn't remember the *how*. It was as if he was looking at his memories behind thick amber glass.

"Come on," he said, and started running again.

"But—" Kirsty began.

"I can't do it again," said Johnny. "It'll never be the right time again."

* * *

Bigmac and Wobbler weren't in trouble, if only because there had been so much trouble just recently that there was, for a while, no more to get into.

"*This* is an air-raid shelter?" said Bigmac. "I thought they were all—you know, steel and stuff. Big doors that go *hiss*. Lights flashing on and off. You know." He heaved on one end of a shed which had smashed into the air-raid shelter belonging to No. 9. "Not just some corrugated iron and dirt with lettuces growing on top."

Wobbler had rescued a shovel from the ruin of someone's greenhouse, and used it to heave bricks out of the way. The shelter door opened and a middle-aged woman staggered out.

She was wearing a floral pinny over a nightdress, and holding a goldfish bowl with two fish in it. A small girl was clinging to her skirts.

"Where's Michael?" the woman shouted. "Where is he? Has anyone seen him? I turned my back for two seconds to grab Adolf and Stalin and he was out the door like a—"

"Kid in a green jersey?" said Wobbler. "Got glasses? Ears like the World Cup? He's looking for shrapnel."

"He's safe?" She sagged with relief. "I don't know what I'd have told his mother!"

"You all right?" said Bigmac. "I'm afraid your house is a bit . . . flatter than it was . . ."

Mrs. Density looked at what was left of No. 9.

"Oh, well. Worse things happen at sea," she said vaguely.

"Do they?" said Bigmac, mystified.

"It's just a blessing we weren't in it," said Mrs. Density.

There was a *clink* of brickwork and a fireman slid down the debris towards them.

"All right, Mrs. Density?" he said. "I reckon you're the last one. Fancy a nice cup of tea?"

"Oh, hello, Bill," she said.

"Who're these lads, then?" said the fireman.

"We . . . were just helping out," said Wobbler

"Were you? Oh. Right. Well, come away out of it, the pair of you. We reckon there's an unexploded one at Number 12." The fireman stared at Bigmac's clothes for a moment, and then shrugged. He gently took the goldfish bowl from Mrs. Density and put his other arm around her shoulders.

"A nice cup of tea and a blanket," he said. "Just the thing, eh? Come along, luv."

The boys watched them slide and scramble through the fallen bricks.

"You get *bombed* and they give you a cup of *tea*?" said Bigmac.

"I s'pose it's better than getting bombed and never ever getting one again," said Wobbler. "Anyway, there—"

"Eeeeyyyyooooowwwwmmmm!" screamed a voice behind them.

They turned. Wobbler's grandfather was standing on a pile of bricks and looked like a small devil in the light of the fires. He was covered in soot, and was waving something through the air and making aeroplane noises.

"That looks like—" Bigmac began.

"It's a bit off'f a bomb!" said the boy. "Nearly the whole tail fin! I don't know *anyone* who's got nearly a whole tail fin!"

He zoomed the twisted metal through the air again.

"Er . . . kid?" said Wobbler.

The boy lowered the fin.

"You know about . . . motorbikes?" said Wobbler.

"Oh, no," said Bigmac. "You can't tell him anything about—"

"You just shut up!" said Wobbler. "You've *got* a grandad!"

"Yes, but there has to be a warder there when I go an' see him."

Wobbler looked back at the boy.

"Dangerous things, motorbikes," he said.

"I'm going to have a big one when I grow up," said his grandfather. "With rockets on it, an' machine guns and everythin'. Eeeooowwmmmm!"

"Oh, I wouldn't do that if I were you," said Wobbler, in the special dumb voice for talking to children. "You don't want to go crashing it, do you."

"Oh, I won't crash," said his grandfather, confidently.

"Mrs. Density's daughter's a nice little girl, isn't she," said Wobbler desperately.

"She's all smelly and horrible. Eeeeeoowwmmm! Anyway, you're fat, mister!"

He ran down the far side of the heap. They saw his shadow darting between the firemen, and heard the occasional "Voommmm!"

"Come on," said Bigmac. "Let's get back to the church. The man said they thought there was an unexploded bomb—"

"He just didn't want to listen!" said Wobbler. "*I* would've listened!"

"Yeah, sure," said Bigmac.

"Well, I would!"

"Sure. Come on."

"I could've helped him if only he'd listened! I know stuff! Why won't he listen? I could make life a lot easier for him!"

"All right, I believe you. Now let's go, shall we?"

They reached the church just as Johnny and the others came running up the street.

"Everyone all right?" said Kirsty. "Why are you covered in soot, you two?"

"We've been rescuing people," said Wobbler, proudly. "Well, sort of."

They looked at the wreck of Paradise Street. People were standing around in small groups, and sitting on the ruins. Some ladies in official-looking hats had set up a table with a tea urn on it. There were still a few small fires, however, and the occasional crash and tinkle as a high-altitude cocktail onion fell back to earth in a coating of ice.

Johnny stared.

"Everyone got out, Johnny," said Wobbler, watching him carefully.

"I know."

"The siren was just in time."

"I know."

Behind him, Johnny heard Kirsty say: "I hope they get counselling?"

"We found out about that," said Bigmac's voice. "They get a nice cup of tea and told to cheer up because it could be worse."

"That's *all*?"

"Well . . . there's biscuits, too."

Johnny watched the street. The firelight almost made it look cheerful.

And his mind's eye saw the *other* street. It was here, too, happening at the same time. There were the same fires and the same piles of rubble and the same fire engines. But there were no people—except the ones carrying stretchers.

We're in a new time, he thought.

Everything you do changes everything. And every time you move in time you arrive in a time a little bit different to the one you left. What you do doesn't change *the* future, just *a* future.

There's millions of places when the bombs killed everyone in Paradise Street.

But it didn't happen here.

The ghostly images faded away as the other time veered off into its own future.

"Johnny?" said Yo-less. "We'd better get out of here."

"Yeah, no point in staying," said Bigmac.

Johnny turned.

"OK," he said.

"Are we going by trolley or are we going to . . . walk?" said Kirsty.

Johnny shook his head.

"Trolley," he said.

It was waiting where they'd left it. But there was no sign of Guilty.

"Oh, no!" said Kirsty. "We're *not* going to look for a cat."

"He went to watch the bombing," said Wobbler. "Don't know what happened to him after that."

Johnny gripped the handle of the trolley. The bags creaked in the darkness.

"Don't worry about the cat," he said. "Cats find their own way home."

The Golden Threads Club occupied the old church on Friday mornings. Sometimes there was a folk singer, or entertainment from local schools, if this couldn't be avoided. Mainly there was tea and a chat.

This was usually about how things were worse now than they had ever been, especially those golden days when you could buy practically anything for sixpence and still have change.

There was a change in the air and five figures appeared.

The Golden Threaders watched them suspiciously, in case they broke into "The Streets of London." They also noted that they were under thirty years old, and therefore almost certainly criminals. For one thing, they'd apparently stolen a shopping trolley. And one of them was black.

"Er . . ." said Johnny.

"Is this the theatre group?" said Kirsty. The others were astonished at the quick thinking. "Oh, no, wrong church hall, very sorry."

They edged towards the door, pushing the trolley. The Threaders watched them owlishly, teacups cooling in their hands.

Wobbler opened the door and ushered the others through it.

"Don't forget, one of them was black," said Yo-less, as he stepped out. He rolled his eyes sarcastically and waved his hands in the air. "We's goin' to de carnivaaal!"

13

Some Other Now . . .

The air outside smelled of 1996. Kirsty looked at her watch.

"Ten-thirty on Saturday morning," she said. "Not bad."

"Er, your *watch* is at ten-thirty on Saturday morning," said Johnny. "That doesn't mean *we* are."

"Good point."

"But I think we are, anyway. This all looks right."

"Looks fine to me," said Wobbler.

"We've been out all night," said Yo-less. "My mum'll go spare."

"Tell her you stopped at my place and the phone was broken," said Wobbler.

"I don't like lying."

"Are you going to tell her the truth?"

Yo-less thought for a few agonized seconds. "Your phone was broken, right?"

"Yeah, and I'll tell *my* mum I was staying at your place," said Wobbler.

"I shouldn't think my grandad's noticed I'm not in," said Johnny. "He always drops off in front of the telly."

"*My* parents have a very modern outlook," said Kirsty.

"My brother doesn't mind where I am so long as the police don't come round," said Bigmac.

Before time travelling to any extent, Johnny thought, you should always get your alibi sorted out.

He stared at the place where Paradise Street had been. It was still the Sports Centre. That hadn't changed. But Paradise Street was still there, underneath. Not underground. Just . . . somewhere else. Another fossil.

"Did we change anything?" said Kirsty.

"Well, *I'm* back," said Wobbler. "And that's good enough for me."

"But those people are alive when they ought to've been dead—" Kirsty began, and stopped when she saw Johnny's expression. "All right, not exactly *ought*, but you know what I mean. One of them might've invented the Z-bomb or something."

"What's the Z-bomb?" said Bigmac.

"How should I know? It wasn't invented when we left!"

"Someone in *Paradise Street* invented a bomb?" said Johnny.

"Well, all right, not a bomb. Something else that'd change history. Any little thing. And you know we left all Bigmac's stuff in the police station?"

"Ahem."

Yo-less removed his hat and produced a watch and a Walkman.

"The sergeant was so flustered he forgot to lock the cupboard after he got the siren out," said Yo-less. "So I nipped in."

"Did you get the jacket?"

"Chucked it in a dustbin."

"That was *mine*," said Bigmac reproachfully.

"Well, maybe that's all right," Kirsty conceded reluctantly. "But there's bound to be some other changes. We'd better find out pretty fast."

"We'd better have a bath, too," said Wobbler.

"Your hands have got blood on them," said Johnny.

Wobbler looked down vaguely.

"Oh, yeah. Well . . . we were pulling at smashed-up walls and things," he said. "You know . . . in case there was anyone trapped . . ."

"You should've seen him grab his grandad!" said Bigmac. "It was *brilliant*!"

Wobbler looked proud.

They met up an hour later in the mall. The burger bar was back to the way it had always been. No-one said anything about it, but from the way he sighed occasionally it was clear that Bigmac was thinking of free burgers every week for the rest of his life.

That jogged Johnny's memory.

"Oh . . . yes," said Johnny. "Er. We've got this letter . . . for you . . ."

He pulled it out. It was crumpled, and covered in vinegar and sooty fingerprints.

"Er, it's for you," he repeated. "Someone . . . asked us to give it to you."

"Yeah, someone," said Yo-less.

"We don't know who he was," said Bigmac. "A completely mysterious person. So it's no use you asking us questions."

Wobbler gave them a suspicious look, and ripped open the envelope.

"Go on, what's he say?" said Bigmac.

"Who?" said Wobbler.

"Y—this mysterious person," said Bigmac.

"Dumb stuff," said Wobbler. "Read it yourself."

Johnny took the paper that had been in the envelope. It contained a list, numbered from one to ten.

" '1) Eat healthy food in moderation,' " he read. " '2) An hour's exercise every day is essential. 3) Invest money wisely in a mixture of—' "

"What's the point of all this junk? It's the sort of thing grandads say," said Wobbler. "Why'd anyone want to tell *me* that? You'd have to be some kind of loony to go around telling people that. This was one of those religious blokes that hang around in the mall, right? Huh. I thought it might be something *important*."

Bigmac glanced at the burger bar again, and sighed deeply.

"There have been changes," said Kirsty. "Clark Street isn't Clark Street any more. I noticed when I went past. It's Evershott Street."

"That's frightening," said Bigmac. "Oooeeeoooeee . . . a street name was mysteriously changed . . ."

"I thought it was always Evershott Street," said Yo-less.

"Me too," said Wobbler.

"And that shop over there . . . that used to sell cards and things. Now it's a jeweller's," said Kirsty insistently.

The boys craned around to look at it.

"It's always been a jeweller's, hasn't it?" said Wobbler. He yawned.

"Well, you're an unobservant bunch, I—" Kirsty began.

"Hold on," said Johnny. "How did you get all those cuts on your hands, Wobbler? You too, Bigmac."

"Well, er, I . . . er . . ." Wobbler's eyes glazed.

"We . . . were messing around," said Bigmac. "Weren't we?"

"Yeah. Messing around. Somewhere."

"Don't you remember—?" Kirsty began.

"Forget about it," said Johnny. "Come on, Kirsty, we've got to go."

"Where to?"

"Visiting time. We've got to see Mrs. Tachyon."

Kirsty waved a hand frantically at the other three.

"But they don't seem to—"

"It doesn't matter! Come on!"

"They can't just *forget*!" said Kirsty, as they hurried out of the mall. "They can't just think: 'Oh, it was all a dream'!"

"I think it's all sort of healing over," said Johnny. "Didn't you see it happening back in 1941? Tom didn't really believe anything that had happened. I bet by now . . . I mean, a few hours after . . . I bet they're remembering . . . I mean, they *remembered* . . . something different. He ran all the way and got there just in time. Everyone was a bit shocked because of the bombing. Something like that. People have to forget what really happened because . . . well, it *didn't* happen. Not here."

"*We* can remember what really happened," said Kirsty.

"Perhaps that's because you're hyper-intelligent and I'm megastupid," said Johnny.

"Oh, I wouldn't say *that*," said Kirsty. "You're being a bit unfair."

"Oh. Good."

"I meant I wouldn't go so far as to say 'hyper'. Just 'very'. Why do we have to see Mrs. Tachyon?"

"Someone ought to. She's a time-bag-lady," said Johnny. "I think it's all the same to her. Round the corner or 1933, they're all just directions to her. She goes where she likes."

"She's mad."

They'd reached the hospital steps. Johnny trudged up them.

She probably *is* mad, he thought. Or eccentric, anyway. I mean, if *she* went to a specialist and he showed her all those cards and ink blots she'd just nick them or something.

Yes. Eccentric. But she wouldn't do things like dropping bombs on Paradise Street. You have to be *sane* to think of things like that. She's totally round the bend. But perhaps she gets a better view from there.

It was quite a cheerful thought, in the circumstances.

* * *

Mrs. Tachyon had gone. The ward sister seemed quite angry about it.

"Do you know anything about this?" she demanded.

"Us?" said Kirsty. "We've just come in. Know about what?"

Mrs. Tachyon had gone to the lavatory. She'd locked herself in. And in the end they'd had to get someone to take the lock off, in case she'd fallen down in there.

She wasn't in there at all.

They were three floors up and the window was too small even for someone as skinny as Mrs. Tachyon to climb through.

"Was there any toilet paper?" said Johnny.

The sister gave him a look of deep suspicion.

"The whole roll's gone," she said.

Johnny nodded. That sounded like Mrs. Tachyon.

"*And* the headphones have vanished," said the sister. "Do you know about any of this? You've been visiting her."

"That's only been because it's, you know, like a project," said Kirsty, defensively.

There was the sound of sensible shoes behind them. They turned out to belong to Ms. Partridge the social worker.

"I've phoned the police," she said.

"Why?" said Johnny.

"Well, she— oh, it's you. Well, she . . . needs help. Not that they *were* any help. They said she always turns up."

Johnny sighed. Mrs. Tachyon, he suspected, never *needed* help. If she wanted help she just took it. If she needed a hospital, she went where there was one. She could be anywhere now.

"Must have slipped out when no-one was looking," said Ms. Partridge.

"She couldn't," said the sister stoutly. "We can see the door from here. We're very careful about that sort of thing."

"Then she must have vanished into thin air!" said Ms. Partridge.

Kirsty sidled closer to Johnny while they argued and said, out of the corner of her mouth: "Where did you leave the trolley?"

"Behind our garage," said Johnny.

"D'you think she's taken it?"

"Yes," said Johnny happily.

* * *

Johnny was quiet on the bus home. They'd gone to the library and he'd wangled a photocopy of the local paper for the day after the raid.

There was a picture of people looking very cheerful in the ruins of Paradise Street. Of course, things were pretty faded now, but there was Mrs. Density with her goldfish bowl, and Wobbler's grandfather with his bit of bomb and, just behind them, grinning and holding his thumb up, you could just make out Wobbler. It hadn't been a good photo to start with and it hadn't improved with age and he had soot all over his face but, if you knew it was Wobbler, you could see it was him all right.

They're all forgetting except me, he thought. I bet even if I showed them the paper they'd say, "Oh yes, that bloke looks like Wobbler, so what?"

Because . . . they live here. They've always lived here. In a way.

When you travel in time it really happens, but it's like a little loop in a tape. You go round the loop and then carry on from where you were before. And everything that's changed turns out to be history.

"You've gone very quiet," said Kirsty.

"I was just thinking," said Johnny. "I was thinking that if I showed the others this piece from the paper they'd say, oh, yeah, that looks like ole Wobbler, so what?"

Kirsty leaned across.

"Oh, yes," she said. "Well? It *does* look like Wobbler. So what?"

Johnny stared out of the window.

"I mean," he said, "it's Wobbler in the paper. Remember?"

"Remember what?"

"Well . . . yesterday?"

She wrinkled her forehead.

"Didn't we go to some sort of party?"

Johnny's heart sank.

It all settles down, he thought. That's what's so horrible about time travel. You come back to a different place. You come back to the place where you didn't go in the first place, and it's not *your* place.

Because *here* was where no-one died in Paradise Street. So here's where I didn't want to go back. So I didn't. So they didn't, either. When the newspaper picture was taken we were back there, but, now we're back here, we never went. So they don't remember because here there's nothing to remember. Here, we did something else. Hung on. Hung around.

Here I'm remembering things that never happened.

"It's your stop," said Kirsty. "Are you all right?"

"No," said Johnny, and got off the bus.

It was raining heavily, but he went and checked to see if the trolley was where he'd left it. It wasn't. On the other hand, maybe it had never been there at all.

When he went up to his bedroom he could hear the rain drumming on the roof. He'd vaguely hoped that he might have been a different person in this world but there it all was: the same bedroom, the same mess, the same space shuttle on its bit of red wool. The same stuff for the project all over the table.

He sat on his bed and watched the rain for a while. He could feel the shadows in the air, hovering around the corners of the room.

He'd lost Mrs. Tachyon's paper somewhere. That would have been proof. But no-one else would believe it.

He could remember it all—the rain on the moor, the thunderstorm, the sting on his whole body when they'd run through time—and it hadn't happened. Not exactly. Normal, dull, boring, everyday life had just poured right in again.

Johnny went through his pockets. If only there was something . . .

His fingers touched a piece of card . . .

The sound of Australian accents from downstairs suggested that his grandad was in. He trailed downstairs and into the little front room.

"Grandad?"

"Yes?" said his grandfather, who was watching *Cobbers*.

"You know the war—"

"Yes?"

"You know you said that before you went in the army you were a sort of aircraft spotter—"

"Got a medal for it," said his grandfather. He picked up the remote control and switched off the set, which never usually happened. "Showed it you, didn't I? Must've done."

"Don't think so," said Johnny, as diplomatically as possible. Before, his grandfather had always told him not to go on about things.

His grandfather reached down beside his chair. There was an old wickerwork sewing box there, which had belonged to Johnny's grandmother. It hadn't been used for cotton and needles for a long time, though. It was full of old newspaper cuttings, keys that didn't fit any door in the house, stamps for one half-penny in old money, and all the other stuff that accumulates in odd corners of a house that has been lived in for a long time. Finally, after much grunting, he produced a small wooden box and opened it.

"They said they never knew how I done it," he said proudly. "But Mr. Hodder and Captain Harris spoke up for me. Oh, yes. Had to be possible, they said, otherwise I couldn't've done it, could I? The phones'd got hit by lightning and the bike wouldn't start no matter what he yelled so I had to run all the way down into the town. So they had to give it to me 'cos they spoke up."

Johnny turned the silver medal over in his hands. There was a yellowing bit of paper with it, badly typed by someone who hadn't changed the ribbon on his typewriter for years.

" 'Gallant action . . .' " he read, " '. . . ensuring the safety of the people of Blackbury . . .' "

"Some men from the Olympics came to see me after the war," said his grandfather. "But I told them I didn't want any."

"How did you do it?" said Johnny.

"They said someone's watch must've been wrong," said Grandad. "I don't know about that. I just ran for it. 'S'all a bit of a blur now, tell you the truth . . ."

He put the medal back in the box. Beside it, held together with an elastic band, was a grubby pack of cards.

Johnny took them out and removed the band.

They had aircraft on them.

Johnny reached into his pocket and took out the five of clubs. It was a lot less worn, but there was no doubt that it was part of the pack. He slipped it under the band and put the pack back in the box.

Grandad and Johnny sat and looked at one another for a moment. There was no sound but the rain and the ticking of the mantelpiece clock.

Johnny felt the time drip around them, thick as amber . . .

Then Grandad blinked, picked up the remote control, and aimed it at the TV.

"Anyway, we've all passed a lot of water under the bridge since those days," he said, and that was that.

The doorbell rang.

Johnny trooped out into the hall.

The bell rang again, urgently.

Johnny opened the door.

"Oh," he said gloomily. "Hello, Kirsty."

Rain had plastered her hair to her head.

"I ran back from the next stop," she said.

"Oh. Why?"

She held up a pickled onion.

"I found it in my pocket. And . . . I *remembered*. We did go back."

"Not *back*," said Johnny. "It's more like *there*." The elation rose up inside him like a big pink cloud. "Come on in."

"Everything. Even the pickles."

"Good!"

"I thought I ought to tell you."

"Right."

"Do you think Mrs. Tachyon will ever find her cat?"

Johnny nodded.

"Wherever he is," he said.

The sergeant and the soldier picked themselves up off the ground and staggered towards the wreckage where the house had been.

"That poor old biddy! That poor old biddy!" said the sergeant.

"D'you think she might've got out in time?" said the soldier.

"That poor old biddy!"

"She was sort of close to the wall," moaned the soldier hopefully.

"The *house* isn't there any more! What do *you* think?"

They scrambled through the damp ruins of Paradise Street.

"Oh God, there's going to be *hell* to pay for this . . ."

"You're telling me! You shouldn't've left it unguarded! That poor old biddy!"

"D'you know how much sleep we've had this past week? Do you? And we lost Corporal Williams over in Slate! We knocked off for five minutes in the middle of the night, that's all!"

A crater lay in front of them. Something bubbled in the bottom.

"She got any relatives?" said the soldier.

"No. No-one. Been here ages. My dad says he remembers seeing her about sometimes when he was a lad," said the sergeant.

He removed his helmet.

"Poor old biddy," he said.

"That's what *you* think! Dinner dinner dinner dinner—"

They turned. A skinny figure, wearing an old coat over a nightdress, and a woolly hat, ran along the road, expertly steering a wire cart between the mounds of rubble.

"—dinner dinner—"

The sergeant stared at the soldier. "How did she do that?"

"Search me!"

"—dinner dinner Batman!"

Some way away, Guilty ambled in his sideways fashion through the back streets.

He'd had an interesting morning hunting through the remains of Paradise Street, and had passed some quality time during the afternoon in the ruins of the pickle factory, where there were mice, some of them fried. It had been a good day.

Around him, Blackbury went back to sleep.

There was still a terrible smell of vinegar everywhere.

By some miracle of preservation, a large jar of pickled beetroot had been blown right across the town and landed, unbroken and unnoticed, in a civic flowerbed, from whence it had bounced into the gutter.

Guilty waited by it, washing himself.

After a while he looked up as a familiar squeaking sound came around the corner, and stopped. A hand wearing a woolly glove with the fingers cut out reached down and picked up the jar. There was a series of complicated unscrewing noises, and then a sound like . . . well, like someone eating pickled beetroot until the juice ran down their chin.

"Ah," said a voice, and then belched. "That's the stuff to give the troops! Bromide? That's what *you* think! Laugh? I nearly brought a tractor!"

Guilty hopped up onto the trolley.

Mrs. Tachyon reached up and adjusted the headphones under her bobble hat.

She scratched at a surgical dressing. Dratted thing. She'd have to get someone to take it off her, but she knew a decent nurse over in 1917.

Then she scrabbled in her pockets and fished out the sixpence the sergeant had given her. She remembered him giving it to her. Mrs. Tachyon remembered everything, and had long ago given up wondering whether the things she remembered had already happened or not. Take life as it was going to come was her motto. And if it didn't come, go and fetch it.

The past and the future were all the same, but you could get a good feed off of a sixpence, if you knew the right way to do it.

She squinted at it in the grey light of dawn.

It was a bit old and grubby, but the date was quite clear. It said: 1903.

"Tea and buns? That's what *you* think, Mr. Copper!"

And she went back to 1903 and spent it on fish and chips. And still had change.

ABOUT THE AUTHOR

Terry Pratchett lives in Wiltshire and writes books—usually about the Discworld, which he is quite sure is not a real place. He's glad that people like them. Sometimes he goes for walks, and finds time for a certain amount of quiet fun. Life is pretty full, really.